OUT OF THE ASHES

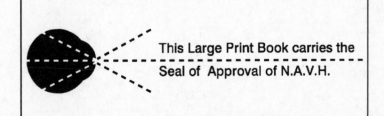

This Large Print Book carries the
Seal of Approval of N.A.V.H.

Out of the Ashes

Tracie Peterson
and Kimberley Woodhouse

THORNDIKE PRESS
A part of Gale, a Cengage Company

GALE
A Cengage Company

Farmington Hills, Mich • San Francisco • New York • Waterville, Maine
Meriden, Conn • Mason, Ohio • Chicago

GALE
A Cengage Company

Copyright © 2018 by Peterson Ink, Inc. and Kimberley R. Woodhouse.
Scripture quotations are from the King James Version of the Bible.
Thorndike Press, a part of Gale, a Cengage Company.

LIBRARY OF CONGRESS CIP DATA ON FILE.
CATALOGUING IN PUBLICATION FOR THIS BOOK
IS AVAILABLE FROM THE LIBRARY OF CONGRESS.

ISBN-13: 978-1-4328-4629-9 (hardcover)
ISBN-10: 1-4328-4629-9 (hardcover)

Published in 2018 by arrangement with Bethany House Publishers, a division of Baker Publishing Group

Printed in the United States of America
1 2 3 4 5 6 7 22 21 20 19 18

This book is lovingly dedicated
in memory of:
Raymond Earl Frappier
My beloved grandpa.

Married for seventy years
to an equally amazing lady,
father to five children — who've all
served in full-time ministry,
grandfather to twelve, great-grandfather
to a continually expanding number
(and soon to be
great-great-grandfather),
godly example, prayer warrior, WWII
veteran, Bronze Star recipient,
lover of mashed potatoes and gravy
and all things sweet,
jokester, and all-around wonderful man.

You never hesitated to be there.
Whether it was in the middle

of the night when I had growing pains
in my legs and you sat with me at the
piano for hours to keep my mind off
the spasms, or the times you told me a
silly story when I needed cheering up,
or when you sent notes of
encouragement before big competitions,
or made me cry at my own wedding,
there are a million beautiful memories
of you being there.

But the biggest and most marvelous gift
you ever gave was your prayers.

You and Grandma prayed for me —
and every single member of our big,
beautiful family — every day, without
fail, for hours on end.

What a legacy you have left us.
Thank you.
I love you and miss you,
oh, so very much.

— Kim

A NOTE FROM THE AUTHORS

Welcome to the second novel in The Heart of Alaska series — *Out of the Ashes.*

As we go back to Curry, Alaska, in the 1920s and the Curry Hotel, we journey with some very broken people. Like so many of us today, they experience pain — physical and emotional — that only our great God can help us endure and overcome. But that's the beautiful part — He is there. Amidst all the junk.

During the writing of this book, Tracie and I both went through some very difficult circumstances. I had an adventurous two-hour ride in an ambulance that led to numerous surgeries and a long road to recovery. Tracie's beloved nephew suffered a seizure, and they ultimately had to say good-bye to a family member who was all too young. It all happened within the same month. And we feel that the title of this book is even more significant in our lives —

7

as we've come out of the ashes ourselves to see the beauty only God can make.

In the Shadow of Denali, book one, started this series in 2017. It introduces the reader to Curry from its inception and tells the love story of Allan and Cassidy, whom you'll see again in this story. Each book in the series is designed to stand alone. You don't have to read each one to enjoy the series; however, reading each in order will definitely add to your enjoyment.

In this story, we have used real historical details and real people intermixed with our fictional characters. And since we didn't know the people personally, we've had to use our imaginations along with our historical research to depict some of their personality traits. Please see the *Dear Reader* letter at the end of the book for more details, links to pictures, and our own research.

Many of our readers have written in asking about visiting Alaska. We definitely recommend taking a trip to the Last Frontier if at all possible. The Alaska Railroad is a wonderful way to see Alaska and the only way to see the remains of Curry at milepost 248.

Denali is just as magnificent as ever and one of the most beautiful sights to behold, but be prepared for him to shroud himself in clouds for weeks on end. While in Alaska, if you hear the beloved phrase "The Mountain is out," make sure you chase the mountain that day in case you don't get the chance again. Take lots of pictures, because it will be a treasure to show your friends and family.

And now, we head back in time to Curry. Our prayer — as always — is that you see the beauty of redemption in this story. But most importantly, we hope you see that God can take our worst circumstances — our shattered pieces — and transform the ashes into an exquisite masterpiece.

Enjoy the journey,

Kim and Tracie

PROLOGUE

August 1925
Al-Mazraa, Syria — roughly 100 km south of
  Damascus

Horrific, gut-wrenching wails brought Jean-Michel Langelier awake. Face-first in the hot sand, he tried to push up from his prostrate position but couldn't lift his head. Where was he?

Syria.

He took a few deep breaths. He'd been stationed in Syria to serve out the rest of his term in the French Army.

The army.

Blinking away grit and sand, he worked to remember his surroundings and all that had happened. He'd offered to serve his country in hopes of helping stabilize Europe after the Great War, the war that had devastated them all. But who was he kidding — in all honesty, he'd run off after the love of his

11

life left France without a good-bye. Not that he'd expected one. Once her father had forbade them to marry, all communication was cut off.

So he found himself in the army. And it brought him to Syria.

All had been peaceful.

Until a rebellion of Druze tribes and Syrian nationalists rose up against French rule little more than a month ago. No one expected it. In fact, the French had been pulling out troops.

But now the rebellion was fighting against the French troops that were left. Jean-Michel shook his head again to clear the fog. Hadn't he heard screaming?

Turning to take in his surroundings, he realized that their ammunition convoy had been attacked as they'd approached the village. Some sort of blast must have rendered him unconscious, which accounted for the pain in his head. He wiped his eyes, hoping to clear them of the grit and smoke. Every muscle in his body protested as he pushed to all fours, and the ringing in his ears grew louder. Blinking against the bright light, he forced himself to focus. But sounds were indistinct — almost muted against the drumming and rushing of his own blood pumping as he pushed himself to stand and move.

Jean-Michel looked down at his torn uniform. There were splotches of blood here and there, but upon inspection he found it was nothing serious. Just small lacerations, no doubt from the explosion.

The explosion. What had caused it? Where was George? And Luc? The two younger men had become dear to him. As their commander, Jean-Michel had earned their respect. However, over time something more had developed — a deep, abiding friendship.

Rapid gunfire and explosions erupted around him. The ringing in his ears gradually subsided, but the pounding pain in his head increased. He staggered to the right, still trying to assess the situation. He was in command, but he couldn't even focus on what should be done.

Desperate screams brought his attention around. Flames engulfed a building several hundred meters north. A bullet ripped past him, bringing Jean-Michel's attention back to his own precarious situation. He staggered toward the small structure that was a gathering place for the women of the area. The desperate cries and screams of those inside made his stomach roil.

Someone had chained the only door in and out. They were trapped!

Jean-Michel tried to pull away the heavy chains, but they had been secured with a lock. He struggled to think amidst the conflict and noise. He had to get help. He needed something to cut the chain. He started off across the compound toward the supply depot.

Just then another explosion sent him to his knees. Looking back, he saw that now the back of the building was on fire. This couldn't be happening. Not now. He'd spent a lot of time around the Syrian people. Earning their trust.

And for what?

He struggled once again to his feet and turned in a circle to survey the world around him. It was as if everyone had gone mad and time stood still. Were those French soldiers igniting other buildings around him? *His* soldiers? No. It couldn't be. Not when there were innocents inside.

Jean-Michel didn't understand what was happening and why they were fighting. So far, all he'd had to do was follow orders and pass them on to his soldiers. But as he watched the flames grow, he couldn't fathom who would order such outright evil.

A figure Jean-Michel recognized all too

well strode around the building, a torch in his hand and a sneer on his face. Phillippe.

Phillippe hated the Syrian people. Hated being posted here. Hated being under Jean-Michel's command when he was fifteen years Jean-Michel's senior. The motivation behind the abhorrence was clear, but his actions were so barbaric Jean-Michel found it difficult to believe. What had made the man snap like this?

This new "war" obviously fueled the man's hate. Phillippe lit another small building and moved on.

"Non!!" The guttural cry exploded from Jean-Michel's lips amidst the raging sounds of war around him and he forced his legs to run faster. He had to free the women and children.

George and Luc emerged from a cloud of gunfire after his shout. Off to the west about a hundred meters, they looked toward his destination and came on the double. Whether they saw Phillippe or the innocent people inside the buildings that were burning, Jean-Michel wasn't sure, but at least they would help stop the madness.

The heat from the fires intensified the heat of the desert and sweat poured from Jean-Michel's body as he ran. There weren't any orders to kill villagers and innocent people.

15

The rebellion hadn't even reached their area yet — at least not until their convoy was attacked. What had happened?

A small face appeared in the tiny window high up the building wall. Mouth open in cries. A small hand beat the glass pane. Someone had to be holding him up to gain that height. Their only hope of escape — a window they couldn't reach.

The face was familiar — the same little boy who'd watched him try a magic trick and giggled when Jean-Michel failed.

They didn't have much time left.

Oomph!

Jean-Michel's right leg buckled underneath him and he crumpled into the sand as his body ignited in pain. Glancing down at his leg, he watched the bloodstain grow on his uniform. He'd never been shot before, and as the agony grew, he ground his teeth. He couldn't think about his own pain right now.

But there was no cover. The rebels had him. Probably thought he *wanted* to see all those people burn to their deaths, since it was his own troops lighting the fires.

"Jean-Michel!" George's voice cut through the gunfire. *"Ne bougez pas!"*

Don't move? He didn't think he could even if he tried. Jean-Michel attempted to wave him off — to convince them to stay put. He couldn't risk anyone else's lives. It was his own fault for taking off into the open. Maybe he could still crawl to the building. But how could he save those people?

Spots danced in his eyes. He shook his head.

Sound began to dim. He heard George's voice again. Then Luc's. But Jean-Michel's gaze was fixed on the building.

A haze filled the outline of his sight as familiar faces entered his vision. George and Luc dragged him backward.

"Non! Non!" They were dragging him away from the building. Didn't they hear him screaming? Didn't they know about those people inside?

Jean-Michel squirmed in his buddies' arms. "Help me save them! Please!"

"We'll get them, but we can't risk you being shot again. You've lost a lot of blood." Luc's calm voice did nothing but grate on Jean-Michel's nerves.

"I don't care about me" — a cough choked him — "save . . . *them!*"

Did they hear him? They were speaking to him, but the words made no sense.

Were his eyes open anymore? He commanded his eyelids to lift, but he couldn't see anything. Only black.

Muffled sounds were the only evidence that he was still somewhat conscious. That and the throbbing pain.

A sudden jerk from side to side released his arms and he plummeted.

Where were George and Luc?

Maybe this was death. And he deserved it.

1

Six months later
February 25, 1926 — New York

Katherine Harrison Demarchis paced the
floor of Grandmother's formal sitting room.
The older woman had once again taken to
arranging her life — *without* consulting her.
Not that she was doing a good job of it
herself or even wanted the job.

Not anymore.

Grandmother was a dear and loved to
keep Katherine on her toes — which used
to make her smile. But now? Did she feel
anything anymore?

It wasn't Grandmother's fault that Katherine didn't care a whit about her future.
The careless thought made her wince. All
the cynicism and negativity swirling in the
dark fog around her had turned her into . . .
what exactly? What had happened to the
carefree, joyous girl of her youth? Always

looking forward to the days ahead . . .

Now, all she wanted was to retreat to a quiet life of widowhood. Alone.

A knot formed in her stomach. Hard like stone and heavier than an anvil, as ugly words — *his* words — rushed in.

Destroyed by the harsh reality of a miserable and loveless marriage, the days of dreams and happy endings were long gone. Katherine straightened her shoulders and stepped to the window to watch the busy, snow-filled street below. How long would it all haunt her? How long would his words continue to wound her? How long before the world realized that everything Randall Demarchis had said about her was true?

She was worthless. A poor excuse for womanhood. She didn't deserve to live.

The gauzy curtain fluttered in the crisp breeze from the slightly opened window and made her take a breath. The chilly air froze her lungs much like her heart. She wanted to matter . . . longed to, in fact, like she used to . . . before she married a monster.

"Katherine?" The sweet voice held just a hint of concern. "I thought you were going to join me in the library."

"I needed a bit of fresh air." That should appease the dear woman for the moment. Until she could rein her thoughts back in.

Grandmother always insisted on having fresh air flowing throughout the house, no matter the temperature outside.

"We need to discuss our plans, dear." The scent of peppermint pierced the air.

Katherine didn't want the discussion, nor the plans. Yet how was she supposed to deny her last living relative — a woman who had become her lifeline over the past few years?

Randall had done all he could to isolate her from her family, but Grandmother would not be managed then, nor now. The determined woman had inserted herself into Katherine's married life, despite her husband's open protests. At one time, he'd threatened Grandmother, but she reminded him she was a powerful woman with friends in high places. If Randall wanted to continue climbing his political ladder, he would do best to humor her and allow for her visits. He conceded, but not without severe punishment meted out on Katherine. Of course, Katherine never revealed that to her grandmother.

When Randall Demarchis died suddenly, Grandmother was the one who'd picked up the pieces. She'd taken Katherine home with her after the funeral and wouldn't let her be alone during any of the night terrors she suffered. The same woman who'd dried her tears as a child now comforted her as an adult. And daily, the woman prodded her to step out of her dark shell and back into the light. Not that Grandmother had much luck, but God bless her for trying.

Katherine turned away from the window to look at her dear elder. "Grandmother, you know I am not interested in taking any trips —"

"You're not interested in much of anything these days." She pointed a knobby finger. "And don't take that irritated tone with me. It won't work, and you know it. One of these days, *my* Katherine will be free to come out again, and I'm looking forward to it." The finger dropped as the older woman squared her shoulders. "And this is not just *any* trip, my child. This is the last trip your dear Grandpapa wanted to take . . . he planned and planned, God rest his soul. You wouldn't deny me that, would you? The last trip *I* would like to take before I leave this earth?"

Katherine braced herself. The guilt trip wouldn't end there. The woman was well into her eighties, but she didn't look like it or act like it, for that matter. Only when she needed to use her advancing years to get what she wanted. "Grandmother, you are too stubborn to leave this earth one second before you choose to. I would imagine even God consults your calendar."

"Don't be blasphemous. Of course, God doesn't consult me, but we do discuss it." She winked and put on a sly grin.

"Be that as it may, I very much doubt that this will be the last trip you *want* to take, nor the last you will take." The woman constantly flitted to and fro between Boston, New York, and Philadelphia. "As to *your* Katherine being free . . . well, I'm quite certain she doesn't exist anymore." The thought tore at her heart.

"It's been over a year since that" — Grandmother always refused to call Randall by his given name — "Senator Demarchis died. Time will heal the wounds. I'm confident of it. I know you don't wish to speak of him or your marriage, but I'm willing to listen if you need me."

"I know." But she couldn't. Wouldn't. Not ever.

Grandmother gave a slight nod and then turned to look at the fireplace. "It's been almost two years since Grandpapa went on to heaven. I've been planning this ever since my beloved passed, and I think I've waited quite patiently." She looked down at the watch hanging from her blouse. "You know, I may not have a lot of time left."

In earlier years, Katherine would have laughed at the swift change to a safer subject — not to mention the dramatic look on the older woman's face. But laughter didn't come easily anymore — it hadn't for a long time — and she really didn't want a scolding about respecting her elders. "I highly doubt that your time here will be so brief, Grandmother."

"Doubt all you want. I just wish you would agree so that we could start fresh. Wash you clean of that man once and for all. Stop allowing him to control you."

Katherine bristled. Did Randall still control her from the grave? She had often thought only death could release her. Her death. His. It never mattered which, so long as she no longer had to abide such a heinous creature.

Apparently, it wasn't that easy.

Randall Demarchis. He'd been her parents' choice. *Not* hers. And she'd never loved the man. But she'd resigned herself to the arrangement out of respect for her parents. At the time, she had little choice.

Her senator husband had been all manners and smooth-talking politician until their wedding day. But as soon as they were alone that first night, his façade fell — and the beast behind the mask came out.

The horrors she faced during those few years of marriage were something she never spoke of — to anyone. But Grandmother had guessed, although never to the degree of severity. And on the evening she persuaded Katherine to be honest with her mother and father, they'd received the news that her parents were dead — killed in an automobile accident.

At that moment, Katherine knew all hope was lost. She was destined to her fate. And refused to ever speak of it again.

After the loss of her parents, Randall's cruelty only intensified. But around town they were the toast and envy of all. He was dashingly handsome and she was classically beautiful. His constituents and peers alike respected and even loved him. Randall was all charm and grace when he wanted to be.

It was all a game. A perverted and hideous game.

The charade continued for three long, miserable years until Randall drank himself into oblivion one night, slipped on the ice outside his club, and fell down the stairs. A broken neck made death instantaneous.

The nightmare was over. The monster was gone. And she didn't shed a tear.

Three years.

And it had changed everything.

Short for a marriage by most people's standards. But it felt like three hundred to her.

Every once in a while, she dreamed of happier times. Back when she *had* hopes and dreams. When she had been in love . . . a long time ago. But those were few and far between now. The reality of her marriage hammered the truth into her heart.

There was no hope of happily ever after.

"Katherine? Don't go into that dark place alone. You can tell me the truth." Grandmother tilted her head in a way that said she knew exactly where Katherine's thoughts had taken her. But the conversation Grandmother wanted to have wouldn't happen. Couldn't happen.

"Katherine . . . dear?" The expression on Grandmother's face changed to worry.

If she didn't steer the conversation back, she'd distress the poor woman, and Grandmother had already been through too much. She knew too much. Even if it was only a fraction — Katherine had to spare her beloved grandparent.

Wherever they traveled, the bleak cloud that was Katherine's existence would follow. It was her fate. Randall had seen to that. But she could spare her grandmother and give her a little peace. "All right, all right. Wherever you want to go. I'll go along. As long as I don't have to dress in any of those crazy new designs that just keep getting shorter." She raised an eyebrow. "And don't think I didn't hear you speaking to your dressmaker about a new wardrobe for me. If I told you the reputation of the girls who don such apparel, you would keel over here and now."

"Agreed. No short dresses." Grandmother's eyes twinkled. "It's nice to hear some spunk back in your voice."

Katherine shook her head. She didn't have the will to argue. Spunk or no spunk, apparently, she was about to travel. "So where are we going?"

"Alaska, my dear." The older woman grinned like the cat that swallowed the canary. "We're going to Alaska."

March 5 — The Curry Hotel, Curry, Alaska

Twenty-year-old Thomas Smith lifted the slop bucket over his head as he navigated his way through the chickens and into the pigpen.

Today, he wouldn't trip. Nor would he spill anything on his clean apron.

And then he would be able to say that he had made it a whole one hundred days

27

without being clumsy. Mrs. Johnson — the head cook at the Curry Hotel — had promised him a cake, and the cook's chief assistant, Cassidy, had promised him that all the kitchen girls and maids would line up and kiss him on the cheek if he made it.

He didn't need any more motivation than that.

But even more exciting was that he'd completed a course with Cassidy's father, Mr. John Ivanoff, and her husband, Mr. Allan Brennan — the two expert wilderness and exploration guides — and they would be presenting him with a certificate of achievement at dinner tonight.

Could the day get any better?

Bessie — the hotel's old sow — made a charge for him inside the pen. With a quick step to the right, Thomas avoided the grumpy pig's first run, but she made another effort with her hind end.

Before he knew it, he was slipping and sliding in the mud as Bessie made another run for him.

Thomas threw the bucket over his head and reached for the fence post to keep from falling. Today of all days. The old girl just had to take it out on him *today*.

Scrambling over the fence, Thomas heard whistles and applause. Great. They were probably all going to laugh at clumsy ol' Thomas.

But as his feet hit the ground and he took stock of his clothing, he was amazed. Not a single smudge. Except for the mud on his shoes. And to make everything even better, the slop bucket had landed squarely in the feed trough and the pigs were enjoying their breakfast.

As the whistles and applause continued, Thomas clapped his hands together and took a bow.

Allan Brennan walked over to him and patted him on the back. "That's what I call thinking on your feet, Thomas. Good job!" He winked at Thomas and walked away.

The praise made him want to puff out his chest. Even though Allan had won Cassidy's heart when Thomas fancied himself in love with her too, the older man had earned his utmost respect. Especially when he and Cassidy came to Thomas a couple years earlier with an offer to help him expand his education.

Growing up in an orphanage until he was fourteen, Thomas had only received a cursory education. The strict religious leaders of the orphanage saw little purpose in teaching the boys anything but physical labor and the restrictions of an angry, harsh, and judging God. The Brennans helped him not only to see God in a different light, but they had made it their goal to give Thomas an education.

Amazingly enough Thomas proved to be a very quick learner. So quick, in fact, that one year later he was able to take the entrance exam for the new college in Fairbanks. The Alaska Agricultural College and School of Mines.

Education had changed his life. He fit in a semester here and there around the busiest seasons of the Curry, but next fall he would attend for the entire fall and spring semesters. Allan and Cassidy offered to pay his tuition and transportation to school. In turn, Thomas offered and pledged to work as a guide for the Curry for the foreseeable future. He also hoped to be able to assist the Brennans with their Seattle-based company by learning as much as he could and offering new ideas for mountaineering equipment they could sell. Especially to all the miners headed to Alaska.

He smiled at the retreating figure of Allan Brennan. The man was his hero, and one day, Thomas hoped to be like Allan. God-fearing, hardworking, and well respected.

Now, if he could just make it until dinner without mishap . . .

Thankfully, there were fewer guests to contend with this time of the year. For Thomas that meant he didn't do so much to help with hikes and camping trips as much as he did upkeep and repairing. But it didn't matter. He loved his work. Loved school too. His studies had opened his eyes to a better understanding of the Alaskan wilderness.

The afternoon passed quickly in his various labors. A glance at his watch made him realize it was, in fact, dinnertime. Heading toward his reward, he smiled.

The downstairs dining room teemed with noise and activity. Happy chatter of the day between all the hotel workers, clanking of silverware on plates, and above all that, Mrs. Johnson's orders. That woman never ran out of steam.

Or orders.

She wasn't a big woman, but she was stout and fierce. He'd heard it said the widow was in her forties, but the years had been hard and she looked older to him. Her reddish-brown hair was equally interspersed with gray, and the lines around her mouth suggested she'd done more frowning than smiling. But she was a fair person and a good judge of character. She could bark out orders like a sergeant in the army, but she would work alongside you with tireless effort.

Thomas admitted he'd come to care about the bossy chef. About all of the staff at the Curry. They were the most important people in his life.

Something like a big family. And he loved it.

Over the years, he'd worked hard. Harder than he ever thought possible. Made more mistakes than he'd ever want to admit, but it had all been worth it. As he looked around the huge table full of staff and workers, Thomas smiled. They weren't like a family — they *were* his family.

Once the needs of the guests were met, the Curry Hotel staff sat down to their own meal in the downstairs dining room. This was the routine they'd followed ever since the place opened in 1923. They took advantage of the leftover food, which was always of the highest quality, and shared their thoughts about the events and happenings of the hotel. Thomas thought it the perfect way to end the day.

The clinking of a glass quieted most everyone and Mr. John Ivanoff scooted his chair back, stood, and cleared his throat. "Everyone, if I could have your attention, please."

Footsteps sounded down the hall and Mr. Bradley — the hotel manager — appeared from the doorway.

Everyone stood.

"Please, be seated." Their manager motioned with his hands. "Well now." He looked straight at Thomas.

Thomas swallowed. A little louder than he intended.

"Dinner upstairs was exceptional, everyone. Excellent job as usual. Our patrons are very happy." Mr. Bradley coughed and then continued. "Mr. Ivanoff and Mr. Brennan have informed me that we have something to celebrate this evening."

Several of the younger staff whispered to each other.

"I'd like to ask a special staff member to come forward." The manager's face was serious and gave nothing away.

More whispers and giggles around the table as most everyone sat up a little straighter.

"Thomas" — he held out a hand — "would you join me up here, please?"

A few gasps were heard around the table and then complete silence.

Thomas took a deep breath and scooted his chair back. It screeched on the hard floor. But he stood up and straightened his

33

shoulders as he walked toward Mr. Bradley.

The manager held his hand out still.

Thomas took it and grasped it.

"As you all probably know, Thomas has been with us for three years now. Since the beginning of the hotel. And even though we've all had challenges to schedules and routines here at the Curry, I haven't seen anyone work harder or longer under sometimes the worst of circumstances."

Gentle applause filled the room.

Mr. Bradley held up his other hand until it was quiet. "On top of his regular duties, Thomas has sought education to further himself and learn a new trade. Not only has he achieved that goal, but he has done it with flying colors and all while fitting in time in Fairbanks to attend college."

More applause.

John and Allan stood as well. Holding out a plaque, Allan handed it to Thomas.

John spoke. "This is your certificate of achievement, Thomas. You've earned it and will one day be the best guide out there — I'm sure of it."

Cassidy had sneaked up behind Mr. Bradley at some point and handed the manager another plaque as she winked at Thomas. The manager grinned. "And this award is for one hundred days —"

34

Cheers and clapping, hooting and hollering drowned out anything else the man might have said.

Thomas gladly took the plaque and raised it over his head as he spotted Mrs. Johnson carrying a massive cake into the workers' dining hall. His mouth watered. This was for *him*. Wow.

John and Allan crouched and each grabbed one of Thomas's legs and lifted him above their shoulders. John's baritone belted out, "For he's a jolly good fellow, for he's a jolly good fellow . . ."

As Thomas looked out across the dining room to all the smiling faces, he couldn't help but be proud.

This was his family.

And he didn't want to be anywhere else.

2

March 6 — France

Gazing down at the coffin that housed his father's physical body, Jean-Michel counted the scoops of dark soil as they hit the lid and began to cover its surface. The two cemetery employees worked their shovels in unison.

Twenty . . . twenty-one . . . twenty-two.

The quiet thumps of dirt plopping on wood became quieter as the coffin disappeared and earth covered earth.

Thirty-four . . . thirty-five.

Thick humidity, rich with the scent of the recent rain, covered the earth. What used to bring him thoughts of being washed clean and fresh starts, now would forever stain his memory with the day he'd buried his dad. His mentor. His confidant.

Pierre Langelier hadn't been that old a man, but a stroke had rendered him helpless just a week earlier. Complaints of blurred vision and fatigue were the only hints that something was wrong with the Langelier patriarch. Everyone thought it was attributed to overwork. But everyone had been wrong.

Jean-Michel wrapped an arm around his sister's shoulders. Other than a few sniffles, Collette had been quiet through the entire funeral and graveside service.

And that worried him.

Collette was never quiet. Since her return from boarding school the year before, she had all but worn him out with her constant flitting about. She had been the apple of their father's eye and could generally get anything she wanted from him. The exception had been where young men were concerned. Collette had encouraged suitors at every point. She wanted to try them on like the silly fashions she and her girlfriends thought so wonderful. Father, however, would not be persuaded. He would find an appropriate suitor for her. Now Jean-Michel supposed that task fell to him.

Another few plunks of dirt. Then the shovels patted the top. He leaned hard on his cane.

Their father was buried. Out of sight. Under a mound. With a wooden cross at the head until the gravestone could be carved and placed.

Too many deaths.

First, the Great War and then the influenza pandemic — every person he knew had lost someone. Only a few years later the Druze Revolt — when he'd failed to save countless lives. Now Father.

He looked up and gazed at the dreary sight before him. Tombstone after tombstone. Mound after mound. And yet Jean-Michel felt they were leaving their father isolated and alone. Without his beloved wife.

Their mother was buried in Quebec — on the other side of the world. They'd been living abroad so the senior Langelier could keep Jean-Michel out of reach of the war. Father paid outlandish fees for Jean-Michel to attend college there, and even though it kept him out of the Great War, they'd all paid the utmost price — Mother contracted influenza and succumbed to the dreaded disease before he could graduate.

Yet another point of guilt.

The reduced Langelier family returned to France after the armistice was signed, and Jean-Michel was stunned to learn that most of his old schoolmates were dead. More guilt piled onto his already heavy heart whenever he looked into the faces of their parents. Did they wonder why he lived when their own sons were dead?

So much sorrow. Too many funerals.

The quiet rustling of movement brought Jean-Michel's attention up from the dark mound before him.

"So sorry for your loss. Pierre was a good man." Someone's soft words reached his ear as they passed by.

"If we can do anything . . ."

"We will say prayers for your family." A woman's voice cracked as she patted Jean-Michel's arm.

One by one the mourners departed with their pittance of encouragement offered. Father had been loved by many as evidenced by the large crowd at the funeral and here at the graveside service. Loved. Admired. Respected. All the things Jean-Michel was not.

Pastor and Mrs. Martin were the only ones left now, and they had moved away about twenty yards — most likely to give Collette and him a few last moments. As much as Jean-Michel felt the tug to speak to someone, to allow all the pain and grief that was buried in him to spew out, he knew he'd never be able to. It would stay locked inside him forever. That was his burden alone to bear.

A shudder under his arm drew his attention back to his sister. She shook again and then fell to her knees and sobbed. "What will we do?" She looked so young and vulnerable — her tiny frame swallowed up in black bombazine. "What will we do without Papa?"

Jean-Michel shifted on his cane and closed his eyes as the words sank into the very depths of his soul. He should have known it was coming. Even vivacious and carefree Collette had broken down.

He'd expected that same shuddering of emotion to overwhelm him. But it stayed submerged and unreachable. He felt only the numbness of his raw existence. Only the depths of his wounds. And he wished he could change that.

"Ahem . . ." The clearing of the throat sounded familiar. "I'm sorry to intrude."

Jean-Michel opened his eyes and looked into the bloodshot gaze of his father's lifelong business partner. "Mr. Dubois . . . um" — he couldn't exactly say it was nice to see him; it wasn't nice to see *anyone* under these circumstances — "thank you for coming."

The man handed him a card. On it a simple phrase was penned. *Je suis désolé pour ta perte.* Words he'd heard countless times that day.

Jean-Michel kept a stoic expression. No doubt Dubois truly was sorry for their loss. He and Pierre Langelier had been more than business partners. They had been lifelong friends. Dubois's tears were real and his sadness no doubt ran deep. But it didn't change a thing.

Mr. Dubois placed a hand on Jean-Michel's shoulder. "Those words are inadequate. I'm sorry. I should have been the one to go first. Not your father." He lifted a handkerchief to his nose. "That was our joke between us."

Jean-Michel didn't wish the man ill, but at the moment he wished those words were true. No response would form on his tongue, so he stared blankly at the man who'd been like family to them. Because reality had set in . . . all the wishing in the world wouldn't bring his father back.

"Can we take a walk?" Dubois wiped his eyes and his nose again.

Looking down at his sister, Jean-Michel shook his head. Collette wasn't a child anymore, but her naïveté and vibrant spirit — untainted or marred by the realities of their dark world — made her age seem that much tenderer. And she was still unmarried.

She needed him. He couldn't leave her alone at a time like this.

But before he could voice his thoughts, Collette stood — mud covering the bottom of her dress — and ran to Mrs. Martin, their pastor's wife.

The pastor nodded toward Jean-Michel.

"I don't feel much like walking, but we can talk for a few minutes. Then, I must get Collette home." Did his words sound as stiff as they felt?

"This is a horrible time to discuss business, but unfortunately, it's necessary. With the death taxes due and our competitors pressing in, I would like to offer to buy out your father's share of the business and factory." He held out an envelope. "As you can see, our lawyers have drawn up the paperwork with a very fair offer." He waited.

Jean-Michel opened the envelope despite feeling there had to be a better time for such matters. Why today?

"I've added in an extra ten thousand francs to the offer. Your father was like a brother to me, and I promised I would see to it that you and Collette were well taken care of." Dubois's voice cracked.

"You sound as if Father knew he was going to die."

Dubois nodded. "He did . . . at least he

42

told me he felt certain he would. He didn't know if it was the fatigue he felt or the blurring of his sight that made him believe this, or some divinely appointed warning, but he felt strongly enough about it that he spoke to me at great length."

"I wish he'd spoken to me."

Again, Dubois nodded. "I wish he would have. However, I want you to know that I made him a promise, and I believe this arrangement will fulfill that in part."

Jean-Michel perused the papers. "This is more than fair, Mr. Dubois." He looked over at his sister, crumpled in the pastor's wife's arms. "You know that I've never had any desire to work at the factory or to run the business, and Father was all right with that." He worked to swallow the lump of guilt down. "He knew I'd had other dreams long ago, and after this" — he looked down at his leg — "he was helping me to find my way."

"He was so proud of you."

Jean-Michel nodded, knowing it was the truth. He stuck out his hand. "I gladly accept your generous offer and thank you for caring so much for our family."

Dubois shook his hand and nodded. "Please let me know if you ever need anything. Anything at all. Yes?"

"Yes, thank you."

The older gentleman walked a few steps and then stopped and turned. "I know how hard the last few years have been." He glanced over at Collette. "The war devastated our nation and it hasn't been easy to recover from that, but your father had a thought that you both might benefit from a trip. He told me how much you all enjoyed traveling when you were younger."

It was true. Jean-Michel had wonderful memories of trips that crossed oceans and multiple countries. His father and mother had wanted their children to see the world. Of course that ended with the onset of the Great War. Poor Collette didn't have the same memories, she'd been so young.

"He thought maybe a trip away would be healing for you both. Mrs. Dubois and I just returned from America — perhaps I could send her over to entice Collette to take a journey? It could take your minds off the grief . . . and America is such an exciting place to visit. They don't bear the physical scars of war as we do."

"Thank you for the offer. Maybe in a few days, she'll be up for a visit."

"Again, let me know if I can help." Dubois patted his shoulder, then took his leave.

Jean-Michel looked back down at his

father's grave. "Was it the right thing to do?" He tapped the envelope against his leg. "Dubois will do right by you, of that I'm sure. But how can I possibly care for Collette when I can't even find my way out of my own pit of despair?" Stashing the envelope inside his coat pocket, he leaned on his cane and walked toward his sister.

No longer a sobbing mess, she smiled at the pastor and his wife. If only he could grab on to a bit of her joy. Her *passion de la vivre.* Passion for living. But his thoughts were too dark.

He couldn't let Collette see the truth. That's how Father handled it all these years. He'd sheltered her and protected her. Jean-Michel wished he could live in that world. But he had little desire to face life another day.

As he neared, Collette reached out a hand to him. "We will make it through together, my brother, yes?"

Pasting on a smile, Jean-Michel nodded. "Yes, my sister. Together we will." He kissed her on the forehead.

If only he truly believed that in his heart.

March 12 — France

Collette Langelier looked down at her black

45

dress and grimaced. She'd never liked black. It was a wretched color. It wasn't even a color — not truly.

Tears sprang to her eyes. How shameful of her. Her father wasn't in the ground but a week. She wore black out of respect for the greatest man she'd ever known. And she would continue to do so.

Even if she hated it.

The clock chimed and she looked around the silent library. Nothing was the same without the effervescence of Father. His personality preceded him when he entered a room and no one ever felt alone or neglected when he was around.

Larger than life. That's how her mother always described him.

She also used to say that Collette's personality was very much like his.

A tear ran down her cheek. She missed him. Missed them both. She'd only been eleven when Mama died. Worse still, Collette hadn't been able to say good-bye. The loss left a huge hole in her heart. Now Papa was gone, too, and the hurt overwhelmed her. Much more than she could say.

Soft footfalls on the carpet brought her attention to the door. She quickly dried her eyes. She didn't want her brother to think she'd been wasting away in despair. Even if she had been. Papa had told her that her brother's strange mood and dark outlook had to do with the pain he felt from his leg, and encouraged her to do nothing to add to his misery.

Jean-Michel walked in and lifted a soft smile in her direction. "How are you this fine morning?" The smile did little to ease the tension in his brow.

"Obviously more rested than you, brother." She poured him a cup of the strong coffee he loved and held it up for him.

"Thank you." He nodded. "Madeleine makes the best coffee, yes?"

Collette allowed herself to laugh. He knew all too well that she couldn't stand the stuff. "If you say so, Jean-Michel. The smell alone is enough to singe my hair." She lifted a hand to her curls and batted her eyelashes. "I'll stick with tea."

At least he chuckled. She'd been working to get him to smile for days now, and nothing had worked. They both missed their father dearly — but how was she supposed to live with a man who wouldn't move forward in his grief?

He settled onto the sofa across from her. "I saw Mr. Dubois again this morning. He gave me some of Father's things and a few sealed envelopes from the lawyer."

She raised an eyebrow. "Was it difficult?"

"No." He looked down at his cup. "It was good. There's a letter for each of us." Reaching into his jacket pocket, he looked her in the eyes. "It was a little difficult at first, but then it was wonderful to read Father's words to me." He handed her an envelope with Father's beautiful script on the front.

The flourish on the *C* made her smile as she ran her hand over it. "I am sure I will cherish it. Father always had a way with words."

"That he did." Jean-Michel stood and leaned on the cane. "I'm going to give you a moment or two to read his letter and then I'll be back. Is that all right?"

"Yes, that's quite all right." He was always so thoughtful — giving her space when she needed it. As she slid a finger under the flap, she thought of Father penning these words — who knew how long ago? — to her, knowing that to read them, he would have had to pass on to heaven. What would she write in a letter like that? The thought had never crossed her mind before, since she tended to live in the moment and enjoy things as they came. There'd never been much need for her to worry. Never much to grieve or be sorrowful over, other than

Mother. Her life had been picturesque. Fun. Happy.

At nineteen years of age, maybe she ought to start taking things more seriously.

She pulled out the single sheet of paper, and it overcame her that this would be the last time she'd receive a handwritten note from her father.

Collette,

Je t'aime plus que les mots ne peuvent le dire . . .

I love you more than words can say. How often he had voiced that declaration and now here it was once again . . . for the last time.

It pains me to think that you are reading this because I am gone, but the prodding to write these thoughts down overwhelms me. I'm sorry for the sadness you will bear on my behalf, but please remember that God loves you more than I ever could. My only true regret is that I found Him so late in life and didn't have the chance to share Him with you like I should.

Which brings me to the purpose of this letter. I have two requests:

1 — Promise me that you will find someone to talk to about God. A man or woman of faith whom you can trust. Your brother has names of several people I think would be helpful. I've also left you two Bibles — one in French and one in English — so that you may study freely. Please pursue this quest. God is everything to me, but I want you to find Him for yourself. He loves you so much. And I want to be able to spend eternity with you, my precious daughter.

2 — By now, Dubois has offered to buy the business. He does it with my full approval and hopes that you will be able to stay in the life in which you are accustomed. There are plenty of funds, and they are dispersed in both your name and your brother's. When you are twenty-five — or when you marry, whichever comes first — you'll be able to manage your own accounts, but until then Jean-Michel will oversee them. I caution you to be careful of young suitors who will come courting just because they know of your wealth. I know you have long desired to find a beau and marry as your friends have done, but I hope you will take your time. Think long and hard about the man who

will be your lifelong companion. Your mother was most precious to me; she completed me. A husband and wife should do that for one another, not simply be someone who looks nice and takes you to parties.

Lastly, be happy. Your brother knows my heart regarding the two of you steeping yourselves in mourning. So, my sweet Collette, I know how you abhor black. Throw off the grieving attire and be the vivacious young woman you are. Convince your brother to travel somewhere and help him come out of the black fog he's been in since the war. I beg you not to mourn me, for I am in a better place.

I pray for happiness for you both — as a father, that is my duty — but more than anything, I pray you come to an understanding with our Lord.

Live life to the fullest, my dearest. Wear your pretty clothes and put ribbons in your hair for me.

As always, your doting Father,
Papa

P.S. I never liked black either.

Collette laughed as tears slid down her

cheeks. He always had a way of lifting her spirits. Oh, how she would miss him.

Jean-Michel leaned around the doorframe. "Is it all right to come back in?"

"Yes." She patted her cheeks with a hankie. "You were right. His words were beautiful to read." Tapping the letter in her hand, she inhaled deeply.

"Would you care to share with me what he said?"

She held out the letter, but he shook his head. "No, just tell me."

"He cautioned me regarding suitors and told me that you would control my money until I turned twenty-five or married. He also told me not to mourn, to wear my pretty clothes and put ribbons in my hair for him." She looked down at the black gown. "He said he didn't like black either."

Jean-Michel nodded. "Did he write to you about God?"

"Yes. And you?"

Her brother nodded, one hand on the mantel, the other on his cane. His gaze seemed to be glued to the fire.

"Well?"

"I don't know what to think of it. Especially since he never really spoke of it to me." Jean-Michel took his hand from the mantel and reached into a pocket. "If you'd like to contact someone on this list, go ahead. It may take me some time before I'm ready to speak of God."

The paper shook a bit in his hand. Collette couldn't stand for her brother to be so miserable. And if talk of God made it worse, then who was she to pursue it? "No. Not now."

He shrugged and tucked it back into his jacket pocket.

"What I would like to do is discuss something that Father said in my letter."

Jean-Michel raised an eyebrow. "You aren't going to speak to me of suitors, are you?"

Collette rose, then crossed to where he stood. "I have no desire to discuss that just now." She smiled. Maybe if she smiled big enough and pleaded long enough, she could convince him. Besides, it was for his own good. Father said so. "I'd like to take a trip."

"A trip." He looked down at the letter. "Exactly what did Father say about a trip?"

"That we should take one. That it would be good for us to have fun." She hesitated a moment. "That we should go off and enjoy ourselves and heal."

Jean-Michel gave her a half smile. "Well, those aren't his exact words, are they?"

"Close enough, brother, and you know it."

She took the letter and went back to the settee. "I think it's a splendid idea. And like Father said, he didn't want us moping about — and he didn't want your sadness and nervousness to worsen."

"You can't do anything about those things, so don't worry over it." He sighed and looked back at the fire. "I can't say the thought of traveling excites me, but if it's something you wish to do . . ."

She squealed and raced over to hug him. "Truly? You would do this for me?"

"But of course."

Ideas formed in her mind. "You know, Mrs. Dubois was just speaking of their trip to America. She told me everything." She sighed. "It sounds so amazing and vast. They absolutely loved it. Could we go?"

"America?" That eyebrow shot up again.

"Pretty please?" She smiled. "I won't ever ask for anything again. . . ."

"Of course you won't."

3

March 12 — The Curry Hotel

Margaret Johnson stared into the mirror. The woman looking back at her was old and weary. More so than her actual age of forty-three. Her once red-brown hair was now dingy with gray. She picked up the brush and began taming the lengthy mane. She remembered back to a happier time when she had been young and her mother had done this task.

"This is your crowning glory, Maggie."

She smiled at the thought of her nickname. No one called her that anymore. No one *knew* to call her that.

With a sigh, she braided the hair into a single plait for bed. Even though it was just nine thirty, the bed beckoned her with promises of a peaceful rest. She'd been up since three that morning, as was her routine. Baking had to be done and readied for the morning meal. Food had to be prepared and staff overseen. It was a job that afforded her few breaks from the routine.

Thanks to Cassidy — that dear girl — Margaret had been able to go to Seattle for a few weeks in January. The first time off she'd taken in three years. But it was still all about her work. Work was what her life revolved around now.

In Seattle she'd visited several well-established restaurants in order to review their kitchens. Wanting to know and see the very latest in equipment was essential so that she could secure similar pieces for her own kitchen at the Curry. The funds afforded by the management were quite generous, and she'd returned to the hotel with wonderful treasures, as well as a few carefully memorized recipes.

Chefs were not known to give out their secrets, but Margaret had a keen eye and good memory. It hadn't been hard to watch the dishes being created as she was told about various equipment. Neither was it hard to sit and sample a meal and guess what ingredients went into the dish. It was something of a gift she had. Her family had always praised her for her tasty creations. Back when she still had a family.

Her husband had told her there was no

finer cook in all the world.

But he was gone now. Taken by the same influenza that took the rest of her dear family.

She tied a ribbon to secure the braid and sighed. Life was so much harder without the people you loved to stand beside you and offer encouragement. Folks at the Curry had taken the place of her family, but even there Margaret kept a tight guard on her heart. She didn't want to get hurt again by losing anyone.

Cassidy was the biggest exception to the rule of keeping people at arm's length. Margaret chuckled. She loved that girl like a daughter. They shared many wonderful conversations about life. Cassidy believed in a loving God, which had been a complete contrast to how Margaret saw Him. Especially after losing all who were dear to her.

Oh, Cassidy prayed for Margaret regularly and hoped that she might one day embrace God as Cassidy did. And while Margaret had to admit she had softened on her views and yielded some of her anger, she was still quite afraid to put her trust in anyone. It was the reason she would never again allow herself to fall in love.

Love was just too painful.

She pulled back the covers and sighed.

This was the loneliest time of the day for her. No one to talk to. No one to listen to. Although her husband, Theodore — Teddy — would have said she did precious little of the latter.

"This is foolishness." With a sigh, she put out the light. "I won't give myself over to brooding. It serves no purpose."

She climbed into bed and hugged her pillow close. "No purpose at all."

A knock at the door made her jolt up in bed. "Who is it?"

"It's Cassidy." The sweet voice floated through the door.

Margaret jumped out of bed as fast as her aching body would allow. When she opened the door, she blurted out, "Is everything okay?"

A huge smile blossomed on Cassidy's face. With a twinkle in her eyes, she pulled a towel-covered plate from behind her back. "Of course, everything is okay. You worry too much." She walked into the room. "I just thought it would be nice to try this new chocolate torte I made, and we can catch up on what's going on." With a whisk of her hand, she uncovered a beautiful and very chocolatey-looking treat. The grin on her face made Margaret laugh.

"You are just what I need, Cassidy Faith.

You do beat all. . . ." Margaret shook her head. All the brooding grief she'd allowed earlier diminished. "When I'm feeling blue, you know exactly what I need."

"A hug?"

Laughter bubbled up out of her. Full, unabashed laughter. It felt wonderful. How did this girl always have so much joy? "You know I could always use a hug. At least from you — we wouldn't want the rest of the staff to think I'd gone soft."

"No, of course not." Cassidy bit her lip, obviously in an attempt to stifle her giggles.

"Exactly. But what was I going to say?"

"What?"

"Chocolate. A woman always needs chocolate."

"Yes, ma'am."

March 12 — France

Jean-Michel rubbed down his right leg. It ached today more than usual. But they'd also had colder temperatures than normal for this time in March. Whatever the case, the ache radiated throughout his body and up into his heart. It was well into the night, but he hadn't been able to sleep.

So much loss. He never expected to be burying his father at such an early age. But as much as the grief threatened to overtake him, he had to at least think of Collette. Father had kept her ensconced in their home amidst friends, parties, and beauty. It wasn't that she hadn't known sorrow or that there were darker things in the world, but she had been taught those things weren't as important as being lighthearted and seeing the good.

Collette's pleas for a trip raced around in his mind. He'd done his best to keep his true feelings to himself at supper that evening as she prattled on about the Dubois's trip to America. But her excitement didn't do anything to spark an urge to go. Everywhere he went, the nightmares seemed to follow.

Perhaps that was it. Maybe a trip abroad wasn't such a horrible idea. America didn't have the traces of the Great War around every corner like Europe did. Maybe there was hope to find a way out of the dark fog that surrounded him. Otherwise, what hope could he give Collette? She deserved to have her only relative be present and part of her life.

He leaned back onto his bed and propped up his bad leg. The voyage was sure to be difficult with his leg — ships were hard enough to navigate on rough seas when you had *two* good legs — but he could at least give it a try for her. Life would never be happy for him again, but he would put his best effort forth to at least ensure Collette was taken care of. Father would want that.

He also wanted Jean-Michel to pursue God — whatever that meant. But Jean-Michel didn't think he could. How could a loving God allow all the atrocities in this world? No.

That request of Father's would have to go unheeded. For now, he would focus on Collette. She was the only one who had a hope for the future.

Exhaustion tugged at him — like gravity sucking him down into the mattress. He laid an arm over his head. He needed sleep.

He was so thirsty. "Water . . . please . . ."

No one heard him. There were too many others in the tent injured like he was and not enough medical personnel.

But he couldn't wait any longer. "Please . . . somebody please . . . I need water!" The words ended on a cry. But he didn't shed any tears. His eyes and face were covered in grit and sand.

A young boy — didn't look any older than twelve years old — came to his side. "Sirotez lentement, monsieur. *Sip slowly."*

Jean-Michel nodded, but as soon as the

cool liquid hit his lips, he wanted to gulp it all down. The lad held the cup back and forced him to take it slower. After more perusal, Jean-Michel recognized the young man as one of their young soldiers. Why on earth did they have mere boys serving? Is this what was left after the Great War? The thought made him want to vomit.

Everything came back in an instant. Fear wrapped its ugly self around his gut.

The water boy turned to leave, but Jean-Michel grabbed his arm. "Where are my friends? George and Luc?"

"I don't know, monsieur. But I'll go ask." He pulled away.

Jean-Michel tried to sit up, but he couldn't. Desperate to find his friends, he turned his head every way possible to search and scan the room but saw no sign of them.

His heart picked up speed and a deep sense of dread filled him. "Non!" He thrashed on the table. "Non! George! Luc!"

An officer he hadn't met ran over and shoved his arms and legs down. "Langelier, calm down or your leg will open up again and bleed the last of your life out onto the sand."

He didn't care. "What happened to the two men who dragged me out? Please, you must tell me."

The officer shook his head.

"What? What does that mean? You don't know where they are?"

The man straightened slowly. "I'm sorry. They were shot rescuing you. They are both dead."

Bolting up in bed, Jean-Michel felt the sweat drip down his forehead. Every time he fell asleep, some terrible memory of the war would surface and take him back to that awful day. He hadn't been able to save anyone. Not the ones burning to their deaths . . . and not his two friends who'd come to save *him.*

Would he spend the rest of his life reliving the horrors? Why didn't God come and save him? Or those people? Or George and Luc, who declared God so merciful and loving? They were so much younger than he and full of life. They should have lived. A merciful God would have saved them. A God of love would never have allowed war in the first place.

Jean-Michel shook his head. "I can't do it, Papa. I can't seek this God of yours. He is a heartless judge — without feeling — without mercy. He leaves us to make our own way — or die."

So many had died and God hadn't been there. Or if He was, then He was even crueler than Jean-Michel believed.

The following morning, Jean-Michel sat in the dining room, drinking his coffee and wondering where the energy to deal with his young sibling would come from. Twenty cups of coffee couldn't even begin to prepare him. Collette would soon burst into the room in her girlish excitement, inundating him with requests — detailing ideas for a trip. Jean-Michel sighed. He didn't have the vigor to deny her. But if he could put her off until he talked to Dubois himself, then maybe he could come up with a suitable plan. At least, he hoped so. The lack of sleep wore him out and made rational thought difficult.

Ten minutes later, Collette danced her way over to him and hugged his neck, kissed his cheek, and smiled. "Good morning, brother. Did you sleep well?"

"Good morning to you too. I slept fine."

"You are lying to me. I can see the bags under your eyes."

He shrugged. "Well, then, why did you ask?"

She tilted her head at him and smiled as she placed her napkin in her lap. "So . . . have you decided about the trip?" Even though she might have been trying to look nonchalant, he knew better.

"I've decided that yes, we will go, but not too soon. I need to speak to Dubois and do some planning, so don't expect to be leaving on the next boat." He lifted his cup to his lips again, hoping that it had been enough to appease her.

She bounced on her chair like she had when she was a young girl. "Oh! That's wonderful. I don't mind waiting. Just the thought of the trip makes me excited, and I will need to prepare as well." She took a sip of tea and looked back to him. "But you will let me know soon?"

"As soon as I am able to make the plans."

"Thank you, Jean-Michel." She got up from her chair. "There's so much to do." With a wave of her hand she headed for the door.

"Aren't you going to eat breakfast?" He raised an eyebrow.

"Non." She flitted back over to his side and kissed his cheek. "I must call Mrs. Hébert and arrange for a new wardrobe, and my friends will no doubt want to throw me a going-away party — so I must help them plan it." As she left the room, she continued listing off things she needed to do.

"Well, at least that will keep her busy," Jean-Michel mumbled and went back to his coffee and newspaper.

Channing — their trusted butler — entered with a tray. "Here you are, sir."

"Thank you, Channing." He lifted the stack of mail — most were condolences. Cards and notes had flooded in since the death of Pierre Langelier became public. Channing thoughtfully provided a letter opener as well, and Jean-Michel took it off the tray, contemplating how he would ever manage to handle all of the replies. Perhaps he could borrow one of the secretaries at the factory to help.

"I will need the car to visit Mr. Dubois a little later."

"I'll have the new driver bring it around. What time should I tell him?"

A letter caught his eye. "Hmm? Oh, in about an hour."

The name Harrison in the corner caused his chest to tighten. Could it be?

Jean-Michel looked up and noticed Channing was gone. His hand trembled as he considered what might be inside the heavy envelope. He decided he didn't want to risk being interrupted and made his way upstairs to his bedroom. Once he was safely behind locked doors, he tore into the packet.

A smaller sealed envelope was inside a letter with instructions on the front.

DO NOT OPEN UNTIL
YOU READ THE LETTER

As he unfolded the pages as instructed, he held his breath.

Dear Jean-Michel,
It has been at least five years since the last time we met. My sweet granddaughter Katherine brought you over to see me at the Ambassador's Ball at the French Embassy and you were quite the charmer. The look of love you two shared made my heart sing. Since I'm not one for beating around the bush, I will get right to the point. Do you still love my granddaughter, Katherine?

Jean-Michel let his breath out in a *whoosh*. He felt as if he'd been punched in the stomach. No, she never did mince any words. But how could the woman ask that? Her granddaughter was a married woman! Too curious to judge the older woman's morals, he read on.

I probably should go back and explain. My son, Mark — Katherine's father — was a fool. And I'm allowed to say that because I was his mother. I loved him, and he was a wonderful man in many

67

ways and did many great things for his country, but he was a fool. And a prejudiced one at that.

Had Katherine's father died? Why would his mother keep speaking about him in the past tense?

I was quite shocked when he took the appointment to be Ambassador to France — knowing full well his feelings toward all things European. But he did seem to thrive and do an adequate job in his posting there.

Then Katherine fell in love with you. He was fine with you paying her attention, since your family was wealthy and of great position in France (which was significantly beneficial to him at the time), but he exploded — as you know all too well — when Katherine wanted to marry you. The thought of his daughter marrying a Frenchman, a foreigner, a European . . . well, it didn't sit well.

What you may not know is that after he forbade you two to marry, Mark booked immediate passage for the whole family. He resigned his post and we exited the embassy in less than two days. He obviously sent quite a bit of communication as well, because as soon as we set foot back in New York, a young senator named Randall Demarchis was waiting for us.

Within the week, Mark had arranged for Katherine to marry the senator. With her heart broken, she didn't much care about anything, and in a short time, they wed.

So that's what happened. All these years, he'd had no idea why Katherine would marry someone else so soon. And the mysteriously anonymous wedding announcement delivered to him was no coincidence. It had angered and crushed him. The letter shook in his hand as he continued.

While I am not at liberty to tell the rest of the story, I will tell you this: that despicable man is dead. And I say, good riddance. Yes, you read that correctly. I don't know the extent of what Katherine suffered, but she is lost and a mere shell of the girl we all knew and loved.

Her parents are also gone — killed in an automobile accident not long before her husband died — so Katherine has only me, but as I age, I worry more for her future. I fear I may lose her to her anguish. She has no desire to go on with life. That Demarchis monster wounded her deeply — mind, body, and soul.

Jean-Michel lifted his hand and covered his eyes. What had Katherine endured? His thoughts ran in too many dark directions. *Non.* He couldn't go there. Lowering his hand, he knew he had to read the rest.

And so, my dear boy, I come to my request.

I have finally convinced Katherine to travel with me to Alaska. This summer, we will spend a few months at the Curry Hotel, in Curry, Alaska.

I'm asking you to come. No. I'm begging you, and if you know anything about me, you know that I never beg. However, Katherine's life hangs in the balance.

You are still unmarried as far as I can conclude, and I'm quite certain you must still love my granddaughter. If I am incorrect, then please send the sealed envelope back. But if I am correct, then please open it to see that I have enclosed everything you need to join us in Alaska. I've arranged everything first class for you to visit America and the great territory of Alaska. A steamer will take you to New York and then a train will deliver you to Seattle. From there you will catch another ship to Alaska and then board a final train to Curry, Alaska, where we will be staying. Your hotel suite is already arranged.

I know it's a lot to ask, but if you love Katherine — please come. I believe it may be the only way to give her a reason to go on.

And so I leave you with the decision. I can only hope and pray that you join us in Curry.

Sincerely,
Maria Harrison

With a long exhale, Jean-Michel lowered the letter. He sat down at his desk and looked out the window without really seeing anything. The world had been gray to him for so long.

He'd never stopped loving Katherine. Even after he knew she'd married someone else, he'd tried to dissect her out of his heart, but it hadn't worked.

They'd been separated by an ocean and an arranged marriage, so he'd gone off to the army to forget her. That hadn't worked

71

either. Now he had a bad leg and a dark past. What good would he be for her?

He glanced at the sealed envelope. He had to do whatever it took to save her. Didn't he? He opened it to reveal various tickets — all first class, as Mrs. Harrison had promised.

But could he ever be worthy of her?

No.

He hadn't been worthy of those poor women and children in Syria. He hadn't been worthy of standing with his childhood friends on the battlefront. And he had a horrible feeling he wasn't even worthy of being the man his sister needed him to be. How could he ever hope to rescue Katherine from whatever pit of despair she had been flung into?

He picked up the letter and refolded it with great care.

"I do love her, but my love cannot save her. It didn't save her then, and it can't save her now, no matter how much I might wish it to be."

He tucked the letter and tickets back into the larger envelope. For a moment, he stared at the handwriting. Despite knowing what had to be done, Jean-Michel hesitated.

Katherine needed him. How could he just let her slip away into the same darkness that threatened to eat him alive? If anyone knew the grip of despair — it was Jean-Michel.

He opened his desk drawer and put the envelope inside. It felt as if he were losing her all over again, and the tightness in his throat threatened to cut off his air. He slammed the desk drawer closed and turned the key to lock it.

He wouldn't be going to Alaska.

4

April 12 — The Curry Hotel

Cassidy Faith Ivanoff Brennan jumped out of bed and looked at the clock. Why on earth would Allan allow her to sleep in? They had far too much to do in the kitchen today to prepare for the banquet tonight. Her husband was no doubt being sweet — after all, she and Mrs. Johnson had stayed late in the kitchen the last two nights working on the perfect menu — but heavens, she was already a half hour behind schedule.

Running around the room to gather her clothes for the day, she mentally made a list of what she could do to catch up. Opening the curtains, she squinted at the brilliant sunlight. The days were getting longer. Almost all the snow was melted and green popped up everywhere.

The wild flowers would soon begin to dot their river valley.

Goodness. Dallying at the window wouldn't get her list accomplished. She needed to focus and not get distracted.

Washed up and dressed in record time, Cassidy locked their room and headed to the main kitchen of the Curry Hotel at a brisk pace. Her braid hit her shoulder blades like a pendulum.

"Fiddlesticks." The huff left her lips as she reached back to wrap the braid into a bun and headed back to her room. Now she'd have to grab a few pins. Why was she forgetting so many little details lately? Getting distracted. Daydreaming. What was going on?

Probably all those things attested to fatigue. She'd been so tired of late. But they'd been busy and there hadn't been time for any breaks.

Still, she needed to work on being more organized and not letting her foggy brain forget things. Maybe it was time to transfer the lists from her mind to paper.

After pinning up her hair, she took some paper and a pencil from the little desk in the corner of their room. She could write a list on the way to the kitchen. Locking the door for a second time, she decided she would just have to scold her husband-of-almost-two-years for not waking her sooner.

With a kiss, of course. She shook her head and smiled. But still, it was entirely his fault that she was in this mess. If he hadn't allowed her to sleep in, she wouldn't be so frazzled.

The Curry — as everyone called it — was situated midway between Seward and Fairbanks on the Alaska Railroad line. It served as the depot for the train as well as the stopover point for crews and passengers. Built in 1923, it was a thing of beauty. Elegant, lavish, and full of modern-day amenities that most of Alaska didn't even have — the Curry was magnificent.

A small community had sprung up around the hotel, but Cassidy's favorite spot was across the suspension bridge over the Susitna River, up the ridge, and in full view of the tallest mountain in North America . . . Denali — or Mt. McKinley as the people in the lower forty-eight were determined to name it.

She longed to head up the ridge today — to see the always snow-covered Alaska Range, bask in the beauty and glory of God's creation, and see if Denali allowed himself to be seen in his entirety. But there wouldn't be time. Maybe soon.

The scent of bacon and sugary-sweet cinnamon rolls greeted her as she scribbled a few last notes on the paper. As she rounded the corner, the din of the kitchen welcomed her as well.

This was home.

She loved it.

For three years, she'd worked at the Curry Hotel as the Chef's Assistant. Although, Mrs. Johnson preferred the title *cook* rather than *chef*. It was backbreaking work at times, but Cassidy loved every minute and was so grateful for all that she had learned.

And it didn't hurt that she had met the love of her life here.

God certainly had blessed her with Allan. He'd blessed her father too — not only with a son-in-law John Ivanoff adored, but with another expert guide. Even now with Thomas's help, the men were hard-pressed to keep up with the schedule of explorations, nature walks, hikes, and fishing trips that guests wanted to take.

"Cassidy Faith!" Mrs. Johnson's harsh voice echoed across the kitchen, "I'm so glad you could join us this morning." In the past, the woman's tone would have made Cassidy cringe. But one look at the older woman's face, and Cassidy knew she was being teased. The tiniest of smiles lifted the corners of Cook's mouth.

"Thank you for having me, ma'am," Cassidy bantered back as she curtsied — ridiculous she knew, but at least it made a few of the girls giggle. While the rest of the kitchen staff still cowered under the barked orders of their commander, she shared a special relationship with the woman, and it brought her great joy. Thankfully, the staff was used to listening to the two women in charge banter, tease — and yes, sometimes even argue — back and forth, and it kept the machine that was the Curry Hotel kitchen oiled and running smoothly.

Cassidy moved to Mrs. Johnson's side and lowered her voice. "I am sorry. Apparently, Allan thought I needed the extra rest. I've no doubt been complaining about how tired I've been."

"I understand, but we've no extra time today. Pretend to be properly scolded and get to work." The gruff tone didn't fool Cassidy.

"Yes, ma'am." She saluted and walked to her station in the center of the kitchen.

The morning passed in a blur of prep for the banquet that would feed two hundred visitors that evening. The yeasty scent of Mrs. Johnson's famous Parker House dinner rolls rose up as Cassidy kneaded the dough. She wiped sweat from her forehead with a work towel and swayed for a moment. Goodness, what was going on?

The room began to tilt and she grabbed the edge of the worktable.

"Cassidy?" Mrs. Johnson's voice was somewhere in the distance.

Tiny pinpricks of light dotted her sight and then a black frame around her vision closed in. "Ummmmmmm . . ."

"She's awfully pale," a voice said from somewhere around the room.

Everything spun and swirled.

"Quick!" Mrs. Johnson's commanding voice again. "Someone catch her!"

Cassidy felt strong arms around her and then nothing.

Someone patted her hand.

Then came a kiss on her forehead.

"Cassidy." Allan's husky voice.

She was in her bed. The familiar comfort and scents surrounded her.

"She's beginning to come around." The voice accompanied a hand wrapped around her wrist. Ah, the new doctor. She recognized his tone. What was his name? "Yes, look, her eyes are fluttering."

"Come on, Cass." Allan's pleading voice washed over her. "Let me see those beautiful brown eyes."

Pulling in a deep breath, she worked to

lift her eyelids and saw her husband's handsome face smiling at her as he sat on their bed next to her. "Hi."

"Hi." He chuckled. "You scared me, honey. Please don't do that again."

She smiled back at him, then furrowed her brow. "What happened?"

"You fainted dead away in the kitchen." Mrs. Johnson came to her other side, pushing the good doctor out of the way. "Excuse me." She didn't even look at him.

The poor man would get used to Cook's no-nonsense ways at some point — he was still new here. But his facial expression was priceless. A bit of shock mixed with "who's in charge here?" mixed with embarrassment to be brushed aside. It made Cassidy smile at the man.

"Are you listening to me?" Mrs. Johnson touched her cheek as gently as her words were in contrast demanding. "Cassidy?"

"Yes, Mrs. Johnson, I'm listening." She nodded.

Allan squeezed her hand.

"You fainted! Clean away!" The woman looked so worried that Cassidy couldn't deny the woman a rant. "If I hadn't moved faster than these old bones should ever move, you would have hit the floor. Hard!"

It all came back and made Cassidy frown.

She peered around Mrs. Johnson to Dr. Reilly. Yes! That was it. His name was Reilly. "Is something wrong with me?"

The man moved forward a smidge and looked to Mrs. Johnson.

The older woman had the grace to step aside a bit, even if only a few inches. She was very territorial.

Dr. Reilly cleared his throat. "From what Mrs. Johnson and your husband tell me, I know you've been working too hard. Your husband further attested that you have been quite tired. Have you been eating?"

Cassidy lifted a palm to her forehead. "I forgot to eat this morning. That must be it."

The doctor chuckled. "That's not all of it, but yes, that contributed."

Mrs. Johnson shook her head. "I wish we had an older doctor." The words weren't quite as hushed as they should have been. But Cook was never one for hushing her thoughts.

The young doctor straightened. "I assure you, Mrs. Johnson, I'm quite capable. I might be only twenty-seven, but I've already been practicing privately for four years and was a medic and surgeon during the war before that."

The older woman gave a huff and gazed toward the ceiling.

Cassidy might have laughed out loud if not for her concern about what was wrong. "What were you saying, Doctor? Not eating contributed to what?" Cassidy's brow wrinkled into worry lines.

He straightened his shoulders and tilted his head just a bit. "Well, I was hoping to tell you privately" — he glanced at Mrs. Johnson — "but . . ."

"You can speak freely, sir. Mrs. Johnson is like a mother to me." Cassidy smiled at Cook's face.

The head chef's eyes blinked in rapid succession. Were those tears?

The blond-haired doctor coughed into his hand. "Well, then, I know I'm new and a stranger to you all, but we will get to know each other pretty well over the next few months."

Allan stiffened, his jaw tight and brow furrowed. "What do you mean?"

The man held up his hands as in surrender. "Nothing bad, Mr. Brennan, I assure you. In fact, I would like to congratulate you both. You see, Mrs. Brennan is expecting."

A gasp behind the doctor. "A baby?" Mrs. Johnson whispered.

"Yes." The young doctor chuckled. "In fact, I'm surprised you all didn't know.

You're at least four months along . . . perhaps more. Have you not had any morning sickness? Or your regular monthly . . . ?" His voice dropped off with the delicate question.

"No, I didn't think about it. I wasn't sick at all, but we've been so very busy." Cassidy did mental calculations in her head. "So the baby will be born in September?"

"That would be my guess." Dr. Reilly's serious expression didn't help him look any older. "Probably late in the month."

Mrs. Johnson began assaulting the doctor with questions, but Cassidy didn't hear any of it. She locked gazes with Allan. A baby. They'd talked and dreamed of this day, and it was finally here.

His eyes conveyed more love to her than she'd ever seen as he leaned close and touched his forehead to hers. "Congratulations, Mrs. Brennan." His words were barely a whisper. "I love you."

"I love you too." She tilted her chin up so she could kiss him.

"Great day in the morning! We're having a baby!" Allan stood up, shook the doctor's hand, ran to the door, and opened it.

In a loud voice she'd only heard him use for getting crowds to quiet down, her husband announced their news to the world. "Everyone, we're having a baby!"

April 15 — New York

Katherine stared into the mirror while the dressmaker walked around her.

"It's lovely, *non*?" The woman's French accent made Katherine's stomach hurt — a sad reminder of a past she needed to forget.

"You did a lovely job, Jacqueline. Truly." She forced some enthusiasm into her voice. "I apologize for my silence."

Jacqueline *tsk*ed. "I know you must miss your husband. It is all right. I understand." She sat on the floor and flipped the hem.

The mention of Randall made Katherine want to scream, but she held her tongue. The only emotion she could feel anymore was anger and outrage — and only when it came to Randall. The man had hurt her more than words could ever describe. To the world, she was a grieving widow. But inside, she was just numb. Unfeeling about anything else. And he had caused it.

"You are so very beautiful, Madam Demarchis. The pink of this gown brings out the beautiful color of your eyes."

"They're just brown." *Like cow dung,* Randall had pointed out on more than one occasion when his temper flared.

"Oh, *non,* they are more than brown, madam. They are like caramel." The dressmaker placed a few pins. "Like velvet. And with the honey color of your hair, it is very appealing. Especially with pink."

Katherine felt a little lift to her spirit. The compliment seemed genuine enough, and it had been so long since she'd even allowed herself to wear anything other than black.

Black for her supposed mourning of her husband.

But in truth, black for the ache in her own soul.

"You like, *oui?*" Jacqueline smiled up at her from her position on the floor as Katherine stared blankly into the mirror.

Fact was, she *did* like the dress. And the color was beautiful and cheery and the length quite modest. She touched the gathered waistline. "Yes, I like it very much."

"*Bien.* Good, good." Jacqueline hopped to her feet and looped her measuring tape around her neck like a scarf. "I will put the finishing touches on the rest of the garments this evening and have them to you by the morning."

"Thank you." Katherine smiled. It had been a long time since she'd spoken any French, but she decided to make the effort for this sweet lady. "*Merci beaucoup,* Jacqueline."

Grandmother tapped her cane on the open door. "May I come in?"

"Of course." Katherine turned to greet her. "Jacqueline just finished up."

Her grandmother's eyes sparkled as she leaned back and looked up and down at Katherine's dress. "It suits you." She smiled. "You look beautiful, my dear."

"Thank you, Grandmother."

The older woman took a seat while the dressmaker helped Katherine out of the dress. "I believe we should depart in two days' time."

"So soon?" Katherine pulled on her dressing gown.

"I will be back tomorrow," Jacqueline interjected as she filled her arms with the various outfits she'd brought to fit.

"See that it's all complete and ready to pack." Grandmother's tone was kind. "And I will give you a generous bonus."

"Oh, *merci, merci*!" Jacqueline hurried from the room, calling over her shoulder. "It will be so."

Katherine finished buttoning her robe and tied the sash. Taking a seat in the rose-and-sage-chintz-covered chair opposite her grandmother, she sighed. "Why so soon, Grandmother?"

"I'd like us to travel and see the country. What do you think? I've always wanted to see the Grand Canyon. Yellowstone and Yosemite. Those giant trees . . ." She tapped her chin.

"The redwoods?"

"Yes, dear. Those. And, of course, the Rocky Mountains." The cane swayed as she talked. "You know, I've been to Denver many times, but I don't believe that you have. There is nothing quite so grand as those mountains. I know they say we have mountains around here, but once you've seen the Rocky Mountains, well . . . those become hills."

"You've said that several times, yes." Katherine squinted.

"Oh, and Pikes Peak. Of course, we need to go there." Grandmother rang the bell for tea but wouldn't look her in the eye. "Maybe we should visit the Alamo too. I've always wanted to see more of Texas."

Katherine crossed her arms over her chest. "What exactly are you up to, Grandmother?"

The woman had the decency to blink several times. "I don't know what you mean."

"You said we were going to Alaska."

"We are." Her face was all innocence, but

her granddaughter knew better.

"So why is it that we need to travel the country?"

"We have to travel across the entire country to catch our ship for Alaska, so we might as well enjoy ourselves and take our time. See a few places. Eat wonderful food. That sort of thing." Maria Harrison was good. Too good. And Katherine knew the woman was up to something.

"Grandmother?" She worked to keep her tone calm and respectful. "I know you. If we're spending the entire summer in Alaska, shouldn't we save the adventure of seeing the rest of the country for another trip?"

"No." Grandmother straightened her shoulders. "Sometimes, you have to take the bull by the horns. Smell . . . the roses."

Katherine's lips curled upward ever so slightly. "Which is better than smelling the bull, I suppose."

The old woman pointed her cane. "See, already it has brought a smile to your face. Just remember, my dear, I don't need to explain myself to you. We're going on a trip. A marvelous trip. A long trip. We will spend our summer in Alaska, where I hope to catch a fish, see Mt. McKinley . . . and a reindeer —"

"And along with the reindeer, a sleigh . . .

and possibly jolly old Saint Nick too?"

"Oh, you! I said no such thing. Everyone knows there's a plethora of reindeer in Alaska." Flustered was too tame a word for Maria Harrison at that moment.

"Really? I don't remember learning that in school." Katherine arched a brow. She could play the game. "I'm not trying to be disrespectful, but you should just admit that you have something up your sleeve."

"I'll do no such thing. But I will leave you to work on your packing." The graceful and ladylike demeanor concealed any hint of discomfort. She rose, using her cane in an overly dramatic way. "You can humor this old lady and accept my wishes. After all, they might well be my last."

"Ha! You will outlive all of us." Katherine felt almost like laughing. Almost.

Her grandmother gave her a sympathetic smile. "One day you will laugh again. Truly laugh. I promise you." It was almost as if she had read Katherine's thoughts. "The pain will pass and you will once again be my happy, sweet Katherine."

Grandmother headed for the door. "Now, where is that silly girl with my tea?" She turned down the hall, leaving the room in a strange silence — almost oppressively so.

Katherine knew Grandmother's words

weren't meant to hurt her; they were meant to uplift. But it brought back all the reasons *why* she hadn't laughed in so many years.

There had been a time when she laughed a lot. Joy filled her life and her heart.

Back when she was in love. Truly in love.

But that love was forbidden and taken away.

Allowing herself a moment to remember, Katherine went to the mirror again. The young woman she saw there was but a shadow of the girl who'd fallen in love in France.

Where was he now? Was he happy — her Jean-Michel?

Oh, he'd been able to make her laugh. So much that it tingled from her toes to the top of her head. So much that it often hurt and she couldn't breathe.

But that had been a lifetime ago.

For a brief moment, she longed for that sense of joy again. Was it possible?

Then Randall's words rushed in: *"Wipe that smile off your face, you worthless piece of trash. . . . I can't have my wife walking around with wrinkles blemishing her face. Besides, you don't deserve to be happy. Ever."*

5

April 20 — France

Collette stood in the middle of Jean-Michel's room with her hands on her hips. He'd sent her up here to find his favorite pair of cuff links. Why the ones he wore weren't good enough, she had no clue. And why she was up here instead of sending for his valet was also beyond her comprehension. But because she couldn't stand being locked up in this house one more minute and couldn't wait to dine at the Dubois's new house in the country, she had volunteered to fetch them. To save time.

Never mind that she hadn't listened when he told her where they were. Where did a man keep cuff links? Didn't the valet normally store them?

Digging around in chest drawers was not a pleasant job. She'd definitely made a mess of things. Where else could she look? Turning in a circle, she viewed the room and let out a frustrated breath. She needed to be done with this dreadful errand.

Aha — over there. In the corner sat her brother's desk, the one he used when he didn't want to traverse the stairs to the study. Maybe they were in there.

The top two drawers on the left held nothing but correspondence. How boring.

The middle drawer was locked.

But Collette had never let that stop her before. Pulling a hairpin from her perfectly coiffed head, she inserted it into the lock.

Voilà! It opened and she began her search. She pushed a thick envelope to the side and tickets spilled out.

First-class tickets.

For a voyage to America.

Forgetting all about the need to tidy up the mess she'd made — or the cuff links, for that matter — she raced down the stairs with tickets in hand.

"Jean-Michel, you sweet brother, you!"

He turned toward her and raised his brows.

"All this time, you've been allowing me to think that you were taking your time with the decision, and yet, you've already purchased the tickets!" She squealed in delight and ran over to kiss his cheek.

But his face turned into a frown. "Where did you get those?"

She bit her lip and attempted to look innocent. That always seemed to help Father forgive her. "They were in your desk —"

"And what, pray tell, were you doing in my desk? Snooping? Collette, you are exasperating. I can't believe you would invade my privacy like that. Riffling through my desk, of all places. Especially in a drawer that was *locked*!"

Tears worked their way to her lashes. It never hurt that she could cry on demand if needed. "But, brother, certainly you can forgive me for such a thing. I was only looking for your cuff links like you asked."

He closed his eyes.

She had him now. "I'm so sorry. But that still doesn't explain the tickets. They are for us, yes?"

He turned toward the window again and sighed. "If you would have noticed, you'd have seen those tickets were for only one person."

She frowned. Surely he wouldn't send her off alone. Or maybe *he* meant to go alone. Oh, this was maddening, but she dare not ask. With his back to her, she couldn't tell if Jean-Michel was angry or just fed up with her.

Should she try another tactic? They were already going to be late, and she really *did* want to get out of the house. "Again, I am so sorry, Jean-Michel. I will leave it alone. I shouldn't have pushed. Let's get to dinner. The Dubois family will be waiting." She ducked her head and saw a slight movement.

"It's forgiven, Collette. But please give me the courtesy of leaving my desk — especially any *locked* drawers — alone." He looked so old as he hobbled toward her. What had happened to her bold and strong big brother?

For a moment, she felt guilty. She really didn't have to be such a trial all the time. But she was *so* bored. All her friends were either married, getting married, or having children. And Collette hadn't gone anywhere or done much of anything, not since the Great War.

Why did everything have to change? First the despicable war ruined everything. Then Jean-Michel was wounded — in more ways than one. Then Father died.

She held out the envelope with the tickets.

He took them and placed them in his jacket pocket. A small smile lifted his mouth. "You're right, we don't want to keep the Dubois family waiting."

Silence kept them company as she put on her wrap and they climbed into the motor-car. Why wouldn't he just tell her what he had planned — why he had tickets . . . for one? She looked over at him. His face was solemn and focused on the road.

Oh, bother. Well, two could play at this game. She crossed her arms over her middle and let out a huff. Let's see how he felt about the silent treatment.

Jean-Michel reached over and patted her knee. "Stop your pouting, and don't for a minute think that I don't know what you are up to."

She turned even more toward the window.

"Well, I guess we should turn around if you're not in the mood to talk."

Why were all men so impossible?

"Oh, well, I thought you'd want to tell the Dubois girls all about our trip to America. We leave next week. But . . . if you're not feeling up to it —"

She sucked in a breath. "Truly?" Like a child, she couldn't help but bounce on the seat.

"Yes."

"Together?" She kept wondering about the single set of tickets.

"Of course, together. I could hardly send someone so silly as you alone." He grinned and gave her a wink.

Collette threw her arms around his neck. "You are the best brother ever."

The terrors that plagued Jean-Michel at night happened almost every time he fell asleep. Most of the time, he relived the same horrible scenes. Over and over and over.

Sometimes with each heartbeat and second lasting much longer — prolonging the agony.

Finding out he was responsible for George's and Luc's deaths.

Watching the people burn inside the buildings.

It was all too real. He'd wake up in a sweat and out of breath.

Tonight he found himself reading and thinking . . . really anything to keep from going to sleep and waking up in a nightmare one more time.

Father's letter lay on the table beside his bed. Jean-Michel had read it every day, but it still didn't change anything.

Underneath his father's letter was the one from Maria Harrison and the tickets Collette had found. Jean-Michel picked up Maria's letter again and read it.

Could the wise old woman be right? Could he be the answer for Katherine?

After all these years, he'd never forgotten her or stopped loving her. He could see her face in his mind just as clearly as if she stood before him now. But did she still love him? And even if she did, would that be enough to heal her from a horrible past — to heal them both?

It broke his heart to think of Katherine suffering. And apparently, she'd suffered a great deal.

Was it all his fault? Five years ago, should he have sneaked her away and eloped — defying her parents?

He shook his head. There was nothing he could do about that now.

Same for him. He'd carry the emotional scars with him until he died.

Then there were the physical ones as well. Would Katherine be disgusted with him now that he was no longer whole?

Rubbing his leg, a little idea niggled at the edge of his mind. The doctor had said if he would just try harder — put his all into it — there might be a chance Jean-Michel could improve. But his heart hadn't been in it.

But now? There was a reason now. Collette needed him. In fact, more so than ever. He'd been noticing her flirtatious and careless attitude toward so much of life. She wanted to have fun and instant gratification. Someone needed to rein her in before she got herself into a heap of trouble. Just two days ago he'd found her making cow eyes at the chauffeur. He'd actually considered sending her off to an expensive finishing school in Switzerland. Then she'd forced his hand by finding the tickets.

That wasn't the real reason, though, was it?

Katherine was. That letter from her grandmother stirred all kinds of new longings and feelings in his heart. Like he was coming back to life. And he wanted to help Katherine to come back as well. With him. He could save her from the darkness that surrounded her. Perhaps their love could save them both.

New resolve in place, Jean-Michel would call the doctor first thing in the morning.

Three days later, Jean-Michel stood in front of the man he'd pinned his hopes on.

"It's good to see you, *Monsieur* Langelier."

Jean-Michel took his proffered hand and shook it. "Same to you, doctor."

"Have a seat. Now, what can I help you with?"

"I'll be brief. We leave in three days' time

for America, and I remembered that you mentioned there was a possibility to do more to help my leg to heal."

The man nodded. "Indeed. Yes." He crossed his arms over his chest. "It will be quite difficult now, though. Much time has passed."

"I'm willing to work hard."

The doctor laughed and pushed his spectacles up onto his nose a little higher. "I'm glad to hear it. In fact, I'm exceedingly glad to see you have the heart to live again. That's what you needed more than any exercises."

Jean-Michel squinted down at the man. "But you do have exercises for me to do — things that will help me strengthen the leg?"

"I do." He reached for a paper and pen off his desk. "But, remember, it will take twice the time now to build it back up. *If* the exercises are even able to work."

Twice the time. That would be six months. Why didn't he listen to the doctor before now? "I'm willing to try. Please."

The man held up a finger as he began to furiously scribble on the paper.

Jean-Michel attempted to read across the desk but couldn't decipher the man's scrawl upside down. Several minutes passed, then he sat in the chair beside him.

After several more minutes, the doctor nodded and brought the paper around to Jean-Michel. "Now, these are the directions for the exercises, but I'm going to show you here how to do them. The directions are just a reminder. Try to do them each thirty to forty times a day."

He felt his eyebrows rise. "That's a great many."

The doctor took in a deep breath. "Yes, it is. But I believe it will work."

Reading over the paper in detail, Jean-Michel realized his work was cut out for him. At this rate of repetition, he'd have to spend a good portion of each day in these rehabilitative exercises.

The doctor reached for Jean-Michel's bad leg. "Let's begin."

Barcelona, Spain

Where was the general?

He must find him. Before anyone else did. The country — no, the world — was counting on him. The new message tucked into his shoe must be delivered. But first, he had to make it out of here alive and find the general.

Around every corner, there were spies. Even though everyone said the war was over, it wasn't.

War was never over.

Never.

The little girl behind the corn cart kept watching him. What if she recognized him? What if she worked for *them*?

He took a few steps back, turned around, and fled through the alley behind him. They wouldn't catch him.

He'd have to risk being seen and send a telegram.

The code would have to be short. Congenial. Like a normal day for normal people doing normal things.

As he sneaked through the streets, he worded it over and over in his mind.

The general would know what to do next.

6

April 30 — Kentucky, USA

As she sat on the edge of the hotel bed, one thought was clear in Katherine's mind. Her feet ached. And their day hadn't even started yet.

For fourteen days, they'd traveled to more states than she could remember and traipsed around looking at anything and everything Grandmother wanted to see. Libraries, cemeteries, interesting-looking buildings . . . the list went on and on.

The beginning of the trip had been lovely, with a visit to Niagara Falls before they left the state of New York. The roar of the falls and the spray of the water on her skin had been invigorating. But as the trip progressed, she had no idea Grandmother would be so adventurous. They took their time and rested often, but still it seemed a great deal of strain for a woman her grandmother's age. However, when Katherine suggested they slow down — perhaps omit a few side trips — Grandmother would hear nothing of it.

They'd been to Philadelphia and Independence Hall, then to Washington, DC — where they must have walked five miles to all the historical and significant buildings. Grandmother had even asked to see the President!

Katherine shook her head. When she'd agreed to go to Alaska, she thought they would simply be going to Alaska. Clearly they were taking the long way. Would they even make it this summer, or would Grandmother have them off to see the pyramids in Mexico? If she did, no doubt they'd have to climb them.

The thought made her chuckle, much to her own surprise.

"Well, my goodness. Listen to that." Grandmother stood at the door between their hotel rooms. "Didn't I tell you this trip would do you good? Now what has so amused you?"

"To be honest, I was wondering if we would ever make it to Alaska for the summer."

Grandmother shook a finger at her as her grin widened. "Now you just hush. We're having fun, aren't we?"

"Of course we are. I just wish I could say the same for my feet." For dramatic effect, she rubbed the bottoms of her feet.

"You can just tell your feet that they better be up for the challenge today, because I have something special planned."

Oh dear.

"You need your most comfortable and sturdy shoes."

Katherine stood and placed her hands on her hips. "Excuse me, but wait just a minute. Before I even put on my most comfortable and sturdy shoes, you need to tell me where we are headed." She smiled at her grandmother. Her heart was in the right place, but if Katherine was going to be along for this adventure, she needed to lay down some ground rules. "While this has been quite entertaining, I think it's time we came to an agreement. No more surprises every day. I need to know how to dress and prepare for the coming 'fun' you have planned."

Grandmother raised an eyebrow and smiled. "And you'll be fine with whatever I choose as long as I tell you each morning?"

Katherine fought the urge to roll her eyes and sighed. "As long as we make it in time to catch our ship out of San Francisco, yes,

I'm fine with that. Like you said, it's an adventure."

"It is. And it wouldn't hurt you to try and show a bit more enthusiasm."

"I'm trying, Grandmother. I am."

"I know, dear." The older woman's aged and wrinkled hand gripped her shoulder.

Their discussion couldn't be allowed to go down any serious route. Katherine's heart wasn't up for it. Even though every day her grandmother tried. "So what are we up to today?" She took a deep breath and put on a smile.

"Mammoth Cave."

Although she would have never chosen to visit a cave, Katherine was so glad they'd come. Their tour guide was full of knowledge and patient with all their questions. The glow of the stalactites and stalagmites in the lantern light was glorious.

Before this morning, she'd had no idea that Mammoth Cave existed. Nor did she know that it was the longest cave system in the world. But now after traveling from "room" to "room" and seeing all the hidden beauty for herself, Katherine was mesmerized. The underground rivers and rock formations were always changing as they explored deeper into the cave. Grandmother had informed her that they were taking the Long Route, which would include a meal, but would take fourteen hours. At the time, she'd been stupefied they would attempt such a thing, but now, she was ever so thankful.

The massive Rotunda Room had been her favorite. Sitting on a rock for a moment, she could imagine instead that she was inside a beautiful opera house and her whispers could be heard across the whole area as several other tourists experimented with her on the travel of sound.

When they'd reached the Bottomless Pit, Grandmother reminded the tour guide that the Bible said Satan himself would be thrown into a bottomless pit. Several of the tourists laughed, while a few others bravely leaned over to look into the mouth of the hole. Katherine shivered with the thought of falling and falling and falling.

"Are you enjoying this, dear?" Grandmother's voice broke through her dark thoughts.

"Oh yes. Very much!" For the first time in a long time, she didn't have to fake the emotion. And it felt really good. "When you mentioned coming to a cave, I thought it would be very small, and I hate small spaces."

"This way, please." The tour guide's voice echoed through the tunnel.

While every other lady had a lantern, Katherine insisted they only needed one between the two of them, so she could carry it and Grandmother could use her cane. But the older woman always seemed to take it from her.

"I guess that means we better continue on our way." Grandmother dusted off her skirt and once again captured the lantern.

Katherine shook her head. She didn't mind following behind and bringing up the rear of their little party. It kept her from having to converse with strangers and gave her time to take in all the breathtaking sights. Grandmother had given her lots of space today, and for that she was thankful. It was refreshing to fully enjoy something again. It had been almost five years since the last time. . . .

Memories of a dark-haired young man with beautiful green eyes filled her mind. Oh, how she had loved him. He'd shown her so many wonderful places in France and always made her feel like a princess. If only she could go back to those days. Before all the ugliness. Before the monster had been unleashed.

Randall had known she didn't love him.

107

He even knew she loved another, but it didn't matter. In fact, he seemed to very much enjoy knowing he had played a part in separating true love. She closed her eyes and drew in a deep breath, trying to will the memories from her mind.

Straightening her shoulders and opening her eyes, Katherine realized she'd stopped walking. Why did all thoughts of Randall turn her into stone? He was gone. For good. But the damage had been done. Grandmother assured her that she could heal and come back from it. But how?

How could she ever move past the violence and the constant barrage of hateful words? He'd drilled ugliness into her every single day for three years.

She'd been relieved when he died. As horrid as that seemed, it was true.

But joy and happiness eluded her. She couldn't find her way back.

Because he haunted her. Haunted her thoughts. Every time she looked in the mirror, she heard his voice. Every time she tried to move past the ugliness, she remembered his words. And she often woke in the middle of the night feeling one of his blows against her back or legs.

Yes, she'd been relieved when he died. But a new torture had only begun.

The silence around her brought her out of her memories. Looking up, all she could see was black.

She wanted to move but couldn't remember what was around her. How many steps had they taken since the Bottomless Pit? Was she still close? Was the path smooth or did it drop off? She couldn't remember. Her thoughts had taken over and she'd pushed the real world aside.

Now there was nothing but darkness closing in. Her eyes couldn't even adjust. There wasn't a bit of light anywhere. And now she couldn't take a full breath. It was like the time Randall locked her in the closet. She'd never known a fear of small places until that moment when the blackness seemed to snuff out all the air.

Her heart plummeted and she decided to sit on the path where she stood so she wouldn't collapse and fall to her demise. How long before Grandmother noticed she wasn't behind her?

The thought made her heart race. If the path ahead was strenuous, Grandmother would be focused on that. Not the fact that Katherine wasn't behind her.

Randall's voice began to ping around in her brain. Every insult, belittling comment, and tormenting bellow competed for an audience.

"No. Stop! No." Katherine threw her hands over her ears. She closed her eyes against the dark that pressed her further and further into the damp limestone floor. It seemed to squeeze the very life out of her, making it harder and harder to breathe. Suffocating her.

Would this be the end? Would she die here in the dark being tormented by the words of a dead man who vowed to love and cherish her?

Why God? Why? Grandmother says that You love me — but how can You? How could You let me experience a taste of love and then snatch it away? How could You allow my father to arrange a marriage to Randall? How could You watch the torture and just let me live through it?

Why am I even here? I'm worthless! Not good for anything.

Katherine dropped her hands from her ears and pulled her knees up under her chin. Let the darkness take her. Her breaths were coming in short gasps now. She had nothing to live for anyway. . . .

A faint sound — like humming — echoed through the silence. It came closer. Katherine knew that voice. Knew the song too. It had been the only thing to get rid of her bad dreams when she was a child.

As Grandmother's voice washed over her, tears ran down her face.

"Jesus loves me this I know . . . for the Bible tells me so . . . Little ones to Him belong . . . they are weak but He is strong."

Katherine opened her eyes and saw a small circle of light pierce through the blackness and come toward her. "Grandmother." The name left her lips on a whisper as the echo of footsteps filled the space around her. Sobs shook her body.

"Yes, Jesus loves me. Yes, Jesus loves me." The song continued on as the light came closer.

"Katherine, I'm here. I heard your cries. But more importantly, God heard them. Before I ever could. He prodded me to turn around."

"Why does God hate me?" The crushing of the darkness from before pressed in again. Harder. Stronger.

"Oh, my dear. He doesn't hate you. He loves you so much."

"No — how could He leave me like that?" Katherine cried. "He left me here with this darkness. It's pushing and pressing all around me."

The footsteps stopped. "In the name of

Jesus Christ who is above every name" — Grandmother's voice was stronger than Katherine had ever heard it — "I say to you, darkness, to flee."

The vise she'd felt around her chest fell away. Katherine took a deep breath and inhaled Grandmother's familiar peppermint scent.

" 'For I am persuaded, that neither death, nor life, nor angels, nor principalities, nor powers, nor things present, nor things to come, nor height, nor depth, nor any other creature, shall be able to separate us from the love of God, which is in Christ Jesus our Lord.' That's from Romans chapter eight." Grandmother nodded and brought the light close to Katherine's face.

The lantern lit up the entire area around them in a beautiful golden glow. The pressure around Katherine was gone. She could fill her lungs again. "How . . . ? What did you do?"

"I believe that the enemy is strong, my dear. But our God is stronger. He is the light. And no matter what hold the enemy has had on you through Randall Demarchis's evil actions or words, we need to give it all to the Savior, who is defeating the enemy as we speak. The name of Jesus is powerful. For He is the King of kings and

Lord of lords."

Katherine put a hand to her chest. "It really is gone. I can breathe." The shock overwhelmed her a bit. She'd never seen or heard her grandmother do anything like that before. But she'd also never felt as dark or oppressed either.

"Do not doubt God, my child. And do not doubt His love for you, even though wicked men may tell you otherwise." She tugged on Katherine's hands. "Let's get moving, we need to catch up with the tour and then later, when we are out in the beautiful sunlight once again, we're going to have a long chat."

7

May 1 — The Curry Hotel

"Now, I know we've been awful busy these past couple weeks and the doctor had you laid up for a week just to be sure everything was okay, but there's something I've been meaning to ask you." Mrs. Johnson wiped down the bread table with gusto and gave Cassidy the look that meant she was in for an interrogation.

Cassidy smiled and finished scrubbing the other prep table. "I'm all ears."

Mrs. Johnson harrumphed. "Now, don't you go sassing me, Cassidy Faith."

"Never." Sarcasm oozed with each syllable.

The older woman ignored her comment but gave her another telling look. One Cassidy had seen a lot over the past few years. "We've only got a little time left alone while the others are at tea. And it's too delicate a subject to broach in front of anyone else."

"Goodness, now you really *do* have my curiosity piqued."

Mrs. Johnson placed both hands on her hips and shook her head. "You better watch your tongue, missy, or I'll have to demote you to washing dishes."

"You couldn't make it without me, Mrs. Johnson, and you know it, so threaten all you like." Cassidy continued to wipe down the other kitchen prep areas. "Besides, who else could you find to put up with your bossy ways?"

The head chef gasped and then started chuckling. "I boss everyone around. And they have to take it because I'm the boss."

"Maybe I do it because I love you."

"Well, then, maybe I won't demote you after all."

"All right, then." Cassidy winked. "Didn't you have a question you wanted to ask?"

Mrs. Johnson tossed a rag at her assistant. "You are exasperating, you know that?"

"Well, if that's your question, I guess I would have to agree. Most people used to get aggravated because I was too happy. And I do recall someone accusing me of thinking that life was all gumdrops and rainbows. . . ."

"Cassidy," Mrs. Johnson groaned. "We've

come a long way since then."

"Yes, ma'am. We have." Cassidy went over and kissed the beloved woman's cheek. Mrs. Johnson might seem prickly and harsh to everyone else, but to Cassidy Brennan, she was like a mother. The two had a bond forged by hard work and tragedy. They'd laughed together, cried together, and worked their fingers to the bone together.

"Now, if you'll let me finish." Mrs. Johnson lowered her voice. "How on earth did you not know you were in a family way all this time? We talked about all of this before you married Allan."

Cassidy smiled at the blush that crept up the older woman's neck. "I noticed my waist was getting firm and maybe a little thick, but I thought it was just from all that good food we cook around here. You're always having me try one of your new creations."

"Well, now we know it wasn't that. Honestly, now it makes me understand your moodiness."

"Moodiness? I haven't been moody." Cassidy frowned. "Have I?"

"Well, let me see. A few months back you were sobbing like a baby over the northern lights."

"They were incredible and all I could think about was the glory of the Lord shining down."

"Then last month you yelled at poor Thomas because he hadn't told you the piglets had been born. Then you cried and cried when he took you to see them."

"Well . . . they were . . . precious." Cassidy shrugged. "All right, so I've been a bit . . . emotional."

"It's typical of your condition. I was a sobbing mess for months."

Everything stopped. What had Mrs. Johnson just said? Cassidy tried to keep her voice low. "You . . . had a baby?"

The cook nodded. "Two. A boy and a girl." Sadness edged her voice. "I lost them with the others."

"When you said you'd lost all your family, I thought you just meant your husband, siblings, and parents. Oh, Mrs. Johnson, I never thought of you having babies. You never told me . . . in all these years." Tears came to her eyes. "Here I go again." Cassidy wiped her eyes with her apron. Now that she thought about it, she *had* been crying at the drop of a hat. "What were their names? How old were they?"

Mrs. Johnson looked for a moment as if she wouldn't answer. She picked up a dish towel and began drying a large glass bowl.

"Jonathan was twelve and Deborah was fif-teen."

"I'm so sorry." Again the tears came. How terrible to lose a child. Cassidy had only just learned of her own baby, but the thought of losing it was more than she could bear.

"Now, don't be crying," Mrs. Johnson commanded. Her gruff tone returned. "I already cried a lifetime of tears over these past seven — almost eight — years."

"Yes, ma'am." Cassidy couldn't help herself. She came and wrapped her arms around the older woman's shoulders. "I'll bet you were a good mother."

"I was a bossy mother, as you can well guess."

Looking up, Cassidy smiled. "And you probably had the cleanest kitchen in the world."

"I did." She patted Cassidy's arm. "Now stop all this. I didn't share it so you would feel sorry for me. I shared it because I wanted you to know that I am here for you to talk to. I can help you with any questions you have about . . . your condition. Usually a girl has her mother to talk to about such things, but since yours is gone, I thought I might offer."

This only caused Cassidy to hug her all

the tighter. "Oh, you sweet woman." The sound of voices coming down the stairs caused Cassidy to release her hold. She stepped away and picked up a couple of potholders. "I'd better check the pies."

Two of the kitchen maids burst into the room, laughing and whispering about something. One look at Mrs. Johnson quieted them, however. The girls hurried through the kitchen and disappeared.

Cassidy closed the oven door. "I appreciate that you care enough to share all of that with me."

"Well, just so you know, I plan to keep a close eye on you." Mrs. Johnson stabbed a finger in the air. "And I will brook no argument when it comes to this, all right, Mrs. Brennan?"

"When it comes to what?"

"Keeping your health and the baby's as my utmost concern."

"Mrs. Johnson, please, the doctor says that —"

"Pishposh, I know what he said, I was there. But *he* is not here with you every day. *I* am."

"Really, I appreciate it, I really do, but I think I can handle us going at our regular pace. I don't see that anything needs to change. I feel fine." So maybe the older

119

woman was a bit overprotective of her. She could handle five more months of that, couldn't she?

"Like I said, I will not tolerate you arguing with me on this point. Besides, Allan and I agree. And we already have a plan."

"A plan? You and Allan have a plan?" Cassidy rarely got angry. But she felt the emotion burning in her gut now. So much for not being moody. "When, exactly, were you going to let me in on this *plan*?" And why was she so fired up about it?

"As you needed to know." Mrs. Johnson grabbed several loaves of bread and started slicing them.

As she needed to know. As if she was a child incapable of taking care of herself. Why all of a sudden did everyone think they needed to tell her what to do? "I cannot believe this. My husband and my boss have conspired against me! They've made a plan without even talking to me."

"You forget, I know how you are. You think nothing of hoisting up fifty-pound bags of flour or running up the stairs two at a time. You need someone to keep you in line so you don't hurt yourself. Mr. Brennan agrees with me."

For the first time since Cassidy could remember, pure rage flowed through her veins. Never mind that she might be over-reacting. She threw that thought out as soon as it entered. Maybe she should've gotten angry ages ago. She untied her apron and slapped it down on the table. "I believe Mr. Brennan needs a good talking-to!"

Cassidy stomped from the room, feeling quite satisfied that she'd shocked Mrs. Johnson speechless.

Thomas joined Allan and John in the dining room after dinner. It was now or never. He had to tell the men the truth. It was only three years ago that he'd shaken the hand of the President of the United States. He'd had his picture taken with him, and the First Lady had commended him. He could definitely face the two men he respected most in the world. Couldn't he?

John's eyes crinkled at the edges as he smiled at Thomas. "Come on in. We've been waiting on you so we could discuss the schedules for tomorrow." Cassidy's father had taken Thomas under his wing when all the boy seemed capable of doing was invoking the wrath of Mrs. Johnson with his clumsy ways. But Thomas had grown out of that, and John taught him well about being a guide around these parts of Alaska.

Allan was all smiles these days. But

121

Thomas guessed that any man would be when his wife was expecting their first child.

Oh, how he hated to wipe the smiles off their faces. He inhaled deeply. "There's something I need to tell you both."

John leaned in and propped his elbows on the table. "Have a seat, son. It can't be all that bad."

Allan simply relaxed back in his chair. "Thomas, you should know us by now. We won't bite. We promise."

Thomas nodded and took the chair next to Allan. He had so much respect for these men. He never wanted to let them down. "I've made a mess out of something, and I don't know how to fix it."

"Well, we can definitely help with that. We're good at fixing things." John reached over and patted him on the shoulder. "Go on."

"Um, well, that is to say . . ." He cleared his throat, but the knot lodged there wouldn't move. "You know that Mr. Karstens asked for me to help for a few days up at the park headquarters?" The superintendent of the Mount McKinley National Park was a great man, but he didn't think it at all amusing when Thomas apparently locked him in the storage room for several hours.

Allan chuckled. "Let me stop you there, Thomas." He picked up a piece of paper off the table and waved it. "Mr. Karstens telegrammed earlier."

Thomas stood up. "So you already knew that I messed everything up? Is that why you were laughing?"

"We couldn't help ourselves," Allan admitted. "We were just imagining you locking poor Harry in the storage room." He burst into laughter anew.

"Allan Brennan!" Cassidy's voice screeched across the room. Thomas had never heard her screech before. Nor had he ever seen her quite so red in the face. "How dare you laugh at Thomas! Don't you pick on him."

Allan stood.

Then John stood.

Thomas looked between the two at their shocked faces and then back to Cassidy.

She charged into the room in a way that spoke volumes. Someone was in big trouble. He just hoped it wasn't *him*. He'd never seen Cassidy in such a state.

"I was not picking on Thomas." Allan lifted his hands as if surrendering a battle. "I was about to tell him that Mr. Karstens' telegram states that *he* was the one who made the mistake that resulted in his being locked in the storage room, not Thomas. He'd given our young man quite the tongue-lashing earlier and wanted to make sure we apologized for him."

Relief flooded Thomas at those words.

Cassidy seemed to calm a bit, but then she started shaking her finger at Allan. "Well, that's all well and good, but it doesn't explain why you and Mrs. Johnson feel the need to plan out my life. I'm quite capable of taking care of myself."

"What are you talking about?" Allan's forehead scrunched.

"The two of you making plans about keeping an eye on me — figuring out what I can and can't do like I'm some sort of child."

Thomas waited for Cassidy to explode, but instead she sank into the nearest chair and began to cry. Thomas eyed her and wondered what could have caused such a change. For him, he only felt relief that what he'd thought was a huge blunder wasn't actually his fault.

Allan moved toward his wife.

John looked over at Thomas. "Maybe we should make our way quietly to the kitchen."

"Don't leave!" Cassidy wailed. "I know you need to discuss tomorrow's schedules and I interrupted you and I'm sorry. I don't know what's come over me." She gasped and put a hand over her mouth. Then she withdrew it. "I was quite short with Mrs. Johnson too."

Allan turned back to them and appeared to be pleading for help with his eyes.

John took a tentative step forward. "You know, Cass, your mother was quite . . . um . . . emotional when she was expecting you. I think that's normal? Maybe? Or we could call for the doctor?"

"No, Mrs. Johnson already explained this to me."

"If you're sure. I know Thomas would go fetch him." John looked worried.

Thomas just nodded as he looked from face to face. He knew his eyes were wide, but the shock of it all scared him. When did sweet, sunshine-smiling Cassidy get a temper?

Allan gripped his wife's hand as she started crying in earnest. "We will figure this out, sweetheart. We will. Just how short were you with Mrs. Johnson?"

Cassidy squinted her eyes at her husband. "Quite. But it's all your fault. Apparently, the two of you have a plan to keep me contained these next few months. A plan that you didn't discuss with me!" Her voice rose.

"Now, honey. Calm down. The only plan we had was to keep an eye on you to make sure you don't overdo it and collapse again. There is no plot against you. And definitely not any plan to keep you . . . *contained.* As if anyone could contain you."

Cassidy began to cry again. This time in great heaving sobs. Allan shook his head and looked back to Thomas. "Would you mind fetching the doctor?"

"I'll go right now." Thomas was pleased with the excuse to leave the room. That wasn't a sight he ever expected to see — Cassidy losing her temper and then bursting into tears. Women sure were odd creatures.

He shook his head as he ran to the doctor's quarters. The incident with Mr. Karstens was nothing compared to the outrage of an expectant mother. He made a mental note to not anger Cassidy Brennan for the next few months.

8

May 12 — Seattle

The deck of the *Alaska II* glimmered in the rising of the sun. Jean-Michel took slow, methodic steps in the wee morning hours, pondering the mess that was his little sister, Collette.

The relatively new ship built by a Seattle company for the Alaska Steamship Co. in 1923 was beautiful and more than comfortable. But all the comforts of the world couldn't take away his dilemma. How had his sister become this . . . self-absorbed? And flirtatious.

For a week on the ship over from France, he'd had to watch her every move. If she wasn't flirting with almost every man aboard, she was risking her safety leaning over the railings, or other such nonsense.

Then they'd spent a week on trains. Traversing the continent of America from east to west. And even after several stern talking-tos, Collette continued in her ways. She stated she was bored. She just wanted to have fun. And why was he being such a stodgy old man about it?

Now they were on yet another ship, headed north to Alaska. He'd had very little sleep and every moment he wasn't reining in Collette, he spent on the exercises for his leg. Which made him bone weary.

Reaching the stern of the great ship, he gripped the railing and inhaled the salty, crisp air. A spray of water reached his face as he heard a deep bellowing sound. Jean-Michel looked down in time to see the tail of a great whale splash the surface. What a magnificent sight. To the left of the giant creature, there swam a smaller one. The mother whale didn't seem to have any issues keeping her youngster in line.

Why couldn't it be as easy for humans?

Especially for big brothers who just wanted to guide and protect their younger sisters.

He rubbed a hand down his face. How he wished Father were still here. Or at least accessible to ask advice. Jean-Michel felt himself floundering.

It wasn't Collette's fault that she was untarnished by the ugliness of the world.

But she was definitely focused on frivolous things. And didn't seem to care too much about how her actions affected other people. If she were even aware. But how could he change that? What could he do?

He was ten years her senior — already away to boarding school when she was born. During his college years in Canada, he'd been far too busy to notice much in regard to Collette's activities. Sickness and war and returning to France had consumed the family after that — and it was Collette's turn to attend boarding school. She'd only just returned the year before, just months before Jean-Michel came home from Syria.

Tragedy and war shaped him. While money, façades, and fake compliments had shaped Collette.

He needed some advice. And fast.

What would Father do in this situation?

He'd probably threaten to cut off all of Collette's funds. Which wasn't a bad idea. She spent money quite freely on the trip. But then she'd probably pout. Perhaps even cry. Could he deal with that?

How had his parents dealt with it?

How was it that a war-torn older brother now inherited the role of guardian? *Ill-prepared* was the only phrase that could describe him and his efforts. But he did have a genuine desire to steer Collette in the correct direction. She needed him. And that kept him going.

Even though he had no idea what he would end up doing with the rest of his life. What was he good for? What all did he really know? He never wanted to return to France. And his sister needed saving from the world and herself.

Collette could be such a sweet girl. Their parents had doted on her and she had adored them. She adored Jean-Michel and he knew she wanted his approval. But something had changed in her the past few months. Even the past year. Jean-Michel couldn't put his finger on it, but he'd have to find a way to reach her with reality before she put herself in a compromising position.

Back in his stateroom, Jean-Michel read through Father's letter once again. Hoping for some tidbit of wisdom he could apply to Collette, he only found the advice to search for God. Maybe one day, he'd be ready. But for now, he'd have to settle for keeping Collette out of trouble for one more day.

May 17

Collette lifted her scented hankie to her nose so she wouldn't have to smell the hor-

130

rendous odors as they disembarked the *Alaska II.* This last leg of the trip hadn't been nearly as fun. Jean-Michel was even grumpier than usual and refused to give her any allowance unless she followed all of his rules. Which made her want to stomp her foot at him in defiance — but she wanted spending money.

About the only good part of their journey from Seattle to Seward, Alaska, had been the scenery. She'd never seen anything so beautiful in all her life. And if she didn't love France so much, she might have decided to stay in this corner of the world forever.

Jean-Michel took her elbow and steered her toward a car. "They will take us to the train quickly. We don't want to miss the train to Curry today."

For someone who hadn't been much too excited about anything on this trip, he now seemed anxious to finish this last leg. Well, she should be thankful. Seward didn't look like it boasted much in the way of shopping or entertainment.

The train ride was much like all the others. Bumpy and noisy. But at least the majority of the smelly passengers were not in first class. Not that first class amounted to much on the Alaska Railroad, but at least there was separation from the many un-washed bodies.

"Est-ce que nous arrivons bientôt?" The question she'd asked Father on countless train trips left her lips and aimed at Jean-Michel.

"Collette, you must remember to speak in English. We're in America and you know it quite well. And no, we will not be there anytime soon, we just boarded the train."

He opened a newspaper and began to read it.

She let out a tiny huff. Why was she always so bored?

"Didn't you bring a book to read?" he said from behind the paper.

"Non." She exaggerated the French word just to annoy him.

He chuckled and flicked the paper straight.

The world had changed, her friends had changed, but had she?

She'd grown up right along with the rest of them. And she must admit that a lot of the world's changes were good ones. Rules were more relaxed. Skirts were — finally — shorter. Women were cutting their hair and being bold and fun. In America they even had the right to vote.

But the restlessness inside her didn't seem

to be satisfied. Something was missing. Something much bigger.

But what was it?

Happiness had never eluded her before. With a sigh, she laid her head on her brother's shoulder and decided to let go of her silly questions and try to go to sleep. Maybe something exciting would happen in Curry.

"Collette. Collette, wake up."

She shifted forward as the train slowed. Blinking against the light, she was shocked that she'd actually fallen asleep for the whole trip. "We're in Curry? Already?"

Her brother nodded. "You snored. It was quite entertaining."

Collette straightened herself and gave him a shove in his seat. "I most certainly did not. Please stop telling tales."

As they gathered their belongings, Collette attempted to get a view out the windows, but all she saw was people.

Jean-Michel offered her his arm and they exited the train together. When she stepped down onto the wooden decking of the train's platform, she got a full view of her home for the next few months.

The Curry Hotel.

The two-toned, dark green building was

two stories with bay windows flanking the canopy and a marquee that read Curry Hotel and Depot.

While not as magnificent as hotels in Europe or New York City, Collette could still see that this was indeed a lavish hotel for the area. She hadn't seen much of civilization since they left Seattle. And oh, how she ached for a bath.

As they walked into the foyer, the beautiful red carpets greeted her along with the dark wood finishes. Deep leather chairs adorned the lobby, and a large fireplace in the corner invited those who wanted to linger and relish its warmth.

Jean-Michel led her to the left of a large staircase. She noted the high counter and assumed they would check in here.

As her brother discussed their accommodations with the clerk, Collette took a few more minutes to explore the lobby. A beautiful dining room was to the left of where she stood, and if the scents emanating from the kitchen across the room were any indication, they would eat well.

Three men descended the stairs together, deep in conversation. But one of them noticed her, smiled, and took a moment to stop and stare.

She smiled back.

This summer could be very interesting.

Jean-Michel tapped her on the shoulder. "If you're done flirting, we can head up to our rooms. There's a boy who is taking our things up." He sighed.

Swallowing a sassy retort when she noticed his face filled with exhaustion, Collette nodded. "I'm ready."

The stairs were beautiful — covered in that rich red carpeting and wide enough for several people to traverse at the same time. They reached the second floor and walked around two large shared washrooms in the center to a hallway that spanned the entire width of the building. Jean-Michel pulled the keys out of his pocket and opened the first door on the right. He spoke to the boy. "This will be the lady's room, if you would be so kind to deliver her luggage here. I'll take the room to the left of hers."

The boy set down the two cases he held and ran back down the stairs for the rest.

Her brother led her into her room. "If you'll notice, we share a private bathroom in between our two rooms. But we have all the modern conveniences. If you need anything, I'll be just on the other side of our bathroom." He walked through the door and left the adjoining doors open as he perused his own room. "Please don't go anywhere. I'd like us to go down for dinner together."

While sparse compared to home, the hotel was indeed a diamond in the rough land of Alaska from all she'd heard. The bed, dresser, and side table were all of high quality craftsmanship, and there was a chair and small bench at the foot of the bed as well. Yes, she could be quite comfortable here. Even without her maid. She'd done fine on the trip without her, and Jean-Michel had convinced her before they left that it wouldn't be necessary to bring their servants.

Her brother walked back into her room. "Do you like it?"

"It's cozy, isn't it?" She watched his face fall and put on a smile for him. The words were meant to be a compliment. "It will be a nice place to stay for the summer." Hopefully the added words would show him she was trying. She knew she'd been difficult to deal with, but she had no idea how to change. And she didn't want to aggravate Jean-Michel anymore. If only she knew how to be more agreeable. How not to get bored. Because if she didn't learn, she'd never be allowed to do anything ever again, and he'd keep her allowance to himself as well.

"Why don't we go down to dinner and

then we can finish unpacking." He held out his arm.

With another nod, Collette walked with her brother out to the hall and he locked her room. "I'm sorry, Jean-Michel. Truly, I am. I know I've caused you great trouble on this trip, but that is not my intention."

He leaned on his cane and looked at her with an eyebrow raised. "It isn't?" His lips curved up into a slight smile.

"*Non.* It isn't. Even though I cause trouble easily, it's not that I want to, necessarily. I'm just . . . I don't know . . . bored . . . restless . . . waiting for my life to begin."

"So you thought to take it out on your beloved older brother, because your rebelliousness and careless attitude wouldn't hurt him at all?" His eyes still smiled at her, but the words hit their mark.

"I said I was sorry."

"I know, Collette. I do. And it is forgiven. But you are almost an adult now. Mother and Father are gone, and I *don't* want to take their place. I want to be your brother and for you to know you can always depend on me." He sighed again. A habit too often used of late. And it was all her fault.

It was true. She didn't want Jean-Michel to fill in as a parent. She loved her brother. More than anyone else. But she didn't

137

understand where she stood now. Didn't know what to do with her life. Through it all, she still needed her big brother — her confidant. But she just felt *lost.*

They started down the steps together.

Collette tried to form the right words to share with Jean-Michel, but they all sounded childish and petty. Even to her own mind. Guilt pierced her heart. She'd forced his hand with the tickets. What if he'd wanted to wait before they traveled? The doctor had given him such strenuous exercises for his leg, and she knew he was still mourning Father's death. What if he wasn't ready?

A grunt beside her pulled her attention back to her brother. His face grimaced as he sank to the steps below.

"Jean-Michel! Are you hurt?"

He sat on the steps for a moment that seemed to last forever, his lips in a thin line. "My leg gave out on me. It's nothing. Just give me a minute."

"Do we need to call for a doctor?"

"*Non.* It is fine."

"Is it all those exercises you've been doing? Maybe you overdid it?"

"*Oui.*" He cleared his throat. "That must be it." He held up a hand. "Just help me up. I'll be fine."

"Are you certain?" Collette saw movement

138

out of the corner of her eye and realized a small crowd had gathered at the bottom of the grand staircase.

"Yes." He flashed her a full smile and straightened his shoulders as he rose to his full height.

Leaning heavily on his cane, Jean-Michel still offered his other arm to escort her down.

Head held high, he led her down each step, and as they reached the bottom her brother greeted people around them. The color in his face showed the pain he was in, but he didn't let on.

And Collette's heart broke. This was all her fault.

How selfish could she be?

9

May 20 — San Francisco

The window in their third-story hotel room in San Francisco squeaked as Katherine opened it for Grandmother. Her need for "fresh air" no matter the outdoor temperature was a bit ridiculous at times. Especially on the train ride through parts of Kansas and Colorado when all they smelled was the smoke from the train and what the cows left behind.

"Fresh air. Hmph." It would take months to forget the stench.

But at least they finally made it to the west coast. They'd traveled the past few weeks, but not in the same way as before. In fact, most of their time had been spent on the trains and in the hotels studying the Bible together and talking. They'd seen the Rocky Mountains and the giant redwoods, but each day, she'd been more enthusiastic about learning than sightseeing.

After her traumatic time in the cave, Katherine had changed. The power she'd felt as the darkness released her, she would never forget. There was so much she still didn't understand, but Grandmother had taken several hours each day to teach her about God's Word and to pray with her. Gone were the hiking expeditions and the things to take Katherine's mind off the past. The older woman admitted she'd used all that time to break the shell around her granddaughter. It wasn't until her grandmother's words in the cave that Katherine truly believed and understood in the power of prayer. As Grandmother had prayed for her there, and then again that night, Katherine knew.

God was there. He'd always been there.

Even in her darkest and worst moments. He was *always* there. Oh, how she ached to have known Him sooner. God had never been important to her father and mother. They were focused on politics and knowing the right people. Her father wanted to change the world, but he'd somehow overlooked the need to change his soul. And then there was Randall. Proudly proclaiming himself to be an atheist not long after they were married. He believed he was god over all his domain, and that included Katherine.

Had she only known the truth . . . understood then what she now knew, perhaps she could have done something to help soften Randall. Perhaps if she'd gone into her marriage with love and kindness, things would have been different. She wasn't sure. Even if in her dark moments she didn't believe he deserved a second chance — God did. Grandmother said the worst and foulest sinner could be forgiven by God.

But this wasn't about Randall. She couldn't allow it to be. Ever again. He was gone and no longer had the power to hurt her . . . unless she let him. And after all she'd come through, Katherine was no longer willing to let him have that power.

That first night, Grandmother had read to her about a man named Saul whom God drastically changed. He became Paul — a completely different person.

Katherine believed she had the same chance. Because she'd felt His power. She didn't have to understand it. She didn't have to understand everything the Bible said, but she knew she was a sinner and that Jesus had died for her.

Grandmother had told her that putting one's faith in God was not the difficult thing so many people made it out to be. She remembered their conversation just hours earlier.

"Katherine, it neither requires cathedrals nor schooling — it's a matter of heart. God cares not for the outward appearance, but He's looking deep into your heart."

"But what if your heart is shattered into a million pieces?" Katherine pushed.

Grandmother's smile had warmed her heart. *"That's when God can do His very best work. That's when He can remold your heart to be exactly as He would have it be. Filled with love for Him."*

Katherine looked out on San Francisco and felt peace wash over her. She had thought her heart long dead, but God brought it back to life. He had collected the pieces, just as He had her tears. Not merely restoring what had been there before. No. He made something completely new. Something whole. Something good.

May 23 — The Curry Hotel

Alaska in May was a sight to behold. Snow covered the tops of the mountains still, but the wild flowers were bursting out of the ground with the long days of sunlight. Jean-Michel's daily routine began with exercises

143

in his room and then a long walk to the Railroad Roundhouse and back. Strength was returning to his leg. And it wasn't just being hopeful. He could *feel* it.

After the night when his leg gave out from under him on the stairs, he took precautions to not sit for too long and allow it to get stiff after all the exercises. The best medicine was to keep it moving and use different muscles. And there was plenty of opportunity to keep him occupied here.

Collette hadn't been quite the challenge as before, although he still had his hands full. Was he this difficult as a nineteen-year-old? He hoped not, but maybe it was just because his sister had always been so sheltered.

The thoughts that plagued him the most were of Maria Harrison and her granddaughter. So far, he hadn't seen them and had no idea when they would arrive. But the anticipation kept him going and gave him motivation to get his leg as strong as possible. Maybe they weren't planning to arrive until June.

That only gave him a few more days.

Days to think about what he would say and how Katherine would respond.

"Hello there!" John Ivanoff waved from beyond the Roundhouse and walked toward him. "I see you're out for your morning stroll."

"That I am." Jean-Michel's heart lifted a little. These men he'd met at the Curry Hotel were encouraging and uplifting. Hardworking and knowledgeable. "It helps the leg every day." Even though he was a guest — and a wealthy one at that — he wanted to spend more time with John and his son-in-law, Allan. They were . . . different . . . than most men he'd known. Their kind spirit seemed genuine — like Father's. Perhaps they too were men of God.

"You injured it in battle?" John reached his side.

"*Oui.* I'm sorry, *yes.*" Jean-Michel cleared his throat. "I was shot during the Druze Revolt in Syria."

"Don't apologize to me, Mr. Langelier. Your English is magnificent, and if it weren't for your accent, I would hardly know it wasn't your native tongue." John reached out to shake his hand. "I'm very sorry about your injury."

Jean-Michel hated to offer his own hand. Not because he didn't want to, but because he didn't want the conversation to end. Somehow he craved what he'd seen in these men. He'd watched their conversations and their interactions. And even though they

145

were always polite, they didn't spend too much time in what the Americans called *chitchat* with him. Probably because they were staff and he was a guest.

So how could he break the barrier?

He offered his hand in return.

John shook it. "Well, I need to go prepare for the trips we have planned for today."

That was his answer. "Mr. Ivanoff?"

John turned back around. "Yes, sir?"

"Do you think I'd be able to go on a few of these trips?" He didn't give the man a chance to give a negative response. "What do I need to do to schedule one with you?"

The man's smile was genuine in return. "Of course. Why don't we meet in the manager's office after lunch?"

Jean-Michel nodded. "Thank you." Watching John walk back to the hotel, Jean-Michel began to form a plan. If he could spend some more time with these men, maybe he could find some answers to the thoughts that plagued him. It would also be good to get Collette out and about.

His cane snagged a rock as he turned around, but for the first time in a long time, it didn't bother him. He realized it was a small sacrifice to pay to be rid of war and death. As he took in his surroundings, he wanted to stay here. The fresh, clean air.

The simpler life. The distance away from every bad memory.

He'd like nothing more than to stay hidden in Curry, but there was Collette to think about. She expected to return to France after the summer and then what? Would she settle down — perhaps marry? As he recalled, she didn't even have a beau. Father had never allowed her to be courted.

Then there was his own future. What was he to do with his life? He'd sold the factory, and because there was plenty of money he'd not given any real thought to doing anything at all . . . after being injured. How could he tell his little sister he no longer wished to return . . . home?

The bullet hole in his leg gave a sudden ache, but he refused to allow the spark of hopefulness to diminish.

He glanced heavenward and noted the clouds that were moving in. That's how it felt in his spirit. One moment there was a bit of open blue sky and the next the clouds blocked out the sun and poured rain down on him.

All around him was such beauty and tranquility. Why couldn't his soul have such peace?

The hike up Deadhorse Hill was invigorating, even if his leg was on fire. Jean-Michel stopped a moment to catch his breath and looked over at Collette. In her white gown, she practically glowed in the sunlight, and the smile on her face proved she was enjoying it. Even if the laundry would have a fun time removing the grass stains from the hem of her dress. It made him feel a moment of guilt. Collette had begged him for some of the shorter fashions, but he'd wanted her to be modest and fully covered. Perhaps if he allowed her to shorten her skirts, the grass wouldn't be an issue. He shook his head and started the rest of the climb. There was so much he didn't understand or know how to handle. He wished that instead of leaving him a letter, his father might have written him a book.

Their little entourage consisted of him, Collette, John Ivanoff, Allan Brennan, and a young man named Thomas. The latter seemed around Collette's age, but Jean-Michel had to give him credit — he hadn't even once tried to flirt with his sister. Always professional and helpful, Thomas seemed the epitome of a gentleman in American terms.

John and Allan led the way with Thomas bringing up the rear. Pointing out flowers, caribou — which a lot of the guests called reindeer — and other significant points of interest, the men made the hike most enjoyable. Even the strenuous parts.

At the top of the hill, Allan began unpacking a sack that contained their picnic lunch. He motioned for all of them to sit, and there were several large rocks placed in a circle where they could rest.

John and Allan sat next to each other with Thomas to Allan's left. Jean-Michel sat between Thomas and Collette, who was seated on John's right. They made a nice little circle and passed the food around.

"Collette." John smiled at her. "Your brother tells me this is your first time to America."

"*Oui.* Yes, it is."

"And what do you think of our great country?" John passed her the jug of lemonade and a cup.

"It is magnificent. And so much bigger than our homeland of France." She sipped from her cup as the wind blew at her hair, and she swiped strands out of her face.

Allan nodded and chuckled. "That's very true. I've been to France — during the Great War — and it's about as big as a couple of states, isn't it?"

She set her cup down and waved her hands. "My goodness, yes! When we had to take the train across the country, I didn't think we would ever make it to the other side."

All the men laughed at her dramatics.

Collette turned to Thomas. "I hear you are quite the expert on flowers now. Mr. Ivanoff said I could ask you my questions."

"Certainly, miss." Thomas cleared his throat.

Collette pulled a few flowers out of her pocket — she must have picked them on the way up — and started drilling Thomas with questions about each.

Jean-Michel allowed himself to relax. At least she wasn't flirting.

John and Allan fell into an easy conversation, and Jean-Michel just watched. And listened. The two seemed close and appeared to have great respect for one another. Both extremely intelligent but with humble attitudes. These were the kind of men Jean-Michel wished he knew. They weren't the kind of men he'd known back in France. Or in the army.

Everything at home was based on money, power, position. At least from the perspective he'd had. If he hadn't lost Katherine, would *he* have gotten sucked into the same mindset? The thought made him cringe, and he looked down at his leg. Was his mindset any better now?

The only man he'd ever wanted to be like was his father. But his father had been a wealthy and very powerful man. Under it all, though, Jean-Michel knew his father loved him. Never cruel, always fair, Pierre Langelier was a man of honor.

Jean-Michel had wanted to be that too. Until his world fell apart.

He had the wealth, and along with it came the power — if he wanted it. But would he ever have the peace of mind — the passion for living that his father had?

He looked over to his sister. So innocent and full of life. Was it a mistake to bring her here? She'd wanted a trip, but Alaska was a choice that was purely selfish on his part. After wrestling with the idea of seeing Katherine again — of doing whatever he could to help her find a reason to live — Jean-Michel had chosen the location in hopes that it might also give him a reason to go on.

Thomas shook his head and laughed at something she said. She pushed another flower at him.

While Collette didn't seem to be running

out of questions — or flowers — the two guides appeared relaxed and comfortable as they sat on the boulders and conversed.

Jean-Michel continued to watch their easy conversation. Like a father and son and very good friends.

Allan's face turned sober and he turned toward John as he spoke.

Jean-Michel couldn't pick out all the words, but he heard "baby" and "worry," and then the last phrase drifted over to him on the wind. "How will I know if I'm going to be a good father?"

The wind shifted and all Jean-Michel could hear was Collette and Thomas. And while their conversation was very educational, Jean-Michel wasn't interested in fire weed and arctic lupine.

When Collette paused for a moment, another word drifted over to him.

"Peace."

The conversations blended together again as the wind blew — the long tundra grass moved and swayed and swished along with it — and Jean-Michel wished he knew what they were talking about. Because peace was something he didn't have.

In fact, as soon as he thought of peace, his mind went in the opposite direction. Images of war, burning buildings, and his friends. Dead. Even though he'd never seen what happened to them, the images of their faces were still burned in his memory.

"Jean-Michel." Collette's hand touched his shoulder.

He wasn't sure how long he'd been sitting there lost in the dark images, but the others were standing.

Thomas offered to take his lunch items and stored them in his bag. He led the way down the hill and Collette followed.

As Jean-Michel stepped in behind her, he heard John talk to Allan in a low tone.

"Give it to God, son. He's the God of peace that 'passeth all understanding' and 'shall keep your hearts and minds through Christ Jesus.' "

The words hit him in the chest and made him take a deeper breath. Peace that passeth all understanding? Was this what his father knew?

Whatever it was, Jean-Michel was perplexed. He didn't deserve it, he knew. But what would it be like to have such peace?

Collette awoke to the sound of moaning. She sat up in bed momentarily disoriented. What was that noise? She'd been warned about the wild animals all around them. Was this one of the bears she'd heard about? She hugged her arms to her body. Mr. Brennan and Mr. Ivanoff said that bears were good climbers. Had one climbed up the side of the hotel? Could they get in through her window?

Then the sound of someone crying out filtered through her closed door. It sounded like Jean-Michel. Perhaps he had fallen.

She threw back the covers and jumped out of bed. The bathroom doors were both open, so she hurried through to the other side. There was very little light, but she could make out her brother thrashing in his bed.

"*Non!* Help them. For the love of all that is good . . . help them!"

Collette had never seen him like this. Father once mentioned that her brother had endured some difficulties while in the army, but he never gave her any details. She knew Jean-Michel hadn't returned with the light-hearted spirit he'd once had, but she attributed that to his wound. But this was something entirely different.

"Don't. Don't let them burn!"

She shook her head. Don't let them burn?

Longing only to ease his misery, Collette sat down on the bed and took hold of his hand. "Jean-Michel. Jean-Michel. I am here. You are safe."

He shook his head from side to side. "You must go to them. You must."

She drew his hand to her cheek. "It's all right, Jean-Michel. It's all right." Tears came to her eyes, but she brushed them away. She had to be strong. She could clearly see that her brother was a broken man, wounded far deeper than she ever knew.

He thrashed and moaned but didn't wake up, and Collette had no idea if it was better to let him work through the nightmare or startle him by forcing him to wake up. No one had prepared her for such a thing, and so she merely held his hand and stayed at his side until the misery passed.

Once he stopped crying out and settled into a more restful sleep, Collette let go of his hand and got to her feet. She walked back to her room, trying to reason through what had just happened. What had her poor brother seen that should leave such horrible nightmares? On their trip here she'd slept soundly each night and couldn't remember ever hearing Jean-Michel having such terrors in his sleep.

She walked to the window and pushed back the drapes. It was already getting light outside, even though it was still quite early. She knew from what Thomas had said that the daylight would last longer and longer into the night and then the sun would rise earlier and earlier. What a very strange land. Strange and beautiful and deadly.

Thomas also told her about the dangers of going out too far from the hotel without someone carrying a weapon — someone who knew their way around. Collette thought perhaps he was just exaggerating, but Mr. Ivanoff had assured her it was true.

"But you mustn't let worries over what might be steal the joy of what is," Mr. Ivanoff told her. "Life is full of both beauty and danger, and we must give attention to both, but we should never let worry steal our focus. Otherwise, we see neither the beauty nor the danger and suffer because of it."

Perhaps in facing danger, her brother had lost the ability to see the beauty — to know the peace and joy life could afford. And in being sheltered from the dangers and sorrows of life, perhaps Collette had lost her ability to feel compassion and mercy for those who suffered.

Well, maybe she hadn't lost it — after all, she felt deep sorrow for Jean-Michel. Still, her sympathy would do little to help him heal. Tears came again, and this time she didn't even attempt to hold them back.

"I don't know what to do. I don't know how to help him."

10

June 1

Cassidy walked out to the gardens at a brisk pace. She couldn't believe the crazy emotions this pregnancy had given her. One moment she was elated, the next she was crying. Then the next — if she wasn't careful — she was ready to unleash her anger on the poor unsuspecting souls who might cross her. *Lord, give me wisdom to feel it coming on, and when it does — glue my lips shut. Please.*

She'd done all right after that first episode, which took her by surprise. And goodness, if Allan didn't get tickled at her every time she got riled up. He probably did it on purpose now just to see it. Well, she would have to work harder to keep her emotions in check.

If that were even possible.

The doctor spoke to her about female

chemicals that changed during an expecting cycle. Well, whatever those chemicals were, they needed some guidance and a little toning down. She was certain that yes, God must have a reason, but it didn't seem fair that she could no longer be her normal self. In fact, she had to start carrying tissues in her apron pocket for those times when the tears began to flow.

As she rounded the corner to the greenhouse, Cassidy spotted a lovely blond woman. Standing there, her shoulders were slightly hunched and shaking. She appeared to be crying.

Cassidy approached. Her heart always ached for anyone lost, alone, or suffering. "Can I help you?"

The woman turned, her green eyes shimmering with tears.

"Oh, my dear." Cassidy pulled out a tissue and started crying herself. "What can I do? Are you hurt?"

"Non. Non." The accent was gorgeous. As was the woman before her. "I am crying for someone else." The words were perfect English but rounded with the sounds of French. Cassidy recognized it immediately.

"I'm a good listener if you need me."

The woman nodded but looked away.

Cassidy dried her own tears and pulled in

a deep breath. She had to stop falling apart every fifteen minutes; otherwise, she'd never make it through this pregnancy without dehydrating.

Thinking the woman wanted to be left alone, Cassidy patted her shoulder and turned to go.

"Have you ever loved someone and not really understood their pain?"

The words caught Cassidy off guard, halting her steps. "Yes, I have."

"*Non.* I don't think you have. Not like this. You are good and sweet. I've seen how you take care of everyone around here." She sat down on a tree stump.

Cassidy shook her head. "You may think I'm good and sweet, but you haven't seen me lose my temper." She made a face and the young woman gave a hint of a smile. Cassidy wasn't sure how old she might be, but she seemed hardly more than a girl . . . so very young and vulnerable in her sorrow. Her clothing depicted great wealth, and all the staff knew they had guests from France that were staying all summer. This must be the sister. Hadn't Allan said something about her brother being wounded in war?

The beautiful blonde looked across the river. "It's so magnificent here."

"Yes, it is."

160

"My name is Collette Langelier." The name was as beautiful as the young woman.

Cassidy held out her hand. "Cassidy Brennan. Call me Cassidy."

"You see, Cassidy" — the woman formed the name slowly as she was trying it out — "I am a selfish person. Everything has always come easy. There's always been money. I've always been happy, but for a few times. My mother died when I was young and that was so very hard. I miss her more than I can say, but Father always did what he could to keep me happy. Until he too died just this last spring."

"I'm so sorry." Cassidy wondered if it would help any to share that she too had lost her mother.

"I'm afraid I've been thinking only of myself and my desires. So much so that I gave little thought to the pain of someone I dearly love."

"I'm so sorry. Are they hurt? Do they need a doctor?"

"*Non. Non.* It's not like that. It is inside." She put a hand to her chest. "The trouble is, I've known for quite some time that this person was hurting inside. But I didn't understand it. It didn't fit into my brightly colored world."

Like gumdrops and rainbows, as Mrs.

Johnson would say. Cassidy felt an instant connection to the young woman.

Collette continued. "But I witnessed some of the suffering the other night. Tormenting dreams that drive him to sweat and thrash and cry out in his sleep."

Tears sprang to Cassidy's eyes again. "You're speaking of your brother?"

"Oui." She nodded. "I know I shouldn't be sharing all of this with a stranger, but I had just prayed for help and you came. Father said he wanted me to seek God, and so I thought I'd pray. I really don't know how to do it very well, but I had heard the pastor pray over my father's grave. He just talked to God and so I did the same. And you appeared." She waved her hankie at Cassidy.

Cassidy didn't know what to say. She wanted to tell Collette that praying was just that easy, but she sensed the woman had much more to say and remained silent.

"You see, our home in France is so large that our rooms are several hallways apart. I never knew . . . about the nightmares." She choked on a small sob. "I knew there must have been death, of course. It was war. I had heard him tell Father of two friends he'd lost, but little else. I didn't know so many had died, and Jean-Michel blamed himself for their deaths. I haven't ever felt that much sorrow or pain." Collette turned those fierce green eyes on Cassidy. "Not until I went through a night at his side as he was troubled by the dreams."

"And now you want to help him heal."

Collette nodded again and bit down on her bottom lip. "But it's more than that. I need to help my brother heal from his broken and wounded heart, while I need to learn how to open up my own. Like I said, I'm selfish . . . and more than a bit spoiled."

"Why do you say that?"

She shrugged. "I traveled all this way with Jean-Michel and never knew about his nightmares. I have always been a sound sleeper, but surely if I cared more about him . . . his pain, then I would have known about them."

Cassidy thought of various reasons why this young woman might never have witnessed her brother's misery, but she stayed on the topic of Collette's concern. "Well, there's a fairly easy way to get over being spoiled and selfish."

"How?" Collette looked at her with a glimmer of hope.

"Think of others first. And not just of frivolous things, but of real needs. Such as children without homes or parents, people without food or shelter, hospitals full of sick people. Think of them, rather than shoes and clothes, money and boys."

Collette seemed to consider that a moment. Cassidy knew thinking of others was simple enough, but acting on it might be a little harder. Especially for one who'd never known need.

"Most important, look to God for help. Ask Him to help you change — to think more on things that aren't about . . . you. Ask Him how you can help others."

"And it is this that makes you so happy?" Collette asked.

Cassidy shrugged. "I think God has given me a glad heart. Sometimes things are difficult — even painful — and I'm certainly not happy then. But I am content in the knowledge that He will always see me through."

"But how do I find happiness? How can I be like you — so helpful and good to others?"

Cassidy laughed. "First of all, don't try to be like me. Just be the best *you,* you can be. I don't go looking for happiness. I live life. All the ups and downs, ins and outs. Appreciating each moment. Finding joy in all the little things."

"But wouldn't that be selfish of me?"

Cassidy shook her head. "There's nothing

selfish about appreciating the good things in life that God has given you. It's when having those things means more to you than helping someone who is in need. Being selfish is when you don't care about the needs of others and think only of how something might benefit you. Finding joy in the things God has blessed us with isn't selfish at all."

Collette gave an exasperated sigh. "I don't know where to begin. There is so much need — my brother is suffering in so much pain. It's like the big mountain you call Denali. I would never know how to climb over it."

Cassidy smiled. "One step at a time, my father would say. One step at a time."

June 5

The train whistled as it began to slow. Katherine let out a sigh. Finally, they'd made it to their destination — the Curry Hotel. Grandmother's strength had begun to visibly fade the last couple weeks and Katherine wasn't surprised. In all her years, she'd never understand how her grandmother had held up the past two months with all the rigors of travel at her age. Katherine felt like *she* could collapse at any moment from the exhaustion of it all.

165

As the railroad cars lurched to a stop, she stood and stretched. "Well, Grandmother, it appears we've finally made it to Curry."

Her grandmother sighed. "It will be nice to spend the summer in Alaska, don't you think, my dear?"

For the first time in a long time, Katherine could agree. "Yes, ma'am." While she couldn't change her past, she at least felt some hope for the future. She didn't have to face it alone — and she had her stubborn grandmother to thank for that. "I'm glad you forced me to come."

"Forced you?" Grandmother shook her head. "That's ridiculous. I never forced you, child."

"How about coerced?" Katherine tried to hide her smile.

"Definitely not." Grandmother straightened her hat.

"Firmly-encouraged-while-making-me-feel-guilty-that-if-I-didn't-go-it-would-break-your-heart?"

Laughter escaped the older woman's lips. "You do beat all, Katherine." She gathered her handbag and book. "I like to think of it as gently steering you in the correct direction."

It felt good to laugh along with her grandmother. Life had not been kind to Katherine for many years, but she knew now that this life wasn't the end. This world wasn't her home. And she would rejoice in that fact. If there was a way to bring joy to others in the days, weeks, and months ahead — she would do it.

Exiting the train, Katherine relished the crisp air and the firmness of the platform. Between all the trains with their rocking, the ships with their rolling, and all the uneven surfaces her feet had landed on, she greatly appreciated a sturdy foundation to stand on.

Grandmother sighed from behind her. "Nice to be on solid ground, isn't it?"

"My thoughts exactly, Grandmother." She took a few steps forward.

The hustle and bustle that surrounded them with passengers scurrying around — most of them men — made Katherine want to shrink and hide. Quiet. She longed for quiet. That's the only way she'd felt truly comfortable the past few weeks. In the quiet, studying the Word and discussing things with her beloved grandparent.

A hand on her arm made her jerk. "Might I help you, m'lady?" The brogue in the man's accent sounded a bit like he was Irish. "I be staying here at the hotel as well."

She blinked several times and stared at

the man in shock. Horrible memories rolled in. It all started with a grip on her arm . . . she shook her head and attempted to move out of his grasp.

His hand remained firmly on her elbow as he smiled down at her. "You look a bit lost, and I know my way around. Maybe we could have dinner together . . . get to know one another?"

This time she yanked her arm away and stepped back. The moment had stunned her, but in that instant, she realized she would *never* allow a man to touch her without her permission. Never. "I'm not a bit lost, sir, and I'll ask you to keep your distance."

His smile diminished slightly. "Is that a 'no' to dinner?"

"You are most correct, young man." Grandmother's cane sliced into the air between them. "Now if you will excuse us, we have a schedule to keep."

The man backed off — not that he had a choice with the cane poised in midair — and Katherine took her grandmother's arm and headed toward the entrance of the hotel.

"Thank you, Grandmother." Tears blurred her vision, and her voice choked.

"Dear, I'm so sorry. I stopped for a moment to place my book in my handbag and had no idea you were that far ahead of me."

Katherine swallowed her discomfort. She needed to get through the next few minutes and get alone so she could deal with these emotions. But not in front of all these people. "It's not your fault. I stopped, and I guess it gave him the opportunity to step in." She had no idea if the man had anything untoward in mind, but her arm still burned from where he'd gripped her elbow. So many times that same action had been Randall's means of controlling her in public. "Please let's just check in. I need a few moments alone."

"Of course." Grandmother took over and strode purposefully to the front desk.

Katherine followed like a small child. In all their travels the past weeks, she'd never had to interact with men. Oh, they'd been around, but everyone must have seen the two women traveling together and left them alone. Even on the tours and during dinners on the ship, people had somehow known that their company wouldn't be welcomed. Katherine swallowed the lump in her throat. She avoided men at all costs since Randall's death. Not that she'd been around people very much, but men in particular terrified her. In her own elite society, Katherine had never had to worry about being accosted as she'd just been. There was an entire mountain of rules and etiquette to observe, and people knew that to do otherwise would bring severe ostracizing. But here in the wilds of America the same rules didn't apply.

Katherine found herself totally unprepared for all the thoughts and emotions flowing through her.

Would she never be able to function around men again?

11

June 6 — Barcelona, Spain

It became increasingly dangerous every time he made his way to the telegraph office. Each time, he took a different route at a different time of day.

He couldn't be compromised. He *must* get the message to the general.

The officer behind the counter today looked over the glasses on the end of his nose. "Perfect timing, sir. A telegram just came in for you."

Glancing around and seeing that no one else occupied the office, he snatched the telegram offered to him. He gave a brief nod and left a coin on the counter.

He turned and tucked the envelope into his pocket. It was paramount that he wasn't watched when he opened it.

Finding an unoccupied hallway to his right, he tore into the message. Not the news he expected, but he would have to make it work. So the general had gone to Alaska. The situation must be grave indeed. But since *his* message had to get to the general as soon as possible, then he would just go to Alaska as well. It would take quite a bit of convincing to the others, but he could do it.

"Sir?" The officer from the telegraph counter waved him over. "If anything else comes in for you, how do you want me to reach you?"

"Don't worry about reaching me." He pasted on a smile because that was what civilized people did. "Hold it for me here and I will come in if necessary."

The officer nodded but looked at him oddly.

Walking out of the telegraph office, he checked his surroundings and then looked back at the building. He couldn't risk the mission. And that officer was too curious. Maybe the man had kept copies of the messages?

The risk was too great.

He'd have to burn the building down.

June 8 — The Curry Hotel

The gentle *ticktock* of the clock on the

172

dresser was soothing in its constant rhythm.

Katherine stared out the second-story window of the hotel, watching the river rush and flow past. She'd hidden long enough. They'd been at the Curry almost three days and she still hadn't left her room — not after the debacle on the train platform.

Why did one man — one touch on her arm — send her into such a tailspin? This whole faith thing was very new to her, but couldn't she be stronger than this?

When the darkness threatened to close in that first night after it happened, Katherine spent the night on her knees in prayer. Grandmother had joined her in the middle of the night. She knew that she was a new creation — that she was safe. But this was harder than she ever thought possible. Letting go of all her fear — all the past — and all the memories that haunted her was proving difficult. Especially when she couldn't even deal with one episode.

A knock at the door told her Grandmother was here for another visit.

"Come in."

The lines in the older woman's face as she entered showed her weariness. "Katherine, we have to talk, dear."

She turned back to the window. It was definitely time, but she felt so frail.

"I'm worried about you."

"I know, and I'm sorry. I didn't mean to worry you."

"It's been three days and you've hardly eaten. I know you're not sleeping well. I can see the dark circles under your eyes." Grandmother sighed. "Please tell me, what can I do?"

Katherine stood, her heart aching. She walked over to her grandmother and wrapped her arms around her. "You've been my rock. You have. Thank you for that. I was just thinking to myself that it was time to join the land of the living again, but it's easier to hide. That was how the old Katherine dealt with things. The new Katherine doesn't know what to do quite yet."

Grandmother hugged her back and then pulled away. She walked over to the chair in the corner. "I don't want to be your rock, Katherine. That's God's job. And I know it's easier to hide, but you grow more when you take the hard path."

Clasping her hands, Katherine nodded. "You know what? When that man first held my arm, it made me freeze. I felt powerless. But then I yanked away and realized that God has made me strong. Physically, I knew I could get away." She sucked in a breath. "But the damage from the past is what immobilizes me. It's emotionally that I don't feel as strong. Those terrible memories will pop up, and I once again feel weak and helpless — in every way."

Grandmother tilted her head as a tear streaked down her cheek. "Well, let's turn it around, then. When was the last time you felt safe around a man? When was the last time you felt cherished or loved?"

Oh, she would ask *those* questions. Taking a moment to collect her thoughts, Katherine knew she had to be honest. "Father never made me feel loved or adored, I'm sad to say. He scared me. But I did *know* that he loved me. In my mind. In his way." She swallowed past the lump in her throat. "And the last time I felt safe around a man would be five years ago. Jean-Michel Langelier. Do you remember him? He always made me feel beautiful and cherished. But he was also my best friend. He knew me better than anyone else." Unbidden tears sprang to her eyes.

"I'm so sorry for all of the pain of the past, my dear girl, I truly am. But let's focus on remembering that there was a man you felt safe with. Next time you find yourself in a situation that brings up all of the bad memories, why don't you try to think of a positive time instead?"

It was worth a try. She nodded.

"But first and foremost, we will continue to bathe it in prayer."

"Yes, Grandmother. Please."

The older woman stood. "Now, if it's all right with you, why don't we freshen up and go down to dinner? I can request a small table for just the two of us."

Another nod. "I'd like that very much. I'm done hiding. At least for now." She attempted a smile.

"All right. I'll come back in about five minutes."

After changing her clothes, Katherine washed her face and applied a little makeup to cover up the circles under her eyes. She was determined to make an attempt at being social. At least she knew she could spend the evening with her grandmother and not worry about making small talk with a bunch of strangers.

But after a brief prayer together and the journey down the stairs, her stomach began to flip-flop. People were everywhere.

Hiding was definitely easier. Maybe she should just stay holed up in her room for a while. No. That was the old Katherine talking. *Lord, please help me. I am a new creation.*

Grandmother tugged on her elbow. "I won't leave your side."

Katherine squared her shoulders. She could do this. With God's help, she could. One breath at a time.

Two gentlemen in suits and ties stood at the bottom of the stairs. As Katherine and her grandmother descended, the men started to move; then one stopped and turned toward her. "You are Senator Demarchis's wife. We met at a party you gave." He held out a hand. "Let me introduce myself. I'm Senator Wesley Jones from Washington State. It is a privilege to see you, and please accept my deepest sympathies for your loss."

She quashed the feeling to turn around and run away. There was no sense in causing a scene and shaming her grandmother. Katherine took the proffered hand and shook it as politely as she could, then quickly let go. But the shock of it all hit her in the face. No matter where she went, she'd always be Senator Demarchis's widow. Even here. In remote Alaska. "Thank you." She forced the words. His sympathies could be thrown out the window. Had Randall truly fooled the entire world? "How long are you in Alaska?"

"Sadly, we leave in the morning. I'd heard

you were here but hadn't had the chance to speak with you yet."

Relief spread through her. At least this link to Randall would be gone. The man seemed nice enough, but she didn't need another jaunt down memory lane. "Well, thankfully, we were able to meet before you head back." It was a lie, but at the moment it was all Katherine could do to paste on a smile. "This is my grandmother, Maria Harrison."

"Pleasure." The senator gave a small bow.

"It was lovely to see you again, Mr. Jones." Katherine nodded and began to walk away. She hoped Grandmother was behind her, because she had no intention of turning back. She could not bear a conversation where she even had to mention her deceased husband's name, and she definitely didn't want to talk to any men, much less shake their hands.

At the entrance to the dining room, she stopped and took another deep breath. She focused on the beautifully set tables and stylish people. It appeared no expense had been spared to make this a luxurious dining experience.

"Nicely done, Katherine. You did well."

"Thank you, Grandmother." She continued to scan the room. "Now if I can just make it through —"

A familiar face stopped her. His dark hair falling across his forehead as it had when they were younger. He stood and she could see his green eyes from the other side of the room. Eyes she would never forget. Eyes that once held so much love for her she'd vowed to follow him anywhere.

"Jean-Michel . . ."

"What are you waiting for?" Mrs. Johnson bellowed to the idle young woman. "Get this fish upstairs at once. Our guests are hungry and there's plenty more to be delivered." The maid nodded and hurried to pick up the tray.

Cassidy felt sorry for the girl. She was new this season and hadn't had that much experience with Mrs. Johnson's manner. But rather than say anything about it, Cassidy focused on making whipped cream for the chocolate mousse they would serve later for dessert.

Her thoughts had ever been on Collette Langelier and her concern about her brother. Cassidy had tried to share a bit of encouragement and what she hoped was godly counsel, but the young woman showed few signs of being comforted.

"And what are *you* daydreaming about?"

Mrs. Johnson asked, her tone softer than before.

Cassidy shook her head. "Just one of the guests. She was unhappy and I tried to offer some encouragement."

"Well, if anyone could do it, it would be you." Mrs. Johnson went to check one of the pots on the stove while the rest of the staff bustled back and forth to see to their stations.

Cassidy finished whipping the cream and went to collect a tray of chilled mousse from the refrigerator. She piped the topping on each of the desserts with expert precision, then returned the tray to the refrigerator and brought out another.

Mrs. Johnson chastised one of the girls for not properly buttering the tops of the rolls. Cassidy smiled to herself. Sometimes she thought if there was nothing to complain about and correct, Mrs. Johnson might very well lie down and die. The woman seemed to thrive on dictating demands, and yet Cassidy knew she could be such a dear.

With the mousse properly topped in whipped cream, Cassidy turned her attention to cleaning up her station when she heard her name being called. She glanced up to find Allan standing near the door.

She smiled and went to see what he

needed. "You know Mrs. Johnson will have your hide for interrupting the kitchen during mealtime."

He shook his head. "Nope. We have an agreement."

Cassidy cocked her head to one side. "And would that agreement involve me?"

"Of course." He kissed her forehead. "You feel much too warm. I think it's time for you to take a few moments outside to cool down."

"But there's work to do."

"We can manage." Mrs. Johnson's words came from behind her. "Now do as your husband says."

Cassidy's joy at seeing Allan quickly faded. "I won't have the two of you playing nursemaid to me. I'm not sick or an invalid and I only fainted that one time. I feel perfectly fine and have far too much to do to go off walking about."

Allan looked at her with a raised brow. "You can walk . . . or I can carry you."

Mrs. Johnson chuckled, making Cassidy all the more frustrated. "You would think I was the first woman in the world to be in my condition."

Allan took hold of her arm. "You're the first wife I've ever had in this condition, and I mean to take care of you. Besides,

I've already cleared this with Mrs. Johnson."

Cassidy had been working hard to control her emotions, but tears came to her eyes unbidden. Truth be told, she was starting to feel rather warm. "Very well. Let's go."

Once they were outside and away from the main building, Cassidy felt her anger ebb. She knew they only wanted the very best for her.

Allan stopped and reached into his pocket. "Here. Blow your nose." He handed her his handkerchief.

"You make me feel like a child." She took the cloth and wiped her eyes.

He put a finger under her chin and tilted her face to meet his gaze. "That isn't my intention. I just care about you — more than you know." He planted a brief kiss on her lips. "I don't know what I'd do if something happened to you."

This brought back Cassidy's tears. "Oh, bother! I'm such a mess."

"But a beautiful one." He grinned.

"I don't know why I think I can help anyone else when I can't even figure out myself."

"What are you talking about now? Who did you try to help?"

Cassidy dried her eyes again. "Collette Langelier. She's worried about her brother.

He was in some battle. It wasn't the Great War, but he got that leg injury."

"Yes, I know. It was the Druze Revolt. He mentioned it briefly."

"Well, Collette said he has horrible nightmares, and she doesn't know how to help him."

Allan shook his head. "I doubt she can. Some things only God can heal."

"She said he feels all this guilt about not saving people, but she doesn't know the details."

"That's a blessing." Allan put his arm around Cassidy's shoulder. "It's best she not know. Otherwise, she'll be having nightmares too. I can tell you from experience, war is a brutal and ugly thing. I pray you never have to see anything of it."

"So is there nothing I can say or do to help her?"

"You can pray for them both, but especially for Jean-Michel. He's troubled to be sure — maybe about more than just the war."

"Can't you talk to him?" Cassidy looked up to find Allan gazing across the field.

"If the man approaches me, of course." He glanced back down at her. "It needs to be his idea — his desire to share what happened. You can't force those memories out of a man. Until he's ready to talk — it's best we just pray."

Cassidy nodded. "I will definitely continue to do that." She drew in a deep breath. "Thank you."

Allan gave her a questioning look. "For what?"

"Caring about me. Enduring my moods and my temper." She turned and put her arms around him. "I think my stomach has doubled in size. Soon I'll be too fat to do this."

He laughed and scooped her up into his arms. "When that happens, then I shall just do this."

Cassidy laughed and held on tight. If only she could always feel this happy and help everyone around her feel the same.

12

For weeks, Jean-Michel had watched and waited for this moment. To be honest, he'd been waiting for years to see her face again.

He grabbed his cane and walked across the crowded dining room.

Katherine.

His Katherine.

His friend and confidante. His first and only love. She was here.

He heard Collette's voice behind him, but he was drawn forward. Conversations and silverware clinking on plates surrounded him as he walked, but none of it mattered.

The head waiter gestured with his arm and appeared to be about to seat the two ladies at a table off by themselves when he noticed Jean-Michel's approach and gave him an odd expression. "Good evening, sir."

"Good evening." Jean-Michel couldn't take his eyes off Katherine's now that he was close to her.

The waiter cleared his throat. "Do you know the senator's wife?" The starched-uniformed man tilted his head.

"I do indeed."

"Well, I don't." Collette's voice behind him shocked him out of his stare.

The waiter raised both eyebrows. "Would you like for me to find a table that would accommodate the whole party, sir?"

"No, that's not necessary." Jean-Michel shook his head, although he would have loved nothing more than to share the evening with Katherine. However, considering the scared look in Katherine's eyes, he knew it was the right decision. It was best not to overwhelm her, even though every instinct within him was crying out to spend every moment with her. "Katherine — excuse me, Mrs. Demarchis — please allow me to introduce you to my sister, Collette Langelier."

The dazed look left Katherine's eyes as she looked over at Collette. "It's lovely to meet you. I've heard so much about you from . . . your brother. Let me introduce you to my grandmother, Mrs. Maria Harrison."

Collette nodded politely. "I'm pleased to make your acquaintance, ma'am."

"You remember Grandmother, don't

you?" Katherine looked at Jean-Michel.

He nodded at Maria Harrison. The woman behind their trip to Alaska gave away nothing. So he decided to keep his mouth shut as well. But the twinkle in her eye told him she was pleased. And his message had been received. He was here for Katherine. "I do. It's a pleasure to see you again, Mrs. Harrison."

"And you, my dear boy. It's been some time. Five years, I think, since we last saw each other. I believe it was at a dance."

"*Oui.* Yes."

"Katherine and I have already run into others we've known. On one of our tours we found ourselves in the company of the Whitmores, and they live just down the street from me. I thought it all very strange to go hundreds of miles away only to have dinner with my neighbors."

"It is a small world sometimes."

"Very small," Katherine murmured.

As much as Jean-Michel longed to remain in her company, he gave a little bow. "Don't let us keep you from your dinner, we must be getting back to ours as well. It is quite delicious. We had the fish." He nodded to the two ladies, turned, and walked back to their table.

Once he had seated Collette again, he

took his own chair and tried not to look at Katherine each second. It took every ounce of determination he had.

"So that senator's wife —" Collette began.

"Widow," he corrected. Probably a bit too abruptly.

"All right, that senator's widow . . . is Katherine. *The* Katherine you wanted to marry all those years ago?"

He nodded and cut another bite of salmon, using every bit of his energy to appear normal.

"Sensationnel. Je n'en avais aucune idée." She sat back in her chair in a stunned manner.

Instead of correcting her to speak English, Jean-Michel was relieved the other patrons didn't understand her words. They'd already drawn enough attention. He was quite shocked himself and knew his sister had no idea that they'd ever run into Katherine. Besides, he didn't have Mrs. Harrison's permission to share their secret.

He couldn't look up at Collette. Or at Katherine. Too afraid his feelings would be obvious. Instead, he focused on his plate and his glass of water.

"Lâche."

"Excuse me?" Jean-Michel lifted his gaze to see his sister's smirk.

188

"I believe the Americans like to use the phrase . . . 'scaredy cat'?" She giggled. "You've attacked your plate with gusto — never once looking up. I know you. And don't look now, but she's watched *you* the entire time."

Whether he wanted to admit it or not, Collette was correct. He was afraid. Scared of messing it all up — of saying the wrong thing. He used his linen napkin to wipe his mouth and then set it on the table. "I'm finished. Are you ready to go up?"

"Not a chance." She set her napkin down as well. "I think I'd like to go for a walk."

"Of course." He stood and offered her his arm.

As they exited the dining room, Jean-Michel looked over at Katherine and smiled. Her eyes had lost the fearful look but now had a guarded appearance. How could he change that?

How could he help her?

The thoughts tumbled over one another in his mind as they walked on a trail behind the hotel to the river, his sister taking slower steps as she stayed at his side. One day, he wanted to venture across the suspension bridge, but he was waiting for his leg to strengthen a bit more.

At the edge of the river, Collette finally

stopped and spoke. "I know I'm your little sister and you've tried to protect me from all the ugliness you faced. But I know about your nightmares, Jean-Michel. I've been in your room almost every night after you cry out to try to help you calm down. I feared you might awaken the other guests."

He opened his mouth to question her, but she held up a hand to stop him. "Please, let me finish. I know I've been selfish and childish and I'm still very young in your eyes. But seeing you suffer has changed me. I want to help. And with everything in me, I believe that beautiful woman in there can help too. Am I correct?"

He shook his head and walked closer to the water. "There's so much you don't know, Collette." He sighed. "I am crippled and war-torn now. A lot has happened to both of us over the past five years."

"But you love her . . . I can see it on your face."

The water flowed by and he kicked a rock into it. Dare he admit it? "Yes. I love her. As much as I ever did before."

"Then you must do whatever you can to win her over. She's a widow and free to love again. Maybe she never stopped loving you to begin with." Collette smiled. "I believe love can do wonders to heal a person."

Jean-Michel looked at her and shook his head. "And what would you know of love?"

She shrugged. "Enough to know it has the power to change a person — to change everything."

Grandmother paced the floor, this time in Katherine's room. "So you refuse to talk about it?"

Katherine pulled the brush through her long hair. So many of the other women were cutting their hair, but she'd kept hers long all because Jean-Michel had told her years ago that he loved her long hair. "No, I'm not saying that I refuse to talk about it. I just don't know what to think or feel. That was quite a surprise."

"I understand the shock, my dear. I do. But did you see his face? He still cares for you."

For twenty minutes her grandmother had worked to get her to open up. Enough was enough. "Of course, I saw his face, Grandmother! I couldn't help looking at him every chance I had." The tears she'd held in check since seeing Jean-Michel started in earnest now. "I know you mean well, but all these questions are just making it worse."

The older woman sat down on the chair. Her mouth dropped open and then shut.

"I'm sorry. I didn't mean to lash out. But don't you understand? Don't you see? I've never stopped loving him. I am so ashamed. I was married and I was still in love with Jean-Michel. What does that say about me?"

"It says that you should never have been parted from one another. Your husband . . . he knew you didn't love him. He knew you didn't wish to marry him and yet he imposed marriage upon you anyway."

"He imposed a great deal on me, but it doesn't change the facts. It is my great shame and I will carry that to the grave."

Grandmother looked at her for a moment. "Did your husband know you loved another?"

"Yes." Katherine twisted her hands together. "I told him the first time we were left alone to discuss our engagement. I made it clear that I didn't wish to marry him — that I was in love with another man. At first, he was ever so gentle and kind. He told me that arranged marriages often separated first loves, but that our love would soon blossom and surpass whatever it was that I thought I had with Jean-Michel. That was his game. He was a complete gentleman before we married. Afterward, however, he often berated me for the love I held for Jean-Michel."

"But he knew the truth. You kept nothing from him and therefore should bear no shame or guilt. You were ripped from the arms of the man you loved and forced into a most unholy union. That was never your choice. You honored your marriage vows and now you are released. You owe it to yourself to rekindle what you once had with Jean-Michel."

"But I can never marry again. Never! Not after what I went through with . . . *him.*"

A knock at the door startled her and she put a hand to her forehead. It was all just too much to bear. She longed for a hot bath and bed.

Grandmother rose and went over and opened the door. "Yes? . . . Thank you." She closed the door. "There's a note here for you."

Katherine took the envelope and recognized instantly the handwriting on the outside. Jean-Michel. She ran a hand over it. If only they could turn back time. But they couldn't. She lifted the seal and pulled out the note.

Katherine,

I was hoping I could convince you to take a walk with me tomorrow. The wild flowers here are beautiful and I know you would enjoy them.

It was lovely to see you again. I pray you are well.

Jean-Michel

"He's asked me for a walk."

"How kind." Grandmother stood and went toward the bathroom that divided their rooms. "I'll give you some time to yourself. I'm really rather tired. I think I'll turn in early. I love you, my dear."

"I love you too." Katherine picked up a piece of stationery and a pen to write a reply. The daylight hours were so long now, she could never tell what time it was. But a glance at the clock informed her it was already 8:00 p.m.

Staring out the window once again, she didn't know what to say.

There'd been a time that the words would have flowed and she wouldn't have stopped until she'd written ten pages. But those days were gone. And even though she still loved him, she'd better take this opportunity to tell him the truth. If he still cared for her as Grandmother suggested, then it was better this way. She would be honest with him and he would have his disappointment and leave her for someone better suited to share his life. Yes, it was better this way — but better for whom, she couldn't say.

Jean-Michel,
    A walk would be nice. How about 1:00
p.m.?

Katherine

What would he think of her if he knew
the whole truth? Would he believe the same
things Randall did? It didn't really matter
anymore, because no matter how much she
still loved him, her life was a pile of ashes.
God may have forgiven her and made her
new, but how could she ask forgiveness of
Jean-Michel?
    Tomorrow she would have to find the
words to tell him.

13

June 9

Collette walked along the river behind the hotel, wondering what would become of her. Oh, there was plenty of money for her future, and she'd love to go back to France, but now that Katherine had arrived, things were bound to change for her brother. Wouldn't they?

Her conversation outside the greenhouse with Cassidy that day came rushing back. Collette had never met such a loving, giving person. A complete stranger, yet she had taken the time to listen to Collette's problems and offer encouragement.

Was that how Christians acted all the time? Was that what Father wanted for her?

Cassidy encouraged Collette to seek God as well. She'd also told her to concentrate on things that weren't about . . . well, *Collette.*

Think of others first. And not just of frivolous things, but of real needs.

Collette had even dared to ask the question on her mind — how did one find happiness?

The laughter of her new friend washed over her. *"I don't go looking for happiness. I live life. All the ups and downs, ins and outs. Appreciating each moment. Finding joy in all the little things."*

Squeals and laughter came up behind her as a group of children ran past her toward the suspension bridge.

Their joy made her want to run alongside them and giggle as well. But at nineteen, she supposed she should act her age.

As far as she could tell, there were three boys and three girls. The two oldest boys seemed to enjoy teasing the oldest girl, who held the hand of the youngest girl. The little troop made their way across the bridge, and they stopped in the middle to look at the water on both sides.

Then the two big boys spread out and started jumping up and down on either side of the four smaller children. The one older girl wrapped her arms around the smallest two, but that left the smaller boy on his own.

What started out as laughter with the

197

bouncing bridge soon became cries of terror.

Collette dashed to the bridge and held on tight as the bridge bounced and swayed. *"Intimidateurs absurdes . . ."* Absurd bullies.

She struggled to stay upright. Just wait until she got her hands on those boys for torturing the little ones.

She was still several yards away when the small boy fell against the cables on one side of the bridge. No longer with sure footing, he screamed and flailed as the bridge swayed.

The largest of the boys picked him up and put his feet on top of the main cable. "Oh, are you scared of the river, Davey?"

"Stop it!" one of the girls cried out.

Since the jumping had stopped, Collette could move quicker. As she reached the group she tried to look as stern as she could. "Stop this now! Put him down!"

But instead of scaring the children into obedience, Collette's words scared the tormentor — who had obviously been so intent on his teasing that he hadn't seen her approach — and he let go of Davey.

The boy fell from the bridge with a cry.

Before she could think to do anything else, Collette jumped into the river after him.

Frigid water rushed over her head. Where

was the boy?

"Help! Help me!" The cry reached her ears.

She let the current of the river help her swim to the child, but when she reached him, his little body sank below the surface. With a swift kick of her feet, she propelled herself underwater and grabbed Davey's jacket.

They came to the surface sputtering and gasping.

"Are you okay?" She looked into his glazed eyes.

He nodded, his bottom lip quivering.

"Bien. Now you help me by kicking your feet and we will get to shore, *oui?"*

Another nod, but now the little tyke's lips were turning blue.

"Keep moving, Davey. You can do it."

The shore seemed a mile away, but only because the current had taken them downriver. With a few last surges of energy, Collette had them up on the shore just as help arrived from the hotel staff.

The sweet little boy looked into her face as someone wrapped a blanket around him. "Thank you, miss." He closed his eyes and leaned on her shoulder.

Collette was sure there was nothing sweeter in the world.

Cassidy huffed and blew a strand of hair off her forehead.

"Everything all right?" Mrs. Johnson made her way to Cassidy's side.

"I'm fine." She sighed. "Let's just say rolling out dough when your middle is growing by inches each day makes your arms a lot shorter. I can't seem to reach quite as far. So then I have to waddle my way around the table to work at it from the other side."

Cook laughed.

A deep voice came from behind Cassidy. "But it's a very cute waddle." Allan walked up beside her and kissed her on the cheek.

She slipped her work towel off her shoulder to swat at him, but he moved.

"Ah, and she also moves slower too."

Cassidy narrowed her eyes. "I would be careful of my words if I were you, Mr. Brennan."

Mrs. Johnson nodded heartily. "Very careful." She pointed her wooden spoon at him. "Remember who feeds you."

He held up his hands in defeat. "I know when I'm licked." He smiled and came close again. "How are you feeling?"

Cassidy loved the sound of his voice.

Especially when he was like this — so concerned about her and their baby. "I'm feeling quite good . . . oh!" The baby moved and she grabbed Allan's hand and put it on her stomach. She'd been feeling the baby move for a few weeks now, and he hadn't been able to feel it yet, but he expressed his desire over and over.

His hand followed a trail across her waist. "Oh, my goodness! Does he do this all the time?" His eyes were wide in wonder.

She laughed at him. One day he'd call the baby a "he" and the next he would say "she" — it didn't matter to Cassidy, as long as the baby was healthy. "Yes, the baby moves a lot. Especially hearing Daddy's voice."

"Hot diggety! That's amazing." He kissed her cheek again and ran toward the stairs. "I have to go tell the guys."

Cassidy glanced at Mrs. Johnson and they laughed together. The rest of the kitchen staff had gotten used to Mr. Brennan's excitement about the baby.

Only about three more months. Although if she kept expanding, she wouldn't fit through the door anymore. And as much as she hated to admit it, she was feeling the exhaustion. Her feet and back ached much more than they ever had before. Even though she'd lost her temper at Allan and

201

Mrs. Johnson early on for cautioning her, she was beginning to feel they were correct. She'd have to slow down soon.

Mrs. Johnson came over and took the rolling pin from her. "Why don't you let me finish that up? You go on upstairs and lie down for a bit."

Cassidy didn't argue. She needed to get off her feet and soon.

Heading up the back staircase, she took the steps slowly and untied her apron. A nap sounded really good about now. After that, she'd work on the list of baby names she and Allan had been compiling.

Was it a boy or a girl? She wished she knew. It would be so much fun to be calling the babe by his or her name now. And it would be nice to plan. Pink for girl. Blue for boy.

Cassidy shrugged and smiled to herself. She had plenty of time.

Her shoe caught on something and Cassidy reached for the bannister. Unfortunately, her actions were too slow. She felt herself go backward in what seemed slow motion.

Tumbling down the stairs, the only thing she could think of was the baby. With a scream that was sure to catch the attention of anyone within a mile radius, she wrapped her arms around her middle and tried to slow her descent before she plummeted all the way to the bottom.

A bone-jarring thud told her she'd reached the floor as heavy footsteps sounded on the stairs. She was afraid to move.

"Cassidy!" Her father's voice made her open her eyes.

"Cassidy!" Allan's worried face was right behind her father.

Her backside ached as well as her left side as she moved her leg. "I'm okay. Just thought the floor needed a hug."

Allan shook his head, "Oh, sweetheart, are you sure you're all right?"

She attempted to move, and everything hurt. "Maybe not."

Dad yelled down the hallway, "I need someone to go for the doctor!"

More footsteps echoed around her, and she decided it was better to keep her eyes closed. Breathe deep. Calm down. Her arms were still wrapped around her middle, and when she felt the baby move, she let a sigh out and opened her eyes. "The baby . . . the baby just moved. I think we're okay. Just maybe a bit bruised."

Her husband knelt in front of her and put his hands on either side of her face. "How far did you fall?"

She looked up the stairs. "Almost the entire way. I was going upstairs to lie down." Maybe he wouldn't look so worried if he knew she was trying to take care of herself.

"Do you think we can move you up there now?"

She nodded.

He wrapped his arms around her, but just as he was lifting, Thomas came bounding down the steps. "Help, we need help right away! Miss Collette jumped in the river to save the little Powell boy!"

Dad looked at her.

"Go. Allan's with me, we'll be fine."

Her father struggled with the decision to leave her — she could see it in his eyes — but she gave him a small smile. "Go."

As the crowd followed Thomas up the stairs, Allan reached down for her again. "Let's get you up to bed and wait for the doctor to check and make sure you're okay."

She nodded. Just rising up to stand hurt, and her head swam. And then . . .

Oh no. She wasn't sure about what she felt. But it scared her. *Please God, no, it's too soon!*

14

June 11

Jean-Michel paced beside his sister's bed, the thump of his cane growing louder with each pass.

Dr. Reilly gave him a pointed look. "Mr. Langelier, your sister will be fine. I've already told you that. I think you can go rest in your room now."

"Non." He shook his head. Collette couldn't be abandoned. Besides, this doctor appeared quite young, so it was entirely possible he didn't know what he was talking about.

The doctor stood and approached him, successfully cutting off Jean-Michel's path. "It's not a suggestion, sir."

"I cannot leave her."

The doctor swiped his face. "Look, I just came back to check on her. The Powell boy is already up and running around again.

Miss Langelier will be soon, I'm sure of it. She just needs a little more rest. There is no indication that anything else is wrong."

Movement from the bed caught his eye, and Jean-Michel leaned to see around the doctor.

"*Frère,* I *am* fine." Collette pushed herself up to a sitting position. "I just got a bit more chilled than little Davey."

The doctor went back over to her and put a hand to her forehead. "Mr. Langelier, she has no fever and no other symptoms. I simply wanted her to take it easy for a few days to ensure her health would return fully."

Collette smiled at her brother. "Truly. Go rest. Every time I open my eyes, you are here." She looked at the doctor. "In fact, maybe after you rest, I'd like to go for a short walk if that is allowed?"

"Most certainly. I would encourage it." The doctor picked up his black bag. "And now, if you will excuse me, I'd like to check on Mrs. Brennan." He exited the room.

Jean-Michel went to Collette's side and sat on the edge of the bed. "I was so concerned. . . . I didn't know what would happen if I lost . . ."

She patted his hand. "Don't allow yourself those thoughts. I am fine, and more importantly, the Powell boy is fine."

"What made you think of jumping into the river?" He knew his tone was cross, but he couldn't help the worry.

"Someone had to save him! He would've drowned!"

Jean-Michel saw his sister with new eyes. Not only had she done an unselfish and truly heroic act, but she seemed all grown up. It couldn't have happened overnight. "I *am* proud of you, Collette."

Tears sprang to her eyes. "*Merci.* But you know what? I think Father would be proud too. I'm beginning to see a hint of what he wanted for me. And I like how that feels. I'm sure I will still make poor decisions and disappoint, but it's a start." She brushed the tears away and smiled at him. "Now tell me, have you had a chance to speak with Katherine yet?"

The question pierced his heart like a dagger. "*Non.* I wrote her a note when they first brought you back to the room and the doctor wasn't sure how long it would take for you to recover."

"What exactly did you say to her in this note?"

"That I wouldn't be able to take our walk."

"That's it?" She sat up straighter and

made a face at him. A face he couldn't decipher.

"Well, I assumed that she'd heard what had happened. What was I supposed to say? I wasn't going to leave you."

Collette sighed one of those sighs that he'd heard many times before. From several different women. Somehow, he felt a scolding would be forthcoming. Something along the lines of how men just didn't understand. Didn't he know better . . . etcetera.

He waited.

She took his hand and squeezed. "You must go write to her now. Then take a nap. You look horrible."

"Grandmother, I really need your assistance with this, please." Katherine packed a small case.

"My dear, I'm not really sure I understand why we need to leave right now. We just arrived in Curry —"

"I can't . . ." Tears choked her throat. How could she explain? She took a deep breath. "I can't see him right now. I just can't. I need time."

"I thought you were going to go on a walk with him?"

"He canceled. Not that I blame him. Collette jumped in the river to save that little

208

boy and Jean-Michel has been by his sister's side ever since. But don't you see? That's what I have to avoid. I can't bear the thought of talking to him just yet. My heart is all over the place. I'm so confused."

Grandmother walked over to her and set a hand on her quaking arm. "I understand, Katherine. I do. Just promise me that you won't avoid him forever."

"I won't. I just need enough time to gather my thoughts and to pray." At least she hoped it was true. Seeking God's help was all so new.

"All right. Let me pack a small case as well and we'll take the train north to Fairbanks. I hear there are some lovely sights to see."

Katherine held up her hands and watched them shake. Why did the thought of speaking with Jean-Michel unnerve her so?

They'd had such a close friendship before. In fact, she'd never felt as comfortable around anyone else. Ever. She could always share her deepest thoughts and secrets with him.

Now all she could do was worry. And shake. And be afraid.

Lord, help my unbelief. Grandmother has told me it's a sin to worry, but I don't know how to stop. I'm afraid, God. Please show me what to do. Give me the words to say. In Jesus' name, amen.

A few days away would hopefully clear her mind and help her heart. If that didn't work, she wasn't sure if anything could.

Grandmother came back in the room with a small suitcase and her cane. "I'm ready, if you are."

"It's okay to leave everything else here?" Katherine hated being a bother.

"Yes, my dear. In fact, I'll speak with the front desk before we leave if that would ease your mind."

She nodded. Following her grandmother out the door, she thought of the way Jean-Michel had looked at her when he first noticed her across the room. Her heart had leapt and for a brief moment, joy filled her.

But then everything else came flooding back. Everything she'd been through. Everything Randall had said. Everything she couldn't have.

If there was a way to move forward without all her troubles of the past, she'd gladly take it. But that was the problem.

It would go with her, like a ball chained to her ankle, for the rest of her life.

The thought crushed her weary heart.

She loved Jean-Michel. But she could never marry again.

■ ■ ■ ■

June 16

Thomas picked up the heavy stock pot and set it on the stove for Mrs. Johnson. "Here you go, Cook."

"Thank you. I can't tell you how much that helps my poor back." The older woman smiled at him and patted his shoulder.

They'd come a long way since his first days helping out in this polished kitchen. Their head chef had just about kicked him out for good because he was so clumsy.

It had been Cassidy who'd encouraged him and stuck up for him. Then her dad had come to his rescue more than once. Without the Ivanoffs, Thomas wasn't sure where he'd be today.

The thoughts of John and Cassidy made his heart twinge. She'd been laid up for a while now after her fall down the stairs. John and Allan had a full schedule with excursions, but somehow they were taking turns being at Cassidy's side. Thomas had been taking her place in the kitchen so they could continue to feed the crowds at the Curry, but they'd need him to return and help with tours. Thankfully, Mr. Bradley told him help was coming.

Maybe it was time he went to visit her. She was his friend after all and he'd love to do whatever he could to cheer her.

"Thomas, would you take this tray up to Mr. and Mrs. Brennan, please?"

He smiled. Perfect timing. "I'd love to, Mrs. Johnson."

"No dillydallying." She pointed a finger in his face and softened. "But I guess it would be fine to spend a few minutes with them and let us all know how she is doing. Let me just add a sandwich or two for you."

He nodded and waited for her to load the tray and then grabbed it. Taking the stairs two at a time, Thomas was excited to see his friends. Even if it was only for a few minutes. They'd poured so much into him that he hoped and prayed he could do something for them in return.

With a knock on the door, Thomas plastered on a big smile and lifted the tray to his shoulder.

"Thomas, how good to see you." Allan welcomed him into their quarters. "Maybe you can help convince my wife that she is wrong."

Thomas laughed and set the tray down. "I highly doubt that would work, sir."

Cassidy lifted a hand in a wave. "Come on over here and catch us up on all the com-

212

ings and goings. Maybe we can distract Mr. Brennan from his current topic."

In all his years, he'd never seen a couple more in love and more fun to watch when they argued. "I'd actually like to hear all about the current topic." He crossed his arms. "Sounds entertaining."

Cassidy rolled her eyes.

Allan took a deep breath. "You see, my beautiful wife here is trying to convince me that it's all right for me to go back to work and leave her —"

"It's not just *my* opinion, Mr. Brennan, and you know it. The good doctor said I was fine. I just am confined to bed rest until the baby comes." She huffed.

Thomas chuckled at the two. "So let me get this straight. You're worried about Cassidy, so you don't want to leave her, but the doctor has said she is fine and you can go back to work?"

"Exactly."

"Exactly."

The married couple exchanged glances.

Cassidy then looked at Thomas. "He's driving me crazy, to tell you the truth. I love the man, but he sure does need something to occupy him. And he hovers. It's bad enough that I have to be bedridden, but I can't even *think* too hard or he'll scold me."

"Wait just a minute — that's not true." Allan tapped the end of their bed and then his brow scrunched up. "I'm not *that* bad . . . am I?"

"Yes, you are." She lifted her chin. "But I love you anyway."

Thomas laughed again at them. "You guys need to do a show for all the staff. It's quite entertaining."

Cassidy picked up a pillow and threw it at him. "You're not helping." But her smile told him she wasn't angry. Maybe a little stir-crazy, but not angry.

Allan sat on the bed next to his wife. "You're determined that you'll be all right without me?" At her nod, he looked at the tray Thomas had brought in. "Okay, then. I surrender. As long as we have someone to check on you every hour, I guess I'll agree to it." He picked up a sandwich. "As long as you promise me you won't get out of this bed for any reason. None at all!"

She put her hand over her heart. "I promise. And Thomas is here to witness it."

Thomas nodded. "I sure am, Mr. Brennan. Now can we please eat?"

15

June 20

Six-year-old Davey held a flower up to Collette, and she crouched down to hug the little charmer. "Why, thank you, *monsieur.*"

"You sure do talk pretty, Miss Langelier. What does *moansure* mean?"

"You may call me Collette, and *monsieur*" — she pronounced the word slower than normal — "means *sir.*"

"That's a right fancy way to pronounce *sir.* Why do you say that?"

Collette tilted her head and thought about it for a moment. "Because it's the French word and I am French. I guess I don't think about certain words that are so . . . hmmm . . . what's the phrase? Everyday normal."

"I think I understand ya. I use the word *ain't* a lot for my everyday normal talking, but Mama hates it. My schoolteacher hates it more than Mama!"

The little guy had worked his way into Collette's heart. She loved their daily conversations by the river. His mother only allowed him to go each day because his father said it would be good for him to not fear the river. Their one requirement was that Collette accompany him if they were unavailable. They had been so very grateful for her actions — even offering her money as a means of paying her back.

Collette had refused, of course. Surely anyone would have done the same, but Jean-Michel told her that wasn't necessarily true. Many people, he had said, would have put their own safety first. He praised Collette for the selfless act.

They walked closer to the river, causing Davey to scoot as close to her as possible. "You know what, Miss Collette?" Davey's little face turned serious.

"What?" Collette had gotten used to his questions each day. And they always started with "you know what?" It took her a while to catch on, but it became their special conversation. At least to Collette it seemed that way.

"I thought you was an angel that day."

"What day? The day you fell?" Up until now, Davey hadn't been willing to talk

216

about his close call. His mother told Collette that he hadn't even shared with them why he had fallen.

"Yep. You had on that pretty white dress with the blue birds on it. So when I saw ya, I thought Jesus had sent an angel to rescue me."

"Why would you think Jesus sent an angel?"

" 'Cause God protects His children. Mama told me so. She said that sometimes Jesus has to send angels to help us get out of the messes we get ourselves into." He nodded and raised his eyebrows.

"But, Davey, you didn't get yourself into that mess, those older boys . . . they are the ones who are at fault for you falling into the river." It still bothered her that those bullies had picked on little Davey. It was little comfort to hear they'd received punishment from their parents. The next time they did something so heartless, there might not be anyone around to save the innocent.

"That doesn't matter, Miss Collette. Don't you believe that Jesus sent you at just the right moment? If you hadn't been there, I woulda drowned and been swept a long ways down the river." His face was so intense, Collette studied him for a moment.

"I don't know what to say to that, Davey.

But if you believe Jesus sent me, then I must agree with you." She had no idea what had brought her to the river at the very time those children would need her. Could Davey be right? *Did* Jesus or God or someone up there send her? Davey was such a slight boy for his age. He wouldn't have had a chance had she not been willing to jump right in after him.

Father's letter came back to her mind. She'd read it so many times lately. Needing a connection to the man she'd so completely adored and wondering what impact his instructions would have on her life. *If* she could follow through with them.

"You *do* believe in God, don't ya?" Davey's face looked shocked that maybe she didn't.

She couldn't let the little guy down. "But, of course, I believe in God. I just need to learn a lot more about Him." Which was all true. But where did she start? The same question had been plaguing her for weeks.

"Well, I can teach ya everything I know."

The thought made her want to chuckle, but she kept her laughter in check. "I would be very honored if you would help me, Davey."

"We ain't . . . aren't going to be here much longer, so we better start tomorrow. Right

218

here by the river. But right now, I gotta go back in. Mama will be upset if I miss nap time." He jumped up and ran off, waving as he went.

Collette waved back and shook her head in wonder. Maybe it was time to learn more about God so she wouldn't look unintelligent to a six-year-old.

Heading back to the hotel, she knew just who she wanted to speak to. Someone who had lots of extra time on her hands right now.

Cassidy.

Margaret Johnson looked over the menu for the third time. Her mind wasn't on it. She was more than a little worried about Cassidy, despite the doctor's assurance that everything was going along just fine.

"Do you have those menus ready for me?" Mr. Bradley swept into the downstairs dining room.

"I'm working on it, as you can see." She motioned to the table. She thought for a moment to take out her frustrations on the man, then thought better of it. The truth was always better at times like these. "I suppose my thoughts have been elsewhere."

He sat down at the table. His expression was sympathetic. "I know you're worried about our Cassidy, but she is doing quite well according to her husband."

"I know. I just know how fragile life can be. A person can be right beside you one minute and gone the next. I've seen it happen."

He nodded. "As have I."

"I didn't realize."

He shrugged. It was late and the man looked exhausted. "You weren't the only one to lose family to the epidemic."

"Of course, I know that." She shook her head. "I doubt there is anyone here who didn't lose someone. Still, when it's someone else, you can sympathize and move on. It isn't the same as when it happens to you." She leaned back in her chair. "Who did you lose, Mr. Bradley?"

"My wife and infant son."

"That must have been devastating." She'd heard the pain in his voice.

"It was. They were fine when I left for work that morning, but dead before I returned home."

"It was that way with my brother and most of his family. My husband and children were several days with it. In fact, I thought they'd turned a corner and were getting better." The memory was still so painful. She had been sure they'd beaten death.

Mr. Bradley nodded. "I think about them both from time to time. My son would have been eight years old had he lived."

"Mine would have been twenty. My daughter twenty-three. Sometimes I think about them and wonder what they would have been like. Would they be married? Have families of their own?"

He nodded. "But it's never good to stay too long in the past."

Margaret squared her shoulders. "No, it isn't. Especially when we have a baby on the way." She smiled. "I believe our Cassidy will make a fine mother."

"As do I." Mr. Bradley stood. "But that does bring me to a point I've been meaning to speak to you about."

"What would that be?"

"I promised you help, and in keeping with that I've hired another cook's assistant to come and help you."

"I don't need any help, and if I did, I would think I'd have the right to hire my own person. I can't have just anybody in my kitchen trying to do things their own way, Mr. Bradley." She grew more irritated with the idea by the minute. "And just what sort of person did you hire without talking to me first? I suppose it will be some flighty, senseless girl who has never lived away from the big city. I can just see her sitting here crying and pining for her home."

"Mrs. Johnson . . ." The manager sighed.

She got to her feet and took up her menus. "Honestly, I don't know why I stay on. No one seems to care at all what I want." She looked at Mr. Bradley as if to dare him to say otherwise.

He smiled. "Mrs. Johnson, I do sympathize, but we have over a thousand people moving through this hotel in the next month alone. Cassidy is not going to be able to return to work, and I had the offer of this cook to come to us on loan. I would have spoken to you earlier about it, but there simply wasn't time. I had to return my answer quickly."

"Just on loan?" She calmed a bit. Maybe that wouldn't be so bad.

"Yes."

She thought about it a moment. They were scheduled to have a larger number of visitors than ever before. Just getting through the year before with Cassidy at her side had been difficult.

"All right. What's her name?"

Mr. Bradley couldn't contain a grin. "It's not a her. It's a him. Daniel Ferguson."

"A man? You want me to put a man in my kitchen? And not just a man, but a Scot?

Mr. Bradley you must be out of your mind. I won't be having it."

"But I'm afraid you must, Mrs. Johnson. Try to remember it's for the sake of the hotel." He headed to the door. "Please try to have those menus to me before you head off to bed."

She'd had all she could take. Without warning she snatched up the menus and crossed the room. With a shove she thrust them at Mr. Bradley's chest. "Here. Maybe you can get your Scotsman to figure them out. No doubt he'll be serving us haggis and scones for every meal."

She stomped out of the dining room and made her way upstairs.

A Scotsman.

In her kitchen!

It was unimaginable.

"I apologize, sir." The manager, Mr. Bradley, handed Jean-Michel an envelope. "This must have fallen behind the mail slot. We found it this morning."

Jean-Michel took the envelope. "It's not a problem, Mr. Bradley. Thank you very much." He nodded and began his trek up the stairs to his room. The handwriting was unmistakable.

Katherine.

Opening his room door, he looked around him. He hadn't seen her for ten days. And it felt like a lifetime of being parched. He hadn't expected the feelings that overwhelmed him as soon as their eyes met. Had it really been five years since her father had forbidden them to marry? Since he'd taken the family and fled the embassy for America? Both Jean-Michel and Katherine lived through a lifetime of agony after that.

He laid his cane on the bed and sat down in the chair to read the letter. All he knew was that they had left the Curry and would be returning to the hotel to spend the summer because that's all the staff knew.

Dear Jean-Michel,

I hope Collette is back to her normal self and recovered and that you are able to enjoy all that the Curry Hotel has to offer. Grandmother and I have been praying for you both.

I apologize for not delivering this in person, but that is part of my difficulty.

It was wonderful to see you again after all these years, but it was also quite a shock.

That is why we left. I needed to think through many things and God is helping me heal. Grandmother has had me traipsing all over the country, and now wants to explore a bit more of Alaska, so I am catering to her wishes and letting God work in my heart and life.

I pray you are well. When I return, I hope we can take that walk.

Sincerely,
Katherine

Her signature hadn't changed and he loved seeing it. But the contents of the letter were not what he'd expected. Why did she have to leave? Especially after they'd just reconnected. What was Maria Harrison thinking? The older lady had orchestrated the whole trip, for pity's sake!

Getting up from the chair, Jean-Michel began pacing. It didn't make any sense. Hadn't Mrs. Harrison thought that *he* was the only hope for Katherine? He couldn't very well help, though, if they weren't even in the same location and especially if they couldn't ever talk.

The question that burned the most was why on earth Katherine would turn to God rather than turn to him? It wasn't like she'd been a religious person all those years ago. As he recalled, her parents didn't even go to church services on Sunday. And it definitely didn't sound like her husband had any interest in such matters.

What changed?

And why did he all of a sudden feel useless? He sank back into the chair.

"Knock, knock."

He looked up to find Collette coming in through their adjoining bathroom. She looked quite lovely dressed in a salmon-colored dress that sported a wide ivory collar trimmed in lace. She'd pinned up her hair in an orderly bun and looked ready for a day of leisure.

"I heard you had a letter."

"News travels fast in this place." Jean-Michel held up the missive.

"Is it from Katherine?"

"No, the King of England."

She scrunched her nose and fixed him with a look. "So what does His Highness have to say? Honestly, Jean-Michel."

"I'm sorry. I'm afraid I'm not good company."

"There's nothing new about that." She came to him and bent down to kiss his head. "But I am always hopeful you will change. I just came by to tell you I'll be visiting with Mrs. Brennan . . . Cassidy."

"Why?"

She straightened and walked toward the door. "Why not?"

"Collette, I'm serious. Why would you bother the poor woman?"

"Because she invited me to." Collette opened the door. "She's bored and needs a friend, and I have questions and need some answers."

"Answers about what?"

"God." She exited, pulling the door closed behind her.

God? Yet another person turning to God rather than him? It was like some sort of strange joke that he couldn't ever hope to be in on. What was happening to him?

Collette sat in the ladder-backed chair beside Cassidy Brennan's bed. "So then it made me wonder if God might have really sent me to that bridge just for the purpose of saving Davey."

"I'm sure He did. The Bible says that He sees even when the sparrow falls. How much more is He going to keep track of little boys?" Cassidy put her hand to her protruding stomach. "Just like He's been watching over me and my baby."

"So God isn't just up there somewhere — doing nothing?" Collette pointed to the ceiling. "Or just waiting to judge us and destroy us for not pleasing Him?"

Cassidy looked at her as if she'd lost her

mind. "Goodness. Who told you that?"

Collette shrugged. "I don't know that anyone in particular has. It's just that our family was never overly religious. My mama used to read me Bible stories. I remember that." She smiled at the memory. "I was especially fond of the one where these two women are fighting over the same baby. They both say they are the mother of the baby. Oh, there was another baby, but he was dead — one of the mothers had rolled over on him in the night. At least I think that's how it went."

"Yes. It's the story of Solomon judging the case and deciding which mother was speaking the truth. When neither was willing to admit the baby wasn't really theirs, he decided to cut the baby in two and give half to each woman."

Collette got excited. "*Oui,* and the real mother fell to her knees and begged him not to do it. She told him to just give the baby to the other woman, and that's how Solomon knew she was the real mother — because she didn't want anything bad to happen to her baby. Mama told me she would give her life for mine." Collette felt a wash of emotion but fought back her tears. "In many ways, she did. I was quite sick with the influenza, and Mama nursed me, even though she wasn't well herself."

Cassidy grew thoughtful and stroked her stomach. "I don't even know my little one yet, but I feel such a fierce love. I would give my life for my child. It makes me stand in awe of God all the more, because He gave His only Son to die for me."

"Just you?"

"Goodness, no. But if I had been the only one who needed a Savior, Jesus still would have died for me. God loves us just that much."

"But why? What have we done that merits such love?"

Cassidy laughed. "We've done nothing and that's the wonder of it. Think about it. Your mother said she'd give her life for you. I would give my life for my baby. Neither you nor this unborn child have done anything to merit such declarations. Just as we did nothing to deserve a Savior. It's not about us, Collette. It's about Him."

16

June 23

"A Scotsman, Cassidy Faith. A Scotsman!" Margaret hadn't wanted to upset the mother-to-be, but she had to talk to someone. "Mr. Bradley said he'd be here today. I can hardly bear it. I ought to just give my notice."

"You can't do that, Mrs. Johnson. We need you. I need you. Besides, you said he's only here on loan for a short time. Just until I'm back up on my feet." Cassidy scooted up in bed, prompting Margaret to hurry over and help her.

"Do you need another pillow behind you?"

"No, I need out of this bed, but no one seems willing to consider that. You have your Scotsman, and I have this." Cassidy waved her hands over the confines of her bed. "And all because Dr. Reilly says I must. I feel like a prized pig in a cage."

Margaret laughed. "More like a princess in the tower."

Cassidy smiled. "It's good to hear you laugh."

"Oh, get on with ya."

"Well, it is. You've been upset ever since you stepped into my room and that was fifteen minutes ago."

She was right. Margaret forced herself to take a deep breath. She grabbed the chair and sat down. "I'm sorry. I never meant to upset you."

"You haven't. Goodness, this is the most entertainment I've had in days."

"So my problems are entertaining, are they?"

"You know what I mean." Cassidy held up a piece of flannel. "Far more entertaining than making diapers."

She couldn't argue with that. "I don't need a man interfering in my kitchen."

"No, nor a Scotsman," Cassidy added with a grin. "But you do need help. It won't be possible for you to manage all those meals without someone to assist — someone who knows what they're doing. Who knows? Maybe he'll be very polite and soft-spoken — willing to take direction without question."

"Ha! He's a man and a Scot. I've never

known either one to be any of those things."

"What about your husband?"

"Ted? He wasn't a Scot, but he was stubborn and ornery. You couldn't tell the man anything — especially the word 'no.' I wouldn't even have married him, but he wore me down. Nagged me to the altar, I used to say."

Cassidy couldn't contain her mirth. It started as a giggle, then burst into a full belly laugh. She held her stomach and laughed so hard tears ran down her cheeks.

Margaret couldn't help smiling. "Well, it's true. You couldn't tell him anything. And if you expected to get something done, you had to make him believe it was his idea."

Her precious Cassidy sobered and gave her a look suggesting she'd just hit upon the solution to the problem.

"No, no, no. I can see what you're thinking. Don't be expecting me to coddle Daniel Ferguson along. I haven't got time or patience for it. This is just going to be a disaster. I know it will. They simply can't expect me to work with a Scotsman."

"For pity's sake, why not, Mrs. Johnson? What have you got against the Scots?"

"Because . . ." Margaret stood and smoothed down her apron. "I'm a Scot. Scots-Irish to boot." She shook her head.

"And you just can't have two of them in the same kitchen without a fight starting up sooner or later."

Given the way Cassidy laughed hysterically, Margaret knew she couldn't convince her assistant that Ferguson was a bad idea. "Oh, I give up. It's time to get back to the kitchen anyway."

"But you know I love you." Tears slipped down Cassidy's cheeks as she continued to giggle.

"Of course, you silly girl. And I love you too." With that, she excused herself and headed out the door. Making her way downstairs, she decided she would just have to deal with the matter in the best way she could. No one was going to listen to her anyway. At least not until there were "wigs on the green," as her Irish grandfather used to say.

Her foot hadn't touched the bottom step when Mr. Bradley came around the corner. "Oh, good, there you are. Please come into my office. Mr. Ferguson arrived on the train and is waiting to begin in the kitchen."

Biting off a retort, Margaret followed the manager with great trepidation. If she'd been a praying woman like Cassidy, she might have asked God for patience or even a spirit of kindness. She threw a quick glance upward.

I don't suppose it would do any good to ask, but I'd be glad if You'd help me.

There wasn't time for anything more.

"Chef Johnson, I'd like you to meet Chef Ferguson."

Margaret found herself face-to-face with a big burly man. He had hair redder than hers had ever been and a beard that matched. His piercing blue eyes looked her up and down as if he were assessing the quality of tomatoes. Finally, he broke into a broad smile and gave a nod.

"Aye, ya'll do just fine, lass."

She stiffened. "The name is Mrs. Johnson. And I will be doing the judging of whether or not *you* will do."

"A widow, Mrs. Johnson, I'm told." He had the audacity to wink. "And a fine figure of a woman. Ya won't be widowed for long, I'm thinkin'."

Margaret felt her neck grow hot and then her face. She knew she must be the color of a beet. "If you know what's good for you, you won't be doing much of your own thinking. You're here to cook, not tell fortunes."

The man roared with laughter and it filled every corner of the room. No doubt people upstairs could hear it. It was worse than a donkey's bray.

She looked at Mr. Bradley, certain he could read her thoughts, because he quickly turned away and looked at the papers on his desk.

"Chef Johnson will show you to the kitchen, Chef Ferguson. I'm sure there's work that needs your immediate attention."

"Then I'll be sayin' good day to ya, sir. And a right bonny day it is." His brogue was thick.

Margaret held her tongue. She marched across the lobby and headed for the stairs that would take her to the kitchen. Her kitchen. Hers alone.

She reached the place where up until now she'd always felt her best. Looking around the large kitchen, Margaret knew it would never be big enough for the two of them.

"So, m'darlin', what would ya have me do first?"

June 28

The beauty of the Mount McKinley National Park around her couldn't squelch the dread in Katherine's stomach. They'd taken this little journey north to Fairbanks and now back south to the park because of her.

Because of her selfishness. Her insecurity.

She'd taken her grandmother off on another trip, knowing full well that the older woman was tired and worn out.

As she laid a hand on Grandmother's forehead, she was thankful she didn't feel a fever, but the beloved woman was pale and hadn't been awake much for almost two days.

It's all my fault, Lord. Please help her to wake up.

Standing to stretch, Katherine wondered what other options she had. The inn here at the park was rustic to say the least, not anything like the lavish Curry Hotel. They should've never left. But she couldn't change the past.

If she could, she'd erase the years of her marriage. Maybe even go back and defy her father and stay in France with Jean-Michel. But where would that leave her today? Would it have changed so much?

One beautiful thing came out of the torment of the last few years.

She was redeemed.

And that changed her life forever.

No matter what, she couldn't allow herself to listen to the lies of the enemy any longer. Grandmother had warned her, but Katherine didn't understand until now. Until she'd seen what her fear and hesitancy caused.

A huge fact remained.

Randall was gone.

That meant his words were gone. His actions were gone. He couldn't hurt her anymore. That meant she needed to grab on to her faith and step forward in it. Embrace it.

"Katherine?" A slight moan from the bed.

She raced back over to Grandmother's side. "I'm here."

"What happened?"

"You collapsed at dinner the other night and have been asleep ever since." She bit her lip. "I've been so worried."

Grandmother attempted to sit up.

Katherine hurried to help her.

"I'm sorry, dear. I didn't mean to worry you. I think it was just my exhaustion catching up with me."

"Don't apologize for anything. It's all my doing. I'm so sorry." Tears filled Katherine's eyes. "If I hadn't . . ."

"Oh, hush, child. Yes, maybe we shouldn't have left the Curry, but remember that I had you traveling all over the country before we even came to Alaska. I'm sure I just overdid it."

"It's still my fault. I shouldn't have pushed to leave like I did. If I hadn't been so afraid to face Jean-Michel with the truth, you might be at the hotel now."

Grandmother patted the bed beside her. "Come sit, my dear. Maybe it's time you tell me what's really going on. What is this truth you can't bear to tell?"

July 3

The ache in his leg made Jean-Michel want to quit the regimen of exercises, but he refused. At least he knew that Katherine would return at some point, and when she did, he wanted to be stronger. To show her that he was able to help her with whatever she needed to heal. Not only that, but strangely enough, he found the exercises seemed to help his spirits as well. It might have only been that he had to concentrate on something other than the past, but at least it was a step in the right direction.

It also helped that John had allowed him to go on a few more hikes with the groups visiting the area. For the most part, Jean-Michel had been able to keep up. The fresh air and scenery also acted as a balm, so much in fact that when he'd come back from yesterday's walk, he'd actually napped without nightmares.

He'd increased the number of exercises he did daily, and would soon need to start the next section the doctor in France had recommended. But he'd need a training partner. Maybe there was a way for young Thomas to help. He could offer to pay the young man — he'd seen how diligent the worker was around the hotel.

Even though the pain was lessening, Jean-Michel wished his strength would return faster. He shook his head. If only he'd listened to the doctor when he first returned from Syria. Maybe he could have bypassed all this misery.

He heard the door to Collette's room open, and she soon appeared at the door between their rooms with a smile on her face. "Where have you been, *mon cher*?"

"With little Davey." Collette smiled and sighed. "He's such a *précieux petit garçon.*"

"Precious little boy or not, are you sure you're not being an interruption to his family?" He grunted. Two more sets on this leg and he'd be done.

"*Non.* They have invited me to spend time with them every day if I wish. His mother said she is most appreciative. Besides, they won't be here but another week."

"What do you do with him — when you go to visit?"

She hesitated and twisted her mouth in an expression he couldn't decipher. "Well . . .

we talk . . . mostly about God."

Jean-Michel stood up straight and wiped the sweat off his brow with a towel. "You are conversing with a six-year-old about God?" The idea sounded ludicrous.

"Oui." She nodded and laughed. "I am." She came over and kissed his cheek and then walked toward her room. "I'll be ready for dinner in a little bit; besides, you need time to get cleaned up yourself. You smell like a *porc en sueur.*"

A sweaty pig? That was it. End of discussion. As she closed the door, Jean-Michel had the urge to throw something.

Since their father died, Collette had come to him for advice, guidance . . . everything. Granted, most of what she needed were words of affirmation about the color of her gown or the style of her hair. On occasion, she even asked him about some piece of news she'd heard from a friend — but that was rare.

Still, why hadn't she come to *him* if she wanted to talk about God? Wasn't that their father's request to them both? And now she was sharing it with a little boy. A child. Who hadn't seen the ugliness of war or death. Who hadn't been there for his sister and held her as she mourned their father's passing.

What was Jean-Michel lacking that he had been trumped by this little boy?

Was it the same reason Katherine turned to God as well?

Thoughts tumbled all over his mind. His father's words came rushing back, but he pushed them aside. He wasn't ready to look for God yet.

But he needed to figure out why he wasn't good enough to save the two women he loved the most.

"You redheaded ignoramus!" Margaret had all she was going to take. "It's to celebrate America becoming a nation. The Fourth of July has always been a huge celebration in this country, and we won't forsake it just because we're a territory and not a state." She looked at her nemesis, Daniel Ferguson. The man was just as impossible as she'd predicted. He had his way of doing everything from making sauces to pastries — and, of course, thought his ways were the best. Well, he wasn't the head chef, now was he? She'd show him who was boss.

"I wasn't suggestin' ya shouldn't celebrate the day. I just find it appallin' that ya'd make a cake that looks like the flag. Have ya no respect, lass?"

Margaret drew a deep breath and planted

her hands on her hips. "This is *my* kitchen and what I say — goes!"

Two of the kitchen maids scurried from the room. Given the fights that had taken place over the last week, Margaret couldn't blame them. She would've liked to have run too, but she wasn't about to give satisfaction to this irritating, ignorant, foolish, stubborn . . . oh, there weren't enough words in the dictionary to describe this man.

Just then Mr. Bradley appeared. He looked hesitant but gave a nod in Mrs. Johnson's direction. "I hope all is going well. The food . . . well . . . it's been wonderful."

"No thanks to him." She pointed to where Daniel stood. He wore a white chef's coat and hat and a broad smile that she wanted to slap off his face.

"I'm glad the folks are enjoyin' the fare." Ferguson nodded to the manager.

"Is everything in order for the celebration tonight?" Mr. Bradley looked to her for an answer.

"It is, if this . . . this . . . Scotsman will follow orders. He doesn't feel our American flag cake is appropriate."

Mr. Bradley smiled and glanced over at the big Scottish . . . oaf. "Well, now, I wouldn't worry overmuch about it."

Margaret wasn't sure if he was speaking

242

to her or the oaf. "No one's going to worry about it, because it's already settled. Now get back to work making icing, Daniel." The name dripped with every bit of the contempt she felt. "I must speak to Mr. Bradley."

She wiped her hands on a towel and headed for the empty downstairs dining room, knowing the hotel manager would follow.

"Do you have an order list for me, Mrs. Johnson?"

"I do, but that's not the reason I needed to talk to you."

His expression took on a look of disappointment. "No, I presumed it wasn't, but had hoped."

"Well, I wake up every morning hoping to find that Scottish barbarian gone. But instead, I find him there trying to take over my kitchen."

"Mrs. Johnson, we've discussed all of this before. When Cassidy is able to return to work, we'll have no need of him and he will return to Seattle. He's only here because we cannot function otherwise. You'll wear yourself into the grave, and then how will you be able to help Cassidy with the baby?"

This caused her to consider the matter a moment. He was right. Having Daniel would free her up to at least make occasional visits upstairs to visit her precious girl.

"I can see you are perhaps understanding the sense of it, Mrs. Johnson."

She crossed her arms. "I can see the sense of it, but I don't like it any better. That man is impossible."

"Is he unwilling to do his job?"

"No. But he's always questioning my way of doing things."

Mr. Bradley nodded. "It's been my experience that everyone has something to learn and something to teach. Perhaps you can benefit each other."

Margaret held her tongue. Mr. Bradley was only trying to help — even if he was a touch out of his mind. The train whistle blew from somewhere down the tracks, alerting them that new guests would be arriving.

"I'm needed upstairs." Mr. Bradley smiled.

She knew he was delighted to have an excuse to leave.

"I don't suppose you have your list ready for me?"

Margaret reached into her apron pocket. "Don't I always?" She handed him the papers, then stormed back to the kitchen. People relied on her to put together a beautiful outdoor buffet for the evening celebration, and she wasn't going to let them down. Who knew — perhaps a bear would come and take Mr. Ferguson out of her sight.

She smiled at the thought for a moment. Not because she wanted to see the man hurt, but because no doubt Daniel Ferguson would simply wrestle the bear into submission, then serve him up for dinner.

"Well, he might be able to manage a bear — but he's not managing me."

17

July 4

The celebration was unlike anything Thomas had seen before. And he'd been at the Curry for three years. Every Fourth of July was better than the last. Mrs. Johnson had outdone herself this year with a huge supper buffet that sported everything from a large selection of delightful appetizers to desserts.

This year, the American flag cake was her crowning glory, measuring five feet by three feet. Everyone agreed that the white cake was so moist it might have floated away but for the heavenly buttercream frosting and berry jam slathered between layers. Thomas had three pieces.

He'd given the head chef his best compliments along with the rest of the crowd. But the poor woman had been miserable ever since Mr. Bradley had brought in Chef Ferguson to help. Thomas heard them fighting at all hours of the day, and even though he was relieved that her harsh words were no longer aimed at him, he did feel a bit sorry for the burly newcomer.

"Well, Thomas, it looks like there's still enough food to feed a small army." Allan walked up beside him.

"Mrs. Johnson always says it's better to have too much than not enough when it comes to seeing folks fed at the Curry Hotel."

"I doubt anyone has ever gone away from here hungry, unless they wanted to." Allan laughed.

"What is the term you Americans use?" Jean-Michel rubbed his stomach as he joined them. "I'm stuffed?"

Allan laughed again. "Good evening, Mr. Langelier. Yes, that's the word. I'm feeling quite stuffed myself. Are you having a good time?"

"*Oui.* It has been very nice." The Frenchman gave a hint of a smile. "I am afraid, however, I have eaten too much cake."

Thomas joined in. "I've had three pieces. But don't tell Mrs. Johnson."

Mr. Langelier held up four fingers.

Allan patted both men on the shoulder. "It's a good thing we didn't have a cake-eating contest. You two would've cleaned it up."

"How is your wife, Mr. Brennan?" Jean-Michel placed his cane in front of him.

"She's doing quite well, thank you for asking." Allan's smile grew. "She's excited, as am I. How have you managed to adjust to the long hours of light? I heard your sister say you were having trouble sleeping."

Jean-Michel shrugged. "Travel is sometimes difficult and sleeping in a bed that is not your own can be hard. I do, however, appreciate the heavy drapes to block out the light."

"You've certainly come a long way since you first arrived." Allan motioned to Jean-Michel's leg. "I believe soon you won't even need that cane."

"I would like that to be so." Jean-Michel glanced back to where his sister laughed with the Powell family.

"Are we still going to have fireworks?" Thomas knew there had been some discussion about whether the weather would hold. John told them a bank of clouds coming off of the mountain was sure to bring rain.

"That's the plan." Allan glanced at the skies, then back to Thomas. "Cassidy even made me move our bed to the window, hoping she might see some of the sights."

Thomas swatted a mosquito and smiled. "I'm surprised she didn't try to get you to bring her out here."

"Oh, she did. She nagged, then sweet-talked, then cried." Allan shook his head. "The woman really should take to the stage."

Thomas noticed that Jean-Michel looked a little pale. "Are you feeling all right, sir?"

"*Oui.* I hadn't known about the fireworks."

"Do you ever have them in France?" Thomas couldn't help asking.

"*Oui.* You have your Independence Day and we have our Bastille Day. It's the fourteenth of this month. There are usually fireworks and military parades. We often have marvelous outdoor orchestras playing well into the night."

"That sounds pretty amazing. We ought to have us an outdoor orchestra." Thomas looked to Allan. "Maybe next year."

"Could be. Although ours would most likely consist of little more than a few harmonicas and some native drums." He grinned.

Thomas laughed and glanced at his watch. It was nearly ten o'clock but still light. The fireworks wouldn't be nearly as pretty as they were in blackened skies, but it was still a celebration and one he truly loved.

"Looks like it's time to get the show started." Allan handed Thomas his plate. "Would you mind getting Cassidy a big piece of cake and taking it up to her? I took her supper earlier, but you know how she loves Mrs. Johnson's cake."

"Sure. I'd be happy to."

Allan started toward the river, then looked back. "You're welcome to come with me, Jean-Michel. You might as well have a front row seat."

Jean-Michel shook his head. "*Non,* I believe I've been on my leg too much as it is. I'm just going to go upstairs and rest."

"But you'll miss the fireworks." Thomas didn't want anyone to miss his favorite part. "Maybe I could get you a better chair?"

Jean-Michel shook his head. "*Non.* I know I will miss the fireworks. But thank you for offering your assistance."

Jean-Michel sat in his room with the drapes pulled. With the first boom of exploding fireworks he felt his skin grow clammy. He gripped the arms of the chair. This wasn't Syria. It was America. This wasn't war, but a celebration of victory.

Another loud boom and this time applause from the crowd outside the hotel. Jean-Michel forced himself to take a deep breath. He could endure this. It was just one night.

His entire body quaked as the explosions continued. Cries of oohs and aahs filled the air. But even as he fought against the memories, those happy cries soon turned into ones of desperation and the explosions became deadly.

Jean-Michel put his hands over his ears and bent forward so low his head was on his knees. The images of that day so long ago flashed before his eyes. He didn't know if God truly offered heaven for His people, but one thing was sure to Jean-Michel.

This was hell.

"Brother?" Collette's voice was only a whisper against the cacophony of war.

He felt a gentle hand on his head and glanced up. Collette looked down on him in obvious concern.

Jean-Michel lowered his hands. "I'm sorry."

She knelt beside him and he straightened. Collette took hold of his hand. "Is this how it was?"

He shook his head. "*Non,* it was so much worse."

She nodded. "And you were all alone."

Jean-Michel considered it a moment. "*Oui.* I was all alone." At least it had felt that way.

She smiled up at him in her innocent way. "Well, you aren't alone now. I won't leave you."

Her kindness touched him. A tiny glimpse of maturity. Collette was beginning to care more for others than for herself. Jean-Michel leaned back in the chair and drew a deep breath.

"Shall I tell you a story?"

"A story about what?" He thought of her love for fairy tales.

"One that Cassidy told me about these terrified men in a boat on a stormy sea."

July 10

"Cassidy Faith, you do beat all." Another lecture from Mrs. Johnson was not what Cassidy had hoped for today, but here she was, in the middle of another one.

"Mrs. Johnson, please, I know the doctor said I couldn't go back to work in the kitchen, but don't you think it would be worth asking if I could at least go sit down there and visit with people?"

"No. No, I do not think it 'would be worth asking' because we're not. You're not. Bed rest means that you are confined to your bed. It does *not* mean that you are allowed to take a jaunt up and down the stairs to go

252

sit in a chair in the busiest room of this hotel."

Mrs. Johnson's reddened face assured Cassidy she should let the matter drop. But how could she? She was half out of her mind with boredom. "Well, I need to *do* something. It's been a month and I've knitted plenty of booties, made an entire wardrobe for this child, and have stitched up four dozen diapers."

The older woman placed her hands on her hips. "Did you copy all those recipes I gave you?"

"Yes." Cassidy sighed. She supposed she should be a tad grateful. "I appreciate you bringing those to me." More than just a tad. Why was she complaining? Because she was bored? "I'm sorry, Mrs. Johnson. I guess I'm just restless, even though I have so much to be thankful for."

"I know, dear." The older woman sat on the edge of the bed. "But you gave us all quite a scare. The doctor is being cautious, and rightly so. The most important thing is that you and the baby stay healthy and safe. Sometimes things like this require sacrifice."

Cassidy nodded. This dear sweet woman was the closest thing she had to a mother figure. She was also her best friend other than Allan. "It was scary. Especially when there was blood. I know it's a delicate conversation, but I don't have anyone else to talk to about it. The doctor said that might happen quite a bit after a fall like that. Just as long as it was only a spot or two here and there, we should be okay."

Mrs. Johnson patted Cassidy's hand. "Oh, my sweet girl, you can always talk to me about whatever you need to." Her soft expression faded back into commander mode. "And this is *exactly* why you won't be going anywhere. Understood?"

It made Cassidy laugh. She couldn't help it. "Yes, ma'am." A new thought came to mind. "You know, Miss Langelier has come by a couple times to visit. She's quite a handful, but I bet you'd love to talk to her too."

"Me? Speak to that wealthy French girl? No, no, no. She's all frippery and finery and I'm all rough edges and orders. You can just keep those visits to yourself. I'm having enough trouble with that loathsome Scotsman."

"Mrs. Johnson, how can you consider him loathsome when you share his ancestry? You're Scottish. You said so yourself."

"I'm also Irish, and the combination of those makes me a formidable opponent, so it's best not to cross me, Cassidy Faith."

She smiled. Whenever Mrs. Johnson used her first and middle names, it made her heart swell. The woman cared for her. "Very well, let me get back to Miss Langelier. She's really a sweet girl, but she's searching for answers. I believe she could use some of your no-nonsense advice. Won't you come more often?"

"I'll come visit *you* more often, but I'll leave Collette Langelier to you." Mrs. Johnson lost her fierce look and chuckled. "Maybe you can teach her your favorite recipes."

"I doubt she can even boil water." The thought made her laugh. "How am I supposed to do that from my bed?"

"Well, that's for you to figure out. You're creative. You wouldn't have to actually use the stove or oven, just teach her the recipes and techniques up here with a few bowls and such."

"That will never work. But thank you for trying and for making me laugh. I'll find something."

"Good. Something to keep you *both* busy and out of trouble."

As if speaking about the girl had summoned her, Collette Langelier peeked in through the open doorway. "Am I intruding?"

"No. Please come in." Cassidy waved her forward. "Collette, this is Mrs. Johnson."

"*Oui.* How are you, Mrs. Johnson? You are the chef, no?"

The older woman gave a nod. "I am, and much too busy to stand here chatting. Good day to you both, and, Cassidy — you stay put."

"Yes, ma'am." Cassidy laughed and motioned to the chair.

Collette quickly took a seat. "Are you sure you don't mind my visit?"

"Not at all. In fact, I'm blessed by it. I cannot tell you how bored I get up here." Cassidy stretched, then put her hands atop her stomach. "I can't believe how big I am. It's a wonder the bed hasn't collapsed."

Collette giggled. "Oh, Miss Cassidy, you are too funny. You are still a very small woman."

"I certainly don't feel like one. But hearing me complain is not why you came today. How may I help you?" Cassidy couldn't contain a laugh. "Perhaps they could just put my bed in the lobby and I could answer guests' questions all day long."

"I don't know why not." Collette played along. "You are much prettier than Mr. Bradley."

Cassidy leaned in closer to Collette.

"Personally, I don't like his mustache. He goes back and forth growing it out, then cutting it off. I told him he looks much better without it, but apparently, he doesn't take store in what I think."

Collette shrugged and held up her hands. "Ah, men. They seldom listen to us, *n'est-çe pas?*" She shook her head. "Isn't it so? I sometimes forget myself and speak French. My brother said coming to America was the perfect way to improve my English, but I'm afraid I tend to forget."

"It's such a beautiful language. I can speak Athabaskan — the tongue of the native peoples in this area, and of course English, but while I've heard quite a bit of French spoken from time to time — I don't understand it."

"I could teach you!" Collette's voice betrayed girlish excitement.

Cassidy nodded. "That might be fun. It would at least give me something to ponder besides my expanding waist size. It could also come in handy when French guests come who don't speak much English."

Collette clapped her hands. "Oh, it will be great fun. You'll see. And maybe you can help me with my English. There are still things I don't understand."

"Like what?"

Collette frowned. "Like when one of the ladies got upset the other night. She jumped up and said, 'Great Caesar's goats.' I looked, but I did not see any goats. My brother said it must simply be something people say in America."

Cassidy laughed. "Ghost. Great Caesar's *ghost.*"

Collette shook her head, looking even more confused. "There were no ghosts *or* goats."

This made Cassidy laugh all the more. "You'll find we say a great many things, and many of them make no sense at all."

18

Thomas watched the crew direct the placement of the last building. A bunkhouse had been moved all the way from the coal-mining town of Chickaloon to Curry, and one crew worked at rebuilding the large structure that could house dozens of people. Then the last of nine cottages was just set in place south of the hotel — also moved from Chickaloon and now rebuilt here for permanent staff at Curry. He'd never seen anything like it.

Their little town of Curry was growing.

Mr. Langelier walked toward him from the hotel and waved a hand. "Thomas, I was just looking for you."

The man's accent was fascinating. "Yes, sir. How can I help?"

"Actually, I was looking to see if I could hire you."

"Oh, I've got a job that I love, sir."

"*Oui.* Yes. I understand that — but I'm asking for your help in exchange for an extra bit of pocket money. As I hear it, you will soon be heading back to school. I thought perhaps a little extra money would help."

Between assisting in the kitchen since Cassidy was laid up and his regular job with John and Allan, he wasn't sure he had much time to spare. But then again, a little extra money would be nice. "I would love to help you, but how much time will you need me?"

"Only about fifteen minutes a day. Would that be acceptable?"

"Yes, sir. I'm sure I could fit that into my schedule, except when we're out on an overnight expedition. What do you need help with?"

The man looked around and then leaned on his cane with both hands. "It's a bit embarrassing, but I have been doing rehabilitative exercises to strengthen my leg that . . . well, it lost a lot of blood when I was shot in battle —"

"You were in battle? I didn't know that, Mr. Langelier." Thomas covered his mouth for a moment. He wasn't a boy anymore, he should behave like it. "I'm sorry, I didn't mean to interrupt."

Mr. Langelier waved a hand. "It's all right,

Thomas. Truly it is. As I was saying, I've gotten to a point where the exercises get harder and I need assistance. Most of it, I just need someone to be a source of resistance. Does that make sense?"

"Yes, sir. I can do that."

"*Spectaculaire!* Would you be willing to begin helping me this evening?"

"Yes, sir. I could come speak to you after dinner."

"*Merci.* Thank you." Mr. Langelier straightened and looked at all the new buildings. "If you could keep this private as well, I would much appreciate it." He held out a hand.

Thomas shook it and nodded.

"Now, if you would be so kind. I'd love to hear all about the National Park and her great mountain. I hear you know a lot about it."

Reaching into his pocket, Thomas smiled and grabbed one of the new brochures. The National Park was one of his favorite subjects. "Take a look at this grand brochure Mr. Karstens put together. He's the park superintendent and one of the men from the first group to ever summit Denali — well, Mt. McKinley — the tallest mountain in North America. He's a sight to behold for sure."

Jean-Michel frowned. "Mr. Karstens?"

Thomas was momentarily confused, then realized what he was asking. "No, the mountain is a sight to behold. If you notice, our train here can take you right up to the entrance of the park where Mr. Karstens has been building the roads into the area. But I agree with Mrs. Brennan — the best view of Denali is from our very own ridge across the river." He pointed toward Curry Ridge.

"How long of a hike is that?"

"Oh, a few miles. We call it the Meadow Lake Trail. It's not too bad though. Cassidy — Mrs. Brennan — and the whole wedding party went up there for their ceremony a couple years ago. It was quite a beautiful day."

"I think I'd like to try that sometime soon — the hike, that is. Will you be taking any groups there?"

"Yes, sir. I'll let you know the next time we schedule the hike."

Mr. Langelier turned back toward the hotel. "I've heard a lot about this Mr. Karstens at the dinner tables each evening. He sounds like he has tamed the area single-handed as you say, *non*?"

"Well, he has done a lot all by himself, that's for sure." Thomas showed him another part of the brochure. "He was the only one for quite a while — he was the first superintendent ever. He's been in charge of the whole place all by himself. Did you know he started the road here with money from the very first official tourist?"

"That's very interesting. Roads cost a lot of money to build."

"From what I heard, the man gave a whopping seven hundred dollars to get it started."

"Indeed. That's very generous."

Thomas watched the man's face. While seven hundred dollars was an amount an orphan like Thomas might never see in his lifetime, this French man didn't seem fazed by the number. Mr. Langelier had money — Thomas knew that — but since he'd never really had any money of his own, it was fascinating to see how the wealthy perceived such things.

"I look forward to seeing this park of yours."

"We take a few trips there each summer, so I can let Mr. Ivanoff know that you'd like to go. The Savage River Camp is remote, about twelve miles from the train, but if you really want to see the mountain in all his glory, you have to trek quite a bit farther west. Mr. Karstens has trails in, but they are still building the road."

Mr. Langelier nodded. "That sounds like quite an adventure. Do people actually climb this mountain?"

Thomas chuckled. "They try, but John . . . Mr. Ivanoff says the mountain is very particular about who he will allow to actually do it. Very few have ever made it all the way to the top."

"Because of the difficulty, *oui*?"

"Yes. Mr. Ivanoff says a man has to have a spirit to match that of the mountain and few do."

"A spirit to match the mountain," Jean-Michel murmured.

"Exactly. Mr. Ivanoff says the key to overcoming any challenge is to have a spirit that can stand up to it — a spirit that can match the challenge."

The train whistle blew and jolted Thomas back into action. "I apologize, sir, but I've got to get back to work. I came out to see them set the last cottage and lost track of time. But I will see you after dinner tonight."

"*Merci*. Thank you, Thomas."

Running back to the hotel, Thomas was grateful for his long legs. A few years back, when he first started at the Curry, they had been a nuisance, making him trip and fall as he grew. But now, he could cover a good bit of ground at a quick pace.

After the train left the hotel depot, he straightened his jacket and walked into the lobby.

"Thomas!" Mr. Bradley waved him over to the front desk.

He approached and steadied his breathing after his run. "Yes, sir?"

"If you're not busy helping John or Allan, I believe Mrs. Johnson could use your help."

"To keep her from killing Chef Ferguson?" Thomas hadn't meant to say the words aloud and quickly put his hand to his mouth.

Mr. Bradley chuckled. "I can't say the thought hasn't come to me as well."

"Sorry." Thomas lowered his hand. "It's just that . . . well . . . things haven't been very easy between them."

"I'm fully aware. Mrs. Johnson comes to me at least twenty times a day to complain about one thing or another." Mr. Bradley glanced past Thomas to the bevy of people waiting to be served at the registration desk. "I see I'm needed." He started across the lobby, then turned back. "Just do what you can to keep the peace."

Thomas nodded. "Yes, sir."

"Mr. Bradley!" Sally, a young maid, approached, a bit of terror on her face.

At least Thomas wasn't the only one heading into battle. He imagined other young men had felt the same as he did now — except they were headed off to a *real* battlefield. Although an argument could be made for the war between Mr. Ferguson and Mrs. Johnson being almost as scary. In both scenarios, the future was unknown, there were certain to be difficulties . . . and probably a little bloodshed. Maybe a lot of bloodshed if Mr. Ferguson didn't stay out of Mrs. Johnson's way.

"Thomas!" The manager's voice cut through his thoughts and made Thomas turn back around.

"Sir?"

Mr. Bradley waved him closer, leaned over the counter, and spoke in a low tone. "I'm afraid we have a delicate situation."

"Sir?"

"One of the guests that who came in on the train is missing. According to the niece, he gets lost often. He's not an old man, though — just a little older than Mr. Brennan — but she said he's got some gray hair at his temples. His name is Mr. Moreau. The rest of his family isn't due here for a few weeks, and the young lady, his niece, is quite distraught. She said he might get worked up if we don't find him soon."

Thomas raised an eyebrow. "I'm not sure I understand, sir."

"Something is wrong with the man, but the niece won't say anything else. She's out searching for him."

"What do you need me to do?"

"Be as discreet as you can, but search the hotel and then the rest of the buildings. We will have to discuss the man's illness with the niece at a later time. For now, we best find him. And quick. The niece was unpacking when she realized he'd left the room without her, so he could be anywhere."

"I'll find him." Thomas lifted his shoulders and took a deep breath. He knew every nook and cranny of this hotel. With a nod to his boss, he took off down the stairs to the basement. He'd start at the bottom and work his way up.

When he reached the bottom of the stairs, he headed to the large laundry room that serviced the hotel and the trains and hospitals from the surrounding areas. Several of the workers lifted a hand and waved, but as Thomas looked around and under tables, their missing guest didn't appear to be there. "Have you seen anyone in here who isn't an employee?" He had to raise his voice to be heard over all the machinery.

Several *no*s and shakes of the head were

all the response, so Thomas headed to the section gang bunkhouse at the back, but there wasn't anyone there.

A few men played cards at a table in the main area outside the bunkroom, and a few of the train workers sat at the men's bar. But Thomas recognized all of them.

He'd just have to search the provisions rooms next.

The hallway to the provisions rooms was quiet, but Thomas decided to check each room thoroughly. The first room was empty of people.

The second room was not.

In the corner, a thin man ran a hand along the wall. He obviously hadn't heard Thomas enter because he didn't turn. Just mumbled, "There must be a secret passageway here somewhere. The general said —"

This must be their guest. Thomas cleared his throat. "We don't have any secret passageways here at the Curry, Mr. Moreau."

The man turned, fear etched into his features.

"Let me help you back to your room. Can I help with anything else, sir?"

The man straightened and his face became a mask. Serene and gentle as if nothing else had transpired. "Yes, thank you. I'd like to make sure my niece is doing well."

268

Thomas held out an arm toward the door. Why would this man think there was a secret passageway here? And who in the world was the general?

July 17

Katherine stepped off the train at the Curry and reached up to help her grandmother down the steps. "How are you feeling?"

"Much improved, thank you. Just in need of a nap."

"Well, I can make sure that happens as soon as you've had a good lunch." She held up her hand. "Please don't argue with me. I insist."

"Bossy girl." Grandmother reached up and patted Katherine's raised hand. "But that sounds delightful. I do need to see to one other matter first, so if you don't mind getting our bags up to the rooms, come back to get me in about ten minutes."

"Are you sure it's not something I can handle for you?"

"No. I'll take care of it. It will give me a few minutes to stretch my legs as well. I assure you . . . I'm just fine."

"All right then, I'll be right back." Katherine turned and nodded to the boy on the platform, and he came forward to take her

269

bags. "Would you assist me upstairs, please, young man?"

"Yes, miss." The young lad appeared to be all arms and legs.

Katherine didn't correct his mistake. It was nice to be called "miss" again. Made her feel young and took her back to days that were happier. She'd hashed out a lot with Grandmother on their trip north. The woman's words had been full of wisdom, but she also pointed Katherine to Scripture. Even though some of the conversation had been hard to hear, it had been beneficial. *"Like roses,"* Grandmother said, *"we all need a little pruning."*

What needed pruning in Katherine's life was a portion of her past. Words that she had believed because they'd been forced into her mind. Darkness that threatened to press in every time she allowed the memories to replay.

One crucial question her beloved grandparent wanted her to ponder was if Katherine truly believed the lies Randall had told her. As she walked up the stairs to their rooms, she mulled it over again. Did she? As Grandmother pointed out, Randall had been a ruthless liar who manipulated everyone for his own benefit. Why should Katherine ever believe a word he had said? She'd honestly never considered it that way.

If she were truly a new creation now, she had to throw off the old.

With new determination, Katherine opened the door to her room and made herself a promise. She would no longer allow anything her husband had said to be believed as truth.

None of it.

It was over.

She had a relationship with her Savior now. The darkness had no power over her.

This was a new life. And she would take it.

She paid the boy a coin and closed the door to head back down the stairs. Just like everything, she would have to take one step at a time. One day at a time. Bad times would no doubt come, but she had to remain strong. *Please God, make me strong.*

At the bottom of the stairs, she heard her grandmother's voice. She looked to her left and saw Grandmother in one of the lovely leather chairs in front of the fireplace, talking to someone.

His back was to Katherine, but she knew who it was.

Jean-Michel.

Her heart skipped a beat as she walked over to them and took a d,ep breath. "Jean-

Michel, it's so good to see you again."

He turned and those green eyes of his latched on to her heart. She thought she was incapable of love anymore, but with him in front of her, all the old feelings — the good feelings — came surging back.

"Katherine."

Just hearing him say her name made her legs feel a bit like jelly. This was much harder than she'd imagined. "I'd still like to take that walk if you'd like to reschedule."

"It would be my pleasure."

Grandmother stood with the help of her cane and Jean-Michel. "Why don't we all have lunch together first, and then Katherine can get me upstairs for a time of rest? This afternoon should be lovely for a walk in the garden."

Katherine nodded, noting the weariness in the elder woman's face. "That is a wonderful idea." She was relieved that the older woman wanted to eat.

Jean-Michel held his arm out for Grandmother. "Shall we?"

The two canes tapped in rhythm along the foyer floor. Katherine put a hand to her churning stomach and watched them as they walked ahead of her. *Lord, give me wisdom. And strength.*

Voices in conversation drifted over her

along with the smells of a delicious luncheon. Katherine's mouth watered. This was comfortable and normal. She could do this. Plenty of people around, good food, and a man she was once madly in love with.

Jean-Michel held out a chair for her grandmother and seated her, then came around for Katherine. "I do believe I smell the chef's signature rolls. I think I've eaten several dozen since we arrived." His smile and casual words broke down the stiff walls around her.

Lunch passed in a blur of chitchat and wonderful food. Several times, she'd even laughed aloud and Grandmother smiled with joy. But the older woman faded fast, so Katherine excused herself for a few moments to take her grandmother upstairs. Jean-Michel told her he would meet her by the fireplace.

She made it through lunch and felt relaxed. She could make it through their walk together too. There was a day long ago when she'd looked forward to walks with Jean-Michel as if they were the grandest event on earth.

"Promise me you'll be honest with him, my dear." Grandmother took the steps at a slow pace.

"I promise." But that didn't mean that she had to tell him *everything,* right? At least not yet.

"I'll be praying." She put her wrinkled hand to her mouth and yawned. "And don't forget to come back to get me for dinner. I understand they are serving fresh salmon this evening. I do believe it's become one of my favorites. Of course, the duck confit and white bean puree they served a few weeks ago is also a favorite, and then we mustn't forget those glorious desserts."

Katherine smiled, a little chuckle escaping. "Oh, Grandmother, I won't forget you."

"I'm quite serious, my girl, so don't you laugh at me." Grandmother winked. "You might get so caught up with your young man that you forget all about little ol' me up here."

"That could never happen." Katherine looked at her grandmother with sincere admiration. "You mean far too much to me. You've helped me find my way back to the living."

The old woman smiled. "I only did what God told me to do. He's the one who gives us life, and He's the only one who can sustain it."

After settling her grandmother in, Katherine made her way back downstairs. Grandmother's words echoed in her head. Why had she never heard such things as a child? Why were her parents not at all concerned with matters of faith?

Jean-Michel stood at the fireplace with his hand on the mantel. "You came back."

His words made her blush. She didn't know if he was referring to just now or her sudden disappearance from the hotel weeks ago. "Yes. I'm very sorry for leaving the way I did last month."

He offered her his arm and nodded toward the door. "Why don't we take that walk now?"

"I'd love to." She slid her hand tentatively around his offered elbow, wondering if the contact would unnerve her. But nothing felt wrong or fearful. Just . . . comfortable.

Several minutes passed as they left the hotel and walked across the train platform. He led her down a well-worn trail that looked like it would reach the river.

Katherine prayed and tried to gather her thoughts, but the familiar scent of his cologne and the simple presence of him at her side made thinking quite difficult.

He stopped them when they were close to the river but kept her arm in his. He patted her hand. "I can't tell you how glad I am to see you again, Katherine."

Heat rose up her neck and into her face. "I feel the same." She cleared her throat. "But I must apologize again for how I left."

"Do not think of it. It is enough that you are here now."

Would he still feel that way after she told him everything? She shook her head to rid herself of the negative thoughts.

"Do you not believe me?"

"It's not that, Jean-Michel. There's just a lot I will need to share with you . . . eventually. I'm not the same girl I was five years ago."

"*Oui.* I know. Just as I am not the same man." He turned toward her and closed the space between them. His face became very serious. "But even though we are different, there's something I must say. To 'get it off my chest,' as you Americans say. I can't bear to go on without you. No matter what has happened, I still love you with all my heart."

Katherine's heart soared. Those words were like a healing balm. But she stepped back a few inches and looked into his eyes. Eyes that seemed a bit tortured and expectant all at the same time. "You may not feel the same after —"

"Nothing could make me stop loving you, Katherine. Nothing." His voice was raspy, desperate sounding. "Do you still love me?"

19

Jean-Michel could tell by her expression that he'd pushed too hard. "I am sorry. Not that I'm sorry to have declared my love for you is unchanged, but I can see that I've caused you distress. That was never my intention."

Katherine turned away from him and stared out across the river. "I have always . . . I . . . never stopped." She didn't seem able to say the words, but Jean-Michel felt certain she spoke of her love for him.

He didn't know quite how to handle the situation. He knew she'd had a great deal of pain in her life these last few years. She wore that misery like a stone around her neck.

"You can tell me about it, Katherine. I promise you that nothing you say will ever stop me from loving you."

She turned. "I am not the same person you loved. So you may not love the woman I am now."

"Nor am I the same man *you* loved, but I believe there is enough of us left to rekindle what once was — what should have been." He reached for her, but her response was to step farther away.

"Please don't misunderstand me, Jean-Michel. It's been a long time . . . and I want to tell you why I left . . . why I ran away."

"Do you mean last month? I thought your grandmother wanted to see more of Alaska."

"No. I mean, she did want to see it, but I was the one who made her go."

"But why? You know I would never do anything to make you unhappy — to hurt you."

"I'm already dealing with so much pain and hurt." Katherine turned to face him. "My husband was a terrible man."

Jean-Michel already knew as much. "But that has nothing to do with us."

"It has everything to do with us, because I'm not sure there can ever be an *us* again."

"But, Katherine —"

"Please stop. You don't understand." She held up her hands and breathed deeply. "Please listen. If you've ever loved me . . . I need you to simply listen."

He nodded and forced his heart to calm. Katherine — his Katherine — needed him. "*Oui.* Go on."

"I faced every day with that man telling me I was an abomination to him — that I was worthless — worse than a dog. He treated his servants better than he treated me. He wounded me, Jean-Michel. Wounded me to the core, and I don't know if those wounds can ever truly heal." She glanced up at him, a sheen of tears in her beautiful brown eyes.

"I'm so sorry."

A shake of her head made a lock of hair come loose from the blue ribbon that held it back. She whisked it behind her ear and sniffed. "No one knew the truth about what I endured. No one. He needed his beautiful wife to appear happily at his side for every prestigious political dinner and engagement. I always wore long sleeves to cover . . ." Her voice cracked. "Forgive me."

"*Non.* It's not your fault."

"That's the thing, Jean-Michel. For years, I've carried it around as my fault. He *told* me it was my fault. It's only by the grace of God that I'm able to begin to get past this."

"What about your parents? Did they never suspect?"

"Father was too enthralled with his senator son-in-law. But I had gained the courage to finally tell them. At least Mother — I was going to share with her what I could.

279

But they were killed in an accident the night I went to speak with them. Things went downhill from there. Randall enjoyed my inheritance almost as much as he enjoyed telling me . . . I was worthless."

"*Mon chérie . . .* I am so sorry."

"No. I am sorry. I'm not doing this very well. Give me some time, please." She didn't give him a chance to answer but hurried away, leaving him baffled and alone.

July 18

The sun seemed to never tire in the summer months in Alaska. Jean-Michel hadn't slept well since coming to this great territory because of all the daylight. But it had kept the nightmares from occurring too often. He could at least be thankful for that. Of course, the lengthy days might only be a part of it. He was no longer sitting around feeling sorry for himself, and he allowed himself to let go of some of the guilt he'd once felt.

Today, the warmth of the rays bore down on him and weighed him down. Katherine loved him — of that he was certain — but something held her back. In his gut, he knew it was something more than what she'd shared. Had she been embarrassed that she told him? Had he pushed too hard?

He walked his daily route down toward the roundhouse and water tower and searched for a way to fix this new mess he found himself in. While his leg was getting stronger, he seemed to be floundering at how to rebuild his relationship with Katherine. Ever since he'd decided to come to Alaska, he'd thought about their reunion. About their love and their past together.

Why was it taking so long?

Maybe because he was impatient. A taste of hope for the future had changed his outlook on life. And he didn't want to waste another minute like he had in past months.

Footsteps sounded behind him as he approached the new cottages. "Mr. Langelier. How are you today?"

Jean-Michel turned and waved at Thomas. The young man had been invaluable in helping him with his exercises, and they'd formed a fast friendship. "I'm doing quite well. And you?"

"Mrs. Johnson sent me with this load of snacks for the men working at the roundhouse today. Apparently, they are working on one of the steam engines." He held out the basket for inspection. "It's just nice to get out of the kitchen today. I miss working with John and Allan out in the fresh air on the days I'm covering for Cassidy. Of course, it's really not as much that they need my help as they need a referee."

Jean-Michel chuckled. "I've heard a bit of gossip about the chef and her new assistant."

"Forgive me. I shouldn't have said anything, Mr. Langelier. That was inappropriate of me. Maybe I'm in need of fresh air more than I thought."

"I can imagine. Especially for a young man like yourself, sometimes it's hard to be cooped up, *non*?"

Thomas nodded. "I was thinking, Mr. Langelier."

"Please call me Jean-Michel."

"I don't know if Mr. Bradley would like that, sir. But I was thinking, while I'm helping with your exercises at night, do you think you could teach me some of those French words?"

"*Oui.* But why do you want to learn French?"

"It sounds educated and refined. And I like to learn."

"But of course. It would be my pleasure —"

Boom!

The explosion made Jean-Michel fall back, hitting the ground hard. Thomas landed beside him.

"What was that?" Thomas murmured and shook his head. "My ears are ringing."

Across the tracks, the engine house and power plant were suddenly engulfed in flames.

Thomas dropped the basket he'd somehow managed to keep upright and jumped up. "Fire!" he yelled out, then raced toward the blaze.

Other men ran toward the fire, not even seeming to notice Jean-Michel.

Jean-Michel got up and looked at the growing conflagration. He should do whatever he could to help. He took a step forward, but his legs felt leaden — impossible to move. People came from all directions to lend their help. Men yelled across the fire for more water — for a ladder.

Screams of women and children began to replace the calls of the workmen. Jean-Michel's vision blurred. The green of the terrain around him turned to brown sand.

Frantic, he tried to get past the front line of men fighting the blaze. "We've got to save them!" The scream tore from his throat.

Arms yanked him back. "Stay back, sir. We've got it under control."

"No! You can't allow them to burn to death! There are people in there!" He forced his way through the men and stumbled outside the burning building. Blasted leg! It gave way again. But he couldn't let those women and children die. Not again.

Terror gripped his heart as he dragged himself along the ground.

"Sir, you have to get away from the building! It's too dangerous." Several men surrounded him and grabbed his arms.

"No, please, save them, can't you hear them?" The smoke choked him. His lungs burned.

"Get that man out of here!" the railroad chief officer yelled.

As two young men dragged Jean-Michel back, he felt hot tears stream down his face. Defeated, he couldn't understand why they were fighting him.

A voice in his ear. "Mr. Langelier, there's no one inside the building." That was Thomas's voice, wasn't it?

Jean-Michel turned to look in the young man's face. Yes, it was Thomas. "No one?"

"Everyone is fine, sir. No one is hurt, thank God."

"There wasn't anyone inside the building . . . no one screaming?"

"No, sir." Thomas helped him to his feet. "Just the men fighting the fire yelling back and forth."

Jean-Michel wiped a hand down his face. His thinking cleared; he wasn't in Syria. He was in Alaska. What had just happened?

The general was nowhere to be found.

And even though he'd checked for secret passageways and looked for his contact, he came up short.

What should he do? If he couldn't find the general and pass on the message, would they lose the rest of their men? Maybe even the whole war?

The responsibility rested on his shoulders, and his alone.

No matter what, he had to find the general. The others weren't helping.

"Uncle? What are you doing out here?" His niece's voice broke through his thoughts.

He thought she'd been occupied in the dining room. "Oh, I'm just watching the crews clean up the mess."

"It's not safe to be this close. Let's get you back inside." She tugged at his arm.

He nodded. He'd just have to sneak out later. The general had to be here.

It appeared almost every hotel guest came outside to watch the commotion. Katherine stepped over a few burnt pieces of wood and tried to get closer to Jean-Michel. His face had haunted her as she watched him trying to get to the building. His cries for help to save people were more than gut-wrenching. They tore at her very soul. Obviously, he'd witnessed something horrific in the past few years. Maybe he was just as damaged as she.

In that moment, a new realization hit her. God had brought both of them through some horrific times. To this place. This time. Two very broken people.

When the men were finally able to pull Jean-Michel back, he'd collapsed and Thomas had spoken to him.

As she made her way to him, the smoke increased and she covered her mouth with a hankie. She just needed to make sure he was all right.

"Miss, you need to stay back." A soot-covered face nodded at her and she stepped away.

Thomas spotted her and said something to Jean-Michel. The young man helped Jean-Michel up and they walked toward her.

Her heart crumbled a little at the look on Thomas's face. Jean-Michel wasn't all right. In her heart, she knew it. But there had to be something she could do. Now she understood his need to help her. That's what people did . . . when they loved each other.

Thomas shook his head and they steered around her back to the hotel.

Well, that wasn't acceptable. He said he loved her still and now he needed help. She wasn't going to stand back and do nothing. Not after everything that had kept them apart. Katherine moved through the crowd with great determination. "Are you all right?" She reached out and took hold of Jean-Michel's arm.

Jean-Michel looked over to her for a moment and then back to the path in front of him. "I'm sorry, Katherine. I should have warned you." He coughed for several moments. "I'm sorry. I can't talk about it right now."

"There's nothing to be sorry about." But his back was to her and he kept on walking. She stood at the edge of the tracks and watched the two men make their way up to the train platform.

Katherine bit back tears and frustration. *Why, God, why?*

A lifetime ago, she and Jean-Michel had shared a special and innocent love. Life hadn't been kind to her since then, and it was apparent that it hadn't been to him either.

But back in the past, she didn't know the

287

Lord. She was pretty certain Jean-Michel didn't either. Things were different now. She wasn't the only broken and beaten-down soul. It looked like her beloved was wounded as well.

She'd been so worried about his reaction to her past, she hadn't thought about *him.*

A new determination swelled in her chest. Good thing she knew Who could help.

Pacing her room after the fire wasn't helping a bit. She'd been praying, as best she knew how, but still she was unsure of the next step. Katherine sat down on her bed and thought maybe if she wrote Jean-Michel a letter . . .

No. They needed to speak in person.

Although there was a major problem — right now, he didn't seem to be willing.

Patience was not her strong suit. When she thought of how she'd left the hotel for a month and made him wait, it made her ashamed. She'd put him through so much.

The look in his eyes as he'd cried out for help would stay with her forever. What could she do?

A knock on the door to the bathroom made her conscious of the tears that streaked her face. Wiping them away, she let her grandmother in and went straight into the gentle woman's arms.

"I heard what happened." Grandmother rubbed Katherine's head. Just like when she was a child. "How about we sit down and pray for Jean-Michel and all the men fighting the blaze right now?"

"I've been praying, but it feels like my prayers are unanswered."

Her grandmother gave a sympathetic smile. "It feels that way sometimes, but never fear. God hears each one and answers. In His time."

Katherine sat on the bed, and Grandmother took the chair and bowed her head. "Heavenly Father, we don't know what has caused so much pain in Mr. Langelier's life, but we know that You do. Please help him to heal — help him to realize that he can lay the past to rest. Thank You, Lord, that no one was in the building when the engine exploded, and please guide all the men who are still making sure that the fire is out."

A knock sounded at Katherine's door. She swiped her face again and went to answer it.

As she opened the door a crack, she recognized Collette and opened the door wide. "Please come in."

"Merci." Collette stood with her hands twisting a handkerchief. "I am sorry to

intrude, but I felt I must speak to you both."

Katherine nodded, returned to sit on the edge of her bed, and patted a place next to her for Collette. "Have a seat."

The beautiful blonde sat down and immediately started crying. "I don't know what else to do other than to tell you the truth."

Grandmother patted the girl's knee. "Go ahead, my dear. We are quite sympathetic and willing to hear what you have to share."

"You see, I didn't know what my brother had been through. I had been quite . . . what is the word? *Inconscient . . .* oblivious to my brother's troubles. Until we took this trip." She sniffed and patted her face and eyes.

"Go on." Katherine needed to know.

"He's terrorized by nightmares. Reliving days during his time in the French army when he was in Syria." She cried in earnest, hiccupping between sobs. "He had to watch a building be burned down with innocent people inside — women and children! One of his own soldiers set the blaze. He was shot trying to rescue them."

"Good heavens, that poor man." Grandmother lifted her own hankie to her nose.

"But that is not all, I'm afraid." Collette stiffened and took a deep breath. "His two best friends came in and dragged him away from the danger . . . but they were shot and killed in the course of it."

Katherine sucked in a lungful of air and covered her mouth. So this is what Jean-Michel lived with. "Today . . . during the fire . . . he was reliving that moment, wasn't he?"

"Oui." Collette stood up. "I did not have my brother's permission to tell you all of this, and he will probably be angry with me — it has not been easy for him since our father died. I am what you Americans say . . . a handful — but I had to let you know. He is not crazy like one of the railroad workers said."

"Is there anything we can do to help?" Grandmother leaned forward.

"Non." She shrugged. "I do not know. Maybe. Jean-Michel had been doing better. Alaska seems to agree with him, but now this. There is a . . . oh . . . what is the English word . . . *démon* —"

"Demon." Katherine barely uttered the word.

"Oui. Demon. It is inside of my brother — keeping him from forgetting. It torments him so." She moved to the door. "I must go."

"Thank you for telling me." Katherine stood and hugged Collette. "You've grown up so much since the last time I saw you in France."

"*Merci.* I fear he'll find out I've come and be angry." The girl rushed from the room as if she'd done something wrong.

Fear began to wiggle its way up Katherine's spine. Collette said she feared Jean-Michel would find out. If Collette was this afraid . . . then maybe she should be as well. But Jean-Michel had shown her nothing but kindness . . . tenderness.

Randall had done the same — before they'd married.

Katherine shuddered. Perhaps she should avoid any relationship with Jean-Michel. One man had already hurt her enough.

As she stood there staring at the door, she could almost feel her husband's fingers tightening around her throat. He often threatened to cut off her air supply, and to this day, Katherine couldn't bear to have anything around her neck. Breathing in through her nose, she prayed silently. He had no power over her any longer.

"Katherine?"

For a moment, she'd forgotten that Grandmother was still in the room. "Hmm?"

"Jean-Michel isn't Randall."

How could the woman read her thoughts?

She put her hands on the door. "I don't know what you mean."

"I've seen you react this way before. When fear takes over." Something tapped on the floor. It must be her cane. "You're afraid that your relationship with Jean-Michel will only spell pain. You want to protect yourself from that."

Katherine turned around and swallowed. "Yes, Grandmother. It scares me, I'll admit it. Watching him today broke my heart."

"You must remember that God has the ability to heal the past. To heal the heart and the mind. Have you considered how He might use you to be instrumental in helping the man you love?"

"But I'm not strong enough." She shook her head.

"God is."

"Of course, God is strong. He's God. But . . . it's hard for me to . . . to understand how that helps me."

"Do you not remember what happened in the cave, my dear?" Grandmother walked over and grabbed her hand and squeezed. "Stop trying to do this all by yourself. God doesn't call you to bear these burdens alone. If you try to carry it yourself, you'll fail every time." With that, she turned and walked toward their adjoining bath. "I'll see you at dinner. I believe I need to lie down for a while."

Katherine walked over to the bed, weary and drained. In a very *un* ladylike fashion, she flopped down on the mattress on her back and looked at the ceiling. It was true . . . she was attempting to do it all on her own. *Again.* And she simply couldn't. Frankly, she was tired of trying. At only twenty-five years old, she should feel young and vibrant, and yet she wandered around like an old lady. Things had to change. It seemed for every step she took forward in her faith, something happened to send her three steps back. She let go a heavy sigh.

God, You're going to have to handle this, because I can't. I don't know what I'm doing. I don't know how to feel. And I'm scared.

She put a hand over her eyes. After her marriage to Randall she had never expected to be happy again. She had believed her life was over — that she would forever be nothing more than a puppet controlled by a cruel master. But everything changed. She'd been handed new life. A fresh start. Was she truly going to allow a man in the grave to dictate the outcome of the rest of her life?

Grandmother once told her that Christians had to take up their cross daily. Katherine hadn't understood until she explained further about Jesus being forced to carry His own cross to the place where they would kill Him.

"He was made to carry the very thing that the Romans would use to end His life." Grandmother had been teary. "And now we are called to take up our own cross."

"And if it kills us?" Katherine pushed.

"It won't," Grandmother assured. "We're called only to take it up — not carry it alone. God will never leave us to bear it alone; otherwise, it surely would kill us."

Katherine considered this for a moment. Jean-Michel was trying to carry this burden alone. Just as she had tried to carry Randall's abuse. Perhaps if they shared each other's burdens, it could truly lighten the load for both.

Maybe she could help Jean-Michel after all. They were just two broken, burdened people in love. And two together was better than one alone.

20

The larger she grew with this baby, the lower Cassidy sank into the bed. She was pretty sure it would have a permanent indentation from her time of bed rest.

Shaking her head, she pushed up with her arms to sit higher.

Allan walked in with her dad. "Good evening, my darling. How are you feeling?"

"Large."

Dad chuckled.

Allan came over and kissed her cheek. "But you're beautiful as ever."

"I'm glad you think so." Cassidy put her embroidery aside. "Tell me about the fire. I've been hearing different stories all day."

"Coal dust got into an overheated engine and it blew. The fire is contained now, no one was hurt, and Mr. Bradley is already talking to the railroad executives about moving the power plant out of the engine house when they rebuild." Allan was good at being concise. She'd give him that.

"Mrs. Johnson told me that a lot of the workers were worried. Because we're so remote, they were afraid a fire could spread and burn down everything before anyone could come help."

Dad came over and patted her hand. "That's true. But we've had some good discussions downstairs. When they rebuild, they're talking of more water lines and fire hydrants to help in case of another fire."

"That sounds like a good idea." Cassidy crossed her arms over her growing middle. It made a nice shelf. "And how is the new annex coming along? I heard that the bunkhouse is done and all the cottages."

"It's fine." Dad shrugged. "But I thought you'd be more excited to know that *your* cottage is ready, and as soon as the doctor says we can move you, you'll have your own home."

She looked at Allan. "Really?"

"Yes." His smile exploded on his face and he leaned down to hug her. "But we will wait to see what the doctor says, right?"

She huffed. "All right." Looking down at her belly, she spoke to it, a common habit now. "You behave yourself in there and promise to wait until it's time to make your appearance, little one."

"It will all be worth it in the end." Dad leaned over the other side of the bed and kissed the top of her head. "I better get back down to the agent's office. Now that they have the new gas car to take people to the Willow and Montana Creeks, we can barely keep up with the scheduling."

"Love you, Dad. Thanks for stopping by." Cassidy turned back to her husband. "You don't have to go too, do you?"

"Not for a few minutes. But since you're laid up, we've had to let Mrs. Johnson have Thomas two days a week. It makes for an interesting time — we've gotten spoiled with all his help."

She tapped the mattress with her hand. "Fiddlesticks, I forgot to ask Dad something."

"What is it? Maybe I can help?"

"Collette was in here earlier. I was wondering if maybe he had some time to spend with her brother. He needs . . . something."

"We did discuss this earlier. Jean-Michel has to be willing to receive help."

"I think maybe he is now. Collette said he was asking her questions she didn't feel she could answer."

Allan kissed her hand. "Always out to help the hurting, aren't you, darling? If I recall, you've always cheered on the underdog."

He leaned back. "I love that about you."

"I love you too." Even after two years of marriage, the looks he gave her could still make her blush. "You'll ask Dad?"

"Yes, I'll ask him. I think Mr. Langelier is scheduled to go on the hike up to Regalvista later this week." He leaned in to kiss her. "I hate to leave you, but I have to get back to work."

He tasted like coffee and chocolate cake. "I know." She licked her lips. "Would you have someone bring me a piece of chocolate cake? I suddenly have a hankering for it."

Just then the door burst open. "I've absolutely had it with that man!" Mrs. Johnson declared as she came into the room with a plate of cake and glass of milk.

"Look, darling, ask and it shall be given." Allan grinned at the sheepish-looking Mrs. Johnson. "She was just asking me to get someone to bring her a piece of cake."

"I'm sorry for my outburst." She hurried to Cassidy's side. "I thought you could use some milk to drink — strengthen the baby — and I thought it might go down better with a piece of cake."

"Well, you two gals have fun settling the problems of the world." Allan gave a casual salute before exiting the room.

Mrs. Johnson went to the door and closed

it. "I can't work with that Scotsman!"

"What's the matter now?" Cassidy picked up the fork and dug into the cake. Oh, but it was good!

"He's rearranged my kitchen. *My* kitchen!" Mrs. Johnson paced at the end of the bed. "The nerve of that man to tell me he was just trying to set it up to be more practical and efficient."

Cassidy washed down the cake with some milk. She dabbed her mouth with a napkin, then asked, "And was it?"

Mrs. Johnson frowned. "Was it what?"

"More practical and efficient?"

The older woman's face reddened. "That's not the point."

Cassidy giggled. "Sorry." She turned her attention back to the cake.

"I can't have a total stranger waltzing into my kitchen and making changes. I can't even find half of my ingredients. He says they're in perfect order and clearly labeled, but there's nothing either perfect or clear about it." She plopped down on the chair by Cassidy's bed.

"So change it back."

Mrs. Johnson looked at her like she'd lost her mind. "I haven't got the time. I'm already meeting myself coming and going."

"I guess you miss me." Cassidy took

another bite.

"Oh, Cassidy Faith, you're exasperating. I don't know what to do with him. He's capable — there's no doubt about it, but he even suggested I change the recipe for my rolls. I want to haul off and slug him a good one."

Cassidy couldn't contain her laughter. "If you do . . . please let me know when."

Mrs. Johnson looked at her with an odd expression. "What? What are you talking about?"

"If you decide you're going to hit him — let me know first."

"Why? So you can risk life and limb to come down and try to stop me?"

"No. See, there's a bet going on with the kitchen staff and some of the laundry girls as to how long it'll be until you lose your patience and wallop him. I just want to know so I can place my bet and win."

Mrs. Johnson's mouth dropped open, and without another word she got up and went to open the door. She turned back and shook her head. "And I thought I might get a little sympathy here."

Cassidy raised her glass toward the woman. "Remember where you told me to look for sympathy."

Mrs. Johnson rolled her eyes and muttered, "In the dictionary."

July 20

Collette had an idea and was on a mission. Maybe if she could get Katherine to spend some time with Cassidy, she could see how happy a married couple could be. Then Jean-Michel could heal, they could get married, and they could all have their happily-ever-after.

After traipsing all over the hotel, she finally found Katherine in the dining room with her grandmother.

"Good morning, Collette." Mrs. Harrison smiled and waved.

"*Bonjour.* How lucky to find you two this morning." She bounced on her toes. "I have an idea for today and was hoping you'd like to come with me to visit Mrs. Brennan."

"Who, dear?" The older woman tilted her head.

"Mrs. Brennan — she's the chef's assistant — except right now she's laid up in her room because she's with child. Her husband and father are the expedition guides."

Mrs. Harrison glanced at Katherine. "Well, we normally don't spend a lot of time with the staff —"

Katherine laughed. "Oh, Grandmother,

the times are changing. I've never known you to act this way."

Collette found her opportunity. "She's a lovely person, and has been a friend to me. You would both like her very much, and since she's confined, I'm afraid she's quite lonely." Well, maybe that wasn't the whole truth, but it might help her cause. "I've even been teaching her a little French to keep her mind off things."

"It would be lovely to meet this friend of yours, Collette." Katherine stood.

Mrs. Harrison sipped her tea. "Why don't you two go on without me? I think I'll enjoy the morning with a good book."

Collette wrapped her arm around Katherine's and they headed out of the dining room. "You'll love Cassidy."

"I'm sure I will. And I apologize for my grandmother. She's been a little on edge lately." The woman hesitated. "How is your brother?"

"He's resting. The doctor said it might take a few days for him to recover from all the smoke he inhaled, but I think he's doing very well. He'll probably come down for dinner this evening. Thomas comes to help him with his exercises every day and you can tell that Jean-Michel is getting . . . how do you say it . . . hmmm . . . antsy."

Katherine laughed. "I can imagine. Please tell him that we've been praying for him."

"I will. *Merci.*"

"Has he been having nightmares?"

"*Oui.* A lot more than before, but I guess that it is to be expected with the events of the fire. He was actually getting better. I think being away from home really helped him." She watched Katherine's face carefully and noted the worry there. "But the doctor says that he will heal and they will go away in time." Again, she hadn't told the whole truth. No need to worry Katherine further by telling her about Jean-Michel's violence as she tried to calm him after his terrors. Hopefully, God would forgive her. Wasn't she doing the right thing by her brother by helping him?

"Well, we will just have to help him recover from the memories, won't we?" Katherine shot her a big smile.

Collette knew she liked this woman. She was perfect for Jean-Michel.

As they reached the Brennans' quarters, Collette knocked on the door.

A muted "Come in . . ." floated through.

She opened the door and grabbed Katherine's hand. Dragging her new friend into the room, she held out her other hand toward Cassidy. "Mrs. Brennan, this is Mrs.

Demarchis."

"It's so nice to meet you, Mrs. Demarchis." The expectant mother tried to sit up straighter. "My husband, Allan, has told me about you."

Collette beamed at Katherine.

Katherine smiled. "It's nice to meet you too. And please, call me Katherine."

"I told her you were learning French, and Katherine also speaks it quite well, so she can help."

"Goodness, that's wonderful." Cassidy leaned forward and rubbed the small of her back. "Collette, could you please grab me another pillow from the blanket box over there?"

"But of course." Collette hurried to the box and retrieved the pillow. She helped Cassidy adjust it behind her back, then waited until she settled back. "Is it good?"

Cassidy sighed. "Yes, much better." She turned back to Katherine. "I think I heard that your husband was a senator?"

"Yes." Katherine's face darkened a bit. "He died last year." She paused and drew a deep breath. "So, how are you feeling? I can imagine it's challenging to be bedridden during this time."

The change of subject was a bit abrupt, but Collette assumed it was because of her loss. She understood that. She did. Father had only been gone a few months and she missed him terribly. The two older ladies chatted, and Collette brought over two chairs.

"So what brings you to my tiny part of the world?" Cassidy asked.

Clapping her hands together, Collette couldn't contain her grin. "I thought we could keep you company a little each day and we could work on projects for your new home, or the *bébé,* or . . . anything. I can embroider quite well."

Cassidy nodded. "Your company is kindness enough. Katherine, what do you like to do?"

Collette looked to Katherine. What did she like — besides Jean-Michel? For a moment Jean-Michel's long-lost love looked blank. Her light brown hair was the color of rich honey in the sunlight, and her brown eyes were a delicious color of caramel. Collette thought her one of the most beautiful women she'd ever known, but at the moment she looked lost.

"I . . . I don't know." Katherine recovered and a smile was back in place. "What could we help *you* do?"

While Collette wanted to pry further, Cassidy obviously understood something else.

She lifted a finger to her lips. "I've got some embroidery to finish on a few things. Collette, you mentioned being good at that."

"*Oui.* What do you have?"

"Some gowns for the baby and some dish towels for the new cottage. After that, I was thinking I could teach Collette a thing or two about cooking, and then when she goes out on expeditions she could bring back more flowers we could press for bookmarks to sell at the hotel."

Katherine's eyes lit up. "I've always wanted to learn how to cook. Could you teach me as well?"

"Of course!"

"From your bed?" Collette couldn't help asking.

"Well, I could get you started from here. You'd have to arrange with Mrs. Johnson about actually practicing down in the section gang kitchen. But we can talk about the various techniques, and you can familiarize yourself with phrases and what they mean."

"That sounds wonderful. And I would be glad to help embroider as well. I used to be quite efficient; it was something my mother insisted on. As to the bookmarks, as long as you teach me, I think I can handle the job."

Collette watched their tennis match of

words go back and forth. Her plan was working. The two were getting along and Katherine would be inspired to marry again.

Jean-Michel could heal.

Then Collette would be free to go on any adventure she pleased.

A conversation with little Davey floated back into her mind. *"But Miss Collette, it's not about how much fun we wanna have. It's about putting other people first. That's what God wants us to do."* How she missed her little friend. And such wisdom from a six-year-old.

Her conscience pricked. But she was putting others first, wasn't she? She was thinking of Jean-Michel's happiness before her own . . . wasn't she?

The stairs were not his friend today. After exerting too much at the fire and then trying to keep up with all the exercises while his lungs choked out the smoke, Jean-Michel felt every muscle in his body protest. But he had to see Katherine again.

Had to convince her he wasn't crazy. He was all right. She needed him.

So he headed to the dining room with Collette in search of Katherine and her grandmother.

"There they are." Collette pointed to the

table across the room. "Come on." She all but pulled him across the dining room, weaving in and around other tables.

"Good evening, Collette . . . Jean-Michel." Katherine nodded.

"Good evening." Collette smiled and curtseyed. "Mrs. Harrison, you look so lovely in blue."

The older woman smiled back. "Why, thank you, my dear. What a sweet thing to say."

Jean-Michel reached for his sister's chair and pulled it out for her.

"Thank you, *frère.*" She lifted the napkin at her place and unfolded it. "Well, it's true, and that peacock blue is one of my favorite colors too."

Mrs. Harrison smiled and motioned him to sit. "Please sit, Mr. Langelier."

Two empty chairs rounded out their table. He chose the one beside Katherine.

The waiter came and chattered about the menu, but Jean-Michel wanted nothing more than to watch Katherine's every move and listen to her every word.

"And for you, sir?" The man waited, his brow tilted up, pen at the ready.

Jean-Michel realized he hadn't listened and now must order. "I . . . uh. . . ."

Collette came to the rescue. "He'll have

what I'm having."

The waiter nodded and quickly stepped away from the table.

Jean-Michel looked at his sister. "And what is it that you're having?"

"Prime rib and poached salmon." She turned to Katherine. "I thought Miss Cassidy to be quite hard on us today with all her utensils and knives."

Had the world shifted its course in the last few days? "Whatever are you talking about?" He gave a pointed look to his sister. What was she up to now?

"We are learning how to handle ourselves in the kitchen so that we can prepare our own meals." Collette tilted her blond head to the side — all innocence and smiles.

Katherine nodded. "I never knew there were so many different utensils that could be used."

Her smile was bright tonight as she shared about the adventures she'd had with Collette as Cassidy made them take notes about cooking. "Collette was completely perplexed when Cassidy held up a whisk and asked what it did."

Since this seemed to make Katherine happy, he decided to ignore the fact that his sister hadn't told him about her new adventure. He turned to Collette. "And what was your answer?"

She blushed and reached for her water goblet. "I thought it was for beating rugs."

Laughter rumbled around their table as the stories continued and Katherine's face lit with happiness. Mrs. Brennan had been good for Collette and it sounded like all the women got along quite well.

"I could never abide cooking." Mrs. Harrison tapped the table with her finger. "I abhor the smell of the gas stove."

"Well, we've been blessed to have others who could cook for us, Grandmother." Katherine reached over and patted her hand.

A French onion soup was served, but Jean-Michel barely tasted it as he listened to Katherine and the others. Mrs. Harrison seemed quite tired. Perhaps she might slip away early and leave him to stroll with Katherine after supper. The thought made his smile widen.

"Fairbanks was quite interesting." Mrs. Harrison spoke as the waiter removed the soup bowls and returned with their entrée.

Conversation flowed around the table, but with each course, Mrs. Harrison seemed to lose strength. In the middle of dessert, she set her fork down. She lifted her glass to her lips and took a sip. "It has been a pleasure to be with you all, but if you don't mind, I think I will excuse myself and retire for the night." She placed a hand on Katherine's shoulder. "Don't worry about me, dear. You stay and enjoy the evening."

"Are you sure, Grandmother?"

"Yes. Quite." She looked up. "Now if you all will please excuse me."

Jean-Michel stood and helped her from her chair. But when he offered the older woman his arm, she shook her head.

"No thank you, young man. I'll make it."

He returned to his chair and chocolate torte.

Katherine and Collette began to discuss the recipe that Cassidy had given them to copy out for themselves, as well as the different techniques used in it. Katherine shook her head. "I have no idea what 'fold' means. I can fold a pretty napkin, but I do not understand how to 'fold in egg whites.' "

"I think she told us, but I can't remember now. Maybe I'll run and ask her after we finish."

The night had been such a joy that Jean-Michel's heart felt like it would explode. There was hope for them after all. Now if he could just convince everyone else at the hotel that he wasn't crazy, he'd be doing even better. Maybe he should just make an announcement. He chuckled to himself.

Collette and Katherine both looked at him.

"I'm sorry — I was thinking to myself. Please continue your story." He placed a hand over Katherine's and squeezed.

She gasped and yanked her hand to her lap. Her eyes went wide. "I'm sorry." She reached out and laid her hand atop his as red crept up her face.

The touch soothed his heart, but the struggle on her face made him want to hurt the man who did this to her.

"I didn't . . . I don't . . ." She stood abruptly. "My apologies. I can't explain right now."

"Katherine?" Jean-Michel jumped to his feet as well.

She waved him off. "I need to check on Grandmother. Excuse me." She put her napkin on the table and rushed out of the dining room.

"Qu'est-il arrivé?" Collette looked across the room, then spoke the question again in English. "What happened?"

"I don't know for sure, my sweet. But I have a pretty good idea." Anger burned in his chest.

It was a good thing Randall Demarchis was already dead.

21

Staying hidden in the Curry Hotel was harder than he'd expected. Thankfully the others were enjoying taking the train to Fairbanks and would spend some time in the park everyone raved about. And his niece . . . well, she was quiet as a mouse to begin with and took her meals in her room to stay close to him.

But getting out and searching for the general or one of his men was proving to be troublesome. There seemed to always be people about. Even in the middle of the night.

The kitchen never slept, and neither did the laundry.

After the fire, they'd had men on watch over the buildings.

So how could this help him?

Maybe the general wasn't actually at the hotel. Maybe he was somewhere in hiding *around* the hotel. Except for the tiny little town area — if you could even call it that — they were in the middle of nowhere. The surrounding area was dense with trees, streams, and lots of mountains.

The perfect spot for the general to hide.

Now to find him and get him the message . . .

July 31

Thomas carried the pitcher of warm milk up to Mrs. Harrison's room. With the long hours of sunlight, the older woman was having trouble sleeping.

He'd worked long and hard this summer so far, and it felt good. But he had to admit he was excited for the fall to get here. He looked forward to returning to school. Everything he learned would help him to do his job better here. Perhaps one day he would even climb Denali. It was a secret desire of his, but one he would never consider without detailed training from someone like John Ivanoff.

He knocked on Mrs. Harrison's door.

Her granddaughter, Mrs. Demarchis, answered and gave him a small smile. "Thank you so much, Thomas. I know this is a lot of extra work for you each night."

She left the door standing open as he entered.

"Not at all, ma'am. I'm just glad I can be of help."

A man's yell echoed down the hallway.

Thomas jerked in that direction.

Another yell.

Mrs. Harrison came out of the bathroom and tied her robe around her. "Ah, Thomas. Thank you."

Again, the sound of someone crying out.

Mrs. Demarchis started for the door. "Jean-Michel."

"Mr. Langelier? Poor boy." Mrs. Harrison took a seat. "I had heard cries before, but always presumed it was a child. Are you certain it is he?"

Her granddaughter nodded. "Yes." Her word was soft. She bit her lip. "I'm sorry, Grandmother. I must go."

Thomas felt quite awkward. "Let me go with you." He set the milk down on the dresser inside the room and followed Mrs. Demarchis out.

Shutting the door, Katherine nodded at him.

Thomas led her down the long hall to the Langeliers' rooms at the far end. Most of the guests who'd been in the rooms closer to the Langeliers had asked to be moved since the fire. Thomas knocked on the door.

Collette opened it in a flurry, her eyes wide.

"We're sorry to disturb you, miss, but we heard yelling." Thomas kept his voice calm.

The French girl's shoulders drooped and she sobbed into her hands. "I'm so sorry, I don't know what to do . . . *Je n'arrive pas à le réveiller cette fois.*"

Thomas didn't understand the last bit, but he understood that she was beside herself. "I'm sorry, could you repeat that?"

She tapped her hand to her head. "I cannot seem to wake him up, nor calm him."

"May we come in?"

"Oui."

He ushered Mrs. Demarchis in before him, and she took Collette in her arms while he went to Mr. Langelier's side. Thankfully the lights were on, and Thomas had no trouble navigating the room.

"He'd been doing so much better before the fire, and usually I can soothe him by speaking softly and holding his hand, but not this time."

Thomas came to Jean-Michel's bedside and tried not to look shocked. The man's face was red, and sweat poured down his forehead as he thrashed back and forth. The covers were twisted around him and seemed to be tightening their hold on the man as he fought.

Perhaps if Thomas tried to still Jean-Michel. He attempted to hold the man down, but it only served to make things worse. Despite the covers' hold, Mr. Langelier jumped up, pushing against Thomas, sending him flying across the room.

Mrs. Demarchis pushed Collette behind her, then walked toward the man. "Jean-Michel . . . my love . . . we need you to wake up and calm down. Everyone is fine."

He stilled. "Katherine?"

"Yes, it's me. I'm here." She took his hands. "Are you all right?"

He sat on the edge of the bed and looked up at her. Then ran his hands through his hair. "Did I hurt anyone?"

Mrs. Demarchis gave Thomas a questioning glance.

He shook his head — Jean-Michel hadn't hurt him, just surprised him.

"No. You didn't." She walked over to Collette and whispered something in her ear. "But it's time we all head back to bed. I don't think it would be appropriate for me to stay." Mrs. Demarchis smiled at Jean-Michel.

Thomas had heard the two had known each other a long time, but the lady's words had shocked him a bit. She'd called Mr. Langelier "my love."

Miss Collette nodded and wiped the tears from her face. "We'll be fine. Thank you for coming. You're the only one who's been able to wake him."

Thomas stayed after the senator's widow left and looked at the man in front of him. "Is there anything I can do to help you, sir?"

"Non." Mr. Langelier sighed. "I'm sorry for troubling you."

" 'Twasn't any trouble, sir. We heard your struggle and came to help."

"I fear it's too late. Look at what the fire has done to my mind. There is little hope for me now."

Miss Collette whimpered. "Oh, *frère.* Katherine was able to bring you out of the nightmare."

"Non. I can't put her through this. I can't."

The young lady began to sob in earnest and ran to the bathroom.

Thomas couldn't bear to watch the man's torment. "Mr. Langelier, if I may be so bold . . ."

"I don't think —"

"Sir. Please. I don't wish to jeopardize the working relationship we have, and I have no desire to hurt you in any way — but there's something that I must say to you. Even if you fire me."

Jean-Michel held his head in his hands.

"I can help you. Well, I can't personally, but I know Who can."

The bed creaked under her as she flipped to her other side.

Again.

Katherine couldn't sleep with the picture of Jean-Michel suffering from the nightmare. She simply couldn't get it out of her mind.

There'd been no rage in Jean-Michel's eyes — just desperation. She wasn't afraid of his hurting her. But her heart ached for him and she knew why — she loved the man. Loved him more than anything in the world. She always had.

The peace that had flowed through her as soon as she saw him gave her the strength to speak to him. She'd known exactly what to do.

Had that been God's divine intervention?

After Randall died, she promised herself she would never let a man hurt her like that again. That she would fight back. And surprisingly, she hadn't felt in danger with Jean-Michel. Yet that had been her fear this whole time — why she'd held back.

"Are you going to keep flopping or would

you like to talk about it?"

Katherine rolled to face the door and saw Grandmother there holding her cup of milk. "I'm sorry. Did I wake you?"

"No, my dear. I never went to sleep. But you *have* been sounding a lot like a fish out of water over here."

The imagery made Katherine laugh. Hopefully she wasn't that bad. All right, maybe she was.

Fluffing up her pillow behind her, she sat up and pulled back the covers for her grandmother to join her. She pulled her knees to her chest. "Jean-Michel was violent in his nightmare tonight."

Grandmother swirled her cup for a moment. "Violent in what way, dear?"

"He thrashed about, yelled. And then when I talked to him, he suddenly stilled. Collette said that she hadn't been able to wake him. But I could. He responded to my voice."

"Did he say anything important during the nightmare?"

"Collette said that he always talks about saving them. It must be the building that was on fire that he couldn't get to and rescue the women and children." Katherine tucked her chin. The image would stay with her for a long time.

"Did he hit you?"

"No."

"Did he push you?"

"No. Although when Thomas tried to hold him down, he got up and knocked Thomas over."

"But he didn't push you? Knock you over?"

"No."

Katherine began to understand. Jean-Michel wasn't Randall.

Grandmother nodded to her. "Sounds to me like the only one dealing with 'violence' is Jean-Michel. And he's got to give that over to the Lord before he can heal."

Katherine nodded. "You know, I'm afraid Jean-Michel doesn't know God. But I'm *not* afraid of him or his terrors."

"Good. I'm glad you finally understand that. *He's* afraid — the events of the past have terrified him."

She closed her eyes and cringed. The other night she'd jerked her hand back from him. His sudden touch — although innocent — had unnerved her. She'd allowed her thoughts to go to an unpleasant place — that old place of fear.

She took a deep breath. "I think I truly do understand now. I've allowed fear a constant place in my life. And yet you've been telling me again and again that true love casts out fear. I was thinking that meant I had to rely on Jean-Michel to cast out my fear. But you meant God's true love, didn't you?"

She trusted Jean-Michel. As much as she trusted the beloved woman beside her. He wasn't a new friend in her life. They had a long history. But every time anything threatened her — reminded her of Randall — she allowed that fear to come in. And fear wasn't trusting God. Fear wasn't of the Lord. Fear *was* unbelief. And she knew better than that — she'd learned and grown a lot. She was a new creation.

Lord, help my unbelief, and please help Jean-Michel to not be trapped by the past. He needs You, Father. Show me how to reach him with Your love.

22

August 1

The beautiful morning light erased the shadows in Jean-Michel's room.

For the first time in years, he didn't feel weighed down by the past as he awoke to a new day.

Thomas — that amazing young man — had stayed with him for hours. Even pulled a small Bible out of his pocket and spoke Scripture after Scripture to Jean-Michel until the truth had finally sunk into his heart.

All this time he'd relied on himself. Thought that Collette needed saving. That Katherine needed saving. When in fact, it was *he* who needed saving.

Papa would be proud. His son had finally sought God.

Did he know? If he did, Jean-Michel was sure his earthly father would be rejoicing.

He finished dressing and picked up his cane. He needed a long walk — away from everything and everyone. Exercise to strengthen his leg and clear his head.

Collette still slept in the other room, and he didn't expect her to wake for hours, since he'd kept her up so late last night with his issues. He'd just leave her a note and meet her for lunch. Hopefully Katherine too — if she'd ever speak to him again after yesterday. But he couldn't wait to tell her. He wanted to talk about it all with the love of his life.

Lord, please help her to forgive me and know that I'm not like her dead husband. I want to cherish her and love her.

The ridge across the tracks from the hotel was Deadhorse Hill. He'd seen John trek up it several times already this summer, and Jean-Michel thought he had enough to work through that the hike would be good for him.

A fresh breeze blew down from the mountains and through the trees. By the time it reached Jean-Michel, the sun had warmed it just enough to make it pleasant. He'd once heard John Ivanoff say the mountain — Denali — made its own weather. It was so massive and so tall it created forces that played out in storms of wind and rain . . .

even snow in summer months wasn't impossible.

As he moved slowly up the hill, he pulled Father's letter out of his pocket. The well-worn sheets of paper felt comforting in his hands, and he reread each line.

Putting the letter back in his pocket, Jean-Michel chewed on the words left by the man he respected most in the world. Now it all made sense — why his father would plead with him and Collette to seek God. There had been a difference in Father the last few months of his life. He'd seemed serene and at peace. Happier even, and he hadn't been happy since losing his wife, their beloved mother. God must have been the source of that peace.

"Hello, up there!"

He turned around. John Ivanoff hiked up the hill toward him.

"*Bonjour,* John. It's good to see you."

"It's a lovely morning, isn't it?" John smiled and shifted the rifle from his shoulder. "I noticed you walking up here and thought I'd join you for a little bit. It's not good to come alone or unarmed." He wasn't at all reprimanding, just pointing out a fact. "What brings you out so early this morning?"

John couldn't have known what door his

question would open. Jean-Michel decided to be honest and stop mincing words around this man. "I couldn't sleep. Had a severe night terror last night — reliving a memory from war — and knocked Thomas across the room." There . . . he'd said it. More like *blurted* it out.

The older man's eyebrows rose. "Want to talk about it?"

Nodding, Jean-Michel kept climbing. "The nightmares have been much worse now since the fire." He pointed to his leg. "You see, when I was in battle — when I was injured — there was a fire. It killed a lot of people. I can't ever seem to forget their faces."

"That's understandable."

"But last night, Thomas stayed with me. He shared his faith, and for the first time, it all made sense."

John stepped with his hands behind his back. "That is wonderful news!"

"The truth is, I came to Alaska — to America, in all actuality — to be able to save someone else from the fear and horrible life she'd endured."

"You came to save Katherine?" The man's question wasn't pushy or arrogant. Just simple. To the point.

"Yes. Her grandmother asked me." He

pulled letters out of his pocket. "It might have been her letter that prodded me to leave France and pursue life again, but I know now that it wasn't for me to save Katherine. It was so the Lord could save *me*."

John nodded and kept climbing up the hill. Slow and steady.

Jean-Michel could do nothing but follow and shove the letters back in his pocket. What was the man thinking?

"So the only reason you came to Alaska was to 'save' Katherine?"

"Yes. But Thomas helped me to see last night that I can't be anyone's savior."

"He's right. And from what you're telling me, I understand you've come to know the true Savior?" John stopped and turned toward him.

"*Oui.* And I've never felt peace like this before."

"But I can see there is something still troubling you." John placed a hand on his shoulder. "Faith isn't always easy. You're not going to have all the answers at once, so if you need to talk to someone, I'll be here for you."

The words touched a place deep in his heart. The man before him reminded him so much of his own father. "Do you mind if we sit for a while, then?"

"Not at all." John walked a few steps up the hill until he reached some logs. Obviously left for seating.

This man could be trusted, Jean-Michel knew that, and now he wanted to learn as much as he could. "The thing I'm struggling with now — is the loss of my friends. The ones who saved me — they sacrificed themselves for me, and I don't understand why God would allow that. They loved Him and I didn't."

"Son, the Bible tells us in John chapter fifteen, verse thirteen, that 'Greater love hath no man than this, that a man lay down his life for his friends.' "

"You're saying they loved me enough to do it. They knew . . ."

"Yes. I believe they did."

John's words made Jean-Michel's head swim. Closing his eyes, a memory washed over him.

"Stay with us, friend. Just a little farther."
George's voice.

His own voice mumbled something he couldn't understand.

"They've spotted us, George. Look out!" Luc pulled faster.

"I'm all right if it's my time to die, my friend. But we know that Jean-Michel is not. Do you

hear me, Jean-Michel? I'm talking about you. Stay awake. You've been holding God at arm's length for too long. And if today is the day you're going to meet your Maker, you need to be ready." It was George again. Pleading with him.

Jean-Michel could feel their arms dragging him. Heard Luc say a prayer for him. The two quoted a verse to him about God sending His Son because He loved the world so that everyone could have everlasting life.

Thwump! Thwump!

He swayed and jerked after the shots. And then he fell. Everything went black.

"Son, you okay?" John stood over him with a hand on Jean-Michel's shoulder. "Are you all right?"

He blinked. He wasn't in Syria. He was in Alaska.

All this time, he hadn't remembered that part of the worst day of his life. Not until now. "You were right. They knew they would probably be killed coming to save me, but they did it anyway."

John sat back down and leaned his elbows on his knees. "That's what true friendship is — what true love is. Laying down one's own life for another."

"They told me I wasn't ready to die."

330

"No, you weren't."

"But I am now." And he meant it. God had done a mighty work in him.

A knock on the door made Cassidy grin. Even if the delivery boy was just coming with the newspaper, it was a welcome distraction. "Come in."

Katherine Demarchis walked in with a half smile. "I hope I'm not intruding."

"Not a bit. I was just hoping for something to take my mind off this bed rest."

Her new friend closed the door. "Well, then, I'll be happy to oblige."

Cassidy pointed to the desk in the corner. "Feel free to bring that chair over here. I forgot to ask Allan to bring it over this morning before he left." She clasped her hands in her ever-shrinking lap. "How are you doing?"

"Well. And you?"

The only way to get past the mundane chitchat was to dive right into honesty. "I feel like I'm about to explode, but the doctor assures me that won't happen. Although he does say I'm quite large for my first child, so maybe we were off on the time frame and I'll have this baby sooner." She shrugged. "That would delight me to no end, but no matter what, I'm happy."

331

Katherine fidgeted in the chair and looked out the window.

"Is something bothering you?"

Her honey-colored hair shone in the sunlight — like a halo as she shook her head. Then a single tear slipped down her cheek.

Cassidy's heart clenched. While they'd only talked a little, she knew that this woman had been through some very difficult circumstances. "Please. Let me help."

She sniffed and focused her brown eyes back on Cassidy. "Grandmother says it's best to be honest, and that the only way I'll learn how to have a deep relationship is to open up, but I find it very difficult." She took a deep breath. "You see, Randall — my deceased husband — was a cruel man. And not just with his words. I couldn't let anyone know the truth. I was too embarrassed and he threatened me, so I kept everything to myself."

"That's understandable, but I hope you know you can trust me. And if you don't yet, I'll pray that we can build our relationship so you feel comfortable."

"Thank you." Katherine sniffed. "I do trust you, though. It's just hard to let things out." She lowered her head and said nothing for what seemed minutes. Cassidy whispered a prayer for God to give the woman strength to say what she'd come to say.

"I've come so far. I have. I'm not afraid like I was. Grandmother has helped me to see that God loves me and will heal me of all those terrible things I went through.

"But this is something else. You see, I always wanted children. In fact, I convinced myself I could put up with almost anything my husband did if I could just have a child. Then one day I learned I was expecting. I was so excited. I thought it would change Randall — that he would be kinder, gentler. And at first it seemed he might, but it was not to be.

"After one particularly bad 'scolding' — as Randall put it — I was in bad shape. He had . . . beaten me . . . kicked me as I lay on the floor. I began to bleed and a doctor was called. He told the doctor I had fallen down the stairs. I passed out from the pain." She raised her head. There were tears in her eyes.

"Later, when I woke up, Randall told me I had lost the baby and the doctor said I could never have children." Tears slipped down and she wiped them with a handkerchief. "He called me wretched names and told me how it was just one more way I had

333

failed him." She paused again and seemed to regain her composure after several deep breaths.

"Oh, Katherine. I'm so sorry."

"He almost seemed pleased to tell me the news. But I felt like my heart had been shredded to pieces. I felt guilty for wanting a child so much. Wanting someone to hold and to love . . . someone to protect. Then I realized I could never protect anyone . . . not from that monster. I was selfish to want a baby so badly."

Her heart ached for the beautiful woman before her. "It wasn't selfish, Katherine. Not at all."

The young woman straightened. "I still long for a child of my own — to love — but that can never be."

"But you have a second chance at love. You never know what God can do."

Katherine nodded. "I now understand that God loves me and made me who I am. I admit that I care for Jean-Michel greatly — he's the only man I ever loved. But what if he can't get past the fact that I can't have children? I know he's always wanted them. We talked about it a lot when we were younger." Katherine stood and walked around the bed pacing.

"You are beautiful, Katherine. Do you

know that — really *know* it? You are one of the most beautiful women I've ever met. And one man — one evil man — cannot overrule what God made you to be." She paused and bit her lip. The thoughts that entered her mind when Katherine was telling her story made her want to jump out of the bed and give Senator Demarchis a piece of her mind. She'd never even met the man, but Cassidy felt such rage — even hatred for him and what he'd done. She took a deep breath. *Forgive me, Lord, for such horrid thoughts. I know it's not my place to judge him.* It was a good thing too.

A thought came to mind out of nowhere. "Katherine, how do we know that what the doctor even said was true? Or that he ever even said it? The doctor didn't tell you directly, did he?"

"No." Her face lit up a little. "In fact, I never saw the doctor while I was awake. Randall only allowed him to come that once . . . when I was unconscious." She shook a little and walked back to the chair. "You think Randall convinced the doctor to tell him that? Or . . ." She stiffened and lowered her brow. "He lied to me. To hurt me." Her face paled with the revelation.

"I'm so sorry."

A bitter laugh filled the air. "I wouldn't

have thought in my younger years that anyone could think or act the way Randall did, but now that I know, I wouldn't put such deception beyond him."

"It sounds to me that the man spoke only lies. Maybe this was one of them." She reached for Katherine's hand.

"Oh, Cassidy, I don't want to get my hopes up."

Cassidy felt the fire within her burn hot. "But our hope is in God. Not man."

The woman's eyes filled with tears again. This needed prayer. And lots of it.

"You are a beautiful child of God and He loves you so much."

"I know that, and I'm hoping Jean-Michel will still love me too. But it scares me. I have battled fear and darkness every day for far too long."

"I'll help you win the battle with prayer. I don't think Jean-Michel needs much encouragement either."

"Well, he also feels responsible for Collette. I think she tried his patience a lot on the trip here."

"But I do see some progress in her, especially after her chats with little Davey."

"Davey has had a better influence on her than any of the adults." Katherine laughed.

Cassidy loved that she and Katherine were

becoming closer but she worried about what Mrs. Harrison thought. "I understand your grandmother wasn't excited about you spending time with the staff. I'm not putting you in any kind of situation by . . . well . . ."

"Being my friend? No. Don't let Grandmother's comment discourage you. She's one of the most genuine people you'll ever meet but she's of that generation where they didn't fraternize with the servants. In Europe, when we lived there, they were always called that, but here we like to use the word 'staff' now. Grandmother needs to adjust to how the times are changing. And they are changing . . . a lot."

The idea of being referred to as a "servant" made Cassidy giggle. She'd always thought of her position at the Curry Hotel as a prestigious one, along with her father's and her husband's. What a different world Katherine had been raised in. "I'm glad you don't have a problem with it, Katherine. I wouldn't want to cause you any shame." No need to tell her that her own husband, Allan, was quite wealthy as well. They enjoyed their simple life.

"Not at all." Katherine finally seemed to relax. She smiled. "I am honored to be your friend."

"Thank you, Mrs. Demarchis."

"You are most welcome, Mrs. Brennan. Now what should we do about Collette?"

23

August 1

Walking the long hallways of the hotel helped Katherine think. Cassidy was amazing. And a friend. It had been a long time since Katherine had a real friend. But when Allan came in to check on his wife, Katherine had been a little uncomfortable. The couple's love for each other was plain, and Allan seemed perfectly at ease kissing his wife in front of others and waiting on her hand and foot.

Katherine's experience being married was nothing like what she witnessed here, and definitely not like her parents' relationship either. They had been distant with each other and definitely not affectionate. But when John came in and joined the conversation, he told some funny story about when Cassidy's mother was pregnant and they'd all laughed. What struck Katherine the most was that the older man clearly still loved his wife and she'd been gone for at least two decades. The time was short with the men visiting, but Katherine found herself longing to see more.

Was that how real marriages worked?

Katherine slowly descended the stairs, lost in her thoughts. Her own mother and father hadn't been all that interested in each other. Katherine couldn't even say for sure that they shared any common interests — except for her. She thought again of Cassidy and her husband. There was such a gentleness in the way Allan spoke to her . . . touched her. It proved to her that love could exist — that it wasn't just a fleeting little-girl notion, as her mother had suggested.

And that thought brought her back to Jean-Michel. Her feelings for him had been so much more than notions. Much more so now. When they were younger, he had been the first person she thought of upon waking and the last one on her mind when falling asleep. Always there were the butterflies in her stomach, the longing to see him, talk to him, touch him.

The stark realization hit her. Those feelings were stronger now than ever. Especially since she'd given up her fear.

She headed into the dining room and

hoped she could find Jean-Michel. There were a lot of things she needed to tell him.

"Katherine."

His voice sent a shiver up her spine. This one warmed her — made her feel young again. She turned to find Jean-Michel watching her from where he stood.

"Good afternoon." Heat rushed up her neck.

He crossed the short distance between them. Smiling down at her, he extended his hand. It was as if he were asking permission to touch her. Katherine smiled and put her hand in his.

His smile broadened. "Would you take a walk with me? There's so much I need to say."

"I was just coming to find you for the very same reason." She held his gaze, unwilling to look away. For so long this was the face that had carried her through bad times. "I'd love to."

He held out his arm for her.

As they strolled out of the hotel, she noticed his gait was stronger now — his limp less pronounced than it had been when she'd first seen him again. The thought thrilled her that he had been able to gain some of the strength back in his leg. His cane thumped a gentle rhythm on the train platform.

He led her down a path to a very pretty field of brilliant dark pink flowers. "They call this fire weed, and I think it's beautiful." Jean-Michel stopped and turned toward her. "But not nearly as beautiful as you, *mon amour.*"

The compliment made her blush. "Thank you."

His face turned serious. "I need to tell you so many things, but this is difficult, so please give me some time."

"Of course." She sat on a bench positioned perfectly to see the flowers and the river and hoped she could keep her stomach from turning itself inside out. "I have quite a bit I would like to tell you as well. But please, go first."

He sat next to her but kept his face to the river. "Katherine, I have loved you for so long. But I know how imperfect I am. I am not whole. I always thought it was you who would make me whole, but I know now that it was God I needed. My father found God before he died, and he wrote Collette and me letters urging us to find Him for ourselves. I was angry at everything that happened during the war and didn't think I needed God. But I was wrong."

Silence covered them for several moments,

and Katherine watched the profile of his face.

"Collette began to understand God when she rescued little Davey. Can you imagine? She had a six-year-old teaching her where her older brother could not." He shook his head. "But I am happy for her. I'm also very pleased you have turned to Him as well. I must admit I was angered at first by your note when you left to go north. But I am stubborn. And God had His work cut out for Him.

"I feel like a changed man already, but you know . . . you witnessed . . ." A deep breath and his shoulders sagged a bit. "You've seen the depth of my anguish in reliving these nightmares. It isn't pretty, and I am so sorry I didn't tell you the truth about them before. Can you ever forgive me, Katherine? I never . . . never wish to hurt you." He rubbed the thigh of his injured leg as she'd often seen him do. "But I can't promise I won't have those nightmares again or how I will react to them. I can only pray and leave it in the Almighty's hands."

She reached out and stilled his nervous action. Intertwining their fingers, she rested their hands in her lap. A sigh escaped Jean-Michel's lips.

"I will love and cherish you for the rest of my days, but I come to you as a damaged man. And you need to know the difficulties." Jean-Michel turned toward her, his green eyes piercing her very heart. "Can you give me another chance?"

She rubbed the top of his hand with her thumb. "Of course I will. But just as you are damaged, so am I." Looking away, Katherine knew she'd never make it through if she stared into his eyes. "You already know that Randall was cruel to me. It wasn't just with his words. He . . . beat me as well. Sometimes — quite severely."

"I wish I could take away that pain. I would never hurt you —"

"I know that. I do." She bit her lip. "As much as I long for us to build our relationship again, Jean-Michel, there's something very important I need to tell you. It's not easy for me to say." Deep breaths . . . she could get through this. And what Cassidy said earlier might also be true. She had to cling to that hope.

"Go on."

"I may not be able to have children."

His face looked like she'd hit him in the stomach. And she might as well have. What man wanted to hear that the woman he loved couldn't bear him any children? With his free hand he did a quick swipe down his face and then he looked back to the river. His silence spoke volumes.

He'd never marry her now.

Words wouldn't come. How could an amazing woman like Katherine survive all this? She was only twenty-five years old and had endured so much.

Why God? What do I say to her?

In his own twenty-nine years, he'd seen horrors firsthand. But he hadn't had to live them like she had. What had that man done to her? His thoughts went to places they shouldn't.

Rage filled him, but he couldn't let it get a grip on him. He knew better than that.

When he turned back to face her, the beautiful smile he'd seen earlier was gone. In its place was a mask of defeat. He'd done that, hadn't he?

He took both of her hands in his and swallowed. "My sweet Katherine, it doesn't matter to me if you can't have children. My love for you will not change."

The sheen of tears glistened in her eyes as she shook her head. "Don't say that to make me feel better, don't. I know how much children mean to you. I remember you telling me that you wanted a houseful."

"But not if you aren't there by my side. Can't you see? God has given us a second chance. He's brought us through fire. And even though we might have only ashes left, I believe we can build from here."

"Truly?" Her face brightened.

"*Oui.* We should do things properly, though."

She raised her eyebrows.

"We know so much about each other from the past, but we need to get to know one another again — the new Katherine and the new Jean-Michel. I want to take our time — all the time you need so that you build trust in me and know that I will take care of you. That I will never treat you as the senator did."

A brief nod and then she tucked her lip between her teeth like she did when they were younger and she was afraid to ask something.

"What is it? Ask anything."

She hesitated, then finally spoke. "Do you . . . have the bad memories every night?"

"I used to have them most every night. Coming here, however, I found some relief — until the fire. But today John Ivanoff prayed for me. I've never felt anything like it. God has the power to help me. I know

346

He does. If He chooses to take away the nightmares, I will be blessed. If He doesn't . . ."

"Then we will get through them together." Her face flushed and she covered her mouth.

He smirked at her — knowing full well that her thoughts had taken her toward marriage. The thought made him very happy. At least she wasn't scared of him.

"I'm sorry. That was very forward of me."

"I like it when you're straightforward like that." He waggled his eyebrows at her.

"Well, then, you should know that I very much want to be held by you — kissed by you." She held up a hand. "But not today. It might take me a while to be ready."

"I've waited all these years, Katherine. I'll wait a hundred more if you'll have me."

24

August 12

Life wasn't fair.

Davey and his family were gone.

Jean-Michel spent all his time either exercising, with Katherine, or with John and Allan.

Collette had picked and pressed enough flowers for bookmarks that she never wanted to see another one in her lifetime. Well, maybe it wasn't quite that drastic, but it felt that way and she was bored.

She'd never make it on bed rest like poor Cassidy.

Maybe she shouldn't have introduced Katherine to Cassidy. Not only was the beautiful widow taking up time with her brother, but she and Mrs. Brennan always had way more to talk about and Collette ended up feeling left out.

That was the problem.

Again, she realized just how selfish she was. But was it too much to ask to have a little attention centered on her again?

With a sigh, she stomped down the stairs to the dining room for luncheon. She had thought America was going to be so exciting. But the most exciting thing this week was the baby moose she saw down by the river. And it was ugly. Why did all the others think it was so cute?

She tapped her forehead with her hand. There she went again. Why must she always revert to her selfish and superficial ways?

Willing the horrible thoughts away, Collette pasted on a smile. Cassidy told her to pray every time she needed help with her attitude or words, so Collette shot a quick prayer heavenward.

Jean-Michel stood as she approached their table and held out the chair for her. *"Chère sœur."* He kissed her cheeks. "Please join us. I'm so glad you made it down. I was just telling Katherine and Mrs. Harrison about a horseback trip into the park I'd like to take next week with John and Allan."

She sat in her chair and placed her napkin in her lap. "That sounds nice."

"We will be gone several days, but I've been told the views of the mountains and glaciers are spectacular."

A lovely plate of luncheon was set before her by their waiter. Collette wondered what it would be like to travel by horseback for several days. "Will your leg be up for the rigors, *frère*?"

"I believe so." He smiled. In fact, he looked more like a little boy than her grown brother. The trip obviously excited him.

She dabbed her napkin at the corners of her mouth. "These berries are delicious."

Katherine leaned closer to her. "They're called salmonberries. Isn't that an interesting name?"

Collette nodded. "Very . . . what is the word? *Aqueux?* Um . . . like water?"

"Watery?" Katherine lifted her brows. "That was exactly what I thought. Like a strawberry, but much more . . . watery."

Laughter rounded the table.

Collette looked back to her brother. "So what will you do on this trip?"

"Obviously ride horses." He took a sip of his coffee. "But also we will look for wildlife, fish, and even walk on a glacier."

"A glacier? How interesting." A new thought invaded Collette's mind and it wouldn't let go. She set her fork down for a moment. "I think I would like to go on this expedition as well." There. She'd said it. Perhaps a bit too loudly, as several people turned to look at their table, but she'd said it nonetheless. If her injured brother could handle the trip, so could she.

Jean-Michel blinked several times at her. "We will be staying in tents, Collette. You've never done that."

"I can learn."

Mrs. Harrison pointed her knife in Collette's direction. "There will be bears, dear. You don't want to disrupt the creatures. Best to leave this trip to the men."

The older woman obviously didn't know that her words would only convince Collette to go. No matter the difficulty. It didn't matter that the thought of bears and sleeping in tents overwhelmed her a bit.

"Collette." Jean-Michel tilted his head. He knew exactly what she was thinking, and so he should. "I've seen that face before. Please. Don't."

"We came here to see Alaska, did we not? You've been on several little expeditions around here while I have done nothing but take a trip down the river. And it wasn't a pleasant one at that."

"And what will you wear, dear girl?" Mrs. Harrison asked. "Did you bring a riding outfit? You can hardly go out into the wilderness on horseback dressed like this."

Collette looked down at her pretty dress.

It had been made just before they'd left for America. The slim straight-lined fashion suited her and made her feel grown-up, but the older woman had a point.

"I will borrow a riding outfit from one of the workers here. If that fails, I shall find a young man as small as me and borrow his trousers."

Mrs. Harrison almost choked on her water. As she covered her mouth with her napkin, Collette recognized the twinkle in the older woman's eyes. "I fear you have a situation on your hands, young man."

Collette turned to Katherine. "Won't you go as well?" She desperately needed an ally.

"No, thank you. I think I will stay here for Cassidy. It's getting harder and harder for her to stay in bed."

"It's the nesting time." Mrs. Harrison nodded. "Happens to every woman. She wants to be up and about preparing for the baby." The older woman looked back at Collette. "Wouldn't you rather stay here and make more bookmarks with Cassidy? I've seen the ones you've made, and they're just glorious. I've even purchased several to take home to friends."

A groan left her lips. Not another bookmark. Please. She sat up straighter and stiffened her shoulders as she lifted her chin.

Just enough to show Jean-Michel she meant business. "I'm finished with bookmarks. I would like to speak to the guides about this trip. I *will* be going along."

August 14

Thomas checked the tents for any tears and looked to his mentor. "Are you sure this is a good idea?"

John shook his head. "You know the tourists these days, Thomas. We can't tell them much if they are unwilling to listen. As soon as Collette said she wanted to go, I had three more women wanting to sign up for the trip to join their husbands. Mr. Bradley says they can handle it, so it's our job to make sure they enjoy it. Even if I do think that having Miss Langelier along just might spell disaster."

The beautiful French girl was about his age, but Thomas didn't understand how the wealthy lived. It always amazed him how much luggage they brought, the shoes they wore, and of course, the crazy outfits they insisted were the style for outings such as the excursions they took. One woman brought her umbrella on one of the short horseback rides and nearly terrified the poor animal when she opened it.

Now they would be going deeper into the park where everything was far more rustic and primitive. There would be no afternoon teas or staff to wait upon them. Worse still, no private accommodations for personal needs. They would have to make all of this clear before the start of the trip, but Thomas had a feeling it wouldn't matter. They would all declare it a great adventure, sure to be fun. As if they knew what it would be like to traipse through tundra grass that was thigh-high or climb craggy rocks. He shook his head. Life must be *very* different in the world in which they lived.

Packing the tent in the special manner John taught him, Thomas thought more about Collette. She was beautiful. And he really liked her brother. But she always seemed dissatisfied, as if she were busting at the seams for something new every day. Like she was bored with life.

Thomas didn't think he'd ever been bored in all of his twenty years. In fact, he could remember plenty of times where he wished he *could* be bored. It was wonderful to work hard and to be busy, but yes, he longed for days where he could lounge around and sip drinks, order food from a fine restaurant, and be waited on hand and foot. The thought made him laugh.

"What's tickled your funny bone?" John was packing up snowshoes for their trek to Ruth Glacier and he smiled over at Thomas.

"I thought for a brief moment about how nice it would be to live as the rich do with people waiting on me."

"Why is that so funny?"

Thomas felt his face flush. "Can you see me holding a cup of tea with one hand — my pinky in the air? I'd probably end up trying to serve dinner."

"That would be a sight to see!" Allan's steady voice came from the doorway. "Good morning, gentlemen. I see we are preparing for our trip into the park. So I'm assuming it's still on? No one got scared and canceled?"

"Afraid not." John sighed. "We've had four more people sign up, and I told Mr. Bradley that was all we could handle."

Allan's eyebrows rose. "Oh, boy. How many total?"

"It started out as three, plus us. Now there are twelve guests plus the three of us, which makes fifteen total." John knelt by the stack of snowshoes and wound rope in a figure eight pattern around his wrist and elbow. "The three of us are going to have to share a tent. We'll have the four women in the large tent and the men can sleep in the other three. Thomas, I'm going to need you to go see Mrs. Johnson and ask for extra bread for sandwiches and anything else that we can carry and don't have to cook. It's going to take a lot to feed everyone for a week. We already planned to fish, so make sure she includes some salt and pepper. You know what we'll need."

"Yes, sir." He jumped up. "The tents are all packed and I've just checked all the sleeping cots over there. Next to the cots we also have five of those . . . what did you call them? . . . Euklisia Rugs — in case some of the men want to sleep on the ground."

"Wonderful, Thomas. Thank you." John stood and patted him on the shoulder. "Oh, and could you check and see if Mrs. Johnson has any of those sweet rolls left? It may take a few of those to keep us going today."

"Yes, sir." Thomas's stomach growled at the thought of the sweet and sticky pastries Mrs. Johnson was famous for. Well, if he admitted it, she was famous for a lot of different things. So was Cassidy.

Thoughts of his friend made him wonder how she was doing. Cassidy was never one to sit still, so all this bed rest must be driving her batty. He'd promised to visit her as often as he could, but since he'd been helping fill in for her, his time had been short.

He hadn't seen her in about a week. Maybe he should try to check in with her today after he spoke with the head chef.

Allan and John kept him up to date on how she was doing, but he sure would like to see her for himself.

As he trekked from the gear shed back to the hotel, he remembered what it had been like when he first came to the Curry. Cassidy had been his champion many times over. Saving him from Mrs. Johnson's or Mr. Bradley's wrath when he was overly clumsy, or just sticking up for him and cheering him on.

A memory trickled in of one particularly disastrous day when the head chef had yelled at him something fierce. Granted, he'd made a huge mess, but it was Cassidy who'd helped him through it.

"We all go through that stage, but I was an exceptionally clumsy child . . . and I loved to hug. Always have, really. And not just people. I hugged our dogs, the pigs, chickens. I even tried to hug a squirrel once. That one didn't go over too well with the squirrel, I'm sorry to say."

Thomas had snickered at the thought of Cassidy imposing her love on the squirrel, but she hadn't minded. Instead she'd continued explaining her own clumsiness.

357

"Anyway, after I would fall down, my dad would say, 'I guess the floor needed a hug.' I can't tell you how many times I hugged the floor . . . or the stairs . . . or a rock, a log, or the grass."

Yep. Cassidy had been the first real friend he'd ever had. For a brief time that first summer, he'd fancied himself in love with her, but she was older and fell in love with Allan. And Thomas was happy for them — he loved Allan and John and was so thankful for their mentoring in his life.

Now, he realized his relationship with Cassidy was special. She was like his big sister. And he'd never had a sibling. He'd been an orphan and all alone until Mr. Bradley hired him.

The Curry was his family now and he wouldn't trade it for the world. He'd become a man here, grown out of his clumsiness, and learned a new trade.

He made his way into the kitchen and sneaked up behind Cook. "Good morning, Mrs. Johnson."

She jumped and put a hand over her heart. "Thomas! You . . . you . . . !"

He leaned down and hugged the woman. She looked like she needed it today. "I was just remembering how much love you've poured into me all these years. Thank you."

Her anger quickly deflated in her eyes and her cheeks turned pink. Every once in a while, he got a glimpse of her softer side. "You do beat all." She hugged him back and stiffened again into her drill-sergeant mode. "Quick, would you like to take a few of those sweet rolls before they're all gone?"

"I thought you'd never ask." He wrapped them up in a tea towel. "Mr. Ivanoff and Mr. Brennan sent me over here to talk to you about the food for this excursion. We've got fifteen people to feed for a week, and since it's so hot and dry, he doesn't want to do too much cooking over a fire — maybe one meal a day at the most. He asked for simple things we could bring with us, like extra bread for sandwiches, crackers, cheese, jerky, you know the drill."

"I certainly do." She shook her head. "It'll be extra work, but I'll make some of those bars you like so much. The ones with the nuts and honey. That will be easy to pack and hold hunger at bay. I'll get the girls working on it all right away."

Thomas glanced around the kitchen. "Where's your helper?"

"You mean that abominable Scotsman?"

Thomas couldn't help grinning. "I heard you two arguing early this morning. It sounded pretty bad. You haven't sent him packing, have you?" He leaned closer. "Or done him in?"

Mrs. Johnson harrumphed. "Would that I could. It still may come to that. The man is the most irritating human being in the world. Thinks he knows it all and has the audacity to suggest my ways are old and outdated."

"Well, yelling doesn't seem to be helping your situation . . . maybe you should try sweet-talking him." Thomas watched in amusement as his comment flustered Mrs. Johnson into momentary silence. It wouldn't last.

"Of all the . . . ridiculous . . . outrageous . . ." She sputtered out several other words that Thomas wasn't even sure of the meaning of before shaking her finger at him. "You'd better never make such a suggestion again. You aren't too big for me to turn over my knee."

Thomas forced down his laughter at the thought of the much smaller woman trying to accomplish such a deed.

"Sorry, Mrs. Johnson." But, of course, he wasn't.

She regained her composure. "Are you all still planning on leaving in the morning?"

"Yes, ma'am."

"Well, then, we'll get right to it. Now scoot

out of here before I put you to work."

He leaned in and whispered, "Thanks for the sweet rolls. You're the best."

"Get on with ya." Her voice was gruff, but Thomas saw the slight shimmy of her mouth. That woman worked so hard not to laugh or smile — he loved seeing her tough veneer crack.

Thomas practically ran up the stairs and over to the building where a lot of the staff lived. Cassidy and Allan's new cottage awaited, but the doctor said she couldn't move into it until she had the baby. When he came to their room, the door was open and Cassidy was all propped up in her bed. Mrs. Demarchis sat in a chair, visiting with her.

"Good morning, Mrs. Demarchis . . . Cassidy."

Cassidy lifted her arms in greeting. "Thomas! How nice to see you. I feel like it's been ages."

"I'm sorry, I know I promised to visit more often, but the hotel has been very busy. How are you doing?"

"As well as can be expected when you're the size of a Zeppelin. If I were allowed out of this room, I'm sure I'd cast a shadow over Denali."

Thomas grinned. "You say the silliest

things. Say, did you know they're finally allowing Germany to start making Zeppelins again? They plan to have transatlantic flights before the year is out. Can you imagine it? Maybe they'll even use them to fly people up here. Wouldn't that be something?"

"It would be." She shifted in the bed. Apparently not an easy feat.

"Can I help?" Thomas asked, stepping closer.

"No. Nothing will until I finally have this baby." Cassidy rubbed her stomach. "So what are you doing today?"

"Finishing our preparations for tomorrow." He looked to Katherine. "We're taking a group out into the park to camp."

Mrs. Demarchis nodded. "I know. Collette tried her best to convince me to go along."

"Yes. I think she's in for a surprise. I can't imagine she'll like it." He wrinkled his nose.

"You might be surprised." Mrs. Demarchis tilted her head. "Collette has been quite bored, and this might very well be the diversion she's needed. Well, then, if you'll excuse me, I should go check on my grandmother. She hasn't been feeling very well of late."

"Of course, but do come back soon." Cassidy smiled. "Please leave the door open as you leave."

Once Mrs. Demarchis was gone, Thomas relaxed. "You don't think I gave her the idea that I talk about guests behind their backs? Do you?"

"I think she understands your concerns, Thomas. I wouldn't worry about it. Now, why don't you have a seat and tell me what's going on in the kitchen. Mrs. Johnson has stormed in and out of my room on multiple occasions to declare Mr. Ferguson to be the bane of her existence. I'd like to hear from someone else how things are going between them."

"Well, this might help put it into perspective. This morning when I went to let her know about the food supplies we'd need for the trip — Daniel was nowhere to be seen. I asked Mrs. Johnson if she'd done him in."

Cassidy giggled and covered her mouth.

"She hadn't, but she made it clear that it still may come to that."

"Oh, dear." Cassidy reached for a hankie. "Poor Mrs. Johnson."

"Ha. I'd say it's poor Daniel. You and I have both been on the receiving end of Mrs. Johnson's wrath."

She nodded and laughed. "Indeed we have. Just remind her next time that he's only here for a short while — just a few more weeks."

Thomas shook his head. "At this rate, we may not have a few weeks, but by then I'll be back in Fairbanks."

"I'm so glad things are going well with school. Even happier that you seem to love it so."

"I do. I never knew learning could be so much fun."

"I am surprised, however, that you haven't met any special young lady."

Thomas looked toward the floor. "I've met some very nice young ladies, but I'm not going to let myself get interested."

"Why not?"

He shrugged and looked back up. "You know it's hard to live out here. It's not for just anybody, and I don't intend to live anywhere else. I figure it'd be best to just get my schooling done and then come back here. I was talking about this to your dad before I left last year. He said it was smart to wait and let God bring the right one to me."

"Sounds like Dad. He's full of wisdom, and it's to your benefit to listen. I'm sure that when the time is right, Thomas, God will bring you the perfect mate. She'll be beautiful and kindhearted and love Alaska."

He nodded and got to his feet. "And God."

Cassidy smiled. "And for certain, she'll love God."

Footsteps pounded down the hall. Then a maid dashed around the corner. "Thomas, Mrs. Johnson asked you to come quick." Her breath let out in a whoosh.

"Don't tell me . . . she's fighting with Mr. Ferguson again."

"Um . . . yes, but this time is different."

25

Katherine stood on tiptoe and kissed Jean-Michel on the cheek. "Have a wonderful time."

Surprise lit his face. "Thank you. I will. I'd like to make a request."

"Go ahead."

"Would you pray for . . . us . . . you and me this week? Maybe write some notes down about your hopes and dreams for the future? The Lord has blessed us with this fresh start, and I want to do it right. And together."

She felt her face flush. "I'd love to. Thank you for asking."

He tipped his hat to her. "I'll see you in a week."

Standing on tiptoe once more, she reached up to kiss him again, but he was ready this time and caught it with his lips.

The brief contact sent tingles down her spine. Which was a good sign. She hoped her affectionate gesture hadn't been too forward, but the past few days she'd really worked at touching and hugging. It had been Grandmother's suggestion, and the older woman had been right. She'd only remembered what it was like to be touched by one person. He hadn't been nice or gentle, but that was all in the past. She needed to trust people around her to love her and be affectionate accordingly. Not everyone had intentions like Randall.

What she'd hoped would come easily to her, since she'd been an affectionate child, was more like having to learn how to walk all over again. She'd jerked a few times when someone touched her, was stiff when she hugged, and even tripped over her own feet at one point. This was harder than she'd thought. But Grandmother encouraged her to keep going. The only thing that kept her working on it was the fact that she loved Jean-Michel.

As long as she was wise in choosing the people she surrounded herself with, she knew she had trust and love. It had taken three years for her to become the old beaten-down Katherine; it might take another three to come out of it. But she was determined to try.

As the group crossed the river by boat with all their gear, Katherine waved. There were horses and more hands to help on the other side and they would start their great adventure.

Last night, she'd prayed with Jean-Michel. It was the first time they had prayed together, and it had set her heart on fire. To think that they could possibly soon start a life together, and they were beginning their new relationships with God as the center. Grandmother said there was no better place to start.

This morning, Katherine had prayed that Jean-Michel would continue to have healing in his heart. The scars would always remain, but she could already see a difference in his eyes since he'd given his life to the Lord. Prayerfully, the nightmares would be minimal on this trip.

And, hopefully, Collette would stay out of trouble.

Katherine wasn't sure what had gotten into the girl, but she'd been quite testy of late. They'd seen such great progress after she'd rescued little Davey, and now it seemed she was floundering again.

But the world was changing and the poor girl didn't know where she fit. Katherine understood that. After all, Collette had been pampered and spoiled and kept from the harshness of the world around her. Without her father in her life, the future would be very different for beautiful Collette. Jean-Michel would do his best for her, but he couldn't keep her from reality. And he'd shared with Katherine that he hoped Collette would marry soon and begin a life of her own. Katherine had asked for only one thing — that he not arrange a marriage for his sister. "Let her marry for love," Katherine begged. Jean-Michel had agreed.

The boat reached the other side of the river and Katherine turned back to the hotel. A visit with Cassidy was in order. The poor dear looked miserable in these last days, but the doctor thought she still had a month or so.

At least while Allan was gone, Katherine could keep the young mother-to-be company.

Passing through the dining room, she hoped to bring a tray from Mrs. Johnson up to her friend.

A conversation brought her up short.

"Amelia, I don't know what to say to you anymore. It's your own fault you're sick. God is punishing you for your sin and you know it. Sickness and hardship are always punishment." The tones that were hushed echoed across the almost empty room. The lady threw her napkin down on the table and stood. "I've had enough. I'm going home. Stay if you like, but I won't take care of you anymore."

Katherine dared a look to the table in the corner of the room as she kept walking. Two ladies, almost identical in looks, wore two opposite expressions. The one sitting looked defeated and pale, while the other stood red-faced, chin lifted and defiant.

Diverting her eyes, she couldn't get through the dining room fast enough. Soft sobs reached her as she pushed on the door to the main kitchen.

"Why, Mrs. Demarchis! Whatever are you doing in the kitchen?" Mrs. Johnson looked stunned.

Katherine put a hand to her stomach and took a deep breath. "I would like to bring a tray to Mrs. Brennan, since I'm headed up to visit with her. I thought I could spare you the trouble."

"How very kind of you." The woman's brows lowered. "Is something bothering you?"

"I'm not sure, but could you have the hotel manager check on the lady in the dining room, please? She's crying."

"Yes, ma'am. Of course." Mrs. Johnson sent one of the kitchen boys to fetch Mr. Bradley. "Let me get that tray together for you."

Katherine took her time walking to Cassidy's room. The tray was heavy, but she could handle it. It was more the weight of the words she'd overheard that kept her steps slow.

"It's your own fault you're sick. God is punishing you for your sin and you know it."

God didn't work that way . . . did He?

She knew that there were consequences for her sin, but it seemed awfully harsh for someone to say that.

While she hadn't gotten a really good look at the woman, she'd seen that the one called Amelia was indeed very thin and pale. The look of defeat in her eyes was one Katherine had seen in her own reflection many a time.

A horrible thought crept in. What if she didn't deserve love? What if her own sin had caused all the horrific events of the past to unfold? What if Randall was right and she couldn't have children? A greater punishment, Katherine couldn't even imagine. Could she have some other sin in her life that God would punish her for?

The thoughts made her stagger and

caused the old fear to come back.

No. Fear wasn't of the Lord. Grandmother kept telling her that, and she believed it. Katherine reminded herself of what happened in the cave. If she needed to put her foot down, she would. She couldn't help but wonder, however, about the exchange between the two women. Did God punish people for their sin? Even sin they'd repented of? What if they did something and didn't realize it was a sin?

When she made it to Cassidy's room, the decision was made. She'd just have to talk about it again.

Knocking on the door, Katherine inhaled deeply through her nose.

"Come in."

Katherine walked in and set the tray down. Before she lost her nerve she decided to just blurt it out. "Do you think God is punishing me for past sin and that's why Randall . . . why he . . . abused me?"

Her dark-haired friend raised her hand to her forehead. "Hold on just a minute. What makes you think that Randall beating you would be punishment for your sin?" Cassidy shook her head. "Katherine, God loves us — He loves you. Randall did what he did because *he* was evil. *He* was sin-filled."

The chair behind her *thunk*ed as she

plopped into it and started crying. "But there were these two women — I think they were twins or very close in age sisters. They were in the dining room and one of them told the other that she wouldn't take care of her anymore because she was sick due to her own sin." All the words fell out in a jumbled, rambling mess.

"What?" Cassidy leaned forward a bit. "Start again. What did the sister say?"

"She said, 'Amelia, I don't know what to say to you anymore. It's your own fault you're sick. God is punishing you for your sin and you know it.' "

"That's terrible! How could someone say such a thing?"

Katherine shook her head. "I don't know, but it made me wonder if it were true. I'm new at this and I don't know Scripture like you do. Oh, Cassidy, what if it's true and I can't have children and it's all because of my sin?" The thought made tears spring to her eyes.

Her friend reached out and pointed a finger in her face. "Now, Katherine Harrison Demarchis, you stop that thinking right now. It's wrong. Yes, we are sinners. Yes, there are earthly consequences for our sin. But no, God isn't up there on His throne waiting for you to sin so He can pour

373

out his wrath and punishment on you. That is *not* how God works." She motioned toward the desk. "Would you bring me my Bible? Allan put it over there this morning when he left."

Katherine wiped her cheeks. She went to the desk in the corner and found the familiar book. Cassidy had it by her every day, and they'd begun discussing different passages together.

"I think it's the perfect time for us to pick up the book of Job. There was a righteous man who was very blessed — with wealth and with family, and he praised God and gave Him all the glory. Satan went to God and told God that Job surely wouldn't continue to praise Him if Satan were allowed to take away those things. So over a short period of time, Job lost everything. Even all his children. His wife even turned against him and said, 'curse God and die.' "

Katherine gasped. "That's terrible."

"It was. Then even his health was taken as his whole body was covered in sores. But that's just the very beginning of the book." Cassidy flipped through page after page. "You see the rest of this? Job had three friends who thought of themselves as righteous, and they came. They sat with him in silence in his misery and mourning."

"Sounds like good friends."

"Sounds that way. But wait — after a week they begin to speak. Chapter after chapter of speeches and Job's responses. My favorite one is where one friend tells Job that he must be suffering because of some sin in his life. So he should examine his life carefully and see what he did wrong and make it right."

Heat filled Katherine's face. "Just like the lady said this morning."

Cassidy nodded. "But at the end of Job, we hear God's response and we see that Job had stood righteous. Even though horrible things happened to him, he stood firm in his faith in God. Job proved Satan wrong. And then God spoke to the friends and said, 'My wrath is kindled against thee, and against thy two friends: for ye have not spoken of me the thing that is right, as my servant Job hath.' After that, God blessed Job even more abundantly than before.

"Bad things are going to happen, my friend. Because yes, we *all* are sinners and we live in a sin-filled world. But —" She flipped to the back of the book. "If we look in Philippians, chapter one, we read, 'And this I pray, that your love may abound yet more and more in knowledge and in all judgment; that ye may approve things that are excellent; that ye may be sincere and without offence till the day of Christ. Being filled with the fruits of righteousness, which are by Jesus Christ, unto the glory and praise of God. But I would ye should understand, brethren, that the things which happened unto me have fallen out rather unto the furtherance of the gospel . . .' "

"I don't understand . . ." Reading Scripture could be so difficult in the old English language, Katherine felt like she was back in school trying to figure it all out.

"He's saying — and this is Paul here, writing from prison, mind you — that even though bad things have happened to him . . . like being thrown in prison . . . he knows that it is for the furtherance of the gospel."

"He was thrown in prison for his belief?"

"Yes, and for preaching the gospel." Cassidy reached a hand out to Katherine.

She took it in hers . . . what a lovely thing friendship was.

"Katherine, listen to me and take a moment to really think about this. Do you see how God has taken the ugliness of your past and how He is making it good now?"

"What do you mean?"

"You and Jean-Michel. Neither one of you knew the Lord a few years ago. Without a relationship with Him you were both condemned to eternal separation from God. But even though God didn't *cause* those horrible circumstances to happen, He has used them now to bring you both to Him and to each other again."

The sun was high overhead by the time they stopped for lunch. Jean-Michel dismounted his horse and found his leg wasn't nearly as stiff as he'd anticipated. But it would be so good to walk around for a few minutes.

He spotted Collette and headed straight for her. She had been an issue this morning. Three times, John, Allan, or Thomas all had to steer her back on the right path. Why she couldn't just follow along, Jean-Michel didn't know. Her spirit wasn't rebellious or mean . . . just . . . frivolous. Thoughtless.

Now that they were off the horses, he could stick closer to her side and prayerfully find out what was going on with her.

Their picnic of sandwiches and homemade pickles from the Curry kitchen was phenomenal. Why did everything taste so much better out in the fresh air? Even the simple fare seemed refined. As the meal concluded, some of the others milled about the immediate area, leaving Jean-Michel and his sister alone.

"I do wish you wouldn't cause us such

worry by wandering off. Try to think of how that makes extra work for the guides."

"I wasn't purposely wandering off. I get distracted and forget where I am."

"Well, as Allan told you the last time, you can't afford to forget. This is a dangerous place, even if it is beautiful."

"I'm not a child, Jean-Michel. I assure you that I can take care of myself. Now, if you'll excuse me." Collette stood.

"Where are you going?"

"Where everyone must go from time to time. Alone."

He understood her meaning. "Just don't go far and keep your eyes open." He'd tried before they left to convince her that it wouldn't be easy to take care of delicate matters. But Collette insisted she could do it if he could. He sighed. If they made it back without mishap it would be a miracle.

Thomas walked over to him. "How's the leg, Mr. Langelier?"

"It's actually doing pretty well. Thank you for asking."

"I noticed the exercises really seem to be helping. You're almost too strong for me to do much good anymore." The young man laughed. "Can I get you anything?"

"*Non.* I believe I am fine. How is the rest of our group holding up?" Jean-Michel got to his feet.

"Oh, the women are already complaining about not stopping enough, and the men are complaining that the saddles aren't comfortable enough. It's normal — we have to deal with the same things every trip."

"Well, I think you are doing an incredible job. *Magnifique!*" He patted Thomas's shoulder.

"If we could get that much encouragement from everyone else, it would be a *magnifique* trip."

Jean-Michel laughed at Thomas trying to speak French. The way he tried to form his lips to mimic him was quite hysterical.

"Oh, it looks like John is rounding us all up." Thomas stood. "I guess we better get ready to head out. Hey, where's your sister?"

Oh no. Which direction had she gone? Jean-Michel shook his head. "I'm not sure. She needed to . . . well . . . relieve herself, but she should have been back by now."

"I'll help you find her." Thomas ran over to John and said something to him. Probably about how the silly French girl had gone off by herself and gotten lost.

The rest of the tourists might complain if he couldn't find her quickly. *"Fille naïve."* Foolish girl.

Thomas and John went north and south

respectively, and Jean-Michel headed to the west. Her name echoed over the hills and valley as they all called out her name.

Jean-Michel cringed when he heard one of the ladies talk about having to wait.

As he crested the first small hill to the west, he spotted Collette's blond head and there she was, strolling back to where they'd picnicked.

With a black bear cub following her like a puppy.

26

Sputtering a thousand different names — that weren't so complimentary — under his breath in French, Jean-Michel walked faster toward his ambling sister.

She hadn't even acknowledged him because she appeared to be enraptured by her new pet. Who, of course, was following because she kept dropping pieces of something behind her.

"Collette." He tried to remain calm, but he knew enough to know that where there was a baby bear, there was sure to be a mama bear. "Collette, stop that."

Her bright green eyes looked up at him and she smiled. "*Frère,* look! Isn't he just divine?"

All around them was the glory and grandeur of God's creation, but in that moment Jean-Michel could only see his sister . . . and the bear cub. He finally reached her side and tugged on her arm. "You need to stop dropping whatever treat you have and come with me right now. Don't you realize the danger you've put yourself in?"

She frowned. "What do you mean? I didn't touch him, I promise. But he started following me, so I gave him some crumbs. He's awfully hungry."

"*Oui.* Just like his mama will be when she finds us."

Thomas came running from the other side of the hill. "Oh, boy." He stopped in his tracks. Cupping his hands around his mouth, he shouted in the other direction. "John, you better bring your gun."

"What?! *Non!* You cannot shoot the baby bear." Collette stomped her foot.

Jean-Michel yanked her arm. "Hush. It's not to shoot it, it's only to protect us if we need it. Now stop feeding the bear and come with me."

Thomas came forward. "We need to get back over that rise. Collette, leave all your crumbs over there — away from us. That should keep the little guy occupied. Then we are going to run as fast as we can over that hill and hope the mama doesn't come until we're out of sight."

"I don't understand." Collette pouted.

"Not another word, Collette. Just do as Thomas said." Jean-Michel gave her a glare that dared her to argue with him.

She crumbled up the rest of the cookies she had in her pocket and left a small pile for the bear to munch on. Then they all took off running up the hill. Thomas grabbed Collette's hand and dragged her as Jean-Michel went as fast as his leg would allow. Thankfully, the exercises had been working.

A loud roaring growl caused them all to fall to the ground when they reached the hill.

"What was that?" Collette's eyes finally showed a bit of sense — and fear.

"That, my dear sister, was the mama."

They watched a large black bear come running out of the copse of trees to the south. She howled and yowled her way toward her baby and scanned the horizon in all directions. Batting her little one on the hind end, she took one last look in the direction of the hill they were hiding on and roared again. She stood on her hind legs and clacked her teeth together, then shoved her little one back toward the trees.

Thomas rolled over onto his back. "Whew. That was a close one. I'm just glad she didn't charge us. She knew we were here. Did you see how she voiced herself directly toward us?"

"Is everybody all right?" John called down.

"We're fine," Thomas replied. "Mama apparently decided she didn't want to go to the trouble of attacking us on such a beautiful day."

Jean-Michel glanced up and saw John standing ready with his rifle. The situation could have been so much worse. Shaking his head, he stared his sister down. "You put every single one of us in danger, Collette."

"*Je suis désolé, je ne savais pas.*" She paused, then repeated it in English. "I'm sorry, I didn't know."

"You didn't know? It never crossed your mind that you should leave wild animals alone?" He shook his head again. How had Father dealt with this? The girl simply didn't seem to have any common sense whatsoever. Maybe she had been *far* too sheltered.

"He was so precious and . . . hungry."

"And you didn't think. You just jumped right in to whatever fancied you at the moment. John and Allan warned you to never try to approach or feed the wildlife. Honestly, do you never listen to anyone's counsel but your own?" His anger toward her was stronger than it had ever been. But how could he help her to understand? She hadn't done anything of malicious intent. She just didn't . . . think.

Thomas stood and offered a hand to Collette. "They might be cute to look at, Miss Langelier, but they are wild and capable of tearing your arm off."

Her eyes went wide. Then the tears started.

Jean-Michel reached into his pocket and handed her his handkerchief. "You needed to hear the truth of it, so dry your eyes. We have a long journey ahead, where you are going to be directly beside me the *entire* time."

She groaned.

"And I won't hear any argument about it."

"I didn't mean to cause harm. I just saw him there in the grass and I wanted to get a closer look."

By now they had climbed to the top of the hill and joined John. Mr. Ivanoff gave Collette a stern look. "You promised to obey the rules we set up, Miss Langelier."

His authoritative voice and position were intimidating. Jean-Michel felt his sister tremble. Good. She needed to be afraid. If she wouldn't respect her authorities, she needed to know there would be consequences.

"I don't want to have to send you back early, but if you can't do as you're instructed, then we'll have no choice." His expression softened a bit. "We only have these rules to keep you safe. Next time you might not be so lucky."

Collette looked miserable. "I am sorry. I didn't think it was so bad."

"You didn't think, and that's the problem." Jean-Michel shook his head. "But I am. I think perhaps you should return."

"Please don't send me away." She looked from her brother to John and then Thomas. "I promise I will listen to every word and obey. I didn't mean to cause such trouble."

John slung his rifle over his shoulder. "Few people get a second chance after encountering an angry mama bear. God's obviously given you one, so I suppose it's only right that I do the same." He cocked his head slightly to one side. "Do I have your word that you'll do as you're instructed?"

"*Oui.* Yes! I promise."

John smiled. "All right. Then let's catch up with the others."

Thomas and John walked ahead and immediately fell into conversation. Jean-Michel couldn't make out what they were saying, but he figured Collette was probably at the center of it.

"Collette, I'm sorry I lost my temper, but I feared you would die and then all of my family would be gone. The thought of seeing you torn apart by a bear was as terrible as the nightmares I suffer."

She looped her arm through his. "I can only say that I'm sorry. I cannot take back my bad judgment, but I will do my best to make better choices in the future."

He paused and looked at her, his anger fading. "I only want to see you grow and mature into the beautiful young woman Papa hoped you would be. But you seem to be going through some sort of growing pains."

She ducked her head.

"What is it?"

"Ever since Papa died, I've felt lost. Sweet Davey helped me to find God, but I make forward progress and then I struggle with all my selfish ways all over again."

"I hear that's quite normal, my pet."

"But don't you see? If you are to be happy, you'll marry Katherine and have a wonderful life. You don't want the baggage of a little sister anymore. And I don't want you to. I want to be able to take care of myself — prove to you that I will be all right. Yet I have serious trouble breaking my bad habits."

"Ah . . . so as the Americans say, we've reached the root of the problem."

"I'm sorry, Jean-Michel. All this time I've wanted to show you that I don't need you to take care of me. But in truth, I very much need my *frère*."

He stopped and turned her face to his. "I am your older brother and I love you, Collette. I will always be here for you — even if I marry Katherine and we have a wonderful life."

"But you won't try to run my life?"

"*Non* . . . I didn't say that. . . ."

August 20

The room felt hot. Much hotter than it had been.

Cassidy looked over at Katherine, who was embroidering a baby cap. The movement caused her head to throb. "Does it feel warm in here to you, Katherine?"

"No, I was actually thinking it might be getting a little cold." Katherine continued to stitch and then her head popped up. "Are you feeling too warm, Cassidy? I could open a window. . . ."

"Yes." She leaned her head back. "In fact, I'm not feeling very well. It just came over me." She scooted herself lower into the bed.

Katherine jumped up from the chair. "You've gone awfully white." She raced to the sink and turned the water on.

Cassidy couldn't see what she was doing, but the sound of the water made her incredibly thirsty. "I need some water, please."

Katherine laid a cool cloth on Cassidy's forehead, then went back to the sink and returned with a glass of water.

The cool liquid felt blessed as it ran down her throat, but she hardly felt strong enough to hold the glass. Katherine seemed to sense this and took hold of the glass just as Cassidy's grip loosened.

"I'm going for the doctor. I'll be right back."

"I'll come too." Cassidy tried to push back the covers but found them much too heavy.

Katherine stilled her hands. "You can't leave the bed, remember? Please don't try to move or do anything that might cause you harm. Do you understand?"

"Yes." She nodded and remembered her condition. What was going on with her mind? Cassidy stared at the ceiling. What was happening? Why did her head hurt so much? The room began to spin, so she closed her eyes and prayed. *Lord, please help. Please don't let anything happen to my baby. . . .*

A hand was on her shoulder. The slight weight of it made her ache.

"Mrs. Brennan. Cassidy, I need you to wake up." The doctor's voice.

Her eyelids felt so heavy, but she managed to lift them. "Dr. Reilly. What's going on?"

"You're very sick. But Mrs. Demarchis has promised to stay by your side and nurse you. Is that all right with you?"

She could barely nod. "Everything hurts." Laying a hand on her abdomen, she was thankful to feel the baby move.

"That's to be expected. Now you need to listen to Katherine. I'm giving her detailed instructions on how to care for you, so you need to drink when she tells you to drink, all right?"

"Yes, doctor."

"Now you rest, and I'll be back in a few hours to check on you."

"Thank you."

As her eyes fell shut again, she heard the doctor whispering to Katherine. She focused on the sound of his voice.

". . . I'm afraid it's the influenza. I had two cases yesterday and didn't think much of it because it was a husband and wife. But apparently another lady had been suffering with it for a day or so prior to that. I now have twelve cases. I'm sorry I can't be of more assistance to you, but I appreciate you staying with her around the clock. Come find me if anything changes."

"So her fever . . . ?"

"It's not too high right now, but we will have to keep an eye on it so it doesn't harm the baby."

A small gasp. "I can do this, doctor."

"Keep fluids going into her. At least every thirty minutes try to get her to sip a little cool water. Keep her in clean, dry linens as much as you can. And keep yourself clean. Wash your hands with strong soap. You've already been exposed, but you lessen your chances of developing the sickness if you maintain sanitary conditions."

"I'm not worried about myself, doctor. I will do everything I can for Cassidy and her baby."

"Thank you. I'll be back."

A door closed.

Influenza? People died of influenza. Cassidy felt her heart race. "Please, please, my baby."

Katherine's hand was on her forehead in an instant and smoothed her hair back. "It's all right. God is going to help me take care of you. I won't leave you."

"Where's Allan?"

"He's out on a trip, remember? He'll be back soon."

"Soon . . ." She didn't want anyone else getting sick because of her. She wanted her baby to be healthy and strong. She wanted Allan at her side, but then he might fall ill as well. *Oh, God, please help.*

Wiping her brow with the cool cloth, Katherine hummed and then began to sing softly. "Jesus loves me this I know, for the Bible tells me so. Little ones to Him belong, they are weak but He is strong.

"Yes, Jesus loves me. Yes, Jesus loves me. Yes, Jesus loves me, the Bible tells me so."

Katherine's voice was soft and soothing like a lullaby. Cassidy began to relax. Yes, Jesus loved her. He loved her and her baby.

"What's all the racket?" Margaret marched into the kitchen. She had kitchen staff who'd fallen ill, and the last thing she needed was problems from her *assistant.*

Mr. Ferguson looked at her from where he stood by the stove. Soup was splattered everywhere — a broken jar lay at his feet.

"What are you doing just standing there?" Margaret crossed the room and quickly began to pick up the glass. Thankfully the jar had broken in three large pieces. There were a few shards, but the bulk of the glass was in her hands. She threw the pieces in the trash can and turned back to see that the man hadn't moved.

"Ferguson, what are you waiting for? Clean up that mess."

To her surprise, he began sinking to the floor. He shook his head, then plummeted like a rock.

The man was sick.

She tried to steady her breathing. The influenza was here. Could she do this all over again? She hurried to his side. Using all her strength, she pulled him back up. His skin was hot — feverish. She wasn't going to be able to keep him on his feet if he lost consciousness, but hopefully she could get him to a chair.

"Come on, you big oaf. Help me out here. Argue with me. Anything. Tell me that my kitchen needs rearranging . . . again. Just walk to the dining room with me."

He mumbled something inaudible, but put one foot in front of the other. By the time they made it to the first table outside the door, she was sweating from exertion.

Easing him into a chair, she patted his shoulder. "I'm going to get some help. You just lay your head down on the table in case you start to faint."

He didn't argue with her, which only proved to Margaret how sick he was. In a flash of memory she saw her husband instead of the Scot. She bit her lip. Not again. She wasn't strong enough.

She hurried and called to the first person she saw — Mr. Bradley. He stood at the front desk, speaking to Dr. Reilly and a couple of the hotel maids. "I need help. Daniel is sick. He nearly collapsed, but I managed to get him to a chair. I don't think he can make it up the stairs."

Mr. Bradley shook his head. "God help us. Not another." He looked at her with a pained expression.

"I'll go see to the man." Dr. Reilly sighed. "Can you send a couple of strong men to help carry him to his room?"

Mr. Bradley turned to one of the girls. "Run down to the roundhouse and get help. Mr. Ferguson is a big man and we'll need some strong arms." The girl nodded and raced from the room.

Margaret turned to go, but Mr. Bradley called her back. She shook her head. "What is it? I need to get back to the kitchen and clean up the mess Ferguson made."

He seemed at a loss for words. "I'm afraid it's bad. There are over a dozen people sick — it's . . . influenza."

"I know." She hoped to never hear that word again. But she knew. Sadly, all too well. How could they ever endure another epidemic? "I'll go see what I can do to help the doctor, then I need to clean the kitchen."

"No. Wait." He reached out and took hold of her arm. "There's something else."

Margaret searched his face. The man looked like he might break into tears. "What is it?"

"Cassidy . . . she . . ."

Margaret felt the blood drain from her face. "No. No, please tell me that poor child hasn't come down with . . . with . . ." She couldn't bring herself to speak the word.

"I'm sorry. The doctor just told me. Mrs. Demarchis is with her — she's offered to take care of her."

Margaret wanted to scream, but the sound stuck in her throat. Where was Cassidy's loving God now?

27

August 22

Easing herself up from her awkward position in the chair, Katherine stretched her
neck. This was the third day since Cassidy
had become ill, and the doctor had just
quarantined the whole of Curry. Over
twenty-five people were down with the sickness, and he said they had to protect the
railroad workers and other visitors.

It made sense to her, but it also worried
her. If they were quarantined, how would
the group off on the camping trip be able to
make it back? They didn't have enough
provisions to stay out in the wilderness long-
term.

Her heart longed for Jean-Michel. The old
saying "absence makes the heart grow
fonder" was certainly true.

The good doctor had instructed her to
stay with Cassidy and not go anywhere else.

Since they were unsure how the disease was spreading, he wanted to try to keep the people he knew had been exposed as far away as possible from the ones who hadn't.

Grandmother was one of those who hadn't been exposed, and for that Katherine continued to thank God. Her grandmother was aging, and this trip had already taken a toll on her.

She glanced at Cassidy. The poor woman had writhed in her sleep on and off for days. Sometimes, it took every ounce of strength Katherine had just to get water down the sick woman's throat.

She knows God.

At least that offered some comfort. Katherine tried not to worry about the expectant mother, but it was hard not to think her situation more critical than that of the others. Cassidy carried a life inside her. A life totally dependent upon her staying alive. How could Katherine ever explain to Allan or Cassidy's father . . . if she died?

She reached forward and felt Cassidy's forehead. Her friend was still quite warm, but it seemed — well, she hoped — that the fever was cooling just a bit.

A slight knock sounded at the door.

Katherine opened it to a red-eyed Mrs. Johnson.

"How is she today?" The cook bustled in with a tray of broth, sandwiches, and some cold milk.

"I'm hoping a little better. At least it seems that way to me."

Mrs. Johnson leaned over Cassidy and kissed the younger woman's forehead. "Oh, my dear, you must stay with us. Keep fighting."

Cassidy's mouth moved as if she were trying to speak, but nothing came out. It only served to make Mrs. Johnson's eyes fill with tears.

Katherine had never seen anything but the no-nonsense side of the hotel's head chef until she came to visit Cassidy. "Would you like to sit down for a few minutes, Mrs. Johnson? Get off your feet for a bit and share with me all the news from downstairs?"

The teary lady nodded. "There's not much to tell. No one is allowed to eat in the dining room. No guests are allowed to leave their rooms except to use the restrooms. The train isn't stopping in Curry, which makes it very difficult, since this is the halfway stopping point and we also do all the laundry for Pullman and the hospitals. The doctor has been quite staunch on all his rules, since it has spread so quickly."

She used her fingers to brush Cassidy's dark locks off her forehead. "Mr. Bradley is beside himself and paces the foyer all day. Many of the guests who aren't sick are beginning to question the reasoning of the quarantine and don't understand why they can't leave. It's all quite a mess down there." She sucked in a little sob and grabbed Cassidy's hand. "Do you really think she's doing better?"

Katherine put her hand on the woman's shoulder. "I do. She hasn't been as uncomfortable the past few hours, and I'm convinced she feels cooler than she did before."

"I can't lose her."

"Mrs. Johnson, I don't think you'll lose your assistant. She's young."

"Don't you see?" Big fat tears rolled down the woman's round cheeks. "She's not just my assistant. I love this girl as if she were my own. Everyone around here knows that I'm hard and rough around the edges — but Cassidy here, she saw what no one else could see."

Katherine didn't know what to do, so she just kept patting the woman's shoulder. "I know she's very fond of you too. She's spoken of you a great deal."

"I lost my whole family to the Influenza Epidemic of 1918. I can't lose Cassidy and the baby. We're so excited about the baby." The tough woman broke into sobs.

Katherine reached out and hugged the chef. "We must have faith. Cassidy would want us to put our trust in God for her recovery."

Mrs. Johnson shook her head. "I don't know how to trust Him when He would allow something like this. I fear Him."

"I know it's hard. Cassidy told me that often in life we endure great trials, not because we've done anything wrong, but simply because we live in a sin-filled world."

"But if God won't protect a trusting child like Cassidy — answer her prayers — then how in the world can I think for one minute He'll listen to *me*?"

Katherine shook her head. "I don't know, but I don't think it's about God choosing one over the other. I know He loves Cassidy. I finally know He loves me, and I feel confident He loves you too, Mrs. Johnson. Maybe you need to just let Him know how frightened you are — how hard it is to trust. I feel certain He will help you."

Another knock at the door was a welcome respite for Katherine. She had no idea how to soothe a woman who had endured the kind of loss Mrs. Johnson had, and she felt inadequate to share the Bible as Cassidy had done for her.

Before she could get up, the door opened and Dr. Reilly stepped in. The doctor's face was grim as he made his way to the bed. "How is she?"

"She's taking fluids as you directed, and I'm wiping her down constantly. I think, in fact, her fever has lessened."

He nodded and took out his stethoscope. He put the instrument to her chest and listened for a moment. "Her lungs sound clear and her heartbeat is strong."

Straightening up, the doctor put the stethoscope in his black bag and pulled out a strange-looking black instrument — something like a funnel. On one end it flared out almost like the bottom of a bell, while the other end had a small circular piece with a hole in the center.

"What is that?" Katherine moved closer.

"It's called a Pinard horn. When I learned Mrs. Brennan was going to have a baby, I sent for one. It arrived on the last train before quarantine. I didn't even realize it, however, until this morning. I opened the box to find it with some other medical supplies."

"How does it work?" Mrs. Johnson moved closer too.

"I should be able to hear the baby's

heartbeat. I can time the beats and should be able to tell if the baby is in distress."

Both women nodded and waited as he pulled back the covers and pressed the horn to Cassidy's lower abdomen. Then he leaned his ear down to the opposite end of the piece and listened.

Katherine and Mrs. Johnson inched and leaned their way in until they all hovered over Cassidy's round stomach.

Katherine found herself holding her breath. The doctor maneuvered the piece several times, positioning it in different locations on Cassidy's belly. It seemed to take forever, but finally he straightened and nodded. "The beats are good — strong."

"Thank God!" Katherine's breath and words spilled out together.

Mrs. Johnson cried into her handkerchief.

"Yes, I'm encouraged. Just keep doing what you're doing. I must keep making my rounds."

"Dr. Reilly, how are the others?" Katherine walked with him to the door.

His blue eyes darkened. "We lost the Griffith girl, and I fear at least two others will pass before the night comes."

Snowshoes were a wonderful invention. Jean-Michel had never seen anything quite like it, and being able to traverse on *top* of a glacier with them was a spectacular thing.

The sparkling white carpet that covered the icy blue layers beneath was a sight to behold. He wished he could share it with Katherine.

So far, the trip had been wonderful . . . and terrible.

Wonderful in the scenery and the companionship with Allan and John and young Thomas.

Terrible in that he missed Katherine . . . and then there were the mishaps with Collette.

First the horrible bear incident about which the group was still gossiping. At least Collette had been properly scared and had been good afterward to obey the rules regarding the wildlife. But there were other things she did out of her lack of common sense. Just after they'd managed to get back on the trail after the bear encounter, Collette fell off her horse while trying to pick a salmonberry off a bush. Then yesterday, she'd gotten herself into a patch of pushki — cow parsnip — and had gotten the sap all over her arms. Of course the sun had been shining, which set off the chemical in the sap and burned her worse than any sunburn he'd ever seen. So now she was traveling with a thick white goo applied to her arms and everyone had to keep telling her, "Don't scratch!" But she insisted the itch was worse than anything she'd ever endured and would everyone please give her a little sympathy.

While the wonderful aspect of the trip was truly wonderful, the terrible part was exceedingly *terrible.* He felt at a complete loss. Was parenting always this difficult?

After the pushki incident, Collette seemed more subdued. For which he would be eternally grateful. Just that morning John and Allan had stressed to her the dangers of climbing on glacial ice. She appeared to understand and be willing to follow the rules, but Jean-Michel feared she'd soon forget or be distracted.

"It's glorious, is it not?" Collette called back to him. Allan had sandwiched her between himself and Jean-Michel on the climb.

"It is — quite incredible," Jean-Michel replied.

They reached a place where things leveled out slightly. John brought everyone to a halt. "We'll rest here a bit and then start back down."

Jean-Michel took his place beside Collette. She shook her head. "You don't have to worry, *frère*. I'm doing my best to obey all the rules."

Her words made him chuckle. *"Merci."*

"I don't know what's gotten into me. I guess after saving little Davey, I felt needed — like I was doing good. Now I just feel . . . I don't know. I see things changing and I suppose I'm trying to find my place." She looked out across the beautiful vista. "I see the love you and Katherine share, and the love Cassidy and her husband share, and I can't help wondering if I'll ever know such love. After all, who on earth would want a selfish little French girl?"

"Collette, you will find love one day."

She turned to face him. "But even you reminded me that men will want me for my money. What if no one ever loves me — just for me? What if I'm too selfish — too silly?"

He wished he could wrap an arm around her shoulders, but the snowshoes made moving closer difficult.

"I don't know where I belong, Jean-Michel. I try to pray like Cassidy taught me. I try to read the Bible, but it's hard to understand. I don't know what I'm supposed to be doing — because nothing I do feels right."

Reaching across, Jean-Michel took hold of her hand. "We have all felt that way. I've struggled too. Sometimes answers take time. Keep praying and reading, but also seek wisdom from those who understand better than we do. I'm sure Cassidy and others would help you to understand the Scriptures. I will try to help too."

"But what if the answers aren't what I want them to be?"

Jean-Michel thought momentarily of Katherine and her concerns about a family. What if she couldn't have children? He wanted a family — sons he could raise to be strong, competent men, and daughters he could dote on and raise to be considerate and wise.

Collette was looking at him for his response, but Jean-Michel wasn't at all sure what he should say. "Sometimes answers aren't what we want them to be. But I suppose that is when we need to rely on God for direction — for understanding of how it all works out to be His plan for us. I don't pretend to know all that, but I'm trying to learn. That's all I want for you. Seek to understand by expanding your knowledge."

"But knowledge of what?"

"I suppose since God is the one who holds the future and knows all things — then we should seek to understand Him and expand our knowledge of the Bible."

She nodded. "I suppose so. But why can't it be easier?"

Jean-Michel laughed. "I wish I knew."

28

Packing up the last of his gear, Jean-Michel was thankful they were on their way back to the Curry. The trip had been amazing. And for two whole days they'd been able to see Denali in his full glory. The mountain loomed in the distance today, his cape of clouds shrouding his top half, and yet, he was still enormous. The Alps were beautiful, but Jean-Michel decided he preferred this Alaska Range even more. Quiet, peaceful, surrounded by caribou and wild flowers bursting open as a carpet across the trail home. It had even come to him last night as he fell asleep — he never wanted to leave this place. He would like very much to remain in Alaska.

But as wonderful and glorious as it had been, he longed to see Katherine again. The days apart gave him time to pray and journal about the future.

He hoped she had done the same and couldn't wait to share together.

As they mounted their horses, Jean-Michel noticed a group of five men walking toward them from the east. John took off toward them on his horse and held up a hand in greeting.

The rest of their little band of travelers waited.

Thomas came over to Jean-Michel's side. "Those are Athabaskan friends of John's."

"Athabaskan?"

"It's a native Alaskan group of people. That's John's heritage."

Collette came closer. "You mean like *Indiens*? Savages?" Her eyes were wide.

Jean-Michel just shook his head at his sister. "Lower your voice, *s'il vous plaît*. You've read too many novels, little sister. It's been a long time since there's been anything of the sort in America. These are native people and we will respect them."

She flushed and backed her horse away a bit.

Thomas scratched his head. "It must be serious. John doesn't look happy." He pointed as John headed back toward their group.

The head guide held up his hand and

asked for everyone's attention. "I'm afraid we have some serious news to share."

Several people whispered as the group came in closer.

John pulled a handkerchief out of his pocket and wiped down his face. His countenance was grave, and he looked to be fighting for control of his emotions. "Forgive me, but we need to head back immediately, and we will take quite a brisk pace. Curry is under quarantine. The influenza has taken three lives already and many are sick. We won't be able to go back to the hotel or our small town, but there may be some way for us to help."

"Where will we go?" one of the men piped up.

"We will camp outside of Curry. We are getting low on provisions as well, so we will have to find a way to get more food without contaminating anyone. The doctor has strict orders in place and the train isn't even allowed to stop. No one goes in or out of Curry."

Katherine bent over the sink and splashed water on her face. She needed sleep. In a bed. But Cassidy still needed her and she couldn't abandon her friend. Not at such a crucial time. The doctor said the next day or so should be the turning point.

Either Cassidy would begin to improve, or . . .

She didn't want to think it. Not after they'd lost one child at the hotel already. Mrs. Johnson had cried and cried when the doctor told them.

Katherine's heart hurt as well, which felt good in an odd way. Every hurt the past few years had been her own. It was almost freeing to be able to carry someone else's burden.

God had done a mighty work in her life. Not for the first time that day, she prayed and thanked Him for all of it. The good and the bad, the lessons and the blessings.

Even in her exhaustion, she felt hope for the future like she hadn't had before.

Cassidy moaned from the bed and Katherine took a clean cool cloth over to bathe her face. The poor woman hadn't taken anything more than a few spoonfuls of broth and a few sips of water each hour. But at least she was still taking fluids, even though she didn't even seem awake.

The doctor walked in — he had stopped knocking, since he came almost every hour now. "How is our patient?"

"She's moaned the past couple hours, which she hadn't done before."

The doctor lifted Cassidy's eyelids and looked at her eyes. "Her pupils look good." He reached down and put his fingers on her wrist. "And her heart rate is better." The doctor wiped his brow and sighed. "I think we have reason to be optimistic."

"How are the others?"

"We may lose a few people today, I'm afraid. And there are some cantankerous guests who seem to care less about their health than their need to 'be seen' out of their rooms for society. I tried to explain to them that no one 'of society' was about, and everyone else was being obedient to the quarantine, but you know how rich people are . . ." He must have realized that he wasn't speaking to a member of the staff because he cleared his throat and his face flushed. "Mrs. Demarchis, please forgive me. I didn't mean —"

She held up a hand. "Dr. Reilly, no apology is necessary. While I understand exactly what you are saying about people of my status, it doesn't offend me in the least. I wish such things were not so important to them." She moved closer to the window to catch the fresh air. The room was so hot and stuffy.

"I do as well." Dr. Reilly smiled. "Still . . . that was completely inappropriate of me. I think my exhaustion is getting the best of me. Please forgive me."

"It's incredible you haven't collapsed yet, doctor."

"You look just as tired. I hope you'll be able to get some rest. Perhaps I could have a cot brought here for you."

Mrs. Johnson walked in. In her no-nonsense manner she seemed to take charge. "Well, I've got the kitchen maids doing all the work from now on, since no one is eating in the dining room. They can handle broth and sandwiches, fruit and cheese. I'm here to take care of Cassidy and give Mrs. Demarchis a chance to rest." She placed her hands on her ample hips and took a deep breath. "What would you like me to do?"

Dr. Reilly chuckled. "Your timing is perfect, Mrs. Johnson. I just mentioned that I would have a cot brought in for Mrs. Demarchis. If you ladies will excuse me, I'll go arrange that right now."

After he left, Katherine hugged the chef. "I don't want to leave Cassidy, but I'm glad you've come. I think I'll go clean up a bit while the doctor arranges for the cot."

"It should be in place by the time you return. I'll see to it that it has bedding."

Katherine nodded. She was so exhausted

that she momentarily considered not even bothering to clean up. She glanced at the sleeping Cassidy. "I'm so tired."

"That's why I'm here, my dear. As I said, Cassidy is like my own daughter. I'd like to be here for her while my duties allow it."

Katherine passed on the simple instructions the doctor had given her. They weren't difficult, but it did take effort and watching the clock to make sure Cassidy got enough fluids.

"Dr. Reilly said she mustn't get . . . he called it *dehydrated.*"

Mrs. Johnson nodded. "I know. I've heard all about it. I'll see that she drinks."

"And it's important to keep wiping her down with cool cloths. He said it's the fever that's most dangerous to the baby."

"I understand." Mrs. Johnson patted her arm. "You look terrible — now go. By the time you get back, the cot will be ready."

When she was confident she'd done all she could, Katherine left the room and closed the door behind her. It had been — how many days? — since she had even been in the hallway. She longed for a walk outside in the sunlight and fresh air, but longed for a bath and her bed even more.

Yawning as she walked to the shared washroom, she stumbled. For a moment she wondered what it was she'd tripped on. She glanced back, but saw nothing. She started again and felt light-headed.

And warm.

So warm that she wanted to unbutton the top buttons of her blouse.

Oh no. This was how it had started with Cassidy.

No. She was simply overtired. She just needed sleep.

But the hallway started to spin.

Then she fell.

29

Margaret sat between Cassidy's bed and the cot on which Katherine Demarchis had been placed. When Dr. Reilly found Katherine on the floor in the hall, he'd brought her back into Cassidy's room.

The cot that had been brought in for her relief now became her sickbed.

Mrs. Harrison hadn't taken the news well. She'd insisted she be allowed to care for her granddaughter, but the doctor refused. The older woman had become so weak, the doctor feared she had taken the sickness, but so far it seemed to be nothing more than her exhaustion from travel. At least that was all Dr. Reilly would tell Margaret.

She wasn't used to having all this time to contemplate. And was pretty sure she didn't like it.

Cassidy stirred, but it was nothing more

than the slight bit of movement Mrs. Johnson had seen before. Once in a while there was a moan — even what sounded to be a few garbled words, but nothing that proved her recovery.

Something inside Margaret seemed to crumble. She went back to her chair and took hold of Cassidy's hand. "You have to get better, my dear girl. You have a babe who needs a mother — a husband who needs a wife." She paused to wipe the tears from her eyes. "And me. I need you too." There was a part of her that wished that weren't true. Margaret had hardened her heart against love for a reason, and now here she was facing the possibility of losing someone she cared about — someone she loved.

"Mrs. Johnson?" a young man called from the doorway.

"Yes?" She looked up. "What is it?"

The man looked hesitant. "It's . . . well . . . Mr. Ferguson. He's speaking . . . uh . . . well . . ."

"What's that to do with me? Can't you see I'm here taking care of these women?"

He nodded. "I know, but he's . . . he's asking for you."

"He's asking for me?" Margaret rolled her gaze heavenward. Why would the man be asking for her?

"He's not doing so good, Mrs. Johnson, and he asked specifically for you. Won't you please come?"

She sighed. The last thing she wanted to do was leave Cassidy and Mrs. Demarchis in order to speak with the Scot, who'd done nothing but give her trouble from the day he arrived. But what choice did she have? It hardly seemed the act of a decent human being to deny the request.

"Very well." She got to her feet. "Where is he?"

"The second room down. I'll show you to him."

"No. You stay here. Sit there." She pointed to the chair. "And don't move until I come back."

He obeyed and took her place between the women. Margaret paused at the door. "If they so much as move, you come get me. I shouldn't be but a moment."

The boy nodded.

She went down the hall and found Daniel's room. Inside, Dr. Reilly stood by the man's bed. "He's been asking for you."

"I heard. Why can't he stay asleep like the others?" Margaret moved closer. "He can't be all that sick if he's talking."

"The sick are all in various states of

consciousness, Mrs. Johnson. Some are speaking, some aren't, but I assure you Mr. Ferguson is quite ill." He lowered his voice. "And perhaps a bit afraid."

She swallowed the lump in her throat and nodded. "What can I do?"

"He's asked for you. Sit with him and hear what he has to say. Half the time he's speaking another language, but from time to time he breaks into English again."

The man looked ashen and small — not at all the feisty, burly man who'd stormed her kitchen like a warrior to battle.

"Daniel? It's me . . . Margaret." She hesitated, then sat down on the side of his bed.

The man opened his eyes. He looked at her for a moment, not seeming to know her. Then a glimmer of recognition crossed his features. He murmured something she couldn't understand. Margaret leaned closer and he spoke again.

Understanding dawned. He was speaking Scottish Gaelic. Margaret hadn't heard this in years, but the words came back to her like it was yesterday.

"I have no family," he whispered, closing his eyes. "I've only you, lass."

Margaret frowned. She was nothing to him but his supervisor, and a bossy one at that. The man must be ranting in his sickness. How could she argue with him now? She felt momentarily awkward and replied in Gaelic, "What is it you want to say, Daniel?"

For several long moments, silence covered the room.

Margaret wasn't even entirely sure he understood her.

He extended his hand. Margaret took hold of it and waited for him to speak again. For a moment, her mind flashed back to 1918 when she'd done the same for her husband and children. For whatever reason, she had been immune from the disease . . . just as she was now. She had held their hands, wiped their brows, and watched them slip away.

Daniel whispered again, a hint of a smile on his lips. "Thank you. Didn't . . . want to die alone."

His words pierced her heart. "Well, you're not alone." The native tongue of her ancestors came easier. "And you're not dying, because I'm your supervisor and I haven't given you permission to die."

His eyes opened and he grinned. "Bossy woman."

"Irritating man."

He closed his eyes and Margaret let go of

his hand. She couldn't help but feel a little guilty for how she'd treated him. The man had been asked to come, and it wasn't like he intended to stay. She tried to push aside her regret. "Now you'd do well to rest and get back on your feet. I . . . we . . . have a kitchen to run."

The only sound was that of his strained, raspy breathing. Margaret thought of all the horrible things she'd said to him. Things she could never take back. She hadn't wanted his help and certainly hadn't wanted his interference, and she'd made that clear to everyone. Especially to Daniel Ferguson.

How could she have been such a hateful woman to him and yet he asked for her in his moments of fear? The thought only served to add to her weight of guilt.

"I'm sorry, Daniel. I should have been kinder," she murmured in English.

He opened his eyes. Margaret wondered if he'd understood her apology. Not that it would matter to him at a time like this, but as much as she wanted *not* to care . . . it mattered to her.

"I am . . . truly sorry."

He gave the tiniest nod. "Will . . . ya . . . pray for me, lass?"

She hesitated. She'd spent so much time keeping God at arm's length — wanting to believe He was good and loving like Cassidy believed — but feeling He was only there to take away what she cared about. Would He even listen to her? The battle raged inside. Perhaps if she'd spent more time asking God to heal rather than railing against Him — Cassidy would be better now and Daniel wouldn't be so sick. Had her own hard heart brought these things on to teach her a lesson? She shook her head. Surely not.

"Pray . . . for . . . me . . . please," Daniel rasped as his eyes closed once again.

It seemed she had no choice — yet she knew the choice was hers and hers alone. "Aye. I'll pray for you."

The general must be sick.

That had to be why he hadn't gotten any word. The four walls of the room were closing in on him and they were all being watched.

And not just by the doctor and hotel staff. There were others.

He could feel it. Maybe *they* had caused the disease. To get to him. To get to the general.

Standing by the window with his hands clasped behind his back, he tried to think of a way to escape their watchful eyes.

"Uncle . . ."

"Yes, my dear." He straightened his shoulders. "What can I do for you?"

"I'm afraid . . . that is . . ." She sank into the chair. "I don't feel too well."

"I'll go fetch the doctor."

"Thank you." She leaned her head back and closed her eyes.

He had no choice — he must leave at once.

August 25

Thomas rubbed his backside. The last seven days on horseback had been good, but today — well, today had been brutal. John asked him to ride ahead as hard and as fast as he could to alert Mr. Bradley — or whoever — that they would be camping on the other side of the river. Since there wasn't a good deal of flat area that low, they'd have to stay up on Curry Ridge but wanted people to know where they were.

They needed provisions, but they could survive in the wild if they hunted and fished — and the rich people didn't complain too much.

When he reached the ridge above the river, he tied up his horse and ran across the suspension bridge. There was a bell on the other end that he was going to ring and leave a note so he wouldn't break the quarantine.

He scribbled what he could on a piece of paper, tied it to the bell, and then rang it.

Then he walked back to the middle of the bridge and waited.

Relief flooded him as he saw Mr. Bradley, the hotel manager, walk out to the bell.

Thomas waved his arm high. "Helloooo!" He watched as his boss took the note. He appeared to read it and looked to be writing on the back. He re-tied the message to the bell, then gave a wave before heading to the hotel.

Thomas ran back across the bridge and retrieved the note.

Glad all are safe and well.
   The notes are a good idea. Do not come near any people.
   More than half of Curry is sick.
   Four dead.
   Please tell John and Allan that Cassidy has been gravely ill but the doctor believes she is improving now.
   Pray.

Thomas's heart clenched. Cassidy was sick? How was he supposed to tell them that? The thought of his sweet friend on death's door tore his stomach apart. He'd heard horror stories about influenza.

As he climbed the hill back to the ridge where they would make camp, he prayed. Cassidy had taught him so much about working at the hotel, how to study the Bible, and how to laugh and look at life positively. God wouldn't take her and the baby to heaven like this . . . would He?

Overwhelmed with sadness and feeling selfish for not praying for the others who were ill, Thomas dropped to his knees.

"Lord, I know You can hear me. You know how I'm struggling to understand and how I'm questioning. But please take care of everyone at the Curry. Don't let anyone else die, Lord. Please. Show us how we can help, and give us wisdom on how to take care of the people in our care out here."

He stood up and looked around him. The group would be coming soon. He'd better do what he could to make their camp setup easier.

Thomas chose a place near one of the small streams that fed into the river. His horse nickered from behind him as he chopped wood. He straightened and prayed again for strength to give Allan the news about his wife. All the while he'd worked putting their camp in order, he'd prayed for wisdom.

Twenty minutes later, the first of the riders entered the open area, and before long the entire camp was filled with complaining travelers. Why were they stuck here? Why couldn't they just go on down to the hotel? The complaints went on and on.

"I'm willing to take the risk," one man piped up.

"It doesn't matter if you're willing to take the risk. The town is under quarantine." Thomas straightened his shoulders. "They have folks who are guarding the perimeter to keep others from getting sick. They've already had four deaths."

One of the women reached for her husband. "Mother is in there — what if she . . . ?"

Most everyone gathered there had someone they cared about inside the quarantine. He understood their concern, but he had to be straightforward with them. "I don't have any names of the . . . dead. So please don't ask."

"Folks, we're going to abide by the law." John's voice boomed over the camp. "If any of you want to make an issue of that, come see me privately. Right now we need to get a fire going and settle in to our assigned tasks. You men who volunteered to catch some fish — get to it. But no one. I repeat . . . no one leaves this camp. Understood?"

While the group didn't look happy, gradually everyone went about their duties.

Thomas took that opportunity to go to Allan and John. "I need to speak with you both."

Allan and John exchanged a look. "What is it?"

"Cassidy . . . she's —"

Allan went white. "She's not dead."

"No." Thomas shook his head. "But she's been sick. The doctor thinks she's on the mend, but I thought you should know."

"And the baby?"

Thomas shook his head. "I don't know."

"I've got to go to her." Allan turned, but John took hold of his arm.

"Son, you can't do that. You know you can't. We'll have a riot on our hands and no hope of keeping these folks on this side of the river if you do."

Allan looked at his father-in-law as if he'd lost his mind. "But it's Cassidy."

John's gaze never left Allan's. "I know. I want to go just as much as you do, but we can't. She's in God's hands, Allan. And she's getting better — at least that's what

427

the doctor believes."

"But . . . what about the baby?"

Thomas didn't know much about such things, but he'd already figured out that it couldn't be good.

"We need to pray." John ducked his head as his voice cracked. "God's brought Cassidy and that baby this far despite her fall down the stairs, and we've got to trust that He'll see her through this. No matter what, Allan, we have to keep these folks calm."

Thomas saw the battle raging in Allan through the expressions on his face. He knew this was probably the hardest thing the man had ever faced. Thomas knew it was hard enough just for him — how much more for a husband and father.

30

August 27

The stack of fish fillets on the plate looked appetizing. Collette nodded to herself. She could eat that. Taking a fork, she pulled off a little piece to taste. *"C'est vraiment bon!"* It was actually good. Even better than it smelled.

She may not have learned much about cooking from Cassidy yet, but she would have to tell her that she'd made fish. All by herself. Well, Thomas had cleaned and filleted it, but she had taken up the task of cooking it. Wouldn't Cassidy be surprised? Tears sprang to her eyes. Thomas had told her and Jean-Michel that Cassidy was among the sick. The thought of losing her precious new friend made her heart ache. She turned back to the fish that still cooked over the fire.

"Look at this!" Jean-Michel walked up

beside her. "My little sister is cooking. I'm so impressed." He peered into the skillet. "But is it edible?"

She poked him and smiled. "I dare you to try it."

He did. "Mmm, *c'est bon,* Collette. It's delicious." He nudged her. "How did you learn to do this?"

"Well, believe it or not, Cassidy taught me from her bed. We talked about recipes and how to do various things. I'll admit not having a stove in her bedroom made it harder to imagine. I had to ask Thomas's advice about cooking over the fire, but now you see I have been able to take all of that knowledge and work it together for our good."

"I'm impressed."

"I'm trying very hard, Jean-Michel."

He smiled and touched her cheek. "And you are doing very well."

"Has there been any word about Katherine?"

He shook his head. "I can't help but be afraid for her and her grandmother. Mrs. Harrison was already quite weak."

Something behind her caught his attention. He frowned.

"What's wrong?" Collette gave a cursory glance over her shoulder.

"Look over there. Who is that talking with John? He looks very familiar. . . ."

"I don't know. I haven't seen him before." She shrugged.

Shaking his head, he looked down. "I must be imagining things." Jean-Michel straightened and patted her shoulder.

"Jean-Michel." Allan's voice took her brother's attention away. "I need some help over here."

"Duty calls."

Collette reached out to stop him. "Jean-Michel, I am praying for them."

He nodded. "Me too. For all of them."

Her brother hurried across the camp while Collette went back to frying the fish in her skillet. If she could master this, she could do just about anything . . . right?

Once all the fillets were cooked, she began to bring plates around to everyone. Who cared if that was normally a job for one of the staff? She was proud of what she'd accomplished, and everyone needed to pitch in to help. Her brother had made that very clear.

John smiled as she drew near. "Why, Miss Langelier, what have you made?"

"Fish!"

He laughed. "And it looks and smells marvelous. Thank you!"

"Would our new guest like some?" Collette peered around. Where had the man gone?

John's eyebrows went down. "He seemed very confused. I had him lay down in a tent over there." He pointed with his fork. "At one point, I thought for sure he was speaking French, but I could be mistaken. When he awakens, I'll need your brother to translate just in case."

"*Oui.* I will tell him." She moved to the next group and offered them some of the fish.

A stocky man she'd come to know as Mr. Samples gave her a look of derision. He'd been known to complain more than anyone about the food. "Is this all there is? Just fish?"

Collette frowned. The ungrateful man. She thought to snap at him and tell him just what she thought of his complaining, but remembered her goal to put others first. "I apologize that there isn't more."

Her soft answer must have taken him off guard. The man shrugged and began to eat his piece. Perhaps soft answers truly did turn away wrath.

For the most part, people had been grateful that they had a place to sleep and food to eat. But there were a few who had complained constantly. Collette realized in watching other people how selfish she must have sounded in the past. Hearing words from others that would have been the same things she might have said in a similar situation opened her eyes. She would double her efforts to be more considerate of others. She glanced momentarily at the sky overhead. *I'm going to need a lot of help.*

After the dishes were done and everyone retired to their tents for the night, Collette stayed out on the ridge looking back toward Denali. The daylight stretched out into the night hours in this land that was so far north. Clouds floated around the very top of the High One and she enjoyed the view of the massive mountain. It was incredible.

Tomorrow they would wait for news once again from Curry. Prayerfully the sick would be on the mend. Tomorrow, she had another opportunity to start anew. She had heard John say that God's mercies were new every day. That gave her hope. She would seek after God. She would focus on other people rather than herself.

She glanced toward the heavens. "I want the heart of a servant, Lord. Show me what I must do."

Even though sleep eluded Collette for most of the night, she still woke up before seven. Probably because the cots they slept on in the tents were not beds they wanted to relish and relax in. They were made for the purpose of sleeping while out on expeditions. Nothing more.

She left her tent that she shared with the other women and found there weren't many people up and around yet. Unusual for the morning. She decided to just hunt down her brother.

She reached the stream and found him filling three buckets.

"I'm glad you're up, Collette. We need your help." Stress etched lines around his face.

"What's wrong?"

"The quarantine didn't work. We have four people sick in the camp."

She sucked in her breath. "Tell me what I need to do."

September 2

Katherine awoke feeling better than she had in days. She opened her eyes and found Mrs. Johnson staring back at her.

"I see you've decided to rejoin the living."

"Yes. I have to say I feel much better."

"Thankfully you only had a mild case. Dr. Reilly said you should be fit as a fiddle in a

434

day or two."

Katherine sat up on the cot. "How's Cassidy?"

"I'm doing just fine." Her friend's voice floated over from the bed.

The older woman grinned. "You just can't keep a stubborn woman down."

"It's a good thing we three have that going for us, then." Cassidy laughed.

"Has there been any word on the rest of the town?" It was taking a while for the fog to lift from Katherine's mind. How long had she been sick?

Mrs. Johnson nodded. "There have been a total of six deaths, but no new cases. The doctor is thinking he just might be able to take us out of quarantine soon. Won't that be a relief for everyone! Many of the guests want to take the first train out of here. I can't say as I blame them."

"It's a terrible thing to endure such sickness, but especially when you're far from home." Katherine stretched and reached for her robe. "Have you had any word from my grandmother?"

"A note came earlier." Mrs. Johnson fished the note out of her apron pocket. "Here you are."

Katherine opened the folded piece of paper. "She's praying for all of us and tells us to keep our spirits up."

Cassidy shifted.

Mrs. Johnson went to her immediately. "I told you I would help when you wanted to move."

"I'm sorry. I've just had this nagging ache in my back all morning. I promise you this — once I'm able to get up on my feet, I may never get back into a bed again."

Mrs. Johnson chuckled. "Katherine, would you hand me one of those pillows at the foot of the bed?"

"Certainly." Katherine reached across the narrow path between her cot and the bed and took one of the pillows in hand. "Here you are."

Mrs. Johnson twisted around, keeping one hand on Cassidy's back. She took the pillow and plopped it down behind the young woman. "There, that should help."

Cassidy nodded and eased back. "I'm glad the doctor said I could have some toast today. I'm starving."

"Well, after days of not eating, while your babe went on feeding from your body, I'm sure you *are* starving." Mrs. Johnson reclaimed her seat. "Now that the two of you are back on your feet — well, as much as you can be — I'm going to get back to my work in the kitchen, while Mr. Ferguson lies around in bed. Just when I get used to having his help, he decides to get sick."

"I doubt he became ill just to irritate you further, Mrs. Johnson." Cassidy smiled.

"Listen to you — sassing me after all the time I've sat here fretting over you." Mrs. Johnson pointed her finger at Cassidy. "You're as bad as he is."

"Maybe Daniel and I shall team up." Cassidy giggled and stretched her arms over her head. "This is misery. I just can't get comfortable." The words were no sooner out of her mouth than she clutched her stomach. "Ow!"

Katherine gasped as Mrs. Johnson jumped to her feet.

"What's wrong?" The older woman put a hand on Cassidy's forehead.

"I think . . . my water just broke."

31

September 5

"The quarantine's been lifted!" Thomas raised the paper over his head and ran from the bridge to the camp.

As the days had passed and they'd received word of people healing from the sickness, many in the camp had taken to walking down to the river each day as Thomas checked for messages.

"The quarantine's lifted!" the young man shouted again.

Cheers were heard throughout their group and folks started for the bridge.

Jean-Michel was as eager as the rest to cross and learn how Katherine and her grandmother were faring, but he wanted to do what he could to help John and Allan break camp and clean up. Thankfully, Collette was of the same mind.

"We'll stay here and help Thomas get

everything packed and down to the river," Jean-Michel told Allan and John. "That way you can go on to the hotel with the others. I know you're anxious to see Cassidy and find out how she's doing."

Both men had a look of exhausted relief on their faces.

"Thank you, Jean-Michel — Collette." John reached out to grip Allan's shoulder. "Under any other circumstances, we would never allow it, but I doubt we could have kept him in camp much longer."

"Me?" Allan shook his head. "I thought I was going to have to tie *you* down to keep you from sneaking over in the night."

"And who could blame either one of you?" Collette ushered the men forward. "Now please go and give Cassidy my love — Katherine too, if you see her. Tell them we'll be back before nightfall."

The two men ran and made their way to the hotel.

Thomas smiled at Collette. "You sure you want to do this? Your brother and I can probably handle it."

"*Non.* I want to help. I'm happy to." She began picking up the pans she'd scrubbed only a few hours earlier. "After all our time on the trail, I think I know the routine."

Thomas laughed and shook his head as

Collette moved to the other side of the camp. "She's sure changed her tune."

Jean-Michel nodded. "It hasn't been easy for her and probably won't be easy in the days to come, but I believe God has finally opened her eyes."

"He has a way of doing that," Thomas replied. "I know He's helped me often enough."

The two men began taking down the tents, and Jean-Michel thought it the perfect opportunity to ask Thomas a few questions. With the scent of wildflowers in the air, he was inspired.

"I have something on my mind and wondered if you might be willing to answer some questions."

Thomas was on the other side of the tent but called back, "Sure. What can I do for you?"

"Tell me about living here in the winter."

For a minute Jean-Michel wasn't sure Thomas had heard the question, but just as he opened his mouth to repeat it, the younger man cleared his throat. "Well . . . it's cold and there's a lot of snow."

"I figured that much. What about the dark?"

"That's something people get wrong. Way up north it stays dark for months in the winter, but here we always get at least five hours of daylight. Of course, a lot of the time that's a cloudy, snowy daylight. But that's better than none."

"It doesn't stay dark for twenty-four hours?"

"No."

They finished with one tent and moved to another. Collette worked in tandem with them, packing up the smaller items as they tackled the larger ones. Jean-Michel smiled to himself. She didn't even have to be told. Would wonders never cease?

"Why all the interest in living here in the winter? You thinking of staying?"

"*Oui.* I am, truth be told."

Thomas straightened and looked at him. "I think that's a wonderful idea. As long as you remember that life up here is all about preparation for any possible problem."

"Wise advice."

"What would you do? Just stay in the hotel?"

"*Non.* I have plenty of finances to start my own business."

"Well, the town has been growing. John or Allan could probably tell you what's needed the most." Thomas stopped and his brow furrowed. "But what about your sister?"

"I don't know." Jean-Michel looked across

the campsite to where Collette was wrestling with a cot. "I don't even know if Katherine would be of a mind to stay, and I certainly wouldn't want to plan a life without her. I just know that there's something about this place that is healing. I felt that even before John prayed with me and I found my sense of who God is and how I needed Him. This last week has done so much to strengthen me physically and spiritually that I find the idea of leaving to be unthinkable."

Thomas nodded. "Alaska has a way of doing that. I can't imagine living anywhere else."

Jean-Michel sighed and looked at the vast and glorious wilderness around him. "Neither can I."

"This is my home and I want no other." Thomas bent down to pull up a stake.

"I want it for my home as well." Jean-Michel sighed and went back to work. He could only hope that Collette and Katherine would feel as he did.

"That's wonderful. We would love to add you to our Curry family." The young man stood and put his hands on his hips. As he looked around the camp, his expression turned grim.

"Is anything the matter, Thomas?"

"Where's PJ? He was still abed last I saw him."

"*Qui*? Excuse me, *who* is PJ?"

"I don't really know who he is. Remember the man who showed up all disheveled and he was sick?"

Recognition struck Jean-Michel. The man who'd looked so familiar. A flash from the war went through his mind. *Non.* It couldn't be. Could it?

"All I know was his name was PJ and he kept mumbling something about the general."

His heart sunk at Thomas's words. Something didn't add up. "He was the one you said I might need to . . . umm . . . *interpréter*?"

"Interpret? Yes." Thomas searched the horizon as he turned in a circle. "But he appears to be gone."

"Cassidy?"

Cassidy heard Allan call through the open window. She smiled at Dr. Reilly. "He's here! Now, we all agreed not to tell him about the babies until the quarantine was lifted. I can't wait to surprise him." She looked at the small bundles tucked in the bed beside her.

"I'm sure that was wise. He'd never have

443

stayed away." Dr. Reilly put his instruments back into his bag and straightened. "You are doing wonderful, Mrs. Brennan."

"Thank you, doctor."

"You gave us quite the scare, but I'm happy to say that everything appears to be just fine."

Footsteps pounded down the hall. The door flew open.

Allan's desperate expression touched her heart. "Cassidy."

She smiled. He looked so tired. "Welcome home."

Allan spotted the doctor. "How is she?"

"Doing very well. I believe she'll be up and running within a week."

Dr. Reilly slipped from the room as Allan moved toward the bed. "Up and running?"

Cassidy opened her arms and he bent over and held her close. "I was so worried. When we heard you were sick . . . I wanted to be here." His murmur against her ear sent chills down her spine.

"I know, and believe me, I wanted you here. But . . . I didn't want you sick. So many were."

He pulled away just enough to kiss her.

Cassidy sighed against his lips. She'd missed this man. This precious husband God had given her. Missed the way he teased her. Even missed his arguments. She rubbed the back of his neck with her fingers.

Thank you, Lord, for bringing him safely back to me and for letting me be here to welcome him home.

A tiny squeak sounded that turned into a cry. Allan jumped back as if Cassidy had put a match to his sleeve.

Cassidy drew the fussy infant into her arms. "Your son would like to meet you."

Allan looked back at her. His mouth dropped open and he stared at her for a moment.

The baby wasn't happy and began to cry in earnest. He was hungry, and Cassidy knew it would only be another few minutes and his sibling would be looking to nurse as well.

"Shhh, now. I'll feed you in a moment." She peered down at the dark-haired infant in wonder, taking in his sweet scent.

Allan sat down on the bedside chair and shook his head. "Nobody told me. When did you . . . when was he . . . ?"

She laughed at his floundering. What a surprise — and his face! "Two days ago . . . on the third of September. Would you like to hold him?"

"I . . . uh . . . what if I don't do it right?"

Laughing again, Cassidy extended the

wrapped bundle. "You'll do just fine."

He took the baby ever so cautiously and tucked him in the nook of his arm. The fussy infant looked up at him with bright blue eyes, and surprisingly enough, calmed. The two stared at each other for several long moments.

Cassidy couldn't help but smile. She had waited for this moment for what felt like forever. She could see the tenderness — the love Allan held for his son. He was going to be a good father. Just then her second baby started to fuss.

Allan looked at his son who had quieted and then to Cassidy. She lifted the twin from beside her and shrugged. "I hope you don't mind . . . but there were two. Although if you do mind, it's too late to send him back."

"Twins?" He stared at her in disbelief. "Boys?"

More laughter bubbled up at the shock on his face. "Exactly. Dr. Reilly said it was no wonder I was as big as a . . . well . . . bigger than he figured I'd be. He didn't learn about it being twins, though, until I was sick. He'd sent away for a special instrument that allowed him to listen to the baby's heartbeat. It came with his supplies just before he had to put the town in quarantine, and when he used it the first time . . . he knew. There were two heart-beats. Twins. But he couldn't tell me because I wasn't conscious." The cries began in earnest and echoed around the room. "And now they are very *hungry* twins." She adjusted her nightgown and brought the baby in her arms up to feed.

Allan continued to stare at her in dumb-founded wonder. She wished she could have taken a picture of his face for later. It was priceless. "I . . . don't know what to say." He shook his head. "You're amazing." He bounced the crying son in his arms.

"Here, hand him to me. I can take them both." Cassidy smiled up to her husband. "God's the amazing one. I don't remember much of what happened while I was sick, but I know so many people were praying for me . . . for them."

"Did you give them names?"

She shook her head. "No. I couldn't keep them from coming into the world before you got back, but I saved the privilege of naming them for your return. After all, we discussed possible names for a boy or a girl, but never for two boys."

Allan touched one son's head with the tip of his finger and then reached over to the other. He traced down the side of his face

447

and smiled. "I guess we've got some decisions to make." He looked up again and his eyes glistened with tears. "Thank you, Cassidy. Thank you for my sons. Thank you for your love." He leaned in and kissed her forehead.

"Ahem!" Dad's not-so-subtle clearing of his throat came from the doorway. "I know I'm intruding, but I couldn't wait any longer."

"You aren't intruding at all, John. Come in." Allan stood with the baby. "Come see your grandsons."

A huge smile split John's face. "Mrs. Johnson told me it was twins. I told her it figured. Our Cassidy never does anything by halves."

Katherine would give it five more minutes, and if Jean-Michel didn't show up, she'd march herself across that bridge and find him herself.

But as she glanced at the door, he appeared.

"I've never been so happy to see anyone in my life." She ran across the lobby.

Jean-Michel opened his arms to her and Katherine stepped in without hesitation. "I was so worried about you." He whispered and hugged her close.

448

Katherine had never known such happiness. She felt the warmth of his arms around her and heard the pounding of his heart as she placed her head on his chest. It didn't matter that they were standing in the middle of the hotel lobby. They could have been standing in Times Square and Katherine wouldn't have cared.

Jean-Michel pulled away first. "We got messages from Mr. Bradley, so I knew you were sick. How are you feeling now?"

"I'm fine." Katherine stepped back to look into his beautiful green eyes. "I wasn't nearly as sick as some."

He nodded. "We heard six people died."

"Yes. And we feared we might lose a great many more, but in the end only six were lost."

"And your grandmother?"

"She never took sick from the influenza, but she's not well. She won't tell me how bad it really is, but I know she's weakening."

"I suppose you will want to get her home very soon."

Katherine shook her head and felt the sting of tears. "I don't think she'll ever leave the Curry alive."

Jean-Michel frowned. "It's as bad as that?"

"Yes. Dr. Reilly says her heart has given

449

out. She had some sort of trouble before even coming here. Didn't tell me about it. I guess she feared I wouldn't come on the trip or allow her to come if I'd known how bad it was. And she's right. I wouldn't have, but I'm glad I did."

"Me too, but I am sorry to hear about your grandmother. I'd like to see her."

Katherine nodded. "Come. I'll take you to her." She held out her hand and he took it into his warm grip. The tingles it sent up her arm made Katherine feel loved and safe.

They found her grandmother propped up in bed and giving orders like a regal queen. Two hotel maids were the focus of her instruction.

"Now I want to make certain you understand. I want the lace gently rubbed with a mixture of baking soda and vinegar. Then let it air-dry and use a warm iron on it afterward. Not hot, mind you. Warm."

"Yes, ma'am." The girls' unison reply echoed in the room.

"And don't forget to bring me an extra blanket."

"No, ma'am. We won't." One of the girls shook her head and they both turned.

"Excuse us, Mrs. Demarchis." She bobbed a curtsy and left the room. The other did likewise and scooted out the door.

Katherine approached the precious woman's bed. "Grandmother, look who's come to see you."

The older woman smiled and motioned them closer. "I'm so glad to see that you've returned safely, Jean-Michel. I had my concerns."

"It's good to see you again, Mrs. Harrison." He went to stand beside her bed and took hold of her extended hand.

"I am glad for that. But I know who you are most glad to see. And it would have caused no end of grief to have you lost in the wilderness."

Jean-Michel laughed. "Although, with the right person at your side, being lost out there might be quite nice. *Oui?*" He winked at Katherine. "But now, I want to know how you are feeling, Mrs. Harrison."

Katherine could see her grandmother's façade of perfection slide into place. "I am in perfect order, just a little tired, but certainly nothing to worry about."

"Grandmother, it's time to be honest."

"Oh, child. I just don't want you two fussing over me."

Katherine leaned in to kiss her on the cheek. "But we like to fuss over you. And you look exhausted. Maybe we should let you rest."

"No . . . there's something I need to tell you." Grandmother placed her hands in her lap and looked determined. "Please sit. On either side of me so I can see your faces."

"All right." Katherine's nerves weren't sure she could take any more bad news. She moved to the left side of the bed and sat next to her beloved grandmother. Jean-Michel took his seat on the other side. The ever-present scent of peppermint floated toward her.

"You see, I need to apologize to you both."

Jean-Michel laid his hand over Grand-mother's clasped pair. "*Non.* There's nothing to apologize for."

"Hush now. You may know part of the story, but you certainly don't know the whole."

Katherine puzzled over this. "What do you mean?"

"Child, I sent a letter to Jean-Michel months ago — before we ever left New York — asking him to join us here in Alaska for the summer. And I will not apologize for matchmaking and seeing the two of you fall in love again . . . but I need to repent for my lack of faith. I took matters into my own hands when I should have left them in God's.

"You see, I couldn't bear to watch you

452

suffer, Katherine. As you shriveled up, my heart went right along with yours. I couldn't make up for what your father did, but I thought I could fix it. Funny thing is, God needed to heal both your hearts before you would ever be ready for each other again. So please forgive me for putting the cart before the horse."

Tears streamed down Katherine's face. "Of course I forgive you. More than that, I bless you for loving me enough to do what you did." She laid her hand over Jean-Michel's and her grandmother's.

"I'm glad you understand my intent. It has been my joy to see you turn to God and grow in a faith of your own. A joy, too, to watch your love come alive again. It has blessed me."

Jean-Michel cleared his throat. "Since we are baring our hearts, it's only right you should know that your letter . . . well, it gave me a reason to go on. After my father passed, it felt like it was all too much. I was lost . . . so lost. At first I was unwilling to even contemplate a reunion because I knew how black my soul had become, but then something happened and I felt I could not refuse."

"You two were meant to be together. I hope you've figured all of that out for yourselves, but in case you haven't . . . I wanted to make that clear. Even if this old woman went about it the wrong way."

Jean-Michel smiled and looked at Katherine.

Her heart melted. Even in all the broken pieces of their lives, God had brought them back together and given them so much more than love. He gave them new life. "Grandmother, your heart was in the right place, and I love you for it." She leaned over and kissed Grandmother's cheek again.

Jean-Michel stood and rounded the bed. As he got down on one knee, he looked at her grandmother. "Speaking of 'meant to be together' . . . Mrs. Harrison, I would request your permission to ask Katherine to marry me."

Katherine blinked back tears. Her heart soared. Could it truly be?

"Of course, you have my permission. Marry the girl and do so quickly. Today, tomorrow. I'm ready."

"Are *you* ready, my love?" Jean-Michel looked up into her eyes. "I don't know how quickly we might arrange for a minister, but Katherine Harrison Demarchis, I would be most honored if you would be my wife."

32

The dining room of the Curry had been transformed into a wedding chapel. Chairs were arranged, fresh flowers adorned the windows, and yummy smells from the kitchen made Katherine's stomach growl. Up to this point, she'd been too nervous to eat anything, but maybe Mrs. Johnson could spare a small snack for her.

Mr. Bradley had arranged for a man named Henry Wilcox to travel up from Anchorage to officiate the wedding, and as the hour drew near, she realized she could hardly wait to become Mrs. Langelier.

How amazing that God had changed her heart so much in just a few short months.

Her stomach rumbled again, and she made a dash for the kitchen. As she went through the door, she looked for the head chef. "Mrs. Johnson, might I trouble you for something small to eat?"

"The bride needs more than something small, lass," Mr. Ferguson called from the corner.

"I agree." Mrs. Johnson's gruff voice echoed from another corner. "I think you need one of my sweet rolls."

Katherine's eyes widened as the two came together and prepared a plate for her in unison and precision. A sweet roll, then a scoop of fried potatoes, then a few slices of bacon. What had happened to the two cooks who always seemed at war?

"Here you are, my dear." Mrs. Johnson handed her the plate and wiped her hands on her apron. "Eat up. You have a big day ahead."

Taking the massive portions back to the dining room, Katherine sat in a chair meant for the guests and looked out the window. Today would be the true beginning of her new life.

"Penny for your thoughts?" Jean-Michel's rich voice reached her ears. "At least, I think that's the correct American phrase."

She laughed. "You got it right. And I was just thinking about the beginning of our lives together today."

"And you're ready for this, *oui*?"

"Yes, my love. I'm ready." She hesitated.

"But we've never discussed . . . well . . . we never finished discussing . . ."

"What is it, Katherine?"

"What if it's true? What if I can't have children?" There. She said it. It was her wedding day, and she just gave the man she loved a way out.

He took her hands. "God is in control. He knows the plans He has for us, and I will be content in that. Besides . . ." He cleared his throat. "I took the liberty of speaking to Dr. Reilly. Under the circumstances, he doesn't know for certain if what you were told was true, but since you don't have any other facts, he said whenever you are ready, you could go see him and discuss it with him yourself. No matter the outcome, I love you. Thomas has told me that he knows of many children who need good homes — so we could still fill a house if we can't have our own."

This precious man. Even broken and shattered, he loved her. Just like God. "I love you, Jean-Michel." The clock chimed. "Let's get married."

Jean-Michel helped Mrs. Harrison down the stairs. The older woman was dressed in her finest. Settling her on the front row, he then walked up to the front of the room and took his place next to Mr. Wilcox.

Thomas walked forward and shook the minister's hand before taking his place at Jean-Michel's side. "Are you ready?"

"Oui." But his heart might just explode, it was beating so fast. He clasped his hands in front of him, thankful his leg was strong enough without the cane on this special day. Another reminder of God's blessings and a day he never thought he'd see a few months ago.

The rest of the chairs filled with members of the staff and other guests they'd come to know.

Then the door to the dining room opened and Collette walked down the makeshift aisle, a bouquet of fresh flowers in her hands. When she reached the front, the guests all stood.

John Ivanoff led Katherine down the aisle on his arm. Dressed in a beautiful pink gown that brought out the loveliness of her hair and eyes, she kept her gaze on Jean-Michel the whole time. Her smile was bright and so were her eyes.

Could he be any happier?

"Dearly beloved," Mr. Wilcox began. "We are gathered here today to join this man and this woman in holy matrimony. Let us pray." The man bowed his head.

Jean-Michel didn't want to take his eyes off Katherine, but he lowered his head.

"Lord, we ask that You would be with us today as we join this man and woman in marriage. We pray a blessing on their life together — that they would grow in love for one another as they draw closer to You. In Jesus' name, amen."

"Amen," the guests murmured.

Jean-Michel felt sweat bead up on his hands as they repeated their vows. He didn't deserve to be this happy, and yet here he stood. Marrying the woman he'd loved for so long.

In the blink of an eye, it seemed it was all over. Mr. Wilcox pronounced them man and wife.

As Jean-Michel leaned down to kiss his new wife, the Curry Hotel dining room erupted in joyful cries.

But all sound melted away as his lips met hers. Innocence, trust, and a lifetime of pain that God turned into joy in that gentle kiss. God had blessed him indeed.

The crowd rushed to congratulate them, and Jean-Michel saw the bliss captured on Katherine's face. He hoped to keep it there for the rest of their lives.

"We've a beautiful cake and punch to do this up right," Mrs. Johnson announced as two of her staff brought in the two-tiered cake on a silver tray.

"I don't believe I'm feeling quite up to staying for cake," Katherine's grandmother announced. "I wonder if someone might escort me back to my room."

Jean-Michel moved forward to assist the older woman, but John Ivanoff waved him off. "I would be honored." He helped her from her chair and placed a protective arm around her. Once they reached the stairs, John lifted her in his arms. Grandmother Harrison offered no protest.

Katherine wrapped an arm around Jean-Michel's back. "Let's stay a few minutes and celebrate with everyone, then we can go check on her. She wants us to have our day." A sheen of tears shone in her eyes. "I promised her we would stay." The corners of her mouth tipped up into a sad smile.

He nodded. This was their day, but they both knew Maria Harrison was not long for this world.

Mrs. Johnson scurried around the room serving cake while Mr. Ferguson disbursed cups of punch. Katherine was still in shock. What had happened between those two? Their fights had become notorious gossip shared around the hotel. And now — well, now, they seemed to *almost* enjoy each other's company.

Maybe it was all a ruse. They could be doing it just for her — to keep her day special.

Whatever the reason, she was forever grateful. The day had been perfect. As she stood next to her husband, they held hands and spoke to the guests.

"So where will you live?" Allan directed his question to Jean-Michel. "Since you're from France and Katherine is from America, will you make both your home?"

Jean-Michel glanced at her. "I'm not sure. We need to talk about it. But I can say quite honestly that there is nothing in France that beckons me back."

"I certainly have no desire to live in New York." Katherine smiled up at him.

"Would you consider staying here?" Jean-Michel turned to her. "The town is growing, we have friends here . . ." He let the sentence hang.

Her heart filled with love for this man. "I would love to stay."

"Excellent!" Allan clapped his hands together. "Now we just need to figure out how to get you a house built before the snow flies."

Collette came up beside Katherine. "Is

this true? You're staying in Alaska?"

Jean-Michel looked a bit fearful. "I'm so sorry, Collette. I had hoped to speak to you on the matter, but yes. It's true. I have no desire to go back to France. However, I will go back to settle you there if that is your desire."

Collette said nothing for a moment, but then she shook her head. "*Non.* I have no wish to go back, but neither do I want to impose on you." She straightened her shoulders and grabbed Katherine's other hand. "I believe I would like to work with Mrs. Johnson and Cassidy."

"You want to work . . . as a staff member?" Jean-Michel sounded shocked.

Katherine looked back to her new sister-in-law and raised her eyebrows.

She smiled and nodded. "Not forever, *frère.* But *oui,* I do. I like feeling useful."

Jean-Michel put his arm around Katherine and smiled out to the crowd. "It would seem we have made a decision to remain in Alaska."

The bell outside rang and brought the room to silence.

The railroad master ran into the room. "Mr. Bradley!"

All eyes turned at the urgency in the man's voice.

"What is it?" The manager set his punch down and became all business.

"There's a tree down on the tracks. A big one. And the next train will be here in less than twenty minutes."

Thomas ran as fast as his legs could carry him. A tree down on the tracks with a steam locomotive headed for it at full speed could be devastating. When he reached the site, he realized that at least it was close enough to the Curry that the engineer would be slowing down, but it wouldn't be enough. And it would be too late.

They had to get the tree off the tracks.

Men worked with chains to try to move the massive trunk, but they needed more man power. Thomas took off his suit jacket and threw it to the ground.

As the crowd began to gather, the railroad master barked orders. "We need all able-bodied men to help lift."

Several more men came forward, including Jean-Michel, Allan, and John. But they needed more.

Mr. Bradley removed his coat and joined them as well.

"Mr. Bradley!" Miss Moreau ran toward them. "I went to get my uncle . . . he may have issues with his mind, but he is very strong . . ." The young woman sobbed. "But he is not there."

"Miss, we've got to get this tree off the tracks. After that, we'll form a search party for your uncle, but at the moment, you need to *move out of the way!*"

Thomas had never heard the manager quite so adamant. But it seemed every time they turned around, this tiny little thing had lost her uncle. They didn't need another crisis. Not now.

"All right, men." The railroad master yelled his command, "Heave!"

The giant trunk moved a few inches.

Grunts and groans were heard through the line of men. The tree had to have been at least eighty feet tall. Were there enough of them to move it?

"Heave!"

Another few piddly inches.

The train's horn sounded in the distance.

"Let's go men, *heave!*"

A shabby form appeared at the edge of the tree line.

Thomas recognized the man. "PJ! Please come help us!"

The disheveled man stared at Thomas with a blank expression. But before Thomas could call out to him again, PJ caught sight of Jean-Michel and hurried to his side. He gave a crisp salute.

"*Mon Général,* I have come to make my report."

Jean-Michel looked at him as if seeing a ghost. Thomas heard the train grow closer. "Get him to help us, Jean-Michel."

"Uh . . . uh . . ." Jean-Michel seemed unable to comprehend what needed to be done.

"The general needs your help." Thomas grabbed hold of the man's arm. "We must move this tree . . . now!"

The man nodded and with surprising agility jumped over the trunk of the tree and stood opposite Jean-Michel.

Thomas gave the man a nod and took his place as well.

The railroad master shouted, "Heave!"

Another blast from the train horn.

"Heave!"

They could see the steam engine now. It wouldn't have time to stop . . . even if the engineer saw them.

"Come on, men! *Heave!*"

Everyone must have had a burst of adrenaline, because the tree moved the last foot off the tracks.

The squeal of brakes pierced all their ears.

As the train passed safely over the tracks and came to a stop, Thomas went to grab

PJ. This had to be the same man he'd seen searching the hotel, mumbling about the general — the mysterious, missing uncle. But he was a mess. How had he gotten in such bad shape?

"PJ?"

The man's eyes opened wider and looked around wildly at the crowd. Thomas grabbed the man's arm before he could run.

"*Un moment,* Thomas." Jean-Michel approached. He searched the man's face. "*Non.* It can't be."

"What do you mean? Do you know this man?"

"*Oui.* I do. His name is *Caporal* — I believe you say, Corporal — Phillippe Moreau."

Phillippe straightened with another crisp salute. "*Mon Général!*" Then his eyes narrowed and a look of confusion came over his face. "General? *Non,* you are not the general. You are . . . you know what I've . . ."

The disheveled man collapsed to the ground in a dead faint.

33

Katherine watched her new husband pace the Moreau family's room back at the hotel while their little crowd watched and waited. What had happened to this poor man's mind?

Mr. Moreau had been carried back and laid in his bed. His niece sat at his side, pleading with her uncle to awaken, but the man hadn't moved.

And now — on her wedding day, no less — Katherine's sweet husband couldn't say a word. Somehow, this man on the bed before them was from the dark past.

The man moaned and shifted on the bed. Then he gasped and sat up with a jolt.

"Uncle!"

Jean-Michel moved forward, as did Mr. Bradley and Thomas. The men had joined them in Mr. Moreau's room, most likely to stand guard over their wayward guest.

Mr. Moreau's wide eyes searched the

room. When they landed on her husband, the man burst into tears and sobbed like a child. "You've come to take me to prison!"

Katherine looked at Jean-Michel. "What is he talking about?"

The niece glanced at them both — fear apparent in her eyes.

For a moment, Jean-Michel appeared twenty years older. He swiped a hand down his face and sighed. "Lord, help me." Moving closer to the bed, he nodded to Mr. Bradley. "This man's name is Phillippe. He was one of the soldiers under my command during the Druze Revolt. One day . . ." He cleared his throat. "Phillippe snapped and he . . . he . . . did some horrible things."

Mr. Moreau cried even louder. "They're all dead. All those people . . ."

In an instant, Katherine understood. The man before them was the man who'd set fire to the building. The reason Jean-Michel had been shot . . . and why his two friends had been killed.

"Oh, please . . . don't take him to prison!" Moreau's niece pleaded.

Jean-Michel let out a long breath. He reached for Katherine's hand but continued to look at the man on the bed. "Nobody will be going to prison, but he needs help. Can't you see that? His mind is being ravaged by the horrible memories."

"No one can save me now . . ." Moreau moaned.

Jean-Michel dropped Katherine's hand and lunged forward, grabbing the man's shoulders. "Phillippe. Phillippe! Look at me!"

The wild eyes focused on her husband. "Captain Langelier."

Jean-Michel nodded. "What you did was wrong. Terrible things. Things that have tormented my dreams for years." He sat on the bed beside the man but didn't release his arms. "But there's something you need to hear from me. Are you listening, Phillippe?"

"Oui, Capitaine." Tears slipped down the man's cheeks.

"There is One who can save you. I know, because I had to be saved myself. No man — no matter what he's done — is beyond redemption."

"It is too late!" The man gripped the sides of his head and pulled at his hair.

Jean-Michel shook him by the shoulders. "Listen to me, Phillippe. *Non.* It is never too late."

The man stilled and watched Jean-Michel.

"It is not too late for you, Phillippe."

Katherine's heart broke as she saw a single

tear slip down Jean-Michel's face.

Her husband let go of the man. "I forgive you . . . I forgive you."

She went to Jean-Michel and wrapped her arms around him.

Mr. Bradley moved to their sides. "I think it's time we got Mr. Moreau the help that he needs."

Standing out on the suspension bridge, Jean-Michel held his bride. "It's been quite a day."

Katherine tilted her head up to him. "I'm proud of you. It couldn't have been easy to forgive Mr. Moreau for his terrible deeds, but you did."

"God did that, Katherine. Not me. It was all I could do not to strangle the man, but then I prayed and God gave me peace. And the power to forgive."

"I'm so thankful He did." She reached up and kissed his lips.

"Thomas told me that he found the man once searching the hotel for secret passageways and muttering about a general." Jean-Michel shook his head. "I had no idea he was here all this time and looking for me." After sorting through what Phillippe had been able to tell them in his lucid moments, they learned he had been inexplica-

470

bly driven to find his commanding officer and confess . . . report his heinous actions. His guilt had compelled him to search for Jean-Michel all the way to Alaska. But too much of the time he'd been confused, thinking he was still a soldier of war on secret missions to destroy the enemy.

The only enemy in reality was his own psyche.

"His mind was definitely not right."

"*Non.* It wasn't. I pity him. I know what I've had to endure all this time, and to think that all these years, it's been eating him up on the inside — the guilt of what he'd done. His mind obviously couldn't take it anymore, and so, as Dr. Reilly explained to me, Moreau had created some kind of new world in his mind. A world where he reported to a general and had a very important mission. Apparently the only true mission was his mind trying to find me. Because I knew what he'd done."

"I can't say I understand it all, but I'm thankful it's over and pray he gets the help he needs. He looks so very old and sick now."

Jean-Michel couldn't believe it — but it showed him what carrying around his burdens could do to his mind. Thank God he'd given his life over before he went down the same dark path.

Katherine pulled away and took a step toward the hotel. "I'm sorry for all you've been through."

Jean-Michel watched her move slowly down the bridge. What was he doing? He caught up to her and pulled her back into his arms. "I'm sorry, my love."

"You have nothing to apologize for." Her sweet smile lit his heart on fire.

"After all we've been through, we're finally married, and I'm neglecting you."

She laughed — a sound that he'd never tire of. "Well, I wasn't going to say anything, but I thought maybe you needed some time."

Leaning down, he caught her lips with his own. "I don't need any more time spent in the past. What do you say we move forward?"

"I'd love that." She pulled away and tugged at his hand to follow.

Morning sunshine filled the room and Katherine turned in her husband's arms.

Her amazing and wonderful husband's arms.

After returning to the hotel, they'd gone to see Grandmother one last time. The beloved woman had declined as the day went on. Katherine cried as she said good night — thinking that it very well could be the last time.

A knock on the door made her jump out of bed and pull on her robe. The only one to disturb them would be the maid who'd stayed up with her grandmother.

Katherine opened the door.

Dr. Reilly nodded. "I'm sorry, Mrs. Langelier. But your grandmother passed peacefully in her sleep."

Jean-Michel was behind her in an instant with his arms wrapped around her. "I'm so sorry, my love."

His arms couldn't take away the pain, and the tears flowed, but Katherine knew it was all right. Grandmother had lived life to the fullest. She'd loved God and done what she could for her fellow man. She had also helped Katherine to live life anew — to have hope in what could be rather than waste away in what had been.

It was because of Grandmother that her love for Jean-Michel had risen out of the ashes of all their pain and suffering to live again.

"Are you certain this is what you want to do?" Jean-Michel wrapped an arm around her shoulder. "The decision was made very quickly and it's not exactly the honeymoon I wanted to give you."

"It will be time with you and that is all that matters." Katherine smiled. It would be hard saying her final good-byes to the woman who'd loved her more than anyone else, but time away with Jean-Michel would be lovely. Then they could return home to Curry. Together.

"We'll be pulling out in five minutes," the brakeman told their small group.

Katherine looked at the train that would take her grandmother's body back to Anchorage. There it would be prepared for burial before traveling back to New York. It was only right to lay her to rest beside Grandfather. The two had loved each other so completely that it would have been wrong to bury her in Alaska. Besides, there would be all of the legal issues to oversee regarding her grandmother's estate. Thankfully, Jean-Michel would be at her side. They'd made the right decision.

"You'll be back before you know it." Cassidy stepped forward and hugged Katherine.

"You'll definitely want to get back as soon as you can," Allan added, "before the snow is too deep."

John grinned. "That could be tomorrow."

The others laughed.

"Thomas! Hurry up or you'll miss the train." Mrs. Johnson's bark resounded off the train platform.

Thomas would ride with them to Anchorage, pick up supplies for the hotel, and then head back. After that, he had to take the train north to school.

Their young friend joined them on the platform, very nearly breathless. "I'm . . . I'm . . . here."

Mrs. Johnson came up behind him. "I don't know how you're ever going to make it in Fairbanks without me to keep you at your tasks." Everyone laughed as Thomas's face reddened.

Allan clapped him on the back. "He'll do fine. He's a good man — getting better by the day."

Collette came from the hotel and threw herself into Jean-Michel's arms. "I will miss you."

"No, you won't. You'll be much too busy," Mrs. Johnson promised.

Jean-Michel kissed her on the forehead. "I have a feeling Mrs. Johnson is right. You will be far too busy to miss me. Who knew? The rich, French socialite taking a job in a hotel kitchen."

Collette let go her hold on her brother

and turned to Katherine. "I love you both so much."

She embraced Katherine and it made Katherine's heart melt a little more. Now she had a sister. "And we love you, and are so proud of you." She smiled as Collette stepped back.

The train whistle blew, signaling the time to go. Everyone bid them good-bye and waved as they boarded the train to Anchorage. Katherine and Jean-Michel climbed into the car, then turned to stop at the top of the stairs.

Jean-Michel took her in his arms. "And so our journey begins."

She touched his cheek. "No, it began long ago and now . . . it continues."

He pressed his lips against hers as a shower of rice fell upon them. Katherine heard the cheers of their new friends as the train began to move. Like a phoenix rising up from the ashes, she felt her heart take flight.

DEAR READER

My husband and I (Kim) traveled back to Alaska last fall to do more research and soak in all the beauty of our favorite places. When we lived in Alaska, we never tired of taking trips off the beaten path. This last trip was no exception.

Walking through the deep, overgrown grass that covers the location of Curry now, it was easy for my mind to wander back to its days of glory. What a beautiful place it must have been to visit and even live!

One of my greatest wishes was that the suspension bridge still stood and crossed the Susitna. I would have loved to walk across it and climb up Curry Ridge. While I've been on Curry Ridge from the other direction, there's just something about imagining what it would have been like to cross the river the same way the people of 1926 did. (We hired a helicopter to take us back to Curry Ridge where the historic lookout still stands, but sadly, the weather never cooperated.)

The scene where little Davey falls into the river from the bridge is every parent's nightmare. The original suspension bridge across the river built in 1924 was very sturdy and quite safe, but the walkway was made of planks and the sides only consisted of cables/ropes vertically and horizontally that connected to the large cables that spanned the river from the towers. A really great look at the original suspension bridge is here: http://www.alaskarails.org/mem/ARR/pc/curry-bridge.jpg. But a later picture of the bridge shows more reinforcement: http://www.alaskarails.org/historical/curry/suspension-bridge.jpg.

The addition of the cottages and bunkhouse at Curry actually happened in 1925, but we fictionalized it for 1926. The buildings were built by the navy back when Chickaloon boomed in the coal industry.

The engine house and power plant had been under the same roof until the fire of 1926. No one was killed in the fire caused by coal dust finding its way into an overheated smokestack of a locomotive. When they rebuilt the engine house, they also rebuilt the power plant — on the other side of the tracks this time.

The Druze Revolt is another incredible piece of world history, but not one that many people know about. Since Jean-Michel was French, we decided to use this little tidbit, but the story about the burning of innocent people is something we created. We don't know if anything like that may have actually happened, and it is not our intention to say that it is a part of history. Please remember this is a work of fiction. But Jean-Michel's war experiences are loosely based on stories my own dear grandpa shared about war and what he went through.

Katherine is named after a dear friend — Katherine Prejean. One of the best people I've ever known. One of the most beautiful hearts I've ever known. And no matter the years or the distance — we will always be kindred spirits. And she'll always be Angi to me.

While there were many men who ran the Curry Hotel kitchen and worked in it over the years (as evidenced in several historical photos), we've chosen to make the head chef be a woman — Mrs. Johnson. She is a feisty character we fell in love with while writing *In the Shadow of Denali*. Her irritating Scotsman Chef Daniel Ferguson is purely fictional.

Senator Wesley Jones was a real Republican senator from Washington State at this time, but we made up his appearance at the Curry. We have no idea if he actually visited Alaska. For the purposes of the story, we needed to bring a politician onstage.

Finally, Cassidy's story is a tribute to Cassidy Hale (see the dedication page in *In the Shadow of Denali*). Precious girl, taken from us way too soon. But God in His infinite wisdom is using her story to further *His* story. Let it shine, let it shine, let it shine.

We hope you join us for book three in THE HEART OF ALASKA, *Under the Midnight Sun,* where a brilliant National Park naturalist and interpreter — Tayler Hale — joins Mrs. Johnson, Collette, Cassidy and Allan, Jean-Michel, Katherine, and Thomas in Curry.

We are so thankful for all of you — our readers.

Until next time . . .

Enjoy the journey,

Kim and Tracie

ACKNOWLEDGMENTS

We could write an entire book about what it takes to bring a novel like this to you, but we won't.

There are many people we'd like to thank:

The incredible people at Bethany House — wow — you are all so amazing, supportive, and brilliant. Every facet from cover design to page layout to marketing is done with the utmost dedication. Thank you all so very much.

Our families. It's truly crazy what the families of authors often have to go through. From reenacting scenes to check their authenticity to strange research questions to frazzled and glazed looks from us during writing and editing . . . you all are wonderful and we love you.

Our Revelationing Daniel Dudes (long story) Bible study and prayer group. Tracie and I couldn't do this without you! Julie, Darcie, Kayla, love and hugs to you all.

My crit group — Becca Whitham, Darcie Gudger, and Kayla Woodhouse. Thank you for holding my toes to the fire. Always. (For instance, Becca's brilliant advice on the prologue for *In the Shadow of Denali* made it shine!)

Tracie — what a joy it is to write with you. You saved my bacon on this manuscript when I went into the hospital and you went above and beyond. But more importantly, your friendship is priceless to me. I thank God for you every day. I love you more than words can say.

Thank you, readers. You give us the opportunity to do this.

To God be the glory in all that we do!

ABOUT THE AUTHORS

Tracie Peterson is the award-winning author of over one hundred novels, both historical and contemporary. Her avid research resonates in her stories, as seen in her bestselling HEIRS OF MONTANA AND ALASKAN QUEST series. Tracie and her family make their home in Montana. Visit Tracie's website at www.traciepeterson.com.

Kimberley Woodhouse is an award-winning, bestselling author of fiction and nonfiction. A popular speaker and teacher, she's shared her theme of "Joy Through Trials" with more than half a million people across the country. Kim and her incredible husband of twenty-five-plus years have two adult children. Connect with Kim at www.kimberleywoodhouse.com.